*Tiger  Bay  Blues*

# Tiger Bay Blues

## CATRIN COLLIER

First published in Great Britain in 2006 by Orion,
an imprint of the Orion Publishing Group Ltd.

A CIP catalogue record for this book is available from the British Library.

Typeset by Deltatype Ltd, Birkenhead, Merseyside

Printed and bound by CPI Group (UK) Ltd, Croydon, CR0 4YY

The Orion Publishing Group Ltd
Orion House
5 Upper Saint Martin's Lane
London, WC2H 9EA

The Orion Publishing Group's policy is to use papers that are natural,
renewable and recyclable products and made from wood grown in sustainable forests.
The logging and manufacturing processes are expected to conform to the
environmental regulations of the country of origin.

www.orionbooks.co.uk

For Margaret Bloomfield, with love and gratitude
for her unstinting friendship and support.
A poor thank you for all her many kindnesses.

# Acknowledgements

I would like to thank everyone who helped me research this book and so generously gave of their time and expertise.

All the dedicated staff of the Butetown History and Arts Centre who are doing so much to preserve the spirit of the old Tiger Bay and chronicle the truly multi-cultural community that existed there before so many of its fine buildings were demolished in the 1960s.

Rhondda Cynon Taff's exceptional library service, especially Mrs Lindsay Morris for her ongoing help and support. Hywel Matthews and Catherine Morgan, the archivists at Pontypridd, and Nick Kelland, the archivist at Treorchy library.

The staff of Pontypridd Museum, Brian Davies, David Gwyer and Ann Cleary, for allowing me to dip into their extensive collection of old photographs and for doing such a wonderful job of preserving the history of Pontypridd.

Absolutely everyone at Orion, especially my editor Yvette Goulden for her encouragement and constructive criticism, Rachel Leyshon, my eagle-eyed copy-editor, Emma Noble, my miracle-working publicist, Juliet Ewers, Sara O'Keeffe, Jenny Page and all the editorial, sales and marketing teams.

And all the booksellers and readers who make writing such a privileged occupation.

And while I wish to acknowledge all the assistance I received, I wish to state that any errors in *Tiger Bay Blues* are entirely mine.

Catrin Collier
August 2005

# Chapter 1

EDYTH WALKED out of the back door of the substantial villa that her father had built on the outskirts of Pontypridd, opened the door to the outside pantry and shivered in the draught of freezing air that blasted out to meet her. At ten o'clock in the morning, the temperature was already high, but the stone-walled pantry had been sunk below ground level. Summer or winter it remained ice-cold, which was just as well for the numerous shrouded bowls and plates ranged on the marble slabs that lined the walls. For days their housekeeper, Mari, had been marshalling all the assistance she could commandeer from family and friends to prepare salads, cold fish and meat dishes, cheeses and desserts.

'A veritable feast,' Edyth's youngest brother Glyn had declared when he'd been allowed to 'lick out' the bowls used to mix the cakes and desserts. Although he was only six, he loved using long words, even when he didn't have a clue what they meant.

Edyth switched on the electric light her father had insisted the builder install, even in the outbuildings, walked down the steps and picked up one of the trays of rosebud buttonholes that she had helped her mother, sisters, aunts and cousins make the night before. To her relief, all the flowers still looked fresh. As did the bridesmaids' posies and bride's bouquet, which stood in buckets of water on the floor.

'God Bless Mari,' she murmured. The housekeeper's idea of wrapping the stems in damp cotton wool had worked, despite her sister's Bella's prediction that the flowers would wither in the heat and the only bridal bouquet she'd have was the faded blue and white wax one that their neighbour, old Mrs Hopkins, kept under a glass dome in her hall.

Edyth balanced the buttonhole trays on one arm, backed out and shut the pantry door before the warm air could reach the food. The plaintive notes of a lone saxophone playing the first few bars of 'The Wedding March' drifted from the front lawn. She stopped to listen. Two hot, clammy hands closed around her waist from behind. She jumped, almost dropping the trays.

'The band's arrived.'

'Let me go, Charlie Moore,' she commanded irritably.

'Didn't you hear me? I said the band's arrived.'

'I have ears.' She set the trays on the kitchen window sill and turned to confront him. Charlie Moore was twenty-one and good looking, in a well-heeled, smooth kind of way. He was wealthy too, courtesy of his family's Cardiff shipping business. But – and she had found this to be an insurmountable 'but', despite his family's friendship with Bella's fiancé, Toby – he was also arrogant and convinced that he was every woman's dream lover.

Instead of releasing her as she'd demanded, he locked his hands even tighter. 'You weren't very nice to me at the reception to unveil Toby's paintings in my grandfather's shipping office.'

'You weren't very nice to me,' she retorted.

'All I did was kiss you. My cheek still hurts from the slap you gave me.'

'You deserved a bruise after jumping out at me like that when I was leaving the cloakroom. You scared me half to death.'

'Be nice to me and I'll show you a good time,' he wheedled. 'My father gave me a sports car last week as a belated graduation present.'

'Bully for you.'

'We could go places. Cardiff, Swansea, Barry Island, Porthcawl . . .'

'I've been to all of them.' She dug her nails into the back of his hands, but failed to dislodge his grip.

'Not with me.'

'I'm particular who I go out with.'

'Come on, Edie, I know you want to kiss me.' He turned her around. 'I can see your lips puckering right now.'

'If they are it's because you've squeezed me so tight I'm going to be sick.' She opened her mouth as if she was about to retch. He stepped back in alarm. She laughed and opened the kitchen door.

'Always joking, aren't you?' he griped.

'Only with clowns.'

'Seriously, Edyth, you will save me some dances at the reception, won't you?'

'No.'

'Come on, stop teasing. You know you're burning to be my girl.'

'When I say something I mean it, Charlie Moore, and contrary to your belief I am not "burning to be your girl". Now, go away, I'm busy.' She picked up the trays again.

'I could carry those for you,' he offered.

'No, thank you,' she refused tartly. 'What are you doing here anyway? All the groomsmen should be next door at Toby's, helping him prepare for his big day.'

'He sent me over.'

'A likely story,' she scoffed.

'It's true,' he protested.

'Do you need help out here, Miss Edyth?' Spatula in hand, Mari came to the door. She looked from Edyth to Charlie.

'Mr Moore appears to have lost his way. But I've just reminded him that he should be next door.' Edyth lifted the tray so the housekeeper could inspect it. 'The flowers are perfect thanks to your idea of keeping the stems wrapped in damp cotton wool.'

'Toby sent me over here to get buttonholes for the groomsmen but Edyth won't give me any,' Charlie complained to Mari.

'You didn't ask for buttonholes,' Edyth snapped.

'You told me to go back next door before I had a chance.'

'Here's one for Toby and one for you.' Edyth picked up two from the tray and held them out to him.

Charlie took them from her. 'What about the rest of the groom's bridal party and the ushers?'

'The best man and one usher are here, but I suppose we can spare half a dozen for anyone who calls in at Toby's before going to the church. If you need any more you'll have to come back to get them. From me.' Mari took six roses from the tray and slipped them into an enamel bowl.

'I'll take these into the hall so everyone can help themselves.' Edyth balanced both trays on one arm so she could open the interior door.

'I'll take them for you, if you like,' Charlie stepped in.

'No, thank you. I can manage, *Mr* Moore.'

'Your wrapper's slipping, Miss Edyth.' Mari retied the bow on the overall Edyth was wearing over her frock. 'You don't want to get your bridesmaid's finery dirty. You still here, Mr Moore?' The housekeeper pushed the bowl into his hands and closed the back door in his face. 'You want to watch that one, Miss Edyth,' she warned.

'Don't worry, I already am, Mari. And he's not my type.'

'Heartbreaker,' Mari teased.

'That's me.'

'Someone will catch you one day,' Mari called after her.

'I'm keeping myself for the Prince of Wales.'

Mari laughed. Unlike Bella, Edyth had never had a serious boyfriend. From babyhood she had been the tomboy in the family, always more interested in climbing trees, riding bikes and horses, and playing football than doll and tea parties.

The porch and front doors were open, and Edyth saw that the saxophonist had been joined by the rest of the band in the gazebo on the lawn. They'd switched from 'The Wedding March' to 'You're Driving me Crazy'. A young, brown-skinned girl with a mature and hauntingly husky voice was belting out toe-tapping notes that drifted in through the windows, which were flung wide in hope of catching a non-existent breeze.

The whole country was basking in a heatwave. The broiling sun and cloudless sky, more appropriate to equatorial climes than Wales in July. Edyth set the trays on the hall stand and checked her reflection in the mirror. Bella was the acknowledged beauty in the family, having inherited their Spanish grandmother's black hair and beguiling dark eyes. But she wasn't too displeased with her own light brown hair and tawny eyes. Both held just enough of a hint of russet gold to lift her looks above the category of mousy.

4

Mindful of Mari's warning about her overall, she slipped it off and studied her gold satin, floor-length bridesmaid's gown. Fortunately there were no smudges or signs of creasing around the waist. But she was furious with Charlie Moore for daring to put his hands on her. Damned man – when she was angry she had no compunction about using the swear words she'd picked up from her male cousins – how dare he untie her overall and take liberties with her?

The frock, cut to the same pattern as Bella's wedding gown, clung to her figure, which she considered rounded in the right places; but was it too rounded? She stood sideways so she could see her profile. Were her hips too large and her bust too small?

A door slammed on the landing and her elder brother, Harry, left the bedroom that had been his before he'd married, and ran down the stairs, whistling an accompaniment to the band.

'Aren't I handsome in a morning suit, and isn't that the perfect piece of music to set the tone for the day?' He swept her up and quickstepped her down the hall.

'If anyone is driving anyone crazy it's you men,' she countered, thinking of Charlie Moore. 'None of you should be allowed near a wedding.'

'Difficult to have one without us,' he observed philosophically.

'I'll make an exception for the bridegroom and father of the bride, no one else.'

'The bridegroom needs a best man and I have the ring all safe.' Harry released her and patted the breast pocket of his morning suit.

'Until you lose it.'

'It isn't like you to spit razor blades so early in the morning, sis. Who's annoyed you? Tell big brother all, and I'll flatten him for you.'

'How do you know it's a him?'

'Because you're only angry with men.' Harry picked up one of the rosebuds and tucked it into his buttonhole. It fell forward at an angle.

'You really would flatten him for me if I asked you to, wouldn't you?' Edyth smiled at Harry's offer and realized that if she wasn't

5

careful she would allow one trivial incident with Charlie Moore to ruin the day, not only for her but for the family.

'Hand me the wooden sword from our old toy box and I will sally forth.'

She took the flower from him. 'Like all men you're as helpless as a baby without the redeeming cuteness.' She winced as a crowd of boys, ranging in age from twelve to four, raced noisily past the front door, whooping and shouting.

'Is that Pirate, or Red Indian language?' Harry asked.

'How would I know?'

'You see them more often than I do.'

The boys disappeared, scattering the chippings on the path in their wake. 'See what I mean about the male sex? They're so excited some of them are bound to be sick. I only hope they ruin their own clothes and no one else's.'

'Better they misbehave now, than later in church.'

'It's difficult to know which are worse: Uncle Victor's boys, Uncle's Joey's, or your brothers-in-law. I've had to help Glyn change his shirt twice this morning because "someone" he wouldn't snitch on stole a plate of chocolate éclairs from the pantry and passed them around. Thank goodness Mam insisted he dress in ordinary clothes when he woke this morning. His pageboy outfit would have been filthy by now.' Edyth opened a drawer, took a pin from the cushion their mother kept there and secured the flower firmly to Harry's lapel.

'I'm on Glyn's side. Weddings can be boring. Especially this waiting around while you girls preen and dress up in your glad rags.' Harry could always be counted on to defend his only brother, who was nineteen years younger than him.

'Glyn is involved, he's a pageboy.'

Given what Harry had overhead Glyn and his youngest brother-in-law, Luke, say about their gold satin knickerbocker suits, he decided a change of subject might be tactful. 'I saw Uncle Victor's twins and Uncle Joey's Eddie sneak into the laundry room earlier.'

'Why would they go in there?'

'They had bottles of beer up their sleeves and cigars sticking out of their top pockets.'

6

'Honestly, they're sixteen going on six!' She took a small bottle from the drawer, unscrewed the gold top, pulled out the rubber stopper and dabbed perfume on to her fingertip.

Harry sniffed. 'Nice scent, sis.' He couldn't resist adding, 'It's better than your usual *eau de* tennis and stables.'

'You have my permission to shout at him, Edyth.' Harry's wife, Mary, led their toddler daughter, Ruth, out of the drawing room.

'Charming, my wife and my sister ganging up on me!' Harry looked down at his daughter. 'Oh, my giddy aunt, Ruthie darling, you look pretty.'

Ruth held up the ballerina-length skirt of her gold satin flower-girl frock and did a twirl. 'And a basket,' she lisped, waving a gold-painted wicker basket in the air.

'Which we're going to fill with roses, aren't we, poppet?' Edyth slipped her overall back on to protect her dress, before picking Ruth up and kissing her.

'My beautiful girl, or is it girls?' Harry kissed Mary's cheek and patted her six-month 'bump'.

'Please have another girl, Mary,' Edyth pleaded, as the boys ran screaming past the front door again.

'Girls are more trouble, especially when they try to keep up with the boys. How many bones have you broken, sis?'

Edyth ignored Harry's question. 'Why don't you do something useful and take all the boys next door so they can annoy Toby? But leave Dad here. He'll be needed to escort the bride.'

'Edyth!' Maggie, the next sister down from Edyth, called from the top of the stairs. 'Bella's asking where you put her bouquet and the bridesmaids' posies.'

'In the outside pantry. I saw them when I picked up the buttonholes. They're perfect. Mari promised to take them out and dry the stems. Do you want me to check to see if she's remembered?'

'Please.' Maggie returned to Bella's bedroom.

'I agree with Edyth; you and the boys would be better out of the way next door at Toby's until it's time to go to the church,' Mary suggested diplomatically to Harry.

7

'As I said, ganging up on me. But I suppose it's time I started on my best man duties.'

Mary's brother, David, emerged from the drawing room. Edyth handed him a buttonhole.

'What do you want me to do with this?' he asked blankly.

'As I just said, boys have absolutely no idea.' Edyth took another pin from the cushion and fastened the rose to David's jacket. 'Now, what do you say to the guests when they enter the church?'

'Bride or groom's side,' he repeated parrot-fashion.

'And which is which?'

'Groom to the right of the altar?' he asked hopefully.

'As you are looking down towards it,' she lectured.

'My father and uncles still "tasting" the wine bought for the reception?' Harry lifted his eyebrows.

'They are.' David's broad smile suggested that the older generation weren't the only ones who'd been sampling the alcohol.

'Round up all the poor superfluous males inside and outside the house, and tell them they've been ordered next door, Davy.' Harry glanced back at Edyth, and realized she had really made an effort. His tomboy kid sister had grown up. 'Didn't know you could clean up so well, sis.'

'Charming!' She stuck her tongue out at him.

'You are to ignore that display of naughtiness from your Auntie Edie, Ruth.' Harry took his daughter from Edyth and set her on the floor. 'Beautiful as you temporarily are, sis, you know what they say: three times a bridesmaid—'

'This is only the second,' Edyth interrupted.

Harry ticked off his fingers. 'Uncle Joey's and Auntie Rhian's wedding, mine and Mary's, and now Bella and Toby's. You need to practise your sums.'

'Belle and I were only flower-girls at Auntie Rhian and Uncle Joey's wedding, so that doesn't count.'

'If you're right, as you're only eighteen months younger than Bella, I suppose you'll soon be following her up the aisle, then,' Harry baited.

He had graduated from Oxford, and all five of his sisters and his brother had been educated with the expectation that they would also attend college. Their father, Lloyd, an ex-miner who had risen through trade union ranks to become an MP, was determined to push every one of his children, girls as well as boys, to the absolute limit of their ability. And although he and their mother Sali had finally given in to Bella and Toby's pleadings that they be allowed to marry shortly after Bella's twentieth birthday, Harry knew his parents saw Bella's early marriage as a betrayal of that ideal.

'I have absolutely no intention of getting married. No disrespect, Mary,' Edyth apologized to her sister-in-law, 'but you won't catch me playing unpaid cook, bottle-washer, laundress, nurse, nanny and housemaid to any man.' She shuddered when she thought of Charlie Moore's clammy hands.

'So *that's* what wives are supposed to do?' Harry winked at his wife. 'How come I drew the short straw, my angel?'

'Davy, at least get the boys to sit down somewhere quiet before one of them breaks a leg or an arm,' Edyth commanded as the noise from outside escalated.

David obediently went to the door. He was the same age as Edyth and had fallen in love with her the first time they'd met. Harry frequently joked that his brother-in-law would cut off his right arm, and cheerfully, if Edyth asked him to.

'Edyth, bring up a couple of pins from the hall table, will you?' Maggie shouted down.

'I'll see to it.' Mary took a dozen pins from the cushion and pushed Ruth gently up the stairs ahead of her. 'Go on, darling; let's see if we can help.'

Edyth frowned. 'I came downstairs to take the buttonholes from the pantry and to do something else . . .'

'Shout at the men?' Harry suggested.

Edyth hesitated, then, as the jazz band Toby had hired for the reception swung into a rousing rendition of 'Walking My Baby Back Home,' she remembered. 'I wanted to ask the band if they'd play "Falling in Love With You" when Bella and Toby return here from the church.'

'"Ain't He Sweet" would be better.' Harry's blue eyes glittered with mischief.

'How about "Ever'thing Made for Love"?' David chipped in

from the porch where he was having no success in calming down the boys. Since Harry had installed a radio in the kitchen of the farmhouse he lived in with his wife and her orphaned brothers and sister, David listened to as many music programmes as he could fit into his working day.

'If you don't go to Toby's now, the best man and bridegroom are going to arrive late at the church, Harry,' Mary cautioned from the landing.

'You see to the flowers, I'll talk to the band, Edyth.' Harry joined David at the door.

'Can I trust you?'

'Wait and see,' Harry answered maddeningly.

Edyth spent a few minutes checking the buttonholes again for sign of wilting. When she was as sure as she could be that all of them would last the day, she went to the door. Harry and David had finally succeeded in collecting the boys but they had gathered in front of the gazebo where the jazz band was playing. Charlie Moore was with them and, to her annoyance, Bella's fiancé, Toby.

'The idiot,' she muttered crossly. 'Doesn't he know it's unlucky for the bridegroom to see the bride before the wedding? All the curtains are open on that side of the house.'

'Talking to yourself is the first sign, Edyth.' Maggie ran down the stairs behind her.

'It's the only way to get a sensible conversation in this house. Do me a favour, Mags – remind Mari to take out the posies and bouquets from their buckets in the outside pantry.' Edyth turned on her heel and charged back up the stairs.

'Harry Evans, brother of the bride and my best man.' Toby introduced Harry to the musicians. 'The King brothers – Tony, Jed and Ron.' He glanced at the crowd of young men and boys standing around them. 'I would introduce everyone to everyone, but as no one would remember all the names, there isn't much point.'

'Pleased to meet you. That was some music you were belting out there.' Harry shook the hands of the three tall Negroes.

'Abdul Akbar on trumpet,' Toby continued, 'Steve Chan on

drums, and the Bute Street Blues Band's talented and beautiful singer, soon to be discovered and swept off to the West End, Judy Hamilton.'

'What Toby means is that I'm auditioning on Monday for a tiny part in the chorus of a tour of *The Vagabond King*. Not that I have a hope of getting it,' Judy explained.

'And when Ziegfeld sees you—'

'The show's touring Aberdare and the Rhondda, Toby, not opening in New York.'

'If you won't dream for yourself, Judy, then I'll dream for you,' Toby said blithely. 'And last but not least, on saxophone, Micah Holsten.'

Harry shook the hand of the only white member of the band. He was very tall and thin, with startlingly white-blond hair. A pair of wire-framed spectacles was perched in front of his deep-blue eyes but even without them he had a keen, intellectual look. Harry found it difficult to gauge his age. At first glance he'd assumed the white hair was a sign of age; close up he recognized it as an indication of Scandinavian ancestry. Micah Holsten could be anywhere between a careworn twenty or a youngish thirty.

'Pleased to meet you, Mr Evans.' Micah had the slightest of accents; his English was clear and almost too perfect, as if he'd practised the pronunciation of every single word.

'Please, call me Harry. There's a buffet laid out in the kitchen for the waitresses and kitchen staff. My parents asked me to invite you all to help yourselves while we're in the church.'

'As long as you're back out here to play for us when we return,' Toby reminded.

'Thank you. Not many people think of the musicians.' Micah turned when a casement slammed noisily against the wall of the house. Edyth, in her long bridesmaids' frock and high-heeled slippers, stood balanced precariously on the sill of the open high window set alongside the staircase. She was reaching above her head to the curtain pole.

'Idiot! You'll fall and break your neck if not your skull again,' Harry yelled.

'Toby's the idiot, coming here before the wedding. Everyone

knows it's unlucky for the bridegroom to see the bride before the ceremony.' She tugged the curtains across the open window, closing them. Seconds later, two loud bangs and a scream echoed from the house.

Harry started running. Aware of someone following him, he turned and saw Toby charging in his wake. 'Edyth won't be the only one screaming if Bella sees you,' he yelled, then darted inside. Edyth was standing on the top step of the long, curving staircase, holding a crossbar gold satin slipper in each hand.

'You threw them on the stairs and screamed to frighten me?' Harry grabbed the newel post to steady himself while he caught his breath.

'I did.' Her eyes glittered triumphantly.

Micah Holsten drew alongside Harry. 'I'm sorry, Harry,' he gasped. 'I would never have entered the house uninvited if Toby hadn't thought you'd need help.'

'My sister, Edyth. Micah Holsten, saxophonist and member of the Bute Street Blues Band. And Toby was right, Micah. Given my sister's history of breaking her bones, I do need help to cope with her idea of a joke.'

'Pleased to meet you, Mr Holsten.' Assuming from the intense way he was staring at her that he thought her a fool for playing such a childish trick, Edyth stepped back into the shadows. 'Be a good best man and keep Toby away from the house, Harry.'

'I'll try. See you in church, sis.' Harry turned to Micah. 'As you're here, I may as well show you to the kitchen.'

The women and girls who had crowded into Bella's bedroom fell silent when Sali draped the veil over her eldest daughter's head. Sali stepped back and Bella stood for a moment, gazing at her image in the cheval mirror through a mist of Bruges lace. She finally turned and faced her sisters, aunts and cousins.

'Well?' she questioned nervously. 'Someone say something, even if it's only, "you look as though you've been dipped in icing sugar, Bella."'

A lump rose in Edyth's throat. Her sister had chosen a plain, white satin, bias-cut frock that clung flatteringly to her bust and slim waist before flaring out below the hips. But her veil and the silver tiara that held it in place were family heirlooms. Lloyd's Spanish mother had worn them when she'd married his father over half a century before, and although the pattern on the lace was ornate, its simple outline complemented the gown perfectly.

'Someone? Anyone?' Bella pleaded.

'You make the most beautiful bride, darling. Toby is a very lucky man.' Sali reached for her handkerchief.

'Auntie Megan? Auntie Rhian?'

'I agree with your mother, the most beautiful bride I've ever seen.' Rhian struggled to keep her voice steady. Her wartime wedding to Lloyd's youngest brother Joey had been a small registry office affair, and for the first time in her life she found herself regretting the sensible 'walking out' suit she'd worn. She'd consoled herself at the time with the thought that it was the marriage not the clothes that mattered. Although she didn't doubt for one moment that Bella would be happy. Toby's besotted devotion to her niece had been a constant source of amusement to the entire extended family for the last four years.

'I can't wait until I'm old enough to get married,' Susie, the youngest of Sali and Lloyd's daughters sighed theatrically.

'And me,' fifteen-year-old Beth and seventeen-year-old Maggie cried in unison.

'One at a time, girls.' Sali attempted to conceal her emotion beneath a veneer of brisk efficiency as she tidied Bella's dressing table, but she deceived no one. 'It's taken four years for your father to get used to the idea of Harry being a husband and father.' She gave Mary, who was sitting on the bed with Ruth on her lap, one of her 'special' smiles. 'It will take him another four to accept that Bella's grown up enough to be a wife.'

'Don't worry, Mam, you'll always have one spinster daughter.' Edyth picked up the gold basket she'd filled with yellow rosebuds and handed it to Ruth.

'Hardly for ever when you go to college in two months,' Maggie reminded.

'Only if I matriculate.' Edyth crossed her fingers superstitiously under cover of her skirt, as she always did when any reference was made to the future that was planned for her. 'And, if I'm lucky enough to pass all my exams, it will only be for three years. I'll come back here to teach and look after Mam and Dad in their old age.'

'That's a comforting thought for you and Lloyd, Sali,' laughed Megan, the wife of Lloyd's other brother, Victor.

'We're not quite in our dotage yet, no matter what you girls think.' Sali tweaked the hem of Bella's dress.

Mari knocked at the door, bustled in with an armful of posies and Bella's bouquet, took one look at the bride and stopped in her tracks. 'Oh, Miss Bella, you look like an angel that's just stepped out of heaven.'

'Doesn't she just, Mari?' Sali agreed proudly.

'And you look just as lovely in that grey silk, Mari.' Edyth was so accustomed to their housekeeper wearing black, it was a revelation to see her in a colour.

'Hardly "just as lovely", Miss Edyth.' Mari gave her a suspicious look. 'What you after?'

'Nothing,' Edyth protested.

'No baskets of food or "old" clothes or books to take down to the Unemployed Institute?' Mari fished.

Everyone laughed. Lloyd and Sali were generous when it came to helping those less fortunate than them, but, to her sisters' annoyance, Edyth was liberal to the extreme. She frequently gave away their precious possessions before they had finished with them.

'Well, ladies,' Mari addressed the room in general, 'there's an impatient crowd of smartly dressed gentlemen and a fleet of cars downstairs waiting to take the guests to the church. The chauffeur of the bridesmaids and mother of the bride has asked me to give a twenty-minute warning. And, as the bride's mother's sons are both involved in the wedding, the twins have offered their services as escort until the father of the bride has given the bride away.'

'Do the twins do everything together?' Edyth asked Megan.

'Sixteen and no sign of them changing their ways.' She shook her head fondly. 'Victor is already pitying the poor girl they'll both start courting.'

Mari saw Sali glance wistfully at Bella. Suspecting there

14

wouldn't be much time for mother and daughter to have a quiet moment together after the ceremony, she took charge. 'Right, bridesmaids, pick up your posies, but keep the tea towels wrapped around the stems until the last minute or they'll leave watermarks on your frocks. Those who haven't yet picked up their buttonholes from the hall, do so. I'll carry that downstairs for you so you can hold up your skirt, pet.' She took Ruth's basket from her, and was so insistent she soon cleared the room of everyone except Sali, Bella and Edyth, who was drying the stems of Bella's bouquet in a towel. 'Perhaps the chief bridesmaid should stay with the bride in case of accident,' Mari declared as an afterthought.

'What kind of accident?' Bella asked from behind her veil.

'Your knickers could fall down, like when you used to snap the elastic to make a funny noise when you were little.'

'Mari!' Bella cried indignantly.

'And no sentimental rememberings or you two will make your mother cry.' Mari took a last look at Bella. 'You do look lovely, Miss Bella, just the way an Evans bride should.' She closed the door quickly, but not quickly enough. Edyth saw a tear in the elderly woman's eye.

'Mari's right.' Sali continued to stare, mesmerized, at her eldest daughter. 'You do look just the way an Evans bride should.' Her eyes clouded as she remembered the day she'd been dressed as a bride. Only her bridegroom hadn't made it to the church. Harry's father had been murdered before he could marry her, but it was a story she and Lloyd had kept from the girls. The tragedy had been hers and Harry's – and today of all days was not the time to remember it.

'You heard Mari: no sentiment and no tears, or we'll spoil our frocks and redden our noses.' Edyth lifted her sister's veil and draped it away from her face. 'I hid a bottle of sherry and some glasses in your wardrobe earlier. Shall I get them?'

'How on earth did you manage to do that without Mari, me or your father seeing you?' Sali asked in amazement.

'Perhaps now's the time to tell you some of Edyth's little dodges.' Bella arranged her dress carefully so as not to crease it before sitting on her dressing-table stool.

'Not if you want me to keep *your* secrets, sister dear.' Edyth produced the bottle and three glasses, and set them on the dressing table.

'Please be careful, Edyth. Sherry will leave a horrible stain on satin,' Sali warned when Edyth uncorked the sherry.

'I haven't had an accident in months,' Edyth protested.

'That's why I'm worried. Whenever you've been quieter for longer than a week, it usually means you're building up to something big. Like that time you fractured your skull.'

'I've broken enough bones for one lifetime.' Edyth filled the last glass and handed two to her mother and sister. 'A toast: to Bella and Toby, and many years of happy married life.'

'And Edyth,' Bella added. 'May she be the first to fulfil Dad's dream of seeing a daughter go to college.'

'If I've passed my matriculation.' Edyth crossed her fingers again before sipping the sherry.

Joey Evans liked to boast that he was the least sentimental man in the family, but Edyth saw her uncle reach for his handkerchief when Lloyd escorted Bella up the aisle to the accompaniment of their mother's favourite Bach concerto. She continued to walk slowly behind her father and sister while keeping a watchful eye on the three small children in front of her. Pageboys Glyn and Luke held Bella's veil stiffly at arm's length and Ruth marched proudly between them, more miniature soldier on parade than flower-girl.

Relieved when they reached the altar without any of the small children tripping up, or getting in the way of the bridesmaids, Edyth looked up to see Toby standing smiling, his arm outstretched to Bella.

She had never been jealous of Bella's dark exotic beauty, but she did find herself envying the look of love and longing etched in Toby's eyes. Not Toby himself – just the way he looked at her sister. And she found herself wishing that a man would look at her that way.

The Reverend Price faced Bella and Toby and the congregation. 'Dearly beloved, we are gathered here today . . .'

To Edyth's annoyance, a mist blurred her vision. She had sat dry-eyed, emotions intact, throughout the rehearsal. Why couldn't she continue to do so now? When Bella handed over her bouquet she buried her nose in the roses, inhaled their scent and wondered if she were dreaming. Could Bella really be getting married and leaving home?

She hadn't felt this way when Harry had married Mary. She adored her big brother, but he was six years older than her and had spent so much time away at school, and later university, that she had never been as close to him as she was to her sisters. And, as she and Bella were the eldest, their relationship had been a special one.

She imagined Bella's bedroom, empty not just for a few hours but, like Harry's, permanently, apart from the odd holiday, and probably not even then as Toby was having a house built for them around the corner from her parents. She would no longer be able to creep in late at night, sit on her sister's bed and devour the picnics they'd sneaked from the pantry while discussing life, art, books and the future.

She and Bella had gone almost everywhere together, both before and after they had grown out of short frocks. School, music lessons, ballet classes, parties, concerts, dances and the theatre, and they had traded insults that everyone outside of the immediate family considered vicious. She hadn't once told Bella that she loved her, or how much she meant to her, or even that she was going to miss her . . .

'I do.' Toby's response rang, loud and clear, to the church rafters.

Bella's 'I do' was softer, more subdued.

The Reverend Price looked expectantly at Harry, who fumbled in his pockets in search of the ring long enough to alarm the groom and send whispers of amusement rippling through the congregation.

Edyth turned in annoyance at a sharp poke in her back. Maggie pointed to the floor. Glyn, Luke and Ruth were sitting in a circle, legs wide apart, feet touching, rolling the basket of rosebuds to one another. She stooped down to take it from them and found herself staring into a pair of unfamiliar, deep-brown eyes.

17

She picked up the basket. The owner of the brown eyes gathered the rosebuds and handed them to her. When he straightened, she saw that he was wearing a cassock, surplice and dog collar. He smiled at her before moving discreetly behind the Reverend Price.

Disconcerted, the warning glare she sent in the direction of the errant pageboys and flower-girl wasn't as stern as she'd intended. She'd heard that the Reverend Price had a new curate. If that was him, he was without a doubt the most attractive man she'd ever seen.

The Reverend Price boomed, 'Those whom God hath joined together let no man put asunder.'

The service ended, the choir began to sing 'Love Divine'. Bella and Toby laughed from sheer relief. The congregation started to whisper and Edyth caught snatches of conversation.

'Such a moving ceremony . . .'

'A beautiful bride . . .'

Edyth crouched down, helped the pageboys and Ruth to their feet, brushed their clothes with the back of her hand and turned to follow Bella, Toby and her parents into the vestry. The Reverend Price's curate stood back to allow the bridal procession to precede him and, to her astonishment, gave her a broad and distinctly non-clerical wink.

Her mouth went dry and her knees weakened. For the first time in her life, she knew beyond a shadow of a doubt that, despite her aversion to all the Charlie Moores she'd encountered, and her assertion that she would remain a spinster, given the right man, just like Bella, she would happily forgo her ambition to attend college in exchange for marriage and – when she looked down at Ruth – children.

# Chapter 2

'YOU CONDUCTED the service beautifully, Reverend Price. There wasn't a dry eye in the church. Your new curate – I didn't catch his name?' Mrs Hopkins raised her voice above the sound of the jazz band playing 'Will You Remember?' in the background.

Edyth stepped out of the line of family that had formed to welcome the guests, and inched closer to the vicar in the hope of discovering more about the stranger. She wasn't disappointed.

'Reverend Peter Slater is not only my new curate, Mrs Hopkins; he's also the son of an old college friend and my godson.' The vicar offered the elderly lady his arm and walked her over to where Peter Slater was holding court in the centre of a group of young and adoring girls. 'Mrs Hopkins, Reverend Peter Slater. Peter, I'd like to introduce you to one of our most dedicated parishioners and church benefactors, Mrs Hopkins.'

Peter excused himself from the girls and shook Mrs Hopkins's hand. While they exchanged pleasantries, Edyth glanced at the queue of guests waiting to greet the wedding party and congratulate the bride and groom. It wasn't diminishing rapidly enough for her liking. She noticed that her younger sisters had already left the line and were talking to their friends, and more alarmingly, that Maggie was eyeing the Reverend Slater, who looked as though he were about to move on from the vicar and Mrs Hopkins.

Edyth muttered an excuse aimed at no one in particular and went into the marquee. Under the pretext of re-arranging the flowers on the top table, she shuffled the place cards. It wasn't difficult. By moving Maggie up one place and banishing her youngest sister Susie to the children's table, she managed to secure adjoining seats for Peter Slater and herself. She left the tent and wandered back into the garden with the intention of waylaying him and introducing herself.

'Edyth,' David ran up to her, 'can I have the first dance after the wedding breakfast? After the bridal dance, that is. Martha said something about you having dance cards . . .'

'Bella decided not to have cards. They're old-fashioned.' Bella's decision had nothing to do with fashion. She like Edyth, had found the crowing of girls with full dance cards over those less fortunate distasteful. Especially when they had first begun to go to parties and found themselves planted firmly among the other gauche young wallflowers.

'But you will save me a dance?' he pleaded.

'Of course,' she murmured absently, her attention fixed on Peter Slater. Standing in sunlight he resembled a matinée idol even more than he had done in the gloomy interior of St Catherine's church. His thick, wavy black hair, regular features and intense expression reminded her of the postcards of the actor Gary Cooper that Susie pinned to her bedroom walls and kissed every night before she climbed into bed.

'I've been practising the steps you taught me,' David added in a tone that might have invoked compassion if her attention hadn't been entirely focused on Peter.

'Edyth,' Susie joined them with David's sister, Martha, 'I don't have to sit at the children's table in the marquee, do I? We're both thirteen and Martha is on Uncle Victor's table with the twins.'

'It's probably a mistake.' Edyth was stricken by an attack of conscience. 'Is there room for you on Uncle Victor's table as well as Martha?'

'Only if we move one of the younger boys to the children's table. Ben's six months younger than me.'

'Swap the place cards over, but don't tell anyone I told you to do it. And if Ben objects, tell him Belle and Toby wanted him to sit with the little ones because he's so good at keeping them in order.'

'Edyth?' Maggie waved to her from the middle of a group of fellow pupils from the grammar school.

'David, be an angel?' Edyth gave him a brilliant smile.

'I'll try.'

The Master of Ceremonies rang a bell. 'Ladies and gentlemen, please take your seats. The wedding breakfast is about to be served.'

'Tell Maggie I'll talk to her after the meal.' She darted over to Peter, leaving David feeling as though she'd slapped him in the face.


'My father died suddenly of a heart attack when I was fourteen and, as the vicarage my parents had lived in all their married life was needed for the next incumbent, Mother and I had to move out of our home less than a week after his death.' Peter Slater murmured thank you to the waitress who set a plate of cold salmon in front of him.

'How tragic, to lose your father at that age, and then your home. You must have been devastated.' Edyth's sympathy was heartfelt. She adored her father and couldn't bear to think of him dying.

'Losing our home was nothing in comparison to losing my father. I miss his guidance and advice even more since I was ordained. But I was born in that vicarage in Mumbles and had lived in the village all my life. However, God provides. People are kind. My mother's eldest sister is also a widow. She offered us a home with her in the village of Sketty, which is only a few miles from Mumbles, so I was able to visit my friends in the holidays. Only in the holidays, because I changed schools after my father's death. The Church offered to pay for my education and I went to boarding school. After I matriculated, they arranged a place for me at the theological college in Lampeter. I was grateful, but I confess, welcoming as the parishioners in Pontypridd have been, I miss the sea after growing up so close to it.'

'I love the sea, too.' Edyth gazed into his eyes and pictured them walking hand in hand along a deserted beach.

'It's never the same two days running. Even when the weather remains fine, the sea changes colour. I used to spend hours on the beach as a child, building sand castles, collecting shells, crabs and other fishy things. Although I'm not so sure Mother appreciated me cluttering my bedroom with them.'

'I'm sure she didn't really mind. If she had done she wouldn't have allowed you to bring them into the house.'

'You're probably right. But then, aren't most mothers tolerant of their children's foibles?'

Edyth fought the urge to smooth away the lines that had appeared at the corners of his eyes when he revisited his childhood memories. 'You left Lampeter at the end of last term?' she fished, hoping he'd tell her how long he'd be staying in Pontypridd.

'No, St Catherine's is my fourth parish.'

'Really?' Edyth abandoned all pretence of eating, cupped her chin in her hand and stared unashamedly at him. 'Where else have you been?'

'Here, there and everywhere. It amuses the Bishop to move curates around at short notice. It saves him the trouble of setting up a chessboard,' he joked. 'I've just come from Llanelli. I was there for six months and before that I spent a year in Brecon, two in Merthyr, and almost three in Bridgend. I like to think the decreasing length of my postings means that the Church is considering giving me my own parish in the not too distant future.'

The Reverend Price was in his early fifties and had been entrenched in Pontypridd for as long as Edyth could remember, so she guessed that if Peter Slater was going to be given his own church soon, it wouldn't be St Catherine's. 'Then you don't expect to be here for long?' She didn't even try to hide her disappointment.

'That depends on the Church. I'm not in a hurry to move until I am offered my own parish. The Reverend Price and my father were close friends and, as my godfather, he's taken his duty towards me seriously. He kept in close touch with my mother after my father died and when he heard that I was looking for a position that would offer more of a challenge to an ambitious curate, he asked the Bishop to send me here. And that, Miss Evans,' Peter gave her heart-melting smile, 'is a brief outline of my short and uneventful life.'

'You see your mother?'

'As often as I can. Swansea is only two train journeys and an hour and a half away, but I get very little free time to travel even that far.'

'And none on Sundays. It must be peculiar to have to work your longest hours on most people's only free day in the week.' Noticing that the waitresses were already collecting plates, Edyth finally cut into her salmon. 'Do you have any brothers and sisters?'

'None. As the saying goes, I'm only, lonely and selfish.' He smiled again and her heartbeat quickened.

'I've never heard that, but then, with four sisters and two brothers, it hardly applies to me.'

'You're lucky to have a large family.' He glanced around the table. 'The only relatives I have in this world are my mother and aunt.'

'There have been times when I would have disagreed with you, but not today. As you may have guessed, we're not only wearing our best clothes but we're all on our best behaviour.'

'Your sister makes a beautiful bride.'

'And Toby a handsome bridegroom. We tease him dreadfully. He's not used to children or girls, and finds us overwhelming.'

'He doesn't seem to have much family,' Peter observed. 'His side of the church was half-empty.'

'He doesn't have any family. His parents died when he was young and his uncle a few years ago. He has no one else, so the only people in his pews were his friends.' Edyth handed her plate of barely touched salmon to a waitress.

'How did he meet your sister?'

'Toby was a friend of Harry's – my eldest brother and Bella and Toby's best man,' she explained. 'When Harry married Mary and went to live with her and her brothers and sister on their farm, Harry asked Toby if he'd like to rent his house, which is next door to this one. You can see the roof over the trees.'

'Very imposing.'

Edyth suspected from the expression on Peter's face that he was wondering how someone Harry's age could afford a house that large, but drilled by her parents never to discuss finances, especially Harry's inheritance from a long-dead great-aunt, she didn't elaborate. 'It is, and as Toby was already smitten with Bella although she was only sixteen at the time, he jumped at the chance. My parents weren't too happy about the arrangement. They hoped we'd all go to college. But Bella gave up on that idea when she and Toby became engaged on her eighteenth birthday.'

'Your father wants to send all of you to college, even the girls?' Peter asked in astonishment.

'*Especially* the girls.' Lloyd caught the tail end of their conversation. 'All women should be educated, and not only so they can keep themselves if necessary,' he said forcefully.

'I agree, sir,' Peter muttered diplomatically. 'But not many men of your generation think that way. My father used to say that it was a waste of time and money to educate women when most of them only end up running a house.'

'Do you have any sisters, Reverend Slater?' Lloyd asked.

'No, sir.'

'That's probably just as well. Tell me, do you think that the education of most children begins at home?'

'Yes, sir.'

'Then a woman's education cannot possibly be wasted if she passes it on to her children.'

'Your father has very definite ideas,' Peter whispered to Edyth when Lloyd turned his back on them to continue his conversation with Toby and Bella.

'Particularly on social justice and the emancipation of women. That's why he became an MP.'

'But women have the vote.'

'Only after a long struggle. And we're still a long way from achieving equal pay and equal rights in all professions.'

'I take it you're a feminist?'

'You're not?' she challenged.

'Of course,' he agreed hastily. 'So, what will you study in college, Miss Evans?'

'English Literature.'

'And then you'll teach?'

'I am going to a training college. Hopefully Swansea, if I matriculate.' Edyth always gave the same answer to any enquiry that touched on her future, although the prospect of teaching had appealed more to Bella than to her. The problem was, other than teaching, nursing or office work, all of which she suspected would bore her witless after a while, there were few interesting occupations open to respectable women.

She looked across the lawn towards the gazebo where the jazz band was softly playing. She would have loved to have become a professional singer or actress, but as her contributions to school concerts had proved that she had absolutely no theatrical talent and even less musical ability, her ambitions in that direction were woefully hampered.

'Did you always want to go into the church, Reverend Slater?'

'Please, call me Peter.'

'I will, if you call me Edyth.'

'I'd be delighted to, Edyth. And, in answer to your question, my parents always assumed that I'd follow my father's choice of career when the time came. To be perfectly honest, after he died, I couldn't think of anything else that I wanted to do. But when I was studying at Lampeter, I did truly feel that I'd found my vocation in life.'

'This is a very serious conversation for a wedding.' She glanced at the jazz band, and the pretty singer. She had skin the colour of milk chocolate, but her black hair, waved in the latest 'loose' style, bore no trace of Afro curl. She wondered about her ancestry.

Peter noticed she was watching the band. 'That girl can really sing.'

'Do you like jazz?' Edyth asked.

'I prefer orchestral and chamber music. Although I occasionally listen to lighter music on the radio and I have been to a few Ivor Novello and Jerome Kern evenings.'

Edyth hid her disappointment. She might not to be able to play a musical instrument but she loved listening and dancing to modern music. 'What about books?'

'I enjoy revisiting the classics. The Brontës, Jane Austen, Dickens and, to go further back, Homer's *Iliad*, but one of the drawbacks of being a curate is lack of time. Not that I'm complaining. In fact, I'm looking forward to taking over the youth club and drama group. I'm recruiting volunteers to assist me. Do you have any time to spare, Edyth?'

'I do, and I would be delighted to help in any way that I can.' Edyth smiled up at the waitress, who was now serving them roast chicken.

'As would I, Reverend Slater.' Maggie leaned across the table, ignored her sister and beamed at Peter. 'Edyth will be going to college at the end of the summer, while I, on the other hand, have another full year of school – and Pontypridd – to go.'

'The final year,' Edyth reminded. 'And the most important one. You'll be busy, Maggie.'

'Not too busy to help the church.' Maggie picked up a jug and handed it to Peter. 'Bread sauce, Reverend, or would you prefer mint sauce with your peas?'

Edyth didn't see her sister as a threat, but she did intend to make the most of her time with Peter, and encourage him to arrange to meet her again outside of the youth club, which wasn't likely to happen if Maggie put an end to intelligent conversation with her blatant flirting. She moved her chair as close as she dared to Peter's, leaned towards him and listened intently to every word he said. It was only embarrassment that stopped her from staring, because every time she glanced discreetly at him from beneath her lowered lashes, she found his soft, brown eyes focused on her.

The main course was eaten, the plates cleared, strawberries and cream served, and the bowls removed. Coffee pots, cheese boards and crackers were placed at intervals along the tables and, throughout it all, Edyth and Peter remained locked in conversation, isolated from and oblivious to everyone around them, in spite of Maggie's attempts to interrupt. When Lloyd rose to make his 'father of the bride' speech, Edyth took the coffee cup the waitress had set in front of her and sipped it absently without putting in her customary cream and sugar.

She tried to look as though she were listening, but she couldn't see or think of anything other than the man sitting beside her. And she couldn't have made it more obvious that she hadn't heard a word that had been said when Harry followed her father and made the traditional toast to the bridesmaids. She lifted her own glass and only realized her mistake when Maggie hissed, 'That's us, you fool.'

Five minutes after the speeches had finished, Edyth couldn't recall a single word that had been said. She resented the polite enquiries that disrupted the flow of her and Peter's conversation – the waitress enquiring as to their preferences; their fellow diners' questions as to what Peter thought of Pontypridd and how he was settling into the town – but worse of all was Maggie, who simply refused to leave them alone. No matter how she glowered, glared and frowned, or how many kicks she aimed at her sister's ankles under cover of the table, Maggie continued to flutter and coo around Peter like a lovesick dove.

'You are *so* right, Reverend Slater. But then, no one in this family has ever voted Tory,' Maggie purred, breaking in on Peter's mild condemnation of the Tory party's demands for a cut in the dole just as unemployment was spiralling out of control across the country. 'Edyth,' she gave her sister a wide insincere smile, 'the jazz band is playing dance music.'

'So we can all hear, Maggie.' Edyth struggled to keep her irritation in check.

'You know how you love to dance,' Maggie commented archly.

'And you don't, Miss Evans?' Peter turned to Maggie in surprise.

'I don't care for jazz or modern music,' Maggie lied. 'I prefer the waltz and foxtrot. But then,' she shrugged and sighed theatrically, 'I have very different tastes from my sisters and am always outvoted by them. However, that won't stop me from asking Father to hire a string quartet to play at *my* wedding.'

Edyth realized that her sister had been listening in on her and Peter's conversation for longer than she'd thought. Normally she would have retaliated, but the last thing she wanted to do was start an argument that might show her in a poor light in front of Peter Slater. 'Isn't it a little early to start planning your wedding, Maggie?' she questioned evenly. 'You are only seventeen.'

'Nearly eighteen.' Maggie tempered her swift correction with a subdued glance at Peter.

Lloyd left his seat and led Bella on to the dance floor. Toby followed with Sali. The musicians played 'What is this thing called love?'

'Even after the ceremony I find it difficult to believe that one of us is actually married – I mean, us girls. My eldest brother Harry has been married for four years, so I am used to the idea.' Edyth felt the need to fill the silence that had fallen after Maggie's sharp rejoinder.

'Your sister is very much married in the eyes of God, the Church, the congregation, and, from the look in his eyes, I'd say her husband,' Peter commented lightly.

'"Those whom God has joined together let no man break asunder,"' Maggie quoted dreamily, gazing at Peter.

Edyth had never wanted to slap Maggie as much or so hard. But before she had time to collect her thoughts, David materialized in front of her, like the genie of Arabian legend. She only wished she could cork him into a bottle and push him out of sight.

'You promised me a dance, Edyth,' he reminded, 'and Toby's asked them to play "The Charleston" next.'

'Edyth and David look *so* good together on the dance floor. People say they should be on stage. But then, being a vicar, I don't suppose you go to the theatre?' Maggie whispered to Peter, although she took care to speak loud enough for Edyth to hear.

'I enjoy shows and concerts, Miss Evans. Only last month I saw *Showboat* in Llanelli.'

Edyth suspected that if she refused David his dance, he'd pout and she'd run the risk of Peter assuming that he was her boyfriend. But if she agreed, she suspected that Maggie or – more likely after the way her sister had behaved – another girl would drag Peter away on some pretext or other to a quiet corner of the house or gardens where she'd have difficulty tracking him down.

'Edyth?' David prompted.

'Could we dance later, please, David? I've just eaten the most enormous meal.'

'You ate hardly anything, Edyth. Besides, it's never stopped you before,' Maggie observed snidely.

'Come on, Edyth, it's "The Charleston",' David reiterated. The dancers finished applauding 'What is This Thing Called Love?', the band took a few seconds' break and Micah Holsten played a solo opening.

Edyth gritted her teeth and smiled at Peter. 'If you'll excuse me, Peter, I'll be right back.'

'Of course, Edyth,' He returned her smile. 'And if the band plays something slower and more my style later, perhaps you'll save me a dance?'

'I'd be delighted.'

'Something slower and more my style!' David mocked as soon as they were out of Peter's earshot. 'The Reverend doesn't look much older than me.' He led the way to the wooden platform Lloyd had hired from the Town Hall and set up on the lawn as a dance floor.

'He *is* a curate.' Edyth sprang to Peter Slater's defence.

'So what?' David demanded.

'Vicars and curates can't be seen doing anything improper by their parishioners.'

'Like this?' David pulled her into the centre of the group of dancers. Normally Edyth set the pace when she partnered David, kicking her legs wide without a care as to whether her skirts flew up or not. But conscious of Peter Slater sitting a few feet away from them, half hoping and half concerned that he was watching, for the first time in her life, she tried to dance sedately, or at least as sedately as 'The Charleston' allowed.

'You're not feeling well, Edyth?' David pitched his voice above the applause when the band stopped playing.

'I told you, I've just eaten an enormous meal.'

'The food was good, wasn't it? But then it would be with your mother and Mari in charge.' David grabbed her hand again as the band started playing the newest hit to cross the Atlantic, 'Dance of the Jungle'. Waving one of his hands high in the air, he grabbed her hand with the other and danced in a circle around her.

Edyth glanced over her shoulder towards the top table. Just as she'd suspected, Peter Slater and her sister Maggie were nowhere to be seen. 'The monster!' she hissed furiously.

'Pardon?' David bent his head close to hers.

'Nothing.' After making sure Peter was nowhere in sight, she began to dance as if she was auditioning for a chorus line.

When she finally managed to escape from David, Edyth made frequent and unsuccessful forays into the house and back garden in search of Peter. Finally, she decided that he must have left. She took what consolation she could in the thought that he was bound to be in St Catherine's church sometime the following day and returned to the party. Determined to make the most of the reception, she partnered every man who asked her to dance and was close to exhaustion when Harry tapped her on the shoulder two hours later. Ruth was lying, eyes half closed, against his shoulder.

'Sorry to interrupt, Edie, but Belle asked me to look for you. She's gone up to change and I think she'd appreciate some help.'

'I'm on my way.' She apologized to her partner and followed Harry back to the marquee. 'Poor little mite, it's tiring being a flower-girl.' She stroked Ruth's hair away from her flushed face.

'Especially when you've eaten as many strawberries, and as much cream, as she has. I'm just waiting for her to be sick over my morning suit,' Harry grimaced.

'Go on, admit it, you love being a father, even the messy bits.' She picked her way over the flowerbed, trying not to let her heels sink into the earth.

'Guilty as charged.' He moved his head and smiled at Ruth, who grinned back at him before sticking her thumb in her mouth. 'If you see Toby, tell him to bring his and Belle's cases down to the car.'

'Of course, I forgot. You and Mary are driving the newlyweds to Cardiff station.' She glanced around the guests in the marquee. 'I must look for the twins.'

'So they can tie things to my car?' Harry guessed. 'I won't thank you if you do.'

'The bride and groom have to have a noisy send-off. It's traditional.'

'Any damage to my Crossley, and I'll send you the bill,' Harry warned.

'I'll ask them to be kind to the paintwork.' She lifted her skirts to her knees and ran towards the house, dropping them quickly when she saw Peter Slater standing on the terrace talking to Reverend Price. He left the vicar and walked over to meet her.

'Edyth, I've been looking for you.'

'You have?' she smiled.

'I admit only for the last five minutes or so.' He dropped his voice to a whisper. 'Reverend Price insisted on introducing me to as many of the congregation as he could find. I've been admiring your mother's greenhouse for the last hour with Mrs Hopkins and a delegation from the Young Wives.'

Her mouth twitched and she turned her back to the vicar lest he see her giggling. 'Mrs Hopkins is a very keen gardener.'

'So I've discovered. Your mother certainly has green fingers. I've never seen such large tomatoes or cucumbers. Or,' he looked down over the lawns, 'well designed flowerbeds.'

'You should have been here last year. Despite all the watering and mulching, the hot summer has killed off some of her best plants.'

'Mrs Hopkins pointed out every single bare spot.' He returned her smile and she suppressed the urge to hug him.

'I'm sorry, Peter, I'd love to stay and talk to you, but Belle sent for me to help her change into her going away outfit.'

'Perhaps we can talk later?' he suggested. 'I always wait to wave the bridal couple off at weddings. It's the best part after the church service.'

'I think so, too.' She looked at him and, to her embarrassment, felt her cheeks burning. She rarely blushed. Why did she have to do it now of all times?

'See you later.'

'I'll look forward to it.' She opened the front door and went into the hall. It was deserted, but an ominous thud resounded from the downstairs cloakroom. Having spotted the twins and a crowd of her younger cousins continuing their drinking and smoking in the shrubbery earlier, she thought one of them might have passed out. She knocked on the door in concern. When there was no answer she shouted, 'Are you all right in there?'

'Go away,' slurred a masculine voice.

'Not until I know you're all right.' She tried the door but it seemed to be locked. She turned the doorknob but someone was holding it fast on the other side. 'Open the door.'

'Go away.'

She put her shoulder to the door and pushed. A blood-curdling scream echoed from inside, ending abruptly in another dull thud.

'What the hell was that?' Toby stood on the landing in his shirtsleeves, his braces hanging down over the trousers of his morning suit, his flies open.

'Someone's in the cloakroom, I thought it might be one of the twins or Eddie . . .'

'That was a woman.'

'I heard a scream.' Harry ran in, with Ruth now asleep on his shoulder. He saw Toby and shouted, 'You're not on honeymoon yet. Button up.'

'Sorry, Edyth.' Red-faced, Toby turned his back to her.

'Someone's in the cloakroom.' Edyth tried the doorknob again but it wouldn't budge.

'They obviously don't want to be disturbed,' Harry commented.

'That's where the scream came from.' She knocked the door again and there was a hollow bang as if something had hit the porcelain sink.

'Here, take Ruth, Edyth.' Harry handed her his daughter and banged on the door with his fist. 'Whoever's inside, open up.'

'What's going on?' Mari walked down the passageway from the kitchen, an apron tied over her finery.

'Someone's in the cloakroom; we're afraid they might be ill,' Edyth explained.

'If they are, it's a sight we don't want to risk this little moppet waking and seeing.' Mari lifted Ruth from Edyth's arms and carried her off as another drunken mumble, came from behind the closed door.

Toby ran down the stairs at the same time as the twins and Eddie entered the porch with a crowd of young boys.

'We heard banging and screaming. Is something going on?' Eddie's eyes shone with excitement – and alcohol.

'That's what we're trying to find out,' Harry answered.

Jed King pushed his way through the mass of boys. 'Has anyone seen Judy? She came in for a glass of water half an hour ago. People are getting fed up with instrumental music . . .'

A second muffled scream echoed from behind the door. Harry didn't wait to hear any more. He ran at the cloakroom door. It shuddered when his shoulder connected with it. He stepped back and hurtled towards it a second time. The lock gave way at his third attempt and splintered open, but the door only moved an inch.

'Here, let me,' Toby slid his foot into the crack.

'After three, push forward with all your strength,' Harry ordered. Jed joined them and they used their combined weight to force it open, although they only managed to move it a couple of inches. But through the gap they could see Judy Hamilton crouched beneath the sink. Tears were running down her face and there were angry red fingermarks on her neck.

'What the hell . . . Judy . . .' Jed, who was behind Harry and Toby, darted forward.

Judy looked up at Jed, Harry and Toby but she didn't move. Her arms were wrapped around her chest, but they could see that the bodice of her frock had been torn to the waist.

'Heave on my count,' Harry commanded. 'One . . . two . . . three . . .'

The three men managed to open the door wide enough for Harry to stick his head through the gap. He looked down on Charlie Moore, who was lying slumped on the floor and jamming the door. He stank of whisky and sweat, his face flushed and scarred by livid scratches on his cheeks and chin.

Harry shouted to the twins, 'Get everyone out of here, close the front door behind you and fetch my mother and father.' He didn't wait to see them run off. Shrugging off his jacket, he said, 'Move, Charlie.'

'I can't,' Charlie mumbled.

'You want me to kick the door down on top of you? Because if that's the only way I can get you to move, I will do it,' Harry threatened.

Charlie slithered into the corner beside the toilet pan. Harry stepped inside and handed his jacket to Judy.

Shaking with rage, Jed followed Harry and crouched in front of Judy. 'Did he hurt you, Judy?'

She shook her head dumbly.

'Are you sure?'

She pulled at the ragged edge of her dress and nodded a reply.

Harry leaned over, sank his fingers into Charlie's collar, hauled him to his feet and shoved him into the hall, as Lloyd and Sali appeared.

Lloyd took in the situation at a glance and closed the front door behind them.

Jed helped Judy to her feet. 'She's my niece . . .'

'She's a bloody half-caste,' Charlie slurred. 'Everyone knows coloured girls are always begging for it. They're not like white girls . . . they . . .'

Jed closed his hand into a fist and squared up in front of Charlie.

'No, Jed.' Toby pushed him aside.

'The bastard . . .'

'I couldn't agree with you more,' Toby said coldly. 'But I introduced him into this house and I'm ashamed to say he's here at my invitation. The honour is entirely mine.' He punched Charlie solidly on the jaw.

Charlie fell backwards and hit the floor.

'The unfortunate thing about drunks is that they never really hurt themselves.' Toby blew on his fist to cool it.

# Chapter 3

'ARE YOU ABSOLUTELY SURE Charlie Moore didn't hurt you, Judy?' Jed King sat beside his niece on the sofa in the Evanses' sitting room and looked earnestly into her eyes.

Judy's voice was huskier than ever. 'He put his hands around my neck and tore my frock, but he was too drunk to do anything else. To be honest, Uncle Jed, I think he even tore my frock by accident. The lace caught in his signet ring. You won't tell the police, will you?' She looked at him in alarm. 'Remember what happened to Diane Robertson?' She turned from her uncle to Lloyd, who was standing in front of the hearth. 'Please, Mr Evans,' she begged, 'don't call the police.'

'We can't simply ignore what Charlie Moore did to you,' Lloyd said firmly. 'He attacked you. He could attack another girl.'

'That's a risk we'll have to take, Mr Evans. For Judy's sake,' Jed interrupted.

'But the man could have killed her.'

'We all know what he had on his mind and it wasn't murder.' Jed glanced apologetically at Sali, who was sitting in one of the easy chairs. 'Diane Robertson was a friend of Judy's. She was . . .' He cleared his throat uneasily. 'She was attacked by the son of one of the high-ups in a bank in Bute Street.' He didn't have to say any more. Lloyd and Sali knew he meant raped. 'Diane's father was a West Indian seaman, her mother Welsh, from Newport. Having faith in British justice, they insisted the police prosecute the boy. But his family are rich; they employed a barrister who painted Diane as a loose woman. She was only fourteen, and worked as a daily maid to two spinsters. One of her brothers walked her to and from work, and she wasn't allowed out in the evenings except with her family. Apart from the one time she ran down to Bute Street in the evening when she wanted to buy some cotton thread and her brothers were out. The character references the family priest and her teachers gave in court didn't make any difference to the judge, or to Diana's employers. They sacked her, she lost her reputation and the boy walked away scot-free.'

'I'm sorry,' Lloyd sympathized.

'That would be bad enough if it was the end of it, but it wasn't. Not wanting to bring any more disgrace on her family, Diane ran away from home. Her mother hoped she'd gone to London or one of the other big cities to look for work. Two months later they found her body in the dock. She'd drowned herself.'

'I can see why you don't want me to call the police,' Lloyd murmured.

Judy stared down at her hands in her lap. She'd spent the last twenty minutes upstairs with Sali and Edyth. Fortunately, Edyth was the same size as her and she'd given her a blue organza frock to replace her torn evening gown. Sali had also made her a present of a lace scarf, which she'd wrapped around her neck to hide the bruises.

'I don't want to think what might have happened if Miss Evans hadn't knocked on the door of the cloakroom when she did,' Judy whispered hoarsely, 'but I'm not badly hurt. The bruises will fade. I couldn't bear to go to the police. They'd ask all sorts of questions. Want to make me out to be a bad girl . . .'

'It's not easy for coloured people to get justice in this country, Mr Evans.' Jed looked Lloyd in the eye.

'Or anyone from the working classes,' Lloyd commented.

Judy rose to her feet. 'I'll go out to the band.'

Jed pulled her back down on to the sofa. 'There'll be no more band or singing for you tonight, Judy. If Mrs Evans doesn't mind, I'd prefer you to stay here and rest for a while.'

'Don't worry, Mr King, I'll look after her.' Sali smiled at the girl. 'Let's go into the kitchen and get you a hot drink. That might soothe your throat.'

'I'd also appreciate it if you keep what happened quiet,' Jed said. 'Obviously your daughter, Toby and Harry saw it . . .'

'Toby told the boys that Charlie had passed out in the cloakroom and Miss Hamilton was trying to help him,' Lloyd answered. 'So I think I can safely say it won't go any further.'

'It's not because of gossip. If my brother Tony ever finds out what Charlie Moore did to Judy, he'd kill him.'

Sali shuddered. There was an expression in Jed King's eyes that told her he was deadly serious. She left her chair at a knock on the door.

Harry walked in. 'I'm not disturbing you, am I?'

'No,' Lloyd answered. 'Mr King and Miss Hamilton don't want to call the police.'

'Toby was afraid they might not. But, given the influence of the Moore family, he can understand their reluctance. That's why I'm here. We have to do something with Charlie.'

'As Toby invited him to the wedding, perhaps he can he suggest something?' Lloyd said drily.

'As we see it, we have two options: you can call the police and have him arrested but,' Harry flashed a quick glance at Judy, 'only for being drunk and disorderly.'

'At a private party?' Lloyd questioned sceptically. 'That reflects badly on our ability to look after our guests. But then, given what happened to Miss Hamilton, we certainly failed miserably when it came to that duty.'

'However,' Harry continued, 'Toby found twenty pounds in Charlie's wallet when we were cleaning him up after he'd been sick. We could call a taxi, put him in it and send him to his father's house in Cardiff. Toby has the address. And Toby's offered to write to Charlie to tell him that after the way he behaved today, he is no longer welcome in this house, or his.'

'What do you think of that idea, Miss Hamilton?' Lloyd asked.

'I don't care what happens to that man as long as I don't have to see him again.'

'I wish you would allow me to call the police. But I understand why you don't want me to.' Lloyd walked to the sideboard and picked up the brandy decanter. 'Can I pour you a drink, Mr King, Miss Hamilton?'

'Please,' Jed answered for both of them. 'There is one other thing that perhaps you don't know, Mr Evans. Charlie Moore is well known down Tiger Bay. His grandfather founded Moore's shipping agency, his father Edward runs it, and most of the seamen in our family as well as our friends and neighbours are dependent on the firm for their jobs.'

'That doesn't give Charlie Moore the right to behave the way he did. Rich and poor should be equal under the law, but as I've discovered, that is often far from the case.' Lloyd handed over the brandies he'd poured.

'If you found that out while working for a white man's union, Mr Evans, imagine what it's like for a black man. The Moores have money and influence. We have none. I love Judy dearly, but I agree with her. A woman's reputation is easily lost, and, once gone, never recovered.'

Lloyd poured himself and Sali brandies, then held up the bottle to Harry.

'No, thanks. Toby and I have taken Charlie next door. I'll ask David and some of the other boys to put him in the taxi and make sure the driver has his father's address. In the meantime, I'd better drive Toby and Bella to the station.'

'What happened to Judy was horrible . . .'

'I'm sorry I told you about it,' Edyth interrupted Bella.

'I'm glad you did. I never liked Charlie Moore,' Bella said vehemently. 'His father and grandfather are nice, but there's something horrid and spooky about Charlie.'

'I agree, but Toby had to be nice to him because of all the work the Moores put his way,' Edyth reminded her.

'Well, Charlie Moore won't be allowed to put a foot over my doorstep, I can tell you.'

'Forget him, Belle. You're going on honeymoon, remember?' Edyth laid the lace veil carefully on the bed and folded it between sheets of tissue paper.

Belle went to the window and gazed out over the lawn. The band was playing 'Someone to Watch Over Me' in slow tempo, and several couples were dancing, arms locked around one another, on the wooden platform. 'I bet the party is going to go on for hours.' She picked up her wide-brimmed, cream straw hat from her dressing table, set it on her head and angled it first one way then another.

'Of course it will.' Edyth handed her sister her pearl-headed hatpin.

'Thank you, for your sisterly consolation.'

'You don't need consoling.' Edyth looked around the room to see if Bella had forgotten anything. 'You're dressed like a film star, you've a suitcase full of brand new clothes that wouldn't disgrace a duchess and in an hour you'll be on a sleeper leaving Cardiff for Southampton. Tomorrow night you'll be cruising across the Atlantic to New York on the *Olympic*. And that's without bringing Toby into the equation. I've never even *seen* a ship with a swimming pool, let alone America.'

'But you can stay at the party and flirt with as many boys as you want.' Bella finally adjusted her hat to her satisfaction and secured it.

'You'd rather change places with me and give up your honeymoon with Toby so you can flirt with boys?'

'No.' Bella's mouth twitched and her eyes glittered, suspiciously damp.

'Sorry you married Toby?' Edyth questioned in concern.

'Of course not.'

'You're worried because tonight's the night?' Edyth ventured.

Bella lowered her voice. 'That night was two years ago, and it was fantastic, but don't tell anyone. Although I think Mam suspects, and I don't doubt she's told Dad. They can't keep anything from one another.'

'You and Toby . . .'

'Wait until you fall in love, Edyth.' Bella exercised all the authority birth had bestowed on her as the eldest sister. 'I promise you, once you find the right one, you won't be able to think of anyone else or keep your hands off him. Or he you. And in this day and age you don't have to. Because making love doesn't have to result in a baby unless you want it to. But that doesn't mean I'm not looking forward to my honeymoon. The best part will be not having to sneak around when we want to make love and waking up next to Toby in the same bed every morning after lying naked next to him all night. There,' she faced Edyth. 'What do you think?'

'I think you look gorgeous and the hat is beautiful. But—'

'We'll have long talks when I come back. Don't forget we'll be living next door until our house is finished and even then we'll only be five minutes away.'

'And I'll be in Swansea teacher training college – if I pass my exams,' Edyth added.

'Of course you'll pass them, and you'll only be there in term-time.' Bella hugged Edyth again. 'Thank you for helping me to choose my trousseau, the wedding dresses and the flowers. And making the buttonholes. And a special thank you for putting up with my grumpy moods for the last couple of months. And looking after the little ones in church and stopping them from tripping up Toby and me with that basket.' Her voice wavered. 'I've been horrible to you over the years, Edie. Bossing you around just because I was a year older. We've had so many fights . . .'

'Haven't we?' Edyth said cheerfully. But her voice cracked when she confessed, 'But I've always loved you, Belle—'

'I hope that isn't crying I'm hearing, because if it is, I'll be joining you.' Sali walked in. She opened her arms and Bella went to her.

'Be happy, darling. You've a good husband who loves you very much.' Sali embraced Bella carefully so as not to crease her coffee and cream wild silk outfit.

'Mam . . .' Bella reached for her handkerchief, 'you and Dad . . . I – we – Toby and me – we can never thank you enough . . . I love – we both love you . . .'

'Your father and I know, darling.' Sali released her. 'But there's no time for speeches. You two have been gossiping up here for far too long as it is. Everyone's waiting to wave you off, and be warned, Auntie Megan and Auntie Rhian have been handing out bags of confetti so you and Toby can expect to get covered.'

'Did I hear someone take my name in vain?' Toby left Harry's room and looked in through the open door. He'd changed from his morning suit into a lounge suit and was carrying his coat, hat and a travelling rug.

Harry ran up the stairs. 'I've put your and Belle's cases in my car, Toby. I thought you two were honeymooning for six weeks.'

'We are.' Toby offered Bella his arm. 'Mrs Ross?'

'From the amount of luggage Belle's taking, I assumed you were emigrating.'

'I'm expecting several climate changes,' Bella replied defensively.

'Toby never said anything to me about taking you to the Arctic Circle. Come on,' Harry chivvied, as Toby gazed lovingly into Bella's eyes, 'if you don't get a move on you'll miss your train.'

'It's good of you and Mary to drive us to Cardiff, Harry, so we won't have to change trains,' Toby said gratefully. 'We appreciate it.'

'You won't be so appreciative if you end up spending your wedding night in the waiting room on Cardiff station.'

Toby and Bella walked along the landing, and Harry shouted loudly down the stairs, 'They're coming!'

Confetti showered down when Toby and Bella stepped on the top stair. They looked up to see Glyn and their younger cousins shaking bags over them from between the banisters on the attic staircase. Laughing, they ran down to the hall, with multi-coloured flecks of paper falling on them from all directions.

'You look like rainbow snowmen.' Joey kissed Bella's cheek and offered Toby his hand. 'That's my niece you've got there, look after her. If you don't, you'll have me to answer to.'

'Not to mention all the other men in the family. But don't worry, I'll take good care of her. Can I call you Uncle Joey now?' Toby joked when he shook Joey's hand firmly.

'Plain Joey will do.'

'Your name may be Ross, but you're one of us, and an Evans now.' Victor looked to the door. 'Lloyd's waiting at the car.'

Bella hugged and kissed Mari and Judy, who was at the old woman's side, and everyone else she could reach.

'Your bouquet, Belle.' Maggie picked it up from the hall stand where Bella had left it when she went upstairs to change. She thrust it at her. 'You have to throw it, so we'll know who is going to be next.'

Bella looked at her sisters and cousins lining the stairs. 'Catch!' She turned her back and flung her bouquet over her shoulder.

Maggie and Beth reached forward at the same time but Maggie knocked it wide and it fell neatly into Edyth's hand. When she looked up, Peter Slater was clapping and cheering along with everyone else. He leaned close to her ear so she could hear him above the noise.

'Congratulations, Edyth.' He winked at her again and her spirits soared. There *was* something between them. And she knew – just *knew* – that he sensed it, too.

Holding the bouquet, Edyth followed Bella and Toby outside. Harry burst into laughter when he saw her.

'That settles it, sis, you're definitely next. So much for college.'

'She's going,' Lloyd growled. He opened the back door of Harry's car, kissed Bella and shook Toby's hand. 'Look after our daughter.'

'I will, sir,' Toby promised solemnly.

'It's wonderful to have another son.' Sali kissed Toby's cheek. Harry helped Mary into the front passenger seat, closed the doors on Toby and Bella in the back, and drove off to the clattering of the tin cans the boys had fastened to the bumper of his Crossley tourer.

The crowd dispersed, with most of the guests making their way to the marquee where the waitresses were serving wine and savouries. The band saw the car moving down the drive and Jed, who'd rejoined them, broke off mid-tune and signalled the others to switch to a jazzed-up version of the old wartime favourite 'Goodbyeee'.

Lloyd wrapped his arm around Edyth's waist. 'Make no mistake,' he warned, 'Reverend Slater or no Reverend Slater, you will be going to college, miss.'

'Reverend Slater?'

'Don't look so innocent, I saw you two talking non-stop throughout the wedding breakfast.'

'We were just talking. And, if I pass my exams, I promise I will go to college.'

He kissed her forehead. 'Good girl.'

'But you have to admit the Reverend Slater *is* very good-looking, Dad,' she teased.

'He's not my type.'

Joey playfully slapped Lloyd's back. 'How about breaking open that bottle of old malt you've been keeping for a special occasion, big brother?'

'His idea or yours? Lloyd asked Victor, who was hovering close by.

'Does it matter?' Victor smiled in anticipation.

Lloyd disappeared into the library with his brothers, and Edyth turned to the kitchen to fetch a vase for Bella's bouquet. Peter Slater touched her arm and she stepped back alongside him.

'Congratulations again on catching the bouquet.'

'Not that I'm superstitious enough to believe it means anything. But I will press it and frame it so Bella can keep it as a reminder.'

'Your sister looked very elegant. The softer lines of the longer skirts in fashion now are more attractive than the harsh silhouettes of the last decade. And she chose her colours well. Coffee and cream go well together, especially when worn by someone as dark as your sister.'

'She did look lovely.' Edyth was astounded. She had never met a man who had been remotely interested in women's clothes before. Certainly not to the extent of daring to express an opinion on an outfit.

'There are more hats here than in your average milliner's.' He flicked through the dozens of caps, panamas and trilbys on the shelf above the coat rack and lifted one down.

'You're not going just when I'm free, Peter?'

'I have no choice. But thank you for your warm welcome. It was kind of your parents to invite a newcomer to a family wedding.' He glanced in the mirror and dropped his panama on his head.

'The pleasure was all ours.' She repeated the standard phrase without thinking. 'I had hoped that we could continue our conversation over supper.'

'As you pointed out earlier, tomorrow's the busiest day of my week.' He moved back against the wall when Mrs Hopkins sallied forth in search of her coat.

'The band is still playing and we're serving light refreshments. Couldn't you stay just a little while longer?' she pleaded.

'Forgive me but Reverend Price has asked me to take the early-morning service and I need to revise my sermon.' He gave her a conspiratorial smile. 'I've found out the hard way that a curate's reputation can be made or broken by the first sermon he preaches in a town. Too long and he's considered pompous and boring; too short and he's slapdash; and pick the wrong subject – well, I won't go into that one until I know you better. Suffice to say that when I preached about Jesus overturning the usurers' tables in the temple, one tally man in Llanelli moved his entire family to a neighbouring parish. But we spoke about the youth club earlier?'

'We did.' Although he had removed his hand from her arm, her heart was pounding erratically.

'Our next meeting is at half past six on Monday evening in the church hall. We have a dozen or so girls among our members. Unfortunately they have a tendency to indulge in horseplay and wear too much cheap scent and make-up. They might respond to the advice of someone like yourself. That is, if you can spare the time to give them a few tips. I noticed that you wear no make-up at all and your complexion is perfect.'

Edyth didn't have the heart to tell him that she was wearing the discreet make-up her mother had taught her and all her sisters to apply. 'I would be delighted to help in any way that you think I can, Peter.'

'See you on Monday evening, Edyth.'

'Until then.' Edyth spotted Maggie bearing down on them. She handed her Bella's bouquet. 'Be an angel and put these in water for me, please, Maggie, while I walk Reverend Slater to the gate.'

Maggie snatched the flowers ungraciously and thumbed her nose at Edyth, just as Peter Slater turned to offer her his hand to say goodbye.

Night had fallen when Harry and Mary returned from taking Toby and Bella to Cardiff station. The air in the garden was warm; thick

44

and velvety, heavily scented with flowers and wax from the candles that Sali and the girls had lit and dotted among the plants in the flowerbeds. The maids were serving coffee, cake and sweet biscuits, but mindful of the noise of the music carrying down to the town, Lloyd had asked the band to stop playing at ten o'clock and most of the guests had left. Harry and Mary found the musicians sitting at a table that had been carried out from the marquee, drinking beer and talking to the family.

'Did the honeymooners make their train?' Lloyd lifted the chair next to his out from under the table and offered it to Mary.

'They did.' Mary sat down. 'But not before Toby and Harry quarrelled about Harry's driving.'

'I gave Toby a choice,' Harry said airily. 'I told him that I could either get him and Bella to Cardiff station on time or drive safely. Toby said he preferred me to drive safely. But Bella asked me to get to the station on time, and everyone knows it's the woman who makes the decisions in every marriage.'

'Well said, Harry. Here's to the legions of hen-pecked men. Poor Toby has no idea what's in store for him.' Joey drained his beer mug and held it out to Harry. 'As you're getting yourself and Mary drinks, you may as well refill all our glasses.'

'Thank you, Uncle Joey. You know I love to play barman.' Harry took the glass and turned the tap on the beer barrel set up on a side table alongside an array of bottles of sherry, wine, raspberry cordial and lemonade.

'I like to make everyone happy.' Joey beamed at the table in general.

'Especially yourself,' Victor quipped. 'How many shorts did you feed our little brother, Lloyd?'

'As many as he fed you and himself, judging by the width of the smiles on all your faces,' Sali answered for Lloyd.

'Whatever you do, Ruth, don't grow up into a nagging wife like your grandmother and great-aunts.' Joey gravely addressed the sleeping child on his lap.

'Let me take Ruth from you, Uncle Joey,' Mary offered shyly. Harry's extended family had welcomed her and her orphaned brothers and sister as if they were long-lost relatives, but her upbringing on an isolated farm in Breconshire hadn't brought her into contact with many people and she still felt a little shy of them, especially when they were gathered *en masse*.

'Absolutely not.' Joey shook his head. 'My children insist they're too old for cuddles these days so I'm making the most of it.'

'Does that mean you're getting broody and there'll soon be another Evans joining the clan?' Victor asked.

'Six is enough for me,' Rhian stated decisively.

'We only have five.' Joey frowned at his wife.

'Five and you makes six, and you're more trouble than all the children put together.' When the laughter died down she said, 'I'm looking to the next generation to provide us with babies.'

'As am I,' Megan added. 'Unless Sali would like to surprise us.'

'There are no surprises coming from this direction but I would like dozens of grandchildren,' Sali said, 'especially if they're all as pretty and sweet-tempered as Ruth. You've done a magnificent job of bringing her up, Mary, as well as teaching her the hardest lesson of all. She understands the word "no". It's a pity you weren't around to tell me your secret when Edyth was small. If you had been, you might have saved her some broken bones.'

'I wasn't that bad.' Edyth handed Harry her empty sherry glass.

'As I recall, you spent more years with your legs and arms in plaster than out of it.' Harry looked around. 'Everyone have a drink?'

'We do. Cheers and good health to the father and mother of the bride for hosting the wedding and hiring us to play here today.' Jed King rose to his feet and lifted his glass ceremoniously. 'And here's to the bride and groom, Mr and the new Mrs Ross.'

'Lucky ducks, going to America,' Susie murmured sleepily.

'Do you play at many weddings?' Joey asked.

'That's something you won't need to know for a few years yet, Joey. You have to keep your girls for a while longer before you can marry them off,' Victor warned.

They all laughed again. Joey's eldest daughter was only ten.

'Parties like this and audiences like your family are unfortunately rare for us, Mr Evans,' Jed answered.

'I've a feeling that much as we all enjoy them, parties will become rarer still in the next few years,' Lloyd said cautiously. 'Times have been hard since the Wall Street crash last October and they will be getting harder. The government is expecting the number of unemployed to reach two million next month, and that's bad news for everyone.'

'It's catastrophic for those of us living on Cardiff docks, Mr Evans,' Micah Holsten said quietly.

'Why worse for those in Tiger Bay?' Harry lifted a chair out from another table and sat next to Mary.

'Because trade is always the first casualty of a recession,' Micah explained. 'Markets shrink, fewer goods are produced, fewer ships sail and hundreds of seamen will find themselves without a berth, which means their families will go hungry. And fewer ships also means a cutback in the number of workers needed to load and unload cargoes. Dockers or seamen, coloured men are always the last to be taken on by those hiring labour and the first to be let go. And a large proportion of the seamen and dockers in Tiger Bay are coloured.'

'It would be naive of us to suppose otherwise,' Lloyd said seriously. 'I've spent my life fighting for workers' rights and an end to discrimination based on class, colour and creed, but I sometimes wonder if we've made any progress since my father and his fellow miners formed their unions in the last century.'

'You're too hard on yourself, Lloyd. We've come a long way in the last fifty years.' Victor opened a packet of cigarettes and offered them around.

'We have further to go than we've come,' Lloyd said thoughtfully.

'There's no discrimination within our community, Mr Evans. Thank you.' Jed took one of Victor's cigarettes. 'We've all sorts living on Bute Street and in the smaller houses behind it. Black, brown, white, yellow, Arab, Muslim, Hindu, Jew—'

'A regular box of liquorice all sorts,' Tony King joked.

'And no one there gives a toss about colour.'

'Except for some of the constables and their families, who live in the Maria Street police station,' Tony chipped in.

47

'Most of them are fair blokes,' Jed qualified. 'Generally speaking, we're like one big happy family.'

'With a few black sheep.' Tony nodded at Micah. 'Take this one, for example. He's too forgiving with the drunks and certain ladies—'

'Tony, you're not in the Pilot in George Street now,' Jed interrupted.

'I heard a lot of stories about Tiger Bay when I went to that party in Moore's shipping offices with Bella and Toby.' Edyth took a biscuit and broke it in half. 'I'd love to walk around there and see the place for myself.'

'What kind of stories?' Lloyd enquired warily.

'One of the clerks was telling us that he and his brother had been invited to someone's house for supper, but they never made it. He said as soon as they left Bute Street and went into the side streets, everyone was singing and dancing, all the front doors were open and he felt as though they'd walked into one enormous street party. They ended up eating supper with total strangers.'

'It can be like that around carnival time,' Jed agreed, as relieved as Lloyd that Edyth hadn't been referring to anything more risqué than the music that was played in the streets around the docks practically every night. 'It only takes one person to bring out an instrument and start playing to get the whole neighbourhood joining in.'

'With spoons, comb and paper, and saucepan drums, if that's all they have.' Micah flicked his cigarette into the ashtray on the table. 'In Tiger Bay, music has an impromptu and international flavour.'

'You're welcome to visit any time you want, Miss Evans. My grandmother would love to make your acquaintance,' Judy Hamilton offered shyly.

'Thank you, Miss Hamilton. After your performance here today I suspect I'll have the life plagued out of me until I bring the entire family down for a visit.' Lloyd glanced at Glyn, who was almost asleep on the chair next to him. 'It's time the little ones were in bed.'

'I'll chase them.' Sali left her chair.

'I'll give you a hand,' Rhian offered.

'We should round up the boys and head for home, Megs.' Victor rose to his feet. 'You did Bella proud, Lloyd, Sali. It's been a wonderful day but my legs feel as though they don't belong to me. I'm getting too old for dancing.'

'Judging by the amount you've done since I met you, I'd say that you were born too old for dancing, my darling.' Megan left her seat and slipped her arm around Victor's waist.

'Stay here, Uncle Victor, Auntie Megan.' Harry finished his beer. 'I'll find the boys for you.'

'I can see the smoke wafting over the shrubs by the gate the same as you, Harry.' Victor squeezed Megan's waist lightly.

'Let me at least go down there and warn them that you're on your way.' Harry set his glass on the table.

'You're not one of the kids any more, Harry. Not now you have one and a half of your own. A grown-up's job is to stop kids from having fun.' Joey looked down at Ruth who was still fast asleep on his lap.

'I'm trying to take over from where Granddad left off. Not that I could hope to fill an inch of his shoes,' Harry said ruefully. 'But he never allowed anyone to get caught doing something they shouldn't at a family party.'

'Possibly because he was usually the one instigating the naughtiness,' Sali recalled fondly. Lloyd's father had died four years ago, yet everyone in the family who was old enough to remember him still missed him, especially at get-togethers at Christmas, weddings and christenings.

'Please, stay and have another drink,' Lloyd pressed the musicians, who were leaving their seats. 'Don't feel that you have to go, just because we're sending the children to bed.'

'It's a long drive back to Butetown, and as it's my van we're using and I have to be up early tomorrow to take services, it's high time we left.' Micah Holsten picked up his saxophone case.

'Take services?' Harry questioned.

'Micah is the Lutheran pastor at the Norwegian mission,' Jed explained.

'But we Catholics forgive him because he makes our kind of music,' Tony joked.

'And, as good Catholics, we also have to be up early. The wife insists on all of us going to first mass.' Jed slipped a protective arm around Judy's shoulders. 'Thank you again for hiring us, Mr Evans.'

'Thank you for making Bella's day special. It certainly went with a swing.' Lloyd shook Tony's hand before slipping his hand into his pocket and pulling out an envelope. 'There's extra in there to replace Miss Hamilton's dress. I'm sorry our cook stained it.' He repeated the story he, Sali and Jed had concocted to explain Judy's change of outfit to the rest of the band and the guests.

'There's no need—'

'Yes, there is,' Sali said firmly. She kissed Judy's cheek.

'I'll send this frock back.'

'Please don't,' Edyth pressed. 'It looks much better on you than me, and to tell the truth it was getting too tight for me.'

'Too many of Mari's chocolate puddings, miss,' Joey teased. 'Well, we all know where to come the next time we need a band.' He stretched his hands above his head and yawned.

'From the look of everyone, it's just as well tomorrow's Sunday.' Rhian lifted Ruth from Joey's lap.

'I can't see anyone in this house getting up for early mass or church,' Lloyd commented.

Edyth didn't contradict her father. But as she said her goodbyes to the musicians, and her uncles, aunts and cousins, she was already planning the outfit she would wear to the early church service at St Catherine's in the morning.

# Chapter 4

JUDY HAMILTON woke with a start the next morning when the church bells started ringing out over Tiger Bay. She threw back the bedclothes and shot out of bed. Hating mornings, especially after late nights, she'd taken the precaution of laying out a clean uniform, shoes, stockings and underclothes before she had left for the wedding the day before. Scooping them from the rickety wooden chair next to her bed, she ran down the uncarpeted wooden stairs into the kitchen.

Pearl, her grandmother, was up, dressed in her flowered work overall, and mixing oats in the porridge pan. The smell of soda hung, nose-stinging, in the air, the flagstone floor was damp from its morning scrubbing and the range gleamed with newly applied black lead.

'Morning, Gran.' Judy dumped her clothes on the only easy chair in the room.

'You'll do yourself an injury rushing around like that.'

'I'm late.'

'No, you're not,' Pearl contradicted. 'It's not half past seven yet. What time did you come home last night?'

'A reasonable hour,' Judy answered evasively.

'I heard you and Jed talking at the door after midnight. But seeing as how Sunday's your half-day, I suppose you can have a nap later.'

'I will, Gran.' Judy kissed her grandmother's wrinkled cheek and went out the back. The family referred to Pearl King's garden as a 'cultivated wilderness'. The sprig of jasmine she had planted next to the ty bach when she had moved into the house as a bride over sixty years before now covered the roof of the outhouse as

51

well as the walls. Knee-high lavender bushes bordered both sides of the crazy paving path below the washing line, and clumps of poppies bloomed, adding splashes of crimson to the shadows beneath the garden walls.

Judy unhooked the tin bath from the back yard wall on her return from the ty bach, carried it into the washhouse and half-filled it with jugs of water that she drew from the cold tap set above the outside drain in the yard. She stripped off her nightgown, stepped into the water and washed as quickly as she could coax lather out of the carbolic soap in the freezing water. After drying herself, she dressed in her plain black cotton maid's uniform. When she'd finished, she dragged the bath outside and emptied it down the drain before wiping it and returning it to the hook on the wall.

'Breakfast is ready.'

'Coming, Gran.' She went into the back kitchen and sat at the wooden table, covered with a darned checked tablecloth that was older than her.

Her grandmother set a bowl filled with porridge in front of her. 'I don't see why Mrs Protheroe has to have you in on a Sunday.'

'I keep telling you, Gran, she likes me to do the fires and make her dinner. I won't be long; she only eats salads in summer.'

'Everybody is entitled to one day off a week,' Mrs King grumbled.

'I had one yesterday,' Judy reminded her.

'From Mrs Protheroe, maybe, but it was no day off for you when you were out singing with Jed's band all day.'

'Singing's fun, not work. You should have seen the wedding.' Judy's eyes sparkled as she concentrated on the early part of the day and pushed Charlie Moore's attack from her mind. 'The wedding breakfast was in a massive house and they'd put up a huge tent on the lawn. The food was out of this world. The family even laid a buffet in the kitchen for the helpers, including us. And the bride was stunning. Her frock was satin and all the bridesmaids were dressed in gold—'

'And you'll have threads hanging from your mouth if you talk any faster,' her grandmother reproved.

'It was a good day.'

'You never have time to rest.'

'I get more time off living out of Mrs Protheroe's than I would have if I lived in. And the chance to eat breakfast with you every day.' Judy sprinkled brown sugar on her porridge and began to eat.

Her grandmother poured a cup of tea, put sugar and a splash of milk in it, and set it next to Judy's bowl. 'Did you get paid yesterday for singing with the band?'

'I put five pounds ten shillings in the box last night,' Judy said proudly.

'Where did you get that kind of money?' Pearl frowned suspiciously.

'Mr Evans, who hired the band, gave Jed five pounds plus petrol money for Mr Holsten's van. My share was ten shillings.'

'And the five pounds?' her grandmother questioned suspiciously.

Judy hung her head. She hated telling lies but this was one that had to be told. 'The housekeeper bumped into me and spilled red wine over my frock. It was ruined. Mr Evans insisted on paying me five pounds to replace it. And his daughter gave me a dress to wear home. She said I could keep it, but I'll wash it and send it back.'

'Good girl. They might be crache but it's as well to show them that we don't take charity. But five pounds is a lot of money for a frock. It didn't cost you that much, did it?'

Judy shook her head. 'You know me. I've never paid more than a pound for a dress in my life. I gave Anna Hughes ten shillings for that one. She said she was too fat to get into it.'

'You stay away from that woman,' Pearl warned severely.

'She's not so bad, Gran.'

'The way she makes her money is. You don't want to get tarred with her brush. A young girl like you just starting out in life can't be too careful about the company she keeps.'

'All I did was buy a frock from her. I wouldn't have got it cheaper anywhere else.' She spooned the last of her porridge into her mouth.

'No wonder you never put on any weight the way you rush

53

around. I'll have dinner on the table at two. Mind you're home to eat it.'

'I will be, Gran.' Judy carried her cup, saucer and bowl into the washhouse and stacked them on the wooden board next to the Belfast sink. She sprinkled a few drops of water from a glass on to a saucer of salt, worked it into a mixture with her toothbrush and cleaned her teeth. She combed her hair, checked her reflection perfunctorily in the mirror and left the house.

'Back at two if not before,' her grandmother shouted after her. 'I'm cooking a beef heart.'

'I'll be home to eat it, Gran.'

The street was full of children dressed in their Sunday best. They were standing around kicking their heels because they'd been warned on pain of dire punishment to stay clean until it was time to walk to church.

Judy greeted them, stopped to admire one small girl's new sandals and ran. If there was one thing Mrs Protheroe hated, it was her maid starting late in the morning, and it was a good mile from Tiger Bay to the quiet suburban street where her employer lived.

Peter Slater uttered the final 'Amen' of the service, faced the altar, bowed and led the procession of servers, candle-bearers, choirmaster and choir into the vestry. The moment the last and smallest boy in the choir closed the door that connected the vestry to the main body of the church, Peter opened the outside door and ran around the building so he could greet the congregation as they filed out of the porch.

More than a hundred worshippers had arrived to hear the first sermon he had preached in Pontypridd, and he had been surprised and gratified to see Edyth Evans among them.

He spoke to everyone in turn, introducing himself to the parishioners he hadn't met and exchanging smalltalk with the ones he already knew. Three-quarters of an hour passed before he reached the end of the queue and he was acutely aware of Edyth's presence in the church the whole time.

'Reverend Price has told me a great deal about you, Mr Chubb, Mrs Chubb. I look forward to becoming better acquainted with both of you.' He shook the hands of the frail, elderly couple, who had remained in their pew until the crowd had dissipated. 'Hello again,' his smile widened when Edyth finally reached him, 'You were the last person I expected to see here this morning. I assumed that all your family would be catching up on their sleep after the excitement of yesterday.'

Edyth hoped he hadn't noticed she'd deliberately hung back and talked to the Chúbbs so she would be the last in the queue. 'None of us were in bed that late, Peter. After Bella and Toby left for Cardiff station, most of the wedding guests went home.'

'But the rest of your family didn't come with you this morning.'

'My sisters will be attending Evensong with my mother. I won't be able to join them because I promised my brother I'd look after his daughter so he and his wife can dine with the family solicitor.' It was the truth, but Edyth hoped he didn't suspect that she wouldn't have contemplated attending the early service if the Reverend Price had been officiating.

'Then I'll look forward to renewing my acquaintance with your mother and sisters this evening when I assist Reverend Price.'

'I enjoyed your sermon.' She had, and tried not to sound gushing. 'The Book of Ruth is one of my favourites. The words are poignant and so poetic. "For whither thou goest, I will go; and where thou lodgest, I will lodge: thy people shall be my people, thy God my God".'

'I think the Book has particular relevance to Wales. Given how few people lived in this country, and especially the valleys before the coal mines were sunk, I doubt there is a family here without at least one foreign-born or English member, if not in their present, then in a previous generation. And just as King David's Moabite grandmother, Ruth, precluded him from being born of pure stock, so do the Irish, English, Spanish and others who came to the valleys and intermarried with the Welsh.'

'I've never thought of it, but you're right. My father's mother was Spanish, although I never knew her. She died before my parents met.'

'As you probably gathered from my sermon, I deplore nationalism when it preaches superiority. My mother is English and

I was teased unmercifully at my primary school because my accent wasn't the same as my classmates'.'

'My father taught us that tolerance takes precedence over religion and nationalism.' Edyth opened her handbag and took out her handkerchief, not because she wanted it, but because Peter's steady gaze was unsettling her.

'I wish there'd been parents like him in Swansea when I'd been growing up.' He ran his fingers through his thick black hair. 'I'm afraid I'm petty-minded enough still to resent the bullying I was subjected to. I'm sorry,' he apologized, 'I didn't mean to bore you with a lecture.'

'You are not boring me. I enjoy discussions, especially theological ones, which is why I opted to study religion along with English and history in the sixth form.' She noticed that his brown eyes looked even darker in the gloom of the stone porch.

'Are you looking forward to going to teacher training college?'

'The place is conditional on my matriculating. The results aren't out yet.'

'I'm sure that an intelligent girl like you has passed.'

'And I'm not at all sure I have.'

But it wasn't that she was unsure about her examination results; without being over-confident, she was fairly certain she'd passed. It was her choice of college and career that she had mixed feelings about. Some days, she felt as though she couldn't wait to get to Swansea and begin studying; other days she was reluctant to even think about leaving her family and Pontypridd. And now there was Peter. 'My maths leaves a lot to be desired.'

'You intend to teach religious education?'

'If I qualify it will be as a primary school teacher, so I'll be expected to teach a little of everything.' She wrinkled her nose. 'But I'm not looking forward to teaching science or maths. They've always been my weakest subjects, although they were my father's strongest. He was a mining engineer before he became an MP.'

'Reverend Price told me he was a member of the Communist party.'

'He has been elected as a Labour MP.' Edyth was instantly on the defensive. 'Reverend Price is aware that he is an atheist. My father has never made a secret of his beliefs to his family, friends or constituents.'

'I didn't mean to suggest otherwise,' Peter said hastily. 'Reverend Price told me that he is one of the most charitable and moral men in the town.'

'My father insists his principles stem from the precepts laid down by Karl Marx, although he will concede that some are similar to Biblical teachings.' Edyth smarted at what she took to be an implied criticism of her adored father. 'Thank you again for the sermon, Peter. Good morning.' She walked out into the sunshine that dappled the trees.

He ran after her. 'Edyth, I apologize if I have upset you. I only mentioned Communism because I am appallingly ignorant about Marxism, which I cannot afford to be with so many miners living in the parish. Do you think that if I asked him, your father would explain Marx's philosophy to me?'

'My father frequently addresses open political meetings and chairs political discussions.'

'Would you be kind enough to let me know when he next speaks publicly, so I can make every effort to attend?' He gave her a conciliatory smile.

'I will.'

He nodded to the verger who was heading for the church to tidy the hymnals and hassocks before the next service. 'If you wouldn't mind waiting a few minutes while I change out of this surplice, it would be a pleasure to walk you home.'

Edyth hesitated. He had apologized for his remarks. And, like everyone in her family, she was over-sensitive when it came to their father's politics. With good reason, because they were always meeting people outside of the mining and working classes who were hostile towards Socialism, and regarded Marxism as heathen, ungodly — and because of what had happened in Russia thirteen years before — incendiary, destructive and revolutionary.

'I wish I could take back my words.' He gave her one of his heart-melting smiles. 'Please, tell me what more I can say to make amends, and I'll say it.'

'I'll wait for you to change so you can walk me home,' she conceded.

'And on the way perhaps you'll tell me about the local beauty spots. I am a keen walker. Reverend Price has mentioned that there are several interesting sights in and around Pontypridd.'

'There are.'

'I don't suppose you would you consider showing some of them to me?'

She had been right yesterday; he was the handsomest man she had ever seen. And it would be so easy to fall in love with him the way Bella had Toby . . .

'Edyth?' he prompted.

Hoping her thoughts weren't mirrored on her face, she gave him the answer he was waiting to hear. 'As I have nothing to do until the results of my examination are posted, when I'll find out whether I need to start preparing for college or not, I would be delighted to show you my favourite walks around Pontypridd, Peter.'

Judy knocked on the door of Mrs Protheroe's sitting room but she didn't dare enter until she heard, 'Come in.'

'I've banked up the kitchen stove, so it will be all right until morning, Mrs Protheroe. I've laid the table for you in the dining room, covered your chicken salad with greaseproof paper and put it on the marble slab in the pantry, and I've made an apple flan for your afters.'

'Dessert, Judy, not "afters",' the widow reprimanded.

'Sorry, Mrs Protheroe, dessert.'

'Here.' Her employer held out an envelope.

Judy's mouth went dry. 'What is it, Mrs Protheroe?'

'Five shillings for last week and two shillings extra to see you through until you find yourself another position.'

'You're firing me?' Judy stared at the widow in disbelief. She had worked for Mrs Protheroe ever since she had left school at the age of twelve, six years before.

'I've taken on the sister of Mrs Davies's maid. She's going to live in. It will suit me better to have someone in the house and you're busy with your grandmother.'

'Please, Mrs Protheroe—'

'Thank you for all you've done, Judy,' Mrs Protheroe cut her short. 'But it's a question of money. Times are hard and I can get a girl to live in for what I've been paying you.'

'I'm sure my grandmother wouldn't mind me living in as long as I could visit her a couple of times a week,' Judy said desperately. So many girls who lived in the Bay hadn't been able to find work of any kind after they had left school; she knew it might prove impossible to find another position that paid five shillings a week plus meals.

'The girl's moving in tonight, Judy. Make up her bed in the box room before you go.'

'Yes, Mrs Protheroe.' Realizing further argument was futile, Judy pocketed the envelope and climbed the stairs. She had the five pounds Mr Evans had given her for her dress. It would be a godsend because she and her grandmother were only just managing to cover the rent, bills and food between them as it was. That gave her twenty weeks – five months. She was prepared to work hard and do anything legal that would bring in a wage. Surely she would find another position in that time . . .

Then she remembered her audition for the chorus of *The Vagabond King*. If she got the part she would be paid thirty shillings a week. She'd have to pay her board and lodge out of that but the company would cover her travelling expenses and if she was careful she might be able to send her grandmother as much as seven shillings and sixpence or even ten shillings a week.

Busy building castles – or rather a career – in the air, she hummed 'The song of the Vagabonds' as she opened the door to the walk-in linen cupboard.

Perhaps Mrs Protheroe firing her might prove to be a blessing in disguise. It would give her the impetus she needed to concentrate on her singing. And if she didn't get a part in the chorus this time, she might get one at the next audition. Then she'd have a profession, not a job, and a better paid one than skivvying could ever be.

'You going to St Catherine's church youth club again, Edie?' Lloyd asked from the depths of his armchair where he was reading the *Pontypridd Observer* and smoking his pipe.

'Yes, Dad.' She lifted up each cushion on the drawing-room sofa in turn.

'And you walked up to Berw Falls with the curate this morning?'

Was it her imagination or did his voice have a slight edge? 'Miss Williams and I took a party of children from the Sunday school to Berw Falls, and Peter came with us. Miss Williams is teaching her class to collect and press wild flowers and I offered to help.' She threw down the last cushion in exasperation.

'You've been to youth club three times a week for the last four weeks, haven't missed a church service on Sundays and helped out at every Sunday school outing the new curate has arranged since he arrived in Ponty. You trying to get the St Catherine's Miss Goody Two Shoes gold medal?' Maggie enquired snidely from the corner where she was sorting through their gramophone records.

'One, as you well know, there's no such medal. Two, you can't expect Peter and Miss Williams to watch all the children from the Sunday school when they take them on an outing. Especially down by the river. As it was, Johnny Edwards nearly fell in, and would have if Peter hadn't grabbed the leg of his shorts.'

'And the youth club?' Maggie persisted. 'You had no interest in it until Reverend Slater came here.'

'That was before I saw my exam results.'

'We all know you passed your matriculation with honours,' Maggie pre-empted sourly.

'As I hope you will when the time comes, Mags.' Lloyd spoke from behind his paper.

'I thought that as I'm going to teach, it was time I spent some time with children.' As an excuse Edyth thought it a good one. She stood in the middle of the room and looked around.

'Then you've definitely made up your mind to teach, Edie?' Lloyd lowered the *Pontypridd Observer* and looked at her over the edge.

'There's not much else I can do with a certificate from a teacher training college, is there?' She realized she'd snapped, but the more she'd seen of Peter the less certain she was about going to Swansea, because it would mean leaving him for at least three years and possibly longer. What if he met someone else, or she hated college and made no friends there?

'As your mother and I keep telling you, in this modern world, the only limit is your own ambition,' Lloyd reminded her. 'And that applies to women as well as men. You can do whatever you want with your life.'

'The church youth club's not like school, so you won't learn much from working with the children there.' Maggie found two records without sleeves and set them aside.

'I know it's informal, but you still need to exercise discipline over the children. And it's been fun working with the drama group. Peter has plans to dramatize some of the simpler Bible stories for the Sunday school this autumn, starting with David and Goliath and Jonah and the Whale.'

'You playing the whale, Edie?'

'I'll pretend I didn't hear that remark, Maggie, because if I had, I'd have to send you to your room.' Lloyd spoke quietly but there was a hint of steel in his voice that they were all wary of. 'If the performances are in the autumn you'll be in college, Edie.'

'Swansea's only an hour and half away by train and I will be home some weekends.' Desperate, Edyth looked at her sister. 'Maggie, have you seen my handbag?'

'I'm looking for record sleeves not handbags, and I've just found them.' Maggie filched two from the magazine stand and waved them in the air.

'I know I brought my bag downstairs. I'm sure I put it on the sofa—'

'Try the hall table, darling.' Sali carried in the crocodile-skin handbag that she and Lloyd had given Edyth for her eighteenth birthday. 'You look nice, Edyth. That shade of green suits you.'

'Thank you, Mam.' Edyth took the handbag from her mother. 'I should have remembered I'd left it with the cosmetics I sorted for the girls in the club.'

'None of mine, I hope.' Maggie returned the last record to the cupboard, slammed the door and dived out into the hall.

'I only cleared my own and Bella's dressing tables of the things we no longer use,' Edyth called after her. 'Although I bet there are just as many abandoned lipsticks, half-empty bottles of scent, and tubs of face powder that aren't suited to your complexion in your bedroom if you'd take the trouble to look.' She checked her reflection in the mirror above the fireplace and adjusted the angle of her straw hat.

'I don't need to look in my room because I'm nowhere near as wasteful as you.' Maggie appeared in the doorway and held open the brown paper and string shopping bag that Edyth had filled. 'Mam, have you seen what Edyth's put in here? There has to be at least ten shillings' worth of bits and pieces. That's an awful lot of money to waste.'

'Everything in that bag is either an unwanted present or has been paid for out of my own or Bella's allowance.' Edyth snatched the bag from her sister. 'And better the things in there are put to some use, than left to spoil until they're no good to anyone.'

'Does Belle know you're giving her things away?'

'She told me to take whatever I wanted from her room.'

'I bet!' Maggie retorted belligerently.

'Girls! Stop bickering, you're disturbing your father,' Sali intervened sharply. 'Maggie, darling, there are times when you sound more like a fishwife than a young lady, and given that Mari was complaining only this morning that she was hard put to find space in your room for your clean washing, it might be an idea for you to follow Edyth's example and clear out the things you no longer need from your wardrobe and dressing table.'

The colour heightened in Maggie's cheeks. She turned her back to Sali and stuck her tongue out at Edyth.

Edyth decided it was more diplomatic to leave than retaliate. 'If I don't go now, I'll be late. Bye, Mam, Dad. Maggie,' she added brusquely. 'See you later.'

'Don't forget to invite Peter Slater in if he walks you home, Edyth,' Sali called after her.

'Must we watch him make gooey eyes at Edie across the supper table every church youth club night?' Maggie complained irritably.

Pretending she hadn't heard her sister, Edyth called back, 'All right, Mam,' and closed the front door behind her.

The weather had, if anything, become even warmer since Bella's wedding. The air was still, hot and devoid of oxygen. Edyth breathed in the scent of the white cabbage roses that her mother loved, and stole a moment to watch the bees and butterflies hovering above the lavender and geraniums.

The church clock chimed the quarter of an hour, she glanced at her wristwatch and realized she was going to be late if she wanted to be in the club when Peter arrived. She raced down the long, sloping drive, hopping, skipping and swinging her bag like a child.

To her surprise Peter was waiting for her at the gate. He lifted his hat when he saw her and offered her his arm. 'Good evening.'

'It is a good evening, isn't it?' Familiarity hadn't lessened the quickening of her heartbeat every time she caught a glimpse of him. In fact, it added to the excitement she felt, even if it was only a momentary sighting across crowded Taff Street. 'What are you doing here at this time of day?'

'If I had no regard for the truth, I would say waiting for you so we could walk to the church hall together, but the Reverend Price asked me to deliver a basket of fruit to Mrs Hopkins.'

'She's suffering from another attack of gout. Mam and Mari called to see her this afternoon. They said she was poorly and very uncomfortable in this heat.'

'I didn't find her at all well. She was—'

'Complaining long and loudly?' Edyth suggested when he paused to search for the right word.

'Constant pain must be wearing,' he answered diplomatically.

'Mrs Hopkins wasn't the happiest of our neighbours even before she had gout.' She hooked her arm into his.

He took the bag she was carrying from her. 'More cosmetics for the girls in the youth club?'

'Just a few odd things that were cluttering Bella's and my dressing tables. I'm glad they can be of use.'

'You've improved those girls beyond all recognition in a few short weeks, and not only in their appearance. They're behaving more like young ladies and less like the hooligans I saw when I first arrived.'

'They were teasing you. A young, good-looking curate should expect to attract attention,' she said lightly.

'That is not the sort of thing an attractive young woman should say to a minister of the church.' There was a hint of seriousness in his voice.

'That's why I said it,' she flirted boldly.

'Edyth . . .'

'Yes, Peter,' she prompted when he didn't continue.

'I waited for you at your gate because I was hoping to speak to you before youth club.'

'About the play?' She swallowed hard. Had she been too forward, too obvious? Was he about to embarrass her by asking her to cool her friendship towards him?

'Not about the play.' He began again. 'Edyth, I . . .'

She braced herself for rejection, but when his voice trailed a second time she said, 'I had hoped that we knew one another well enough by now to say almost anything, Peter.'

'You are only eighteen,' he blurted uneasily.

'Guilty.' The comment made her all the more certain that he wanted to tell her that they could never be more than friends.

'There's ten years between us. I will be twenty-eight on my next birthday.'

'When will that be?'

'The twentieth of August.'

'I'll put it in my diary and bake you a cake,' she rejoined flippantly, in a desperate attempt to lighten the heavy atmosphere that had fallen between them.

'I'm not one of your brothers or cousins.' He slowed to a halt.

She released his arm and looked into his eyes, but found it difficult to read the expression in them. 'Does that mean you won't allow me to tease you any more?'

'No.' He didn't even smile. 'But the Reverend Price spoke to me this morning. He said there's been talk in the town.'

'About us?'

'He reminded me that I'm a curate and you are a lively and attractive young woman. He went on to talk about my position in the Church and my hopes for advancement, and finished by saying that the last thing I can afford to do is attract gossip or cause a scandal.'

'Reverend Price thinks it's scandalous that you walk me home from youth club and occasionally stay to supper?' she questioned indignantly.

'Of course not. But—'

'I hope you reminded him that this is nineteen thirty not eighteen thirty,' she broke in heatedly. 'Surely even curates are allowed friends of the opposite sex in this modern day and age?'

'I didn't dare remind him of anything of the kind. But then my parents were middle-aged when I was born, and compared to yours they brought me up in an old-fashioned way. One of the first lessons they taught me was not to question my elders and betters. As you know, my father was a vicar and the Church has always moved slower than the era it finds itself in.' He clasped her hand and replaced it in the crook of his elbow. 'But we might pre-empt damaging rumours if you allow me to ask your father's permission to call on you and court you formally with a view to our becoming engaged in the future.'

'Engaged!' she exclaimed in astonishment. 'I thought you were going to suggest that we didn't see so much of another.'

'Surely you must have realized how fond I have become of you.'

'I . . .' She was completely taken aback. Then she realized that, although she had fallen head over heels in love with him, he hadn't attempted to kiss her, or mentioned love once. Not that she'd minded too much. After fighting off Charlie Moore, and a few other boys who'd tried to 'take liberties' she hadn't been prepared to give, she'd found his gentlemanly conduct refreshing – at first. But he had said 'fond' – and fondness was a long way from love. She was fond of the family's cat.

'If I've misunderstood our friendship, please tell me now, before I say anything more that will embarrass us both.'

65

'No, you haven't misunderstood me,' she said quickly, setting aside her thoughts until later.

'I dared to hope that you felt the same way about me that I do about you. And, I realize that to someone of your warmth and spontaneity, "fond" might seem a cold word. But, as you know, my father died when I was young and I had to assume responsibility for my mother's affairs as well as my own. I have always been wary of rushing into anything. And we have only known one another a month, although it seems longer. In fact,' he smiled broadly, 'I can't imagine life without you now.'

'That's a beautiful thing to say.' She was still reeling at his suggestion. If that wasn't rash after an acquaintance of only a month and not one single kiss, she didn't know what was.

'I could tell you I love and adore you and it would be the truth, Edyth,' he said earnestly. 'How could any man not love and adore someone as attractive and lively as you. But you are young—'

'A fault time will correct,' she interrupted, hers spirits soaring. He did love her. *He loved her*!

'And there is the practical side to consider. My father left me a small annuity, which is a welcome addition to my income as a curate, but combined they're barely enough for one person to live on. And the Church lodges married curates in rooms, hardly the best place for any couple to start married life. We couldn't even consider marrying until after I am given my own parish.'

'Have you forgotten that I've promised my father I'll go to college in September?'

'No, and I know you won't qualify for three years,' he said thoughtfully. 'Edyth, have you any idea what I'm asking you to give up? If you became a teacher you would earn an excellent salary, be able to keep yourself in comfort and, in time, even buy your own house. If you marry me, I couldn't possibly hope to offer you the same standard of living. Vicars' stipends have never been generous. They have to pay rent to the Church and can only live in their vicarage as long as they are able to carry out their duties. My salary will provide for our needs but few if any luxuries.'

'You're warning me that we will be poor?'

'We certainly won't be rich,' he said decisively, 'even after I get my own parish. Not if we remain in Wales.'

'With my family here, I can't imagine living anywhere else.' Edyth meant it. She had never considered moving away from her parents.

'You know Reverend and Mrs Price. You've seen how hard she works for St Catherine's.'

'She sits on as many charitable committees as my mother and father combined,' she agreed. 'And that's without running the jumble sales, Mothers' Union and Young Wives, organizing the Sunday school and its annual outings, and overseeing all the parish's Christmas activities. You know her nickname in the town is Mother Jesus.'

'That's very Welsh – and disrespectful.'

'It's not meant to be,' she explained. 'People are very *fond* of her.' She couldn't resist repeating the word he'd used, but if he saw the joke he didn't smile or comment on it.

'Some people say it's unfair of the Church to expect vicars' wives to act as unpaid secretaries and helpers to their husbands, but that's simply the way it is. I can't see things changing. I'm asking you to sacrifice a great deal, Edyth. Your own career and social life in favour of mine,' he continued soberly.

'I know that, Peter.'

'Do you, really?' he asked seriously.

'Yes.'

'And you still want to continue seeing me?'

'More than anything else in the world.' She lifted her face in the hope that he'd finally kiss her. But he simply began to walk on again.

'This last month, working alongside you with the parish children and in the drama group has been wonderful. I would have spoken sooner if I hadn't been concerned that I was asking you to give up too much.'

'Nothing is too much to ask of the person you love,' she said softly.

'Then I have your permission to ask your father if I can call on you?'

'Yes, although I warn you, I don't know what he'll make of your request after the rather obvious way Toby chased Bella.'

'Toby didn't ask your father's permission to court Bella?'

'To get engaged and marry her, yes. But court her?' She laughed. 'No. Toby didn't need to. He followed Bella around with a hangdog expression on his face from the very first moment he saw her – or so my mother and father say.'

'I can't believe that you love me.'

'I do.' She laughed again, when she realized that she had unwittingly repeated the vow from the wedding service.

'If we don't hurry we'll be late.'

He quickened his pace and she fell into step alongside him. A curtain moved in one of the bay windows when they passed a terrace of houses. The Reverend Price was right; she and Peter had attracted gossip and she realized that meant Peter would never risk kissing her in public. But if he stayed for supper after he had spoken to her father, and she walked him to the gate when he left, anything could happen under cover of darkness.

She recalled the confidences Bella had entrusted to her, glanced at Peter and wondered what he would look like naked. She blushed when she caught him looking back at her. It was only then she considered her parents. She had no idea how either of them would react to Peter's proposal that he 'court her with a view to becoming engaged'.

She consoled herself with the thought that it wasn't as though she was asking their permission to forgo college for marriage, only courtship. A courtship she was 100 per cent certain would lead to a perfect and wonderful new life with the man she loved.

As for college – how could she bear to leave Peter in Pontypridd and go to Swansea? Forty miles and an hour and a half away by train had never seemed so distant.

# Chapter 5

JUDY HAMILTON tied the laces on her tap shoes, straightened her shorts and blouse, and joined the two dozen girls vying for position in front of the long mirror fixed to the wall of the dressing room. Before she had a chance to catch more than a glimpse of her reflection, a brisk, businesslike woman, dressed in a black skirt and white blouse, shouted, 'Numbers eighteen through to twenty-three, inclusive. Follow me to rehearsal room nine.'

Judy knew her number was twenty-one, but she checked the card she'd been given before joining the other girls rushing out of the door.

Rehearsal room nine was a large hall at the end of a long corridor. Three walls were covered in mirrors with practice bars screwed in front of them. Two men sat on chairs close to the door. Both were holding pencils and notepads. An enormously fat woman flowed over a stool in front of an upright piano that had been pushed into a corner. She ground out the cigarette she'd been puffing when the girls clacked, taps ringing, into the room.

'You're all third recalls, right?' one of the men asked. He waited for the girls to answer.

'We're doing "What France Needs", chorus and King. You've all had the score and practised the dance steps?'

Judy nodded earnestly along with the others.

'King?' the man shouted.

A middle-aged man wearing thick theatrical greasepaint, which made him look positively geriatric, walked in front of the line of girls.

'And piano . . . go!'

Judy sang, danced and acted for all she was worth. She tried to practise all the maxims her dance teacher had taught her, but it wasn't easy. She wasn't in the mission hall of Old Angelina Street now, and the stern-faced producers were very different from kindly Mrs Rossiter who had taught her and the other Bay girls basic ballet and tap.

She could hear Mrs Rossiter's voice in her head: 'Head up, chest out'; 'Shine, but not so much that they mark you as an individual, or they won't want you in the chorus'; 'Smile as though you're having the time of your life – so what if your feet are killing you? So are everyone else's'; 'Acting is reacting to everyone else on stage'; 'Sing for the man in the back row of the Gods.'

The piano player hit the last note, the 'King' walked off without glancing at the girls. The two men conferred. After five minutes the younger of the two shouted.

'In a straight line. Numbers at waist height.'

Most of the girls, Judy included, were still gasping for breath after the energetic dance, and she found it an effort to hold her number steady. But she was determined not to show any sign of nervousness.

The two men carried on whispering and making notes. Judy saw them looking at her several times. Once she even thought that they were going to comment on her performance, but they merely carried on pointing and scribbling.

'Thank you, girls, you can go and change. But don't leave yet. Miss Hedley, we'll have the next half-dozen in.'

Miss Hedley led the way back to the dressing room and the girls trooped after her. Judy held her head high and tried not to look dejected. She was the only coloured girl there, although there had been three at the first audition. But, she reminded herself, it was a call-back. And no theatrical impresario ever invited a performer to a call-back unless he was seriously considering that person for a role.

She slipped off her blouse, buttoned her dress over her chemise and pulled off her shorts under cover of the skirt. She was untying her tap shoes when she saw the make-up artist working on one of the first half-dozen girls who'd been called in.

The girl was white with black curly hair and the make-up girl was blacking her face. Judy sat back and waited, watching the artist turn the girl into a black minstrel figure. Half an hour later Miss Hedley called her into the corridor.

'Mr Lyme and Mr Purgis want you to know that they think you're very talented, Miss Hamilton.'

'But?' Judy knew there had to be a 'but' when a sentence began that way.

'It's nothing personal, and no reflection on your suitability for the chorus, but we'll be travelling for twenty-six weeks, staying in digs, bed and breakfasts, and small hotels. You being what you are,' Miss Hedley coughed in embarrassment, 'could make it difficult for us all. Some landladies won't take coloured people. On behalf of myself and the company, I'm sorry. Good luck with your career.'

'Thank you for being honest.'

Too ashamed to reply, Miss Hedley returned to the dressing room. Judy picked up the bag she'd left by the door and walked down the stairs. The sky was blue, the sun shone, and all she could think about was the unfairness of life. Where aptitude and hard work counted for nothing and the best she could hope for was a job as a skivvy. But not living in. For the first time she understood why Mrs Protheroe hadn't offered her that option. A coloured daily maid was one thing. It was quite another to have one sleeping under the same roof as an employer.


'Good evening, Mrs Evans, ladies.' Peter greeted Sali, Maggie, Beth and Susie when he and Edyth joined them in the family's drawing room at half past nine.

'Peter, how nice of you to bring Edyth home again.' Sali set aside the matinée jacket she was knitting for Mary and Harry's new baby. 'Maggie, switch off the radio, please.'

Maggie made a face but she did reach out and turn the knob. The click silenced a chorus from Gilbert and Sullivan's *Pirates of Penzance*.

'Won't you sit down, Peter? Supper will be ready soon,' Sali invited.

'Peter wants to talk to Dad, Mam.' Edyth unpinned her hat.

'He's in his study.'

'Is he busy?' Edyth ignored her mother's suspicious frown.

'When have you known him not to be?' Sali turned to Peter. 'Like every Member of Parliament, Lloyd always has more constituency business to attend to than any one man can fit into a working lifetime.'

'I'll knock on his door.' Edyth walked down the hall to Lloyd's study at the back of the house. She emerged a few minutes later, called to Peter and showed him in before returning to the drawing room.

'What's happening?' Maggie asked Edyth.

'Private business between Peter and Dad.' Edyth tried to check her irritation with her sister.

'Maggie says the curate is sweet on you, Edie.' Susie dropped the book she had been reading.

Edyth picked up a magazine that was littering the sofa and returned it to the rack. 'We are friends.' She knew her mother was watching her but she couldn't look her in the eye.

'Help Mari lay the table, darlings, and warn her Peter is staying for supper, so we'll need a few extra dishes on the table. Tell her to put out the cold ham as well as the beef and pork pie.'

'And the lemon cake I made for tomorrow's tea,' Edyth added.

'You want to show him how well you can cook?' Maggie mocked when she passed Edyth's chair. She spoke quietly, but not quietly enough.

'I heard that, Maggie, and I gave you something to do,' Sali reproved.

'Yes, Mam.' Rebuked, Maggie followed her sisters.

'Well?' Sali asked Edyth after Maggie closed the door.

'Peter's asking Dad if he can call on me.'

'"Call on you"?' Sali had difficulty concealing her amusement. 'That's a quaint phrase. Especially when I consider the amount of time you two have been spending together lately.'

'He said a vicar can't be too careful when it comes to avoiding gossip. He wants to court me with a view to getting engaged,' Edyth divulged uneasily. It was a relief to repeat what Peter had said.

'Engaged! Edyth, darling, you know you won't be allowed to go to college if you're engaged.'

'We both know that, Mam. It's just that he wants to court me with a view to getting engaged . . .' Edyth fell silent when she realized how foolish that sounded. Wasn't every courtship the process of getting to know someone you were attracted to before taking the relationship one step further?

'It seems to me that Peter Slater is living in another age, darling. You know your father and I believe that all young people should have a good time. Courting someone should be about fun and enjoyment. A courtship "with a view to getting engaged" sounds so serious. Tell me,' she caught Edyth's hands in her own. 'do you love Peter?'

'I think I fell in love with him the first time I saw him at Bella's wedding,' Edyth replied truthfully.

'You think?' Sali repeated. 'Thinking you're in love is not the same as being in love. You are very young . . .'

'I'm two years older than Bella was when she met Toby,' Edyth pointed out defensively.

'But your father and I still insisted that Bella go out and meet other boys.'

'It didn't do any good. Bella persuaded you to allow her to get engaged to Toby on her eighteenth birthday.'

'Only because we could see how much in love they both were. And don't forget, they had known one another for two years by then, not one month.' Sali stroked her hand. 'Darling, the last thing I want you to do is to rush into anything that you may regret later.'

'I won't,' Edyth said firmly.

'But a courtship does sound as though Peter is more serious about you than you are about him.'

'No, Mam,' Edyth said soberly. 'I promise you, I do love him. More than any other man I've ever met or could hope to meet.'

'If that really is the case then, even if we wanted to, and I'm not saying we do, your father and I couldn't stop this courtship "with a view to getting engaged" of yours, could we?'

Edyth thought of Peter and smiled. 'No, Mam, much as I love you and Dad, I don't believe you could.'

The ten minutes Peter spent closeted with her father were the longest in Edyth's life. She glanced up nervously when the door opened. Peter walked in first but Lloyd followed close on his heels. He closed the door behind him. 'You know what's going on, Sali?'

'Edyth's just told me.'

'I've warned Peter that he and Edyth cannot get engaged while she is in college.'

'I am aware of that, sir.' Peter hovered close to the door.

'Please, sit down, Peter.' Sali indicated the chair opposite her own.

'Thank you.' He perched on the edge of the seat of an easy chair and stared at the hearth. The grate had been filled with a pretty arrangement of dried flowers, but it wasn't striking enough to warrant the attention he was bestowing on it.

'So, let me understand you – both of you.' Lloyd remained standing and looked from Peter to Edyth. 'You are asking my permission to start "courting formally" whatever that means, with a view to an engagement that will not take place until Edyth leaves college in three years' time?'

'Yes, sir.' Peter avoided meeting Lloyd's eye.

'A formal courtship you intend to inform Reverend Price and your superiors in the Church about?' Lloyd guessed perceptively.

'Yes, sir.' Peter squirmed uneasily.

'Few men in this day and age would bother to tell their employers that they are about to start courting a girl,' Lloyd continued flatly.

'With all due respect, Mr Evans, the Church is no normal employer.'

Lloyd sighed and Edyth knew he was struggling to contain his annoyance. 'I am aware of that, which is why I am so concerned about your relationship with my daughter. Would it be fair of me to say, Peter, that the Church prefers married to unmarried clergy?'

'I am aware of the saying that the Church prefers married vicars because it gives them four working hands for the price of two. But a vicar's wife is second only to the vicar when it comes to parish business. She is highly regarded and respected—'

'But not in her own right,' Lloyd interrupted. 'Only in her husband's shadow. And she will live her entire life that way. Also, two for the price of one isn't the only reason why the Church prefers married clergy, is it?'

'No, sir.' Peter's cheeks flamed bright red. 'The Church demands the highest morality from all the clergy.'

'And this, I take it, is where the formal courtship comes in?'

'To be blunt, yes, sir. I try to be open and honest in all my dealings.'

'Have you considered how you'd react if Edyth changes her mind in six months or a year from now?'

'I rather hope she won't, sir,' Peter replied.

'You are very quiet, Edyth.' Lloyd locked his hands behind his back and looked to his daughter. 'Do you want to continue seeing Peter?'

'Yes, Dad,' she answered decisively.

'And if I give my consent . . .' A bemused expression crossed Lloyd's face. 'I'm not entirely sure what I'm giving my consent to, other than a courtship. Will you promise me that you won't put your college career at risk by getting engaged to Peter before you qualify as a teacher?'

'I promised you that I would go to college if I matriculated, Dad, and I will.' Her voice didn't waver, but her resolve was already crumbling. It was simply too cruel to expect her and Peter to live in separate towns for three years while they were getting to know one another.

'You know she gained high honours, Peter,' Lloyd said proudly.

'Dad . . .' Edyth protested, acutely embarrassed whenever either of her parents mentioned her success. Sali was shaking her head at Lloyd and Edyth knew her mother was warning her father not to continue lecturing her.

'All right,' Lloyd said softly. 'If there's one thing I've learned in life, it's that it's futile to try to stop two people from seeing one another if they believe themselves in love. I won't even try. You do love one another?' he asked suddenly.

'Yes, Dad,' Edyth replied swiftly.

'I would never have asked your permission to court Edyth if I didn't love her, sir,' Peter answered.

'I won't pretend to be glad at your association. You know my views on organized religion, Peter?'

'I do, sir.'

'And yet still you want to court – and eventually marry – my daughter?'

'Edyth has been confirmed as a member of the congregation of St Catherine's.'

'That was none of my doing' Lloyd hesitated. 'I had hoped that all my daughters would wait until they had finished their education and gained some experience of the world before embarking on romance. Perhaps it was optimistic of me, but whatever else, I am not at all certain that you are suited to the life of a vicar's wife, Edyth.'

Peter appeared to be so browbeaten by the interview with her father that if it hadn't been for the presence of her parents Edyth would have kissed him. 'I love Peter and want to share his life, Dad. And, as his life is the Church, then it will be mine.' She thought back to the first sermon she had heard Peter preach:

'*For whither thou goest, I will go; and where thou lodgest, I will lodge: thy people shall be my people, thy God my God.*'

How apt and prophetic those words had turned out to be.

Lloyd held out his hand to Edyth. 'Then there's nothing more to be said, Edie.'

Edyth took it, left her seat and hugged her father.

Lloyd offered Peter his hand. 'You have my permission to visit my daughter in this house as often as you like, and in view of the situation between you, regard it as your own. But only if you give me your word that you will not press her into a formal engagement or give her a ring without discussing the matter with me, while she remains under age.'

'You have my word, sir. Thank you.' Peter shook Lloyd's hand.

'Shall we go in to supper?' Sali suggested.

Lloyd held the door open. Peter was the first to leave the room. Edyth followed but something prompted her to glance back at her parents, and she intercepted a strange look between them. She had what she wanted, their agreement – if not their blessing – to her courtship. But that was small compensation for their lack of warmth towards Peter.

She wished that they had welcomed him to the family in the same loving, open-hearted way that they had welcomed Mary and Toby. But then Peter was a clergyman. And given her father's antipathy towards the Church she could understand his reluctance to see her become a vicar's wife. Even one as handsome, kind and forward-thinking as Peter.


'Can you imagine how I felt, Uncle Jed?' Judy demanded. They were in the upstairs sitting room of the Norwegian Mission. Judy knew her uncle was usually there around six o'clock every evening, whether he'd been fortunate enough to find a day's work unloading or loading a cargo or not. And she had gone straight there from the audition in the hope of finding some sympathy.

'Yes, I can,' he said quietly.

'Sitting there, watching them black up a girl so she looked like a pier minstrel in front of me. And then to be told that I had the talent but landladies might not want me staying in their house . . .'

'Forget it, Judy.' Jed knew it was easier said than done. He had lost more days work on the docks because of colour prejudice than he had found. And every single rejection had hurt.

It had pained him to be passed over, to see less skilled and dedicated men be given the jobs he wanted, simply because their skin was a different colour to his. Most of all, it hurt him to know that his beloved children would forever be regarded as second-class citizens in the country of their birth.

'There's only one thing to do, Judy.' Micah Holsten brought a tray of coffee over and set it on the table in front of them.

'What's that, Mr Holsten?' she asked.

'Forget it, like your uncle said. And if you can't, pick yourself up, dust yourself off and sing with us in the upstairs room of the Ship and Pilot this coming Friday.'

'You've a booking?' Judy cried excitedly.

'The Bute Street Blues Band has a booking. Unfortunately not at the same rate of pay as the wedding, but it's only for a couple of hours. Two bob do you?' Micah asked.

'Very nicely.'

'The way things are going, Judy, love, before long, the band's bookings might be the only work any of us have,' Jed said grimly.


'Goodnight, Peter, I expect we'll be seeing a lot more of you in future.' Lloyd followed Peter into the hall and handed him his hat and coat.

'I'll walk Peter to the gate, Dad.' Edyth opened the front door.

'Take your jacket, Edyth. It's been so hot today you could catch a chill,' Sali called from the dining room where she and Mari were clearing the table.

'It's still warm, Mam.' Edyth followed Peter outside, and Lloyd closed the door behind them.

'Your father hardly said a word at supper,' Peter commented when he and Edyth walked down the drive.

'You'll have to give him time to get used to the idea of me . . .' she almost said 'marrying' before amending it to, 'courting a curate.' They reached the wooden gates that were always left open, except when sheep came down from the mountain. At the first sign of a woolly coat Mari rushed to close them to protect Sali's precious plants.

He glanced at the sky. 'There's cloud tonight, I hope that doesn't mean the weather is breaking.'

'Mam was right to tell me to take a jacket. It's definitely cooler than it has been.' Suddenly cold after the almost unbearable heat of the day, she shivered. It was impossible to decipher the expression on Peter's face in the darkness. When he moved, he was little more than a silhouette beneath the shadows of the trees that her father had planted along the garden walls.

'How long do you think your father will need to get used to the idea of my courting you?'

She shivered again, and hoped that he would put his arms

around her. When he didn't, she crossed her arms tightly. 'As long as it takes him to get to know you.'

'I hope that will be sooner rather than later. The prospect of three years of strained visits to your family when you come home from college in the holidays is rather daunting.'

Still hoping he would at least hug, if not kiss her, she moved even closer to him. 'It might have been better if we hadn't said anything to him or my mother just yet.'

'If we hadn't, I would have felt that we were sneaking around behind your parents' backs.'

'Perhaps you're right. At least this way everything is out in the open.' Edyth recalled what Bella had said about the clandestine visits she'd made to Toby when they were engaged, and trembled from more than the chill in the air.

'Possibly too much in the open, as far as your sisters are concerned. Did you hear Maggie tonight? "Isn't Edyth spending a lot of time in the church and youth club helping you out, Reverend Slater?"'

'That's just Maggie,' Edyth dismissed. 'She can't bear anyone else in the family to be the centre of attention. First it was Belle with her wedding, now it's me and my matriculation. She'll grow out of her mood when she matriculates herself next year. She's bound to get honours. She's brighter than the rest of us put together.'

'That's magnanimous of you considering the way she behaves towards you.'

'You've noticed?'

'I couldn't help it.'

'I'm not always very nice to her,' she confessed.

'You're not?' he asked, in surprise.

'My sisters and I are always squabbling, which is why my father insisted the builder put in a third floor so we could each have our own bedroom. We've fought one another since cradle days. Bella and I were probably the worst. We've said and done the most awful things to one another but we didn't really mean them. We're absolutely the best of friends now. And when there's a real problem that affects the family we stop bickering and work together to solve it.'

'That seems a strange way to live,' he commented, 'but I'm hardly qualified to pass judgement when I've no brothers and sisters.'

'Given the families I know well, like my Uncle Joey and Auntie Rhian's and my Uncle Victor and Auntie Megan's, I'd say it was normal. All my cousins fight and argue with one another.'

'You should have put on your jacket.' He held out his right hand. She took it and, to her dismay, he shook her hand. 'Goodnight, Edyth. You'd better run back into the house before you catch cold.'

'Will I see you tomorrow?' she asked hopefully.

'Mrs Hopkins asked me to administer the holy sacrament to her at her home. I could hardly refuse.'

'The last time she had gout she didn't leave her bedroom for six weeks,' Edyth warned. 'You could be visiting her for quite a while.'

'Reverend Price suggested that I make an allowance for a daily visit to her in my diary when he asked me to call on her this morning. But it is convenient for us.'

'It is,' she agreed.

'So, may I call and see you after I have visited her tomorrow?'

'What time are you likely to be here?'

'Around four o'clock?'

'Just in time for tea?' She made a mental resolution to bake another cake to replace the one they had eaten at supper.

'That would be nice, thank you. I'll see you then.'

'I'll look forward to it.' She stood on tiptoe and kissed his cheek.

He stepped smartly away from her. 'They can see us from the house and the curtains are open.'

'So?' she challenged. 'We're courting, aren't we?'

'Not in public, Edyth.'

'It's dark.'

'I'd prefer it to be darker still, and more private.' He held her hand between his for a few seconds. 'Until tomorrow.'

'Until tomorrow,' she repeated, then turned and raced back into the house.

Maggie was in the hall, ostensibly tidying the coat rack, but Edyth knew she'd been waiting for her.

'You weren't out there long,' Maggie observed slyly. 'Doesn't the handsome curate go in for long goodnight kisses?'

'When are you going to stop nosing into my private life?' Edyth retrieved the jacket she'd hung on the hall stand when she'd come home from youth club and slipped it on. She went into the dining room, but only the cloth and napkins were left on the table.

'You weren't long.' Sali stowed the silver cruet in the sideboard.

'You were right, it is chilly out there. Is there anything I can do?'

'No, everyone helped. Mari and the girls are already washing the dishes. But your father would like a word with you in his study – nothing bad,' Sali reassured her when Edyth's face fell. 'You look tired. Why don't you go on up to bed after you've seen him? I'll call in to kiss you goodnight. Would you like a glass of hot milk?'

'She'd prefer hot chocolate.' Mari carried in a tray of clean silverware, set it on the sideboard and gathered the tablecloth and napkins into a bundle.

'You'll clean your teeth afterwards?' Sali returned the candlesticks to the mantelpiece.

'I'm not seven years old now, Mam,' Edyth retorted.

'More's the pity. If you were, I wouldn't be losing you to Swansea in September.' Sali winced as a crash resounded from the kitchen. 'I hope that's a cup or tea plate and not one of the expensive serving dishes.'

'Mam, Susie's broken the meat plate *and* the butter dish,' Maggie shouted gleefully.

'Can I slap maddening Maggie? *Please*?' Edyth begged.

'Slapping her would only make her worse,' Sali said philosophically.

'Poor Susie probably feels dreadful. No one breaks dishes on

81

purpose.' Edyth lifted a rose bowl from the sideboard and set it in the centre of the table.

'The number you've broken, you should know. I suppose it's to be expected that one of your sisters would take over from where you left off, now you've outgrown your clumsy phase.'

'Don't tempt fate by talking too soon, Miss Sali,' Mari warned. 'Only this morning I—'

Edyth held her finger to her lips until Sali left for the kitchen.

'It was such a pretty little china figurine,' Mari said regretfully.

'It was grotesque, Mari,' Edyth contradicted. 'Bella bought it for me when she was five years old and even she outgrew pink cupids and shepherdesses by the time she was six.'

'You'll miss it.'

'I won't.'

'What won't you do?' Maggie appeared in the doorway.

'Miss your snide remarks when you get struck by a lightning bolt of niceness.' Without giving Maggie time to think of an apt rejoinder, Edyth walked along the passage to her father's study. The door was open and he was sitting at his desk, an ash tray in front of him and the pipe he had recently taken to smoking instead of cigarettes in his hand.

He saw her and smiled. 'You look exhausted, my sweet.'

Edyth returned his smile. Her mother was right, he wasn't cross with her. Ever since she could remember he had called her mother, 'sweetheart' and she and her sisters 'my sweet', except when he was angry with them for breaking one of his few cardinal rules, all of which were centred around consideration and respect for others.

'I feel tired. It's probably down to the fresh air and long walk to Berw Falls this morning.' She sat on the long sofa that faced his desk.

'This courting business? Was it Peter Slater's idea or yours?'

'Peter's, but to be honest, I've chased him – not too noticeably, I hope – since Belle's wedding.'

'I suppose a curate is not difficult to chase. Head for the church and he'll turn up sooner or later, if he's not already there.' Lloyd packed a wedge of tobacco down in his pipe with the end of a pencil and lit it.

'You knew I was chasing him?' She had the grace to blush.

'I've never known you to be so interested in church activities. You had me worried. I thought you'd been infected by a case of religion and were heading for a convent.'

'I'm not Anglican nun material, Dad.'

'I didn't bring you up to be Church fodder, that's for sure.' He puffed his pipe slowly and she knew better than to hurry him. 'You really love him?'

'Yes, Dad.'

'In that case I only have one more thing to say to you before closing the subject, until you or Peter bring it up again. If there should come a time when you feel that you have fallen out of love with him, promise me you will put an end to this formal courtship of his.'

'I won't need to because I know that one day we'll make the perfect married couple.'

'Promise me?' he reiterated solemnly.

She sensed that he wouldn't be happy until she had given him her word. 'I promise, but I do love him, Dad, and we will be happy together – you'll see.'

'I hope you're right, Edie. Because I want nothing less for any of my girls.' He left his desk, went to the sofa and offered her his hand. She took it, and allowed him to pull her to her feet.

'Thank you, Daddy.'

'You haven't called me that in years.' He kissed her forehead. 'And why are you thanking me?'

'For being you and not flying off the handle like so many fathers would have done at the prospect of losing a second daughter to marriage so soon after the first.'

'I hope I won't ever lose you, or any of the others. And you won't be walking down the aisle for three years yet.'

She pushed her doubts about college to the back of her mind. 'I'll try to be a credit to you.' She hugged him.

'You already are Edie. But if you are determined to improve

yourself in any way, you could try to be a little less accident-prone. I hate to see you hurt yourself.'

'I've never broken a bone deliberately, Dad.'

'I know that, my sweet. Sleep well.' He followed her into the hall and watched her walk up the stairs. He returned to his study. Sali was sitting on the sofa, waiting for him.

'I saw Edyth hug you, so I take it that went all right.'

He shrugged. 'Our talk went fine. As for her and the curate, time will tell. Is it so terrible of me to hope they won't get married?'

'No,' she said quietly. 'But you do know that the girls won't allow you to pick their husbands for them, don't you, darling?'

'I know. But Edyth and Peter Slater are so . . .' Maggie laughed in the kitchen and Lloyd realized that if he could hear her, she could hear him. He left the sofa and closed the door. 'Mismatched,' he declared quietly.

'You can't stop a girl from falling in love with a man, however unsuited they may be, any more than you can stop a starving miner from striking. If Peter should prove to be Edyth's choice of husband, it's out of our hands, Lloyd.'

'Prove to be?' he repeated. 'Then you don't give her your blessing, either?'

'For all that she believes herself grown up, she is still very young.'

'The hardest thing about having children is allowing them make their own mistakes. It's torture to stand by and watch, knowing they're heading for disaster and won't take a blind bit of notice of anything that's said to them until it's too late. And even if you try to warn them, they'll take it the wrong way, clam up and probably never come to you with their problems again.'

'It's late, you're maudlin.' She left the sofa and went to him. 'Let's go to bed and leave Edyth and the curate to live their own lives.' When Lloyd hesitated, she added, 'They will anyway, with or without our blessing.'

'You're a wise woman in many ways, Sali Evans, but I sometimes wonder if the biggest mistake you made was to marry me. I see a streak of Joey's wayward stubbornness in Edyth.'

'Poor Joey. He's the hard-working director of the largest and most successful chain of department stores in South Wales, a charitable pillar of the community, respectable married man and father of five, yet you and Victor still see him as your wild, womanizing younger brother.'

Lloyd refused to be mollified. 'He almost messed up his life.'

'But thanks to Rhian, he didn't, and Edyth won't.' Sali tried to inject more conviction than she felt into her voice in an effort to hide her own concern about Edyth's choice of suitor.

But a frown furrowed her forehead when she knocked on Edyth's door later and went in to kiss her daughter goodnight. Edyth was already asleep. The cup of chocolate Mari had brought her stood untouched, cooling on her bedside cabinet. Sali kissed Edyth's forehead before removing the cup. She couldn't help wishing that her daughter was a child again, with nothing more serious on her mind than the next picture she would draw and which frock to wear in the morning.

# Chapter 6

MICAH HOLSTEN lowered his saxophone. 'You sing like a lovesick angel, Judy. That is absolutely the best "Crying the Blues Away" I've heard, but,' he glanced at his wristwatch, 'I have to be at a meeting of the seaman's relief committee in the Sailors' Home in Stuart Street in ten minutes.'

'Same time tomorrow, Micah?' Jed asked.

'It suits me if it suits everyone else. Let's see if we can get a couple of these new numbers in when we play the White Hart on Saturday. It's great playing in a different pub every weekend but we don't want to stick to the same repertoire. The landlords may not have heard us before, but chances are the audience will have.' He laid his saxophone gently in its case, closed it and opened the door of the room that served as a cloakroom to the Norwegian mission church during services, and Bute Street Blues Band rehearsal room during the week. A crowd of seamen, who'd been sitting on the stairs, applauded when he appeared. Micah bowed as if he were the conductor of a grand orchestra and held out his arm to his fellow band members.

'I'll walk you home, sunshine, and call in on Mam.' Jed slipped his arm around Judy's shoulders. 'How's she been lately?'

'Suffering more than most of us in this heat, Uncle Jed.' Judy picked up her handbag. 'But, you know Gran, heat or no heat, she won't stop cooking and cleaning. She's on her feet from morning till night.'

'You two all right for money?'

Judy knew what it had cost her uncle to ask her that question. With six growing children, a pregnant wife, no regular work and only his earnings from playing in the pubs and clubs during the last few weeks, he didn't have enough coming in to keep his own family, let alone his niece and mother. And none of her other uncles was in a better position to help.

'We managed before I lost my job. And I still have the five pounds that Mr Evans gave me to replace the frock that was ruined at that wedding. With what I've been making with the band and helping out two mornings a week peeling potatoes in the chip shop we're managing.'

'You're a good girl, Judy. You've looked after Mam better than most daughters, let alone granddaughters.'

'What goes around comes around.' She followed him out of the mission. 'Gran didn't have to keep me when Mam died and Dad went to sea and never came back.'

'She didn't, but you've long since paid back any dues you owed. Bye, Micah, Tony.' Jed shouted his goodbyes to the rest of the band, Judy blew them kisses and they walked down the street.

'I have never known a summer like this one. In Wales, that is.' Jed took his handkerchief and mopped his face. 'Crossing the equator, yes. Docking in Mombasa, yes. The Caribbean, yes. But Cardiff, never.'

'It must be wonderful to travel,' Judy said wistfully.

'If you want to do it, sunshine, nothing can stop you. But a word of advice: try to do it first class. A seaman sees very little beyond a port. Some are smaller than others, some are dirtier, but most of them are much of a muchness.'

'First class costs money.'

'No one can go anywhere, first or third class, without a ship. If this Depression bites any harder, they may as well close the docks because nothing will be sailing in or out of Cardiff. There's no point in shipping coal when no one has the money to pay for it.'

They crossed the road and skirted a crowd of boys playing football with a tin can. They were in no hurry and neither were their friends and neighbours who were out taking the early evening air. Jed and Judy walked slowly through the network of terraces and side streets, exchanging gossip, admiring new babies and making preposterous plans for the band which they both knew would never happen. But that didn't stop them from trying to outdo one another.

'One day we'll play the Waldorf Hotel in New York,' Jed declared. He knew a man who had worked there as a bellboy and waxed lyrical about its luxurious rooms.

'And the Ritz in London.'

'The Moulin Rouge in Paris,' Jed rejoined swiftly as if they were playing a game of snap.

'The Casino in Monte Carlo.'

'The Coliseum in Rome.'

'Bands don't play there,' Judy countered. 'Only gladiators, and they fought there hundreds of years ago.'

'We'll travel back in time,' Jed continued.

'And play for the Roman Emperors,' Judy laughed. 'It's good to have dreams.' She turned the key that was always left in the lock of Pearl King's front door, and walked in.

Jed frowned. 'Mam should be sitting out on the step on a nice evening like this.'

'She said it was too hot.' Pearl and Judy's next-door neighbour, Mrs Francis, had carried out her kitchen chair and was sitting chatting to Mrs Hawkins, who lived on the other side of her, while darning her sons' and husband's socks.

Judy walked down the passage and called out, 'Gran?'

Jed followed and saw Judy run to his mother, who was lying slumped on the kitchen floor.

Peter slipped a key from the enormous bunch he had been wrestling with into the lock of the door of the church hall, and turned it.

'At last, the right one.' He withdrew it and tested the door by putting the weight of his shoulder against it.

'It was a good rehearsal tonight.' Edyth waited for him to finish checking the hall was secure. 'You've succeeded in firing the children's imaginations. Did you hear them practising their "giant" voices? I can't wait to see their finished papier mâché Goliath head.'

'I caught a glimpse of their drawings for a flannel-covered

whale. No seamstress could create anything so elaborate.' He pocketed the keys. 'You've done a good job of writing the play, Edyth. It's brought the story to life. Every member of the group has identified with David, which is what I was hoping would happen.'

'It's easy to work with children when they're enthusiastic.'

'Do you think they'll be ready to perform it before you leave for college?'

'I don't see why not if all the rehearsals go as well as tonight.' She took the arm he offered her. 'Provided that is, Goliath is ever finished. He's taking an awful lot of newspaper.'

'I can't believe the summer is almost over.' He raised his hat to a passing schoolteacher.

'In less than three weeks I'll be setting off for Swansea.'

'Are you looking forward to it?' He stopped suddenly and looked back at the hall.

'I checked all the windows, twice,' she assured him. 'And yes, I am looking forward to going to college,' she answered, hoping he'd drop the subject. In fact she wasn't looking forward to leaving him behind in Pontypridd, and she was also beginning to wish that she'd never promised her father that she would go to college if she matriculated.

'But you're just a little apprehensive?' he ventured.

'How do you know?'

'Because it's how I felt before going to Lampeter. It's nerve-racking to go to a strange town when you know no one there and haven't a clue what to expect.' He stopped at the kerb to allow an empty coal cart, drawn by a tired old horse, to pass.

'I've been to Swansea on holiday lots of times so it's hardly a strange town, and I'm not going alone. Two other girls from the sixth form will be first years as well. Although they weren't special friends of mine and won't be studying English, I've a feeling we'll cling together until we find our feet. And it's bound to be fun living in a dormitory full of girls my own age. Miss Jones – she's my history teacher and only six years older than me – told me that her college days were the happiest of her life, which is hardly surprising as she cares for her elderly mother now, and the only time she leaves home is to go to school.'

What she didn't tell Peter was she'd called in on Miss Jones and her elderly mother because she'd wanted to talk over her doubts about going to college with someone. For the first time in her life, she felt that she couldn't confide in either of her parents, although she had written to Bella care of the hotel she and Toby were staying at in New York, to tell her about Peter's courtship – and her reluctance to leave him for three long years.

'Did Miss Jones say why her college days were so happy?' He escorted her across the road and they began to climb the hill.

'She said that she and her friends used to go for long walks around Swansea Bay in the evenings. And on summer weekends they used to bathe in the small bay behind Mumbles Head. 'And of course there are all sorts of cafés and ice-cream parlours in Mumbles as well as the town, and two really good theatres, not to mention the cinemas and the shops—'

'You do realize you haven't mentioned studying once,' he teased.

'The studying part is easy,' she dismissed. 'I had my book list last week. I've read most of them and I've always enjoyed writing essays. That probably comes from being one of a large family. With everyone talking at once, writing was often the only way I could express my thoughts.'

'I enjoy writing as well. To my tutor's astonishment I even liked writing sermons in college when I knew I would probably never get a chance to deliver them. It's stood me in good stead. The more preparation I do before a service now, the more confident I feel about delivering it.'

'Are you giving a sermon again on Sunday?'

'Yes,' he smiled. 'And I have a small surprise for you.'

'What?' she asked eagerly.

'It wouldn't be a surprise if I told you. Reverend and Mrs Price asked me to invite you to dinner on Saturday evening, if you are free.'

'That's the surprise?'

'No.'

'You know I keep my Saturday evenings free for you.' She stopped to breathe in the scent of a rose bush in bloom. 'Should I write Mrs Price an acceptance note?'

'No need, I'll tell them you'll be delighted to be their guest. Although you won't be, once you're there.'

'I like Reverend and Mrs Price. They're lovely people and good company,' she remonstrated.

'I couldn't agree with you more.'

'Then why shouldn't I be delighted to accept their invitation?'

'I can see you haven't dined with them.' He looked over his shoulder to make sure no one was close enough to listen in on their conversation. The street was deserted but he still lowered his voice. 'I will never admit I said this in public, but Mrs Price has one fault: the way she treats food is sinful.'

Edyth burst out laughing. 'She can't cook?' She took his arm again and they moved on.

'I didn't say any such thing.'

'But you meant it. It also explains why you visit us so often around mealtimes.' She stepped closer to him as a crowd of young men dressed in shorts and football boots ran past, their middle-aged trainer panting breathlessly behind them. 'Do you want me to ask Mari to pack you a picnic of cake and sandwiches so you can have a midnight feast?'

'Don't joke. You have no idea how tempted I am to take you up on that offer. I've lost count of the number of times I've woken in the middle of the night suffering from stomach pains. I'm never quite sure whether they're hunger or indigestion.'

'You poor man,' she sympathized.

'I'd like to find my own accommodation. The problem is it suits the church and the Reverend and Mrs Price to have me live at the vicarage, so I can be close at hand in case of an emergency.'

'Will there be any other guests at the dinner?'

'The Bishop, the Dean and their wives.'

Her eyes widened. 'They want to meet me to see if I'll make a suitable vicar's wife, don't they?'

'They want to meet you, because I've told them about you and your father's consent to our courtship. But there's no need to be concerned. They're people, the same as you and me.'

'They're anything but the same as you and me,' she contradicted. 'The Bishop can make or break your career.'

'That's for me to worry about, not you, Edyth. All you have to do is be yourself and they'll love you.'

'Most of my parents' friends are union people and politicians. I've never met a bishop or a dean, not outside of church anyway. What on earth do I talk to them about?' she demanded in panic.

'Knowing the Bishop and the Dean, they'll monopolize the conversation. All you'll have to do is follow it and be ready to contribute if they ask your opinion. And if I were a betting man, which I'm not, I'd stake money on them spending the greater part of the evening on a post-mortem of the last test match at Headingley. Your father is well known for his left-wing sympathies so I don't think they'll be insensitive enough to bring up the subject of the Soviet persecution of the churches.'

Mentally she ran through her wardrobe. One or two of her evening dresses were too elaborate for dinner at a vicarage, but she had a plain navy silk that Peter hadn't seen; only it had a low neck. Would the Bishop be offended . . .

'What should I wear?' she asked, but before he had time to answer, she realized clothes and conversation weren't her only problems. 'Should I bring anything?'

'Gifts aren't necessary, although Mrs Price may appreciate a bunch of flowers from your garden.'

'Roses,' she said decisively. 'A dozen long-stemmed cream buds. And for Reverend Price?'

'As I said, please don't feel that you need to bring anything, but one of your apple flans or a lemon cake might go down well. He has a sweet tooth, and the only cakes Mrs Price bakes that deserve the name are rock cakes. And, if you give him a cake, he'll feel duty bound to share it with me so you'll make two people happy.'

'You haven't said what I should wear?'

'You always dress beautifully but . . .'

'But?' she repeated uneasily. It was the closest he'd come to criticizing her and she was instantly on the defensive.

'How about the brown suit and cream blouse you wore the other evening?' he suggested.

'The linen Mam bought me for college that Maggie calls my dowdy schoolmarm outfit?' Edyth tried not to sound disappointed. She adored pretty clothes and loved wearing silk in the evening.

'The Bishop and the Dean's wives dress plainly and I've never seen Mrs Price in anything other than black.'

'According to Mari, not since her brother was killed in the Great War. He was in the same regiment as my Uncle Joey.'

'I didn't know.'

'You're right, there's nothing worse than being overdressed,' she agreed, reminding herself that it was Peter's career not her clothes that was important. And, as everything in her wardrobe had been bought at cost price because her mother worked in the department store Harry had inherited, her wardrobe was bound to be more extensive than that of Mrs Price and possibly even the Dean's wife. 'I'll make sure my brown suit is clean and pressed.' They reached the end of her road. 'Are you coming in for supper?'

'I can't tonight – unfortunately.'

'Mari was making Cornish pasties and sausage rolls when I left,' she tempted.

'That remark, Edyth Evans, is torture to a starving man. But the answer still has to be no.'

'Shall I ask her to save some for your tea tomorrow?'

'Please.' He smiled. 'The surprise is that Reverend Price has asked me to give the sermon again on Sunday, but not in the morning. At Evensong.'

'That's wonderful. People must have told him how good your morning sermons have been.' A frightening thought occurred to her. 'Is the Bishop coming to dinner because he's considering moving you from Pontypridd?'

'I told you when we first met that the Bishop's hobby is moving curates around the chequerboard of parishes.'

She quelled a rising tide of panic. 'Where's the furthest parish from here and Swansea?'

'I prefer not to think about it.'

'Have you no idea where you might be going?' she persisted.

'Absolutely none. And, there's no point in my asking Reverend Price to find out. The Bishop is notoriously tight-lipped about the movement of clergy. No one will know anything until he gives me my marching orders, or not, as the case may be. If he has made a decision about my future, the one thing I am certain of is that it's known only to him, and God.'

'Do you think that he might be considering giving you your own parish?'

'If he is, he hasn't discussed it with me, or Reverend Price.'

'But it's your career,' she protested.

'Which hopefully God is directing.' He fell serious. 'When I was ordained, I put my trust in Him. And He hasn't let me down. He has brought us one another.'

'What if they move you miles away? I may not see you for weeks on end. Months possibly . . . Peter, I couldn't bear it . . .'

They reached her drive. He looked up and down the road; there was no one in sight when he led her inside the gate. Gripping her by the shoulders, he looked into her eyes. 'One step at a time, Edyth. There's no point in panicking until we know the situation.'

'It's bad enough having to wait three years to marry you without being separated as well.'

'We haven't been − yet. And who knows, if I go back to the vicarage and write a brilliant sermon of publishable standard and you bake extra-delicious cakes for the Bishop and Dean as well as Reverend Price, not to mention dazzling them with your charm, wit, conversation and eminent suitability to become a vicar's wife, they may consider placing me closer to Swansea.'

She refused to be mollified. 'You have an over-inflated opinion of me and my cooking.'

'No, I don't.' Secure in the knowledge that the trees prevented them from being seen from the house or the road, he brushed his lips against hers, so lightly that afterwards she couldn't be sure whether he'd actually kissed her for the first time or not.


The doctor rose from the chair Jed had carried in from the kitchen and set next to the parlour sofa. Pearl King was lying, stretched out, twitching uncontrollably, on her 'best' sofa where Jed had tenderly laid her after lifting her from the kitchen floor. He'd considered the parlour to be the closest and most obvious place for his mother to await the arrival of the doctor, but Judy knew that if her gran could speak, she would have given her son a telling-off for entering the most hallowed room in the house.

The doctor snapped his bag shut. 'It's a stroke, a severe one,' he added superfluously. Judy and Jed had determined before he'd answered their call that Pearl had lost her speech, the use of both legs and become incontinent.

'Can you do anything for her?' Jed asked.

'Very little. It's a question of waiting to see if the body recovers. She should be kept quiet and given plenty of water and liquids. Solid food could choke her. Don't move her more than you have to. It might be an idea to bring her bed down here and shift some of this furniture out. She's going to need round-the-clock nursing and it'll be easier if she's downstairs.'

'I'll look after her,' Judy volunteered. She thought of the money she had left. It wouldn't be anywhere near enough to cover the cost of medicine and the doctor's future visits. 'Can we have your bill?' she asked, needing to work out the weekly cost.

'I'll give it to you later, Judy. In the meantime,' he scribbled a note on a pad, and tore off a sheet of paper, 'get this tonic made up in the chemist's. Feed her two spoonfuls three times a day.'

'Is that the red or the green tonic?' Jed asked. In his experience the doctor only prescribed two and neither worked. They certainly hadn't helped his eldest son who'd succumbed to meningitis, or his sister who died of diphtheria shortly after she'd given birth to Judy.

'The green. I wish there was more I could do, Jed. You could try the Chinaman. I don't know what's in half his medicines but some of them seem to work.'

'For a stroke?' Jed looked the doctor in the eye. After checking that Judy's attention was fixed on Pearl, the doctor shook his head.

'I'll walk you to the door, Doctor.' Jed waited until they were out of Judy's earshot before saying, 'My mother's dying, isn't she?'

Knowing Jed wouldn't thank him for any platitudes or meaningless reassurances, the doctor said, 'She is.'

'How long does she have?' Jed asked bluntly.

'Considering she's probably aware of the state she's in, for her own and all your sakes, I hope the end will be soon. It's what I'd want for my own mother if it had happened to her.'

'Thank you,' Jed said simply. 'Don't forget to give us your bill.'

'I won't. I'll call again tomorrow. If you need me sooner, send for me.'

'We will.'

The doctor held out his hand, Jed shook it and watched him walk to his car.


'Reverend Price tells me your father is the Labour MP Lloyd Evans, Miss Evans.' The Bishop leaned across the Prices' table, cut into the cheese and helped himself to a sizeable portion.

'He is,' Edyth answered cautiously, wary of elaborating. So far the conversation at dinner that had included the ladies had been general and innocuous. As Peter had predicted, the Bishop and the Dean had discussed cricket, apparently oblivious to the boredom of their wives and, she suspected, Peter and the Reverend Price, neither of whom had made a single observation on the match or its outcome.

Peter had finally managed to steer the discussion away from sport by describing their work with the church drama group and the children's attempts to make a Goliath head. He had also praised her efforts to teach the local girls grooming and dress sense, and encouraged her to talk about the forays that she and Miss Williams had made into the local countryside with the Sunday school pupils in an effort to keep them occupied during the long summer holidays.

Superficially the evening had been pleasant enough but Edyth couldn't help feeling there was an undercurrent beneath the small talk that she wasn't privy to. She had turned her head more than once to see the Bishop studying her intently. His wife, a large, florid woman who favoured floral pastels, had spoken to her as if she and Peter were engaged and about to set the date. It was only consideration for Peter's career that prevented her from correcting the woman. The Dean, however, stared openly at her for so long that he made her nervous, and she ended up dropping her knife and hitting her wine glass against her plate. Whenever her childhood clumsiness returned, it did so with a vengeance.

The meal had been as dreadful as Peter had predicted. Reverend Price reminded them frequently throughout the evening that his wife had only the assistance of a 'tweenie' – a rough maid of all work – and no cook, which was evident from the dishes the poorly trained girl brought to the table.

The first course of leek and potato soup was lumpy and principally flavoured with flour. The saddle of mutton was burned on the outside, raw and bloody on the inside, the roast potatoes were pale, soggy and greasy, the stuffing had come from a packet, the Yorkshire puddings would have been better served as pancakes, the gravy was as full of solids as the soup had been, and the cauliflower and string beans boiled for so long they had turned to mush.

Fortunately Mrs Price had chosen to serve fresh strawberries and raspberries with clotted cream for dessert, but delicious as they were, they weren't filling. Edyth wished she had the Bishop's courage when he reached out a second time and helped himself to another quarter of a pound of cheese and fistful of crackers.

She laid the thin slice of Caerphilly cheese she had cut for herself on a digestive biscuit and bit into it.

'So what do you think of our Reverend Slater's new post, Miss Evans?' the Dean enquired the moment her mouth was full. His voice had grown heartier over the course of the evening, which Edyth attributed to the liberal quantity of wine the Reverend Price had poured into his and the Bishop's glasses.

'I didn't know that Peter – Reverend Slater – had been given a new post.' Edyth looked apprehensively at Peter who was sitting opposite her.

'Of course you wouldn't.' The Dean laughed loudly. 'He only found out about it himself half an hour before dinner.' He nodded sagely at Peter. 'As His Grace said, it will be a challenge, my boy. A real challenge,' he repeated. 'But one I hope you will rise to. Do your duty, serve your flock as well as you have served the ministers and parishioners in all your postings, and I'll lay a pound to a penny that you will be vicar of your own parish within six months.'

'I hope you haven't taken up gambling, Dean.'

Even Edyth could see that the Bishop was joking, but the Dean thought it necessary to reply.

'Just an expression, Your Grace, just an expression.'

'May I ask where the parish is?' Edyth asked.

'Certainly, my dear. After all, you will have as much interest in the place as Peter.' The Bishop beamed at her, obviously extremely pleased with himself, and she had a feeling that it wasn't only Peter they had been discussing earlier, which explained the looks he had been giving her throughout the evening. 'Our Reverend Slater is such a dedicated clergyman we have decided to send him to a parish that has been sorely neglected of late by the failing health of the present incumbent, Reverend Richards. The place is ripe for Peter's brand of enthusiasm. The present vicar will retire within six months, an interim period perfect for a curate to take over the onerous duties, while being eased into a position of complete responsibility. Show the same dedication to duty that you have over the past few years, my boy, and as the Dean said, six months from now you will be leading your own flock.'

'That's wonderful news. Congratulations, Peter.' Edyth turned to the Bishop. 'But you still haven't said where the parish is, Your Grace.'

'I haven't, have I?' He reached for the cheese again. 'It's Butetown.'

'Or, as it's more commonly known, Tiger Bay. A tough one even for our talented Reverend Slater here.' The Dean waited until the Bishop had taken another hefty lump of cheese before helping himself to a chunk of Stilton. 'But whether Peter will be vicar there or not is entirely dependent on you, Miss Evans.'

'Me?' She looked at him in confusion. Then she noticed Peter was as red-faced and uneasy as he had been when he'd asked her father if he could formally court her.

'The curacy is assured,' Peter said quietly.

'But not the post of vicar,' the Dean added.

'I don't think Miss Evans understands the situation.' Mrs Price made her first contribution to the conversation. 'The Reverend Slater will only be appointed vicar of Butetown if he is a married man.'

'The Church couldn't place a bachelor in Tiger Bay,' the Dean boomed. 'Too many temptations down there for a single man, Miss Evans. Far too many. Even for someone as upright and moral as our Reverend Slater,' he laughed, oblivious to the silence that had fallen over the table.

'It was a pleasure to meet you, Miss Evans. I trust the next time we see you there will be cause for celebration. As I said to Peter earlier, it would be a personal as well as professional pleasure to join two such dedicated Christians in Holy Matrimony.' The Bishop shook Edyth's hand. The Dean, their wives, and the Reverend Price followed suit, but Mrs Price kissed her cheek. Edyth noticed that the vicar's wife looked drawn, tired and years older than her husband, although she knew from town gossip that Mrs Price was ten years younger.

'Take care of yourself, my dear,' Mrs Price whispered, when she walked Edyth to the front door.

'Thank you for a lovely evening, Mrs Price, Reverend Price.'

'It was our pleasure,' the vicar answered.

The Reverend and his wife stood on the step to wave them off. Peter escorted her down the path in silence. When they reached the gate they turned and waved back. Edyth didn't speak to Peter until she heard the door close behind them.

'You didn't tell me that promotion to the post of vicar would be dependent on you having a wife,' she said.

'But I did tell you that the Church prefers vicars to be married. Don't you remember? It was when I asked you if I could speak to your father?'

'You mentioned something about it but I didn't think you meant it personally.' She wondered why she hadn't connected the conversation with his declaration that he loved her, when both had happened on the same day.

'I didn't know I was going to be offered a curacy in Butetown today with a view to taking over from the incumbent within six months. I didn't even know the Reverend Richards's wife had died before Christmas or that he was in failing health. You heard the Dean and the Bishop, it's a challenge. It's also a testament to their faith and confidence in me.'

'Why shouldn't they have faith in you? You're talented, enthusiastic—'

'As are a hundred other curates in South Wales, all of whom are older and more experienced than me,' he broke in brusquely. 'Please believe me, Edyth, I had absolutely no idea the Bishop was considering me for the curacy, let alone the post of vicar, until he arrived this evening. I know what you're thinking—'

'Do you?' She slowed her step and looked at him.

'You're assuming my suggestion that we embark on a formal courtship was a selfish one, made in the hope of furthering my career. Well, you couldn't be more wrong. The moment I looked at you I knew you were the only woman for me.'

It was one of the most romantic things he had ever said to her. But she had to ask the question uppermost in her mind: 'What happens to your career if you don't get married?'

'I can take the curacy, but if I'm still single when Reverend Richards retires, as the Bishop expects him to do within six months, the Church will look for someone else to take over the parish.'

'That's unfair,' she cried out. 'It's you who will be appointed, not the woman you marry.'

'It may be unfair, but the Bishop's decision is final. He couldn't have made it clearer when he spoke to me before you arrived tonight. No wife – no parish.'

'It's that important for you to be married?'

'Edyth, I know you've led a sheltered and privileged life, but you must have some of idea what Tiger Bay is like.'

'I went to Moore's shipping offices in Bute Street with Toby and Bella to see some of his paintings. The offices, Port Authority, Banks and Exchange buildings are magnificent. As for the streets behind them, I saw working-class homes, no different from the Rhondda. Presumably the people in them work on the docks or aboard ships instead of in the pits,' she replied.

'Not all the sailors live in your working-class homes'. A fair number of foreigners disembark with money in their pockets which they are looking to spend before their next voyage.'

'Which means lots of pubs, drunks, houses of ill-repute and women who make a living in ways that aren't discussed in polite society. I haven't led that sheltered a life, Peter,' she retorted testily.

'The Bishop – wrongly in my opinion, although I would never dare say it to his face – is convinced that the temptation of living in close proximity to that particular kind of sin would be too much for any bachelor.'

'He thinks you would become a drunk or—'

'You don't need to spell it out, Edyth,' he interrupted prudishly.

'All I can say is that he doesn't know you,' she muttered, furious with the Bishop for insisting that Peter's advancement depended on him being married. 'No one, not even a Bishop, should have the right to tell anyone when they should marry. It is a private and personal decision that should only be made by the people concerned.'

'It might be better if we talked about this tomorrow. It's been a long evening, and I can see you're angry.'

'With the Bishop, not you,' she snapped. 'How dare he pressurize us? We promised my father we wouldn't even consider marrying for three years, yet tonight I had the distinct impression that the Bishop and the Dean were planning to conduct our wedding service without even consulting me.'

'If they were, they were only thinking of me.' He grasped her gloved hand. 'Consider the situation from their point of view, Edyth. Their first duty is to the Church. It's their responsibility to train, place and advise the clergy, and use the people at their disposal to the best advantage. They aren't thinking of themselves but the parishioners in Butetown, my advancement and – you.'

'The last person they are thinking about is me,' she said dismissively.

'They know I love you, because I told them.'

'What exactly did you say?'

'What I just said to you. That I knew you were the one for me the first moment I set eyes on you at your sister's wedding. They realize that it will only be a matter of time before we are man and wife. And they also realize that our future, comfort and standard of living depends on my position within the church.'

'You told them that you wouldn't marry me until you had your own parish?'

'I didn't need to tell them that. It's Church policy to discourage curates from marrying. For one thing we're always being moved about and for another our stipends are too small to support a family.'

'And they thought they'd hurry things along for you.'

'We discussed it at some length, Edyth. I told them that you had matriculated with honours and had a place waiting for you at Swansea teacher training college. I also told them that your father wanted you to take up that place. But as the Bishop said, 'what purpose would it serve to delay our marriage for three years?'

'I hope you told him that it will give me time to qualify as a teacher,' she retorted caustically, her anger with the Bishop momentarily demolishing her own doubts about attending college. 'I think that's purpose enough, even for a Bishop.'

'Yes, you would have your certificate,' he agreed, without answering her question. 'But we intended to marry after you qualified, and as a married woman you would not be allowed to teach. So in effect that would be a waste of the next three years, not only of your life, but also mine. Years that we could both put to good use working together for the people of Butetown.'

She considered for a moment. 'I hadn't thought of it that way,' she conceded.

'The Bishop made me see that we have a choice, Edyth. Either I spend the next three years as a curate, and you as a student being supported by your father. Or we could both be doing useful work, earning our living and making a home together. Just think of the difference you and I could make in an area like Cardiff docks. There are children there in even more desperate need to have their energies channelled into useful occupations than there are in Pontypridd. And if this depression lasts or gets worse, as your father seems to think it will, more and more people will be turning to the Church: the poor for the basics they need to live, the unemployed for societies and voluntary work to keep themselves occupied until they can find work again, and the wealthy in the expectation that we will distribute their charitable donations where they are most needed.'

'You really think we should get married right away?' She tried to decipher his expression in the thickening twilight.

'I think our future is more important than you acquiring a teaching certificate you will never use,' he said resolutely. 'And your father has already said that he has no objections to our marrying when you are of age. But if you don't want to marry me just yet—'

'I do,' she broke in earnestly. 'But I resent the Bishop ordering us to marry.'

'He didn't, Edyth. All he did was offer me the opportunity to run my own parish, which is the reason I joined the church. Butetown parish could be the realization of all my ambitions.'

'My father was dreadfully upset when Bella gave up her academic plans to marry Toby,' she murmured, more to herself than Peter.

'What is more important, Edyth,' he asked baldly, 'your father's disappointment or our future?'

'It's not as simple as that.'

'Yes, it is. This is the golden opportunity that I have been waiting for all my life. If we aren't married, the Bishop will appoint someone else vicar of Butetown. And then it's anyone guess as to how many more years I'll remain a curate, doing someone else's bidding. The Reverend Smith in Burryport didn't get his own parish until he was forty-five. I don't want to wait that long, Edyth, because it would mean delaying our marriage as well as putting my career on hold. Please, I'm not asking you to disobey your father; all I'm asking you to do is think about it before I visit you tomorrow. Will you do that much for me?' His eyes glittered in the moonlight.

'I will.'

They reached her drive. He drew her back beneath the trees.

'I'll be here tomorrow at teatime after I have seen Mrs Hopkins. We'll talk some more then?'

'Yes.'

He kissed her, and that time she was left in no doubt that it was a real kiss and their first. 'You know that I love you, Edyth?'

'As I do you.'

'Then trust me.'

Suddenly he was gone. She walked up to her front door, her mind a kaleidoscope of rotating images. The Dean smirking at her, gloating in his superior knowledge of Peter's appointment to Butetown. The Bishop cutting ever larger pieces of cheese. Mrs Price finally speaking in her timid, tired voice.

*'I don't think Miss Evans understands the situation. The Reverend Slater will only be appointed vicar of Butetown if he is a married man.'*

Peter looking at her in the moonlight.

*'You know that I love you, Edyth?'*

*'As I do you.'*

He was right. She hadn't really wanted to go to college anyway. It was her father's ambition for her, not her own. Maggie, Beth and Susie were bright. They would go to college in her and Bella's place. Her father would soon recover from any disappointment. Especially when he saw the work that she and Peter would be doing in Tiger Bay.

# Chapter 7

'NO! NO! NO! Absolutely not.' Lloyd paced from the hearth to the bay window, turned on his heel and glared at Edyth and Peter, who were sitting side by side on the sofa. Edyth's hand was beneath Peter's and the sight infuriated him. It was as though she had already adopted the role of submissive, subservient wife. 'I agreed that you two could "court formally" – not that I had the faintest idea what that meant. I did not agree that you,' he pointed at Edyth, 'could marry before you came of age. Or that you could give up your place at college.'

'Sir, please, if you would listen, just for a moment—'

'Not for one second!' Lloyd rounded on Peter. 'You give your word lightly, Slater. Even for a clergyman.'

The curate's colour heightened, but Sali was too busy watching Lloyd to be concerned with Peter Slater's feelings. She had seldom seen Lloyd angry and then only when he had been fighting the blind stubbornness that had affected men on both sides of the miners' strikes. He had never lost his temper with her or one of their children. She knew he was thinking of Edyth and wanted the best for her. But she also realized that his exasperation would only serve to exacerbate the situation and make Edyth even more determined to follow her heart.

'Lloyd, please sit down so we can discuss this properly,' she begged, when he continued to stalk restlessly around the room.

'There is absolutely nothing to discuss,' he said flatly. 'Edyth gave me her word that she would go to college if she matriculated. She has matriculated – with honours – and she *will* go.'

'But, Dad, don't you see that even if I go to college, I will never use the qualifications I gain.' Edyth spoke softly, in the hope of defusing the tension that hung, tangibly in the air. 'As soon as I am of age, I will marry Peter.'

'Even if you are halfway through your final year?' Lloyd challenged. When she didn't answer his question, he said, 'So, you won't complete your course in college, no matter what. Is that what you are saying?'

'No, Dad. But as a married woman, I wouldn't be allowed to teach, so my going to college would be a complete waste of the next three years. Better that Peter and I spend that time working together for the people who live in Tiger Bay.' She unconsciously reiterated Peter's argument.

'You are only eighteen,' Lloyd reminded testily. 'The law recognizes that no one of that age knows their own mind.'

'But I do,' Edyth insisted earnestly. 'Making Peter and I wait won't change the way we feel about one another. But it will lose him this parish. Please, Dad, I love Peter and he loves me. It's not as if we're asking for anything besides your and Mam's blessing. The Church will give us a house once Reverend Richards retires, and then we'll have Peter's salary as a vicar to live on. We'll be able to work together—'

'We?' Lloyd interrupted her. 'You've been ordained now?'

'Being a vicar's wife is a vocation just as much as teaching. And now that I've met the man I love, it's what I want to do with my life.' She lifted her chin defiantly.

'I may not be able to support Edyth in luxury, sir, but I will be able to provide her with a reasonable standard of living.' Peter found the courage to meet Lloyd's disapproving eye.

'But will you be able to give her a teaching certificate?' Lloyd mocked.

'You know I can't do that, sir.'

Lloyd returned to the fireplace, leaned against the mantelpiece and gazed at Edyth. When he finally spoke, all trace of anger had left his voice. But Sali knew him too well. Lloyd's temper was quick to flare and just as quick to cool. He appeared calm and detached but she realized from the ice in his eyes that this time he had gone from fiery rage to iron frost. And there would be no thawing or talking him round. Not now.

'Have you considered what kind of life Edyth will lead in Tiger Bay?' Lloyd enquired conversationally of Peter.

'As the wife of the vicar, she will be looked up to and respected by everyone in the community. She will help with the church groups, chair the Young Wives, act as secretary to the Mothers' Union, run the Sunday school, Bible classes, temperance society, youth club and drama group—'

'Temperance society?' Lloyd ran his fingers through his greying hair. 'Have you the slightest idea what kind of people live down the docks? Have you met the men and women she will be mixing with?'

'We are all God's people, sir.'

Knowing the effect the phrase would have on her father, Edyth winced.

'God's people?' Lloyd raised his eyebrows questioningly. 'Office workers, port officials, dockers, seamen and their families aside, have you considered the flotsam and jetsam that wash up in every port? The homeless, the drunks, the gamblers, the gangsters, the prostitutes—'

'With all due respect, sir,' Peter turned crimson at Lloyd's mention of prostitutes, 'I have heard the stories about Tiger Bay but I also know people exaggerate. Many decent families live in Butetown.'

'I said office workers, officials and working classes aside. But I don't believe they will need the services of a vicar as much as the unemployed and destitute. Do you intend to ignore them?'

'It is my intention to reach out a helping hand to everyone in my parish.'

'How?' Lloyd enquired sardonically. 'By praying for their souls? Or by running a mission and doss house that you will expect my daughter to work in? One where she will be exposed to all kinds of vermin. And I don't mean the human kind. A place where diseases brought in by sailors from every continent will thrive: tuberculosis, diphtheria, typhoid, plague—'

'Dad, please!' Edyth jumped to her feet.

'I'm outlining the life of drudgery this man is offering you in the cause of furthering his career in the Church. I know his kind of religion—'

Peter finally retaliated. 'I don't think you do, sir.'

'What did you say?' Lloyd's voice was soft. Ominously so.

'You are a Communist, sir.'

'A pagan who is going straight to hell, is that what you think?' Lloyd's eyes narrowed and Sali trembled, because the one thing guaranteed to incense Lloyd was someone lecturing him on religion. 'I don't need you to tell me what your Church stands for. Or what kind of people work for it. I have lived through too many miners' strikes in the Rhondda Valleys to fall for your theological propaganda. I have seen the bodies of women and children who starved to death laid out in unfurnished rooms without even a blanket to cover them, because their families had pawned every possession they owned to buy food, and there wasn't a farthing left to bury them. It was the pennies from the miners' unions that bought their last resting place, not the coins from the churches' poor boxes. I have seen pregnant women and babies with bellies and eyes swollen from malnutrition stand in line in soup kitchens set up by your Church in Wales – and other religious establishments – and watched while ministers made them sing hymns to God's glory before they would hand over a bowl of watery soup. So, don't lecture me on your Church – or your God, Slater. If he exists and sits watching us from a throne in heaven, he either spends a great deal of time sleeping or looking the other way.'

Edyth closed both her hands over Peter's and tightened her grasp, willing him not to answer her father back. But if he understood her warning, he chose to ignore it.

'Man is responsible for the misery in this world, Mr Evans, not God.'

'Really?' Lloyd questioned sceptically. 'Then all I have to add is your God is very selective in the things he takes responsibility for. But I have no wish to argue doctrine with you. I believe in tolerance and free speech and gave my children the freedom to make up their own minds about religion and which, if any, church they wished to attend. But listen well, Edyth.' He looked sternly at his daughter. 'I will not sign a piece of paper that will put you at the mercy of this man so he can turn you into his and the Church's drudge. You're far too intelligent to waste your life. If you can't see that it would be a waste, you're not the girl I thought I'd raised. And I'll be damned before I'll give you permission to ruin yourself.' Clenching his fists, Lloyd walked out of the room.

Silence closed in, warm, thick and suffocating. Edyth was the first to break it.

'Mam?' She looked to her mother.

'I will talk to your father, Edyth. But don't hold out any hope that I'll try to change his mind. Peter,' Sali turned to the curate, 'I believe my husband is right. Edyth is too young to marry. She should go to college and when she has her teaching certificate she will have the means to support herself and be in a position to decide what she wants to do with her life then. In the meantime, for all our sakes, you should leave this house.'

'Thank you for the courtesy of listening to me, Mrs Evans.' Peter rose to his feet.

'You can't throw Peter out,' Edyth cried, her anger surfacing now that Lloyd was no longer in the room.

'I am not,' Sali demurred.

'But you've just told Peter to leave,' Edyth argued. 'And he'll be going to Cardiff soon. I'll never see him again—'

'Don't be melodramatic, Edyth,' Sali rebuked. 'Of course you will see him again. But we need to give your father time to calm down. And he's not going to do that while Peter remains here.'

'Would you have any objection to my writing to Edyth, Mrs Evans?' Peter asked.

'None whatsoever.'

'You will allow her to receive letters?'

'It's not a question of "allowing", Peter. We have always respected our children's privacy and their right to lead their own lives.' An icy note entered Sali's voice at the inference that either she or Lloyd would keep Edyth's mail from her. 'You will be welcome to visit us another day. Edyth, show Peter out.'

'I'll walk to the gate with him.'

'As you wish.' Sali followed Lloyd out of the room.

It was late afternoon but the heat hadn't abated and the temperature was as unbearable as it had been at midday. Edyth was sweltering in her thin cotton frock and she wondered how Peter could stand wearing his black serge suit, grey shirt and dog collar. She leaned against the conifer next to the gate and stared down at a clump of lilies of the valley growing in its shade.

'They didn't even listen to you,' she complained bitterly.

Peter looked around; there was no one in the street so he slid his arm around her shoulders. 'Do you think that your father will change his mind in the next few weeks and give us permission to marry?'

She shook her head. 'I've never seen him so angry as he was just now. It's not just us – it's the Church. After what he said, I don't need to tell you what he thinks of organized religion.'

'It's not going to be easy having an atheist for a father-in-law.'

There was an inflection in his voice, but Edyth was too miserable to pick up on it. 'That's supposing he ever allows us to get married.' She screwed her handkerchief into a tight ball.

He slipped his fingers beneath her chin and lifted her face to his. 'We will marry one day, Edyth, I promise you.'

'I only wish I could believe you.' She gazed into his soft brown eyes.

'Trust me, we will be man and wife.' He gripped her hand, lifted it to his lips and kissed it. 'You'll write?'

'I'll go to my room and start a letter right away. Where shall I send it?'

'St Catherine's vicarage, care of Reverend Price. I expect the Church to move me to the docks in the next few days, but he will know where I am and forward my mail. It should only be delayed by a day or two at most. I'll send you my new address as soon as I have it. I don't know yet if I'll be staying at the vicarage in Butetown or not.'

'I'll miss you.' Tears pricked at the back of her eyes.

'I love you.'

'I love you, too, for all the good it does us.'

'Put your trust in God, Edyth. He will watch over us.'

She waited at the gate while Peter walked away, but tears

blurred her vision long before he turned the corner. She took a few minutes to compose herself then looked up at the house, feeling as though it was home no longer, but a prison that was keeping her from the man she loved.

Judy sat on a stool beside her grandmother's bed in the stifling front parlour. She had come to dread the nights, which seemed to have doubled in length since Pearl's stroke. In the day, neighbours, her uncles and their families were in and out of the house, bringing flowers from their gardens and homemade cakes, and brewing cups of tea she rarely had time to drink.

Their visitors were kind, well-meaning and anxious to help, but she realized and reluctantly accepted that there was nothing she nor anyone else could do, except to allow death to take its inevitable course.

She had made up a bed for herself on the floor, but as her gran was noticeably more agitated during the hours of darkness, if she had the energy, she preferred to sit up. As usual, she had lit a candle when dusk had fallen and it flickered on the mantelpiece, casting tentacle-shaped shadows on the walls. It wasn't just that she didn't have a shilling to spare for the electric meter – although she didn't; her grandmother couldn't bear the glare of the electric light shining down on her.

There had been little change in Pearl King's condition since the afternoon she had collapsed. She lay, as comfortable as Judy could make her, in the vast double bed that almost filled the room, unable to make an intelligible sound, or do the smallest thing for herself. Asleep or awake, her left arm twitched continuously, her fingers plucking at the patchwork cover she had stitched from scraps of the family's discarded clothes.

Judy had spent hours staring at that quilt. She not only found it comforting, but preferable to looking at the ravaged face of the woman who had brought her up and whom she loved so much. And every single piece of fabric reminded her of some small instance in her grandmother's life, or her own.

There were plain serviceable grey patches from her three uncles' school shorts interspersed with beautifully embroidered white cotton patches, double-stitched for strength, from her own baby dresses. The striped pieces of flannel from her West Indian grandfather's nightshirts had to be more than a quarter of a century old, as it had been over twenty-five years since her grandmother had received the telegram to say that he'd died in a fire on-board his ship. There were pieces of aprons she could remember her grandmother wearing, and borders from old tablecloths and tea towels. Fabrics that had once been a part of their everyday life together, a life Judy knew was fast ebbing away.

When Pearl was awake, her eyes came brightly, vividly alive, at odds with the wreck of her body, as she gazed keenly around the room. Her uncles had spent a day moving the furniture around the tiny terraced house, turning the front parlour into a bedroom, and Judy sensed her grandmother's anger and frustration both at the desecration of her 'best room' and with the body she could no longer control.

But most of the time she was too busy – and tired – to spend much time thinking. Washing, dressing and feeding her grandmother, who was loath to eat or drink – as if she actually wanted to hasten her end – took up every minute of the day. Including the ones she should have spent sleeping. The money from the Evanses had dwindled to a few shillings after she paid for the medicine the doctor prescribed and met his bills. And both she and her uncles knew that if it hadn't been for the bookings Micah Holsten negotiated for the band every weekend, she wouldn't have been able to pay the rent.

Her uncles' wives did what they could: taking it in turns to look after one another's children, so Judy could practise and sing with the band; making soups and stews that they brought round at meal-times, not only because Judy couldn't spare the time to cook, but also because they knew she had no money for food.

A knock at the door echoed down the passage, which Judy found strange. Her uncles' families, the neighbours and even the doctor walked straight in. It was common practice in the Bay. She lifted the light quilt to her grandmother's chin, concealing her twitching hand beneath it in case someone wanted to see her, then went to the door.

A middle-aged, fair-haired, balding man stood on the step. He looked her up and down, and she instinctively clutched at the neck of her blouse.

'Are you Judy Hamilton?'

'And if I am?' she answered abruptly.

'I'm Joshua Hamilton. Your father.'

'This room is hotter than a bread oven.' Lloyd set his knife and fork down on the remains of his cold ham and wilted salad. Sali and Edyth were sitting opposite him. At his insistence, they were in the upstairs dining room of the Mermaid Hotel in Mumbles, one of the most fashionable and expensive hotels in the small seaside village outside Swansea.

'We are in the coolest spot next to the window.' Sali smiled at him, but Edyth continued to study a painting of a sailing ship on the wall above his head.

Lloyd had watched Edyth during the meal and was convinced she'd only swallowed a forkful of her prawn salad. Aware that her father was looking at her, she pushed the food aside on her plate and set down her own knife and fork. Lloyd refrained from making a comment. The forlorn hope he'd nurtured, that she would break her silence of the last few weeks towards him, had dissipated. Not only had she picked at her meal, she'd ignored all the remarks he'd made to her, and answered her mother's gentle enquiries in monosyllables.

'Can I bring you anything else, sir, madam, miss?' The waitress moved behind Edyth's chair, took her pencil from her pocket and held it over her notepad.

'Would either of you like dessert or coffee?' Lloyd asked.

'I couldn't eat another thing, thank you, the salads were very good.' Sali smiled at the girl.

'Nor I.' Edyth spoke to the waitress, not her father.

'Then it will just be the bill, please,' Lloyd said.

'I'll make it up and bring it over, sir.' The waitress walked over to the cashier, who was sitting at a desk by the door.

'Well, darling, your accommodation is comfortable and, from the look of the girls we met when we carried your things into the dormitory, you'll soon make plenty of friends. Take things slowly. I'm sure you'll find your feet and settle down in no time. The views are so beautiful from your bedroom you might find it difficult to concentrate on studying but after all the times we've holidayed here, I think you've picked the right place . . . You know Swansea and the Mumbles well enough to find your way around, but as you've only ever been here for a few weeks at a time it's new enough to be interesting. You'll have lots of fine walks . . .' Sali was conscious she was saying anything and everything that came into her head to fill the crushing silence that had fallen between father and daughter.

The last month had been unbearable. Lloyd had prided himself on being close to all his children, constantly telling them that whatever their problems, they could count on him to do all he could to help without being critical. But Edyth had refused to look at him or answer a single question he had put to her since the afternoon he had turned his back on her and Peter Slater, and walked out of the sitting room.

Their embittered and prolonged quarrel had affected the entire household. Edyth had continued to speak to the rest of the family, but had restricted her conversation to the absolutely essential. And not even Mari had been able to coax her to acknowledge Lloyd's presence.

Sali knew Edyth was in touch with Peter because letters arrived for her every day bearing Cardiff postmarks. But Edyth hadn't volunteered any information about the contents and Sali felt too dispirited to enquire. Meals, once the highlight of family life, had become torture. Edyth poked at the food on her plate, barely eating a mouthful before making her excuses and leaving the room. And neither Sali nor Lloyd wanted to escalate the tension by forcing her to stay.

Using the excuse that she was studying in preparation for college, Edyth had become uncharacteristically solitary, shutting herself up for hours in her bedroom, all the while growing thinner and paler as the heatwave continued into late summer, browning the countryside, triggering a nationwide drought and draining the energy of everyone forced to venture out of doors.

Desperate, Sali had turned to Lloyd's brothers and their wives for help. But although Victor and Megan and their four boys, and Joey and Rhian and their five children had visited them more often than usual, they had no more success than she, Mari, the girls and Glyn had in drawing Edyth out of the shell she had retreated into.

Joey hadn't needed to warn her or Lloyd that even if they succeeded in getting Edyth to college, they wouldn't be able to force her to stay there, much less study, and Sali suspected that Edyth might be planning to deliberately flunk her exams at the end of her first term.

Lloyd checked the bill the waitress presented to him, paid it and added a ten per cent tip. He left his seat, shrugged on the linen jacket he had hung on the back of his chair and glanced at his watch.

'The Cardiff train will be leaving Swansea station in half an hour. I'll go downstairs and ask the receptionist to order us a taxi.'

Sali nodded. After he left, she took Edyth's handbag from the floor and handed it to her. 'You have enough money, darling?'

'I also have my bank book. If I need more, I will draw some out. There's no need for you to send me any.' Edyth picked up her straw hat from the empty chair next to her and jammed it on her head.

'You will look after yourself?'

'You don't have to worry about me, Mam.'

'Please, won't you at least say goodbye to your father?' Sali pleaded.

Tight-lipped, Edyth shook her head. 'He knows how I feel. I have nothing more to say to him.'

'You're breaking his heart—'

'If you're going to catch your train, you should go.' Edyth led the way out of the room and ran down the stairs. The taxi had arrived and Lloyd was outside, holding the door open. He made one final attempt to talk to Edyth.

'We can catch a later train, if you'd like us to drive you up to Townhill and drop you outside the college, Edie.'

Edyth didn't answer him. She hugged and kissed Sali and, ignoring Lloyd, walked swiftly across the road. Seconds later her slight figure was lost in the crowds walking beneath the shade of the trees opposite.

Lloyd continued to stand and stare, as though he were searching for a glimpse of her.

Sali touched his arm. 'The sooner we go, the earlier the train we'll catch.'

Lloyd leaned forward and spoke to the driver through the cab window. 'The railway station, please.'

'Very good, sir.'

Sali stepped into the cab, Lloyd followed and Sali reached for his hand.

'I didn't think we'd succeed in getting her here. At least we achieved that much,' she consoled.

'The question is whether she will stay,' he said disconsolately. 'Sweetheart, I have a feeling we have a long three years ahead of us, and I am not at all sure that our Edyth will have a teaching certificate at the end of it.'

After checking there was no train in sight, Edyth crossed the tracks of the Mumbles railway that followed the curve of the bay and looked down at the beach. Small boys and girls were playing hide and seek amongst the rows of small boats and sailing dinghies that had been dragged above the tide-line. In the distance on the far left, she could see the silhouettes of the tall cranes and hoists of Swansea docks. To her right, Mumbles Head stretched out to sea. The lighthouse perched on the furthermost point reminded her of a long white finger, its glass nail pointing upwards to a cloudless, sun-baked sky.

Gulls screeched, a singularly mournful sound, as they swooped low over the breaking waves in search of prey. The tide was incoming, swirling fast, carrying a crust of seaweed, driftwood and shells that crowds of young boys, armed with nets and buckets, paddled through in search of fishy treasures. Edyth imagined a young Peter among them and, for some unaccountable reason, the image brought tears to her eyes.

She made an effort to block out the raucous sounds of laughter and noise around her and concentrate on the natural beauty of the bay: the water that sucked and gurgled like a living being through the pebbles on the tide-line; the frothing of the dirty grey foam, flecked with blacker streaks of coal dust, that topped the breakers dissolving on the shore; the peculiar tracks made by crabs scuttling sideways over compacted, wet sand.

She stepped down on the rocks, spread her handkerchief on an outcrop and perched on it before opening her handbag and drawing out the letter she had received that morning. She had read it so often she could have quoted it line for line, but that didn't deter her from reading it again.

*My dearest Edyth,*

*I do hope you are well and in better spirits than when you wrote your last letter. Unfortunately, Reverend Richards continues in poor health and is unable to perform his ecclesiastical, administrative or pastoral duties. At the Bishop's suggestion, and in the absence of close family and friends, I have taken it upon myself to speak to his doctor. He believes Reverend Richards's illness owes as much to his depressed spirits as a physical cause. The poor man lost heart when his wife died suddenly following a seizure before Christmas, and I only have to think of the effect that our present separation is having on my state of mind to understand a little of what he is suffering.*

*Aside from weakness, loss of appetite and trembling in his limbs, Reverend Richards has no medical condition his doctor can diagnose, but he is lethargic and has little interest in parish affairs, his parishioners or indeed life.*

*The Bishop visited us yesterday. He spent the entire afternoon here, first talking to Reverend Richards, and then myself, before joining both of us for tea in the vicarage. As I have told you in my previous letters, our housekeeper's culinary skills rival those of Mrs Price.*

She smiled at the reference that no one not acquainted with Reverend and Mrs Price would understand. It added an intimacy to her relationship with Peter. Already they shared secrets.

*The Bishop is arranging for the Reverend Richards to be taken to a retreat on Monday week. There, he will be cared for by a professional* nurse employed by the Church. The Bishop and I prayed that care, rest and good food will restore him to his previous robust health, but given that Reverend Richards is sixty-four, the Bishop thinks it best to retire him now, so the years left to him can be spent in well-earned rest and quiet contemplation.

This leaves the church with the problem of what to do with the Butetown parish. The Bishop told me that he was impressed with what I have achieved in the few short weeks since he appointed me curate here. I have resurrected the youth and temperance clubs and enrolled over twenty members in each. I have held an inaugural meeting of a drama group, although the people who turned up were more interested in music than theatre. I also arranged a picnic for the younger parishioners with the help of a few of the mothers and a local fruit merchant who loaned us his lorry to take the children to Leckwith Hill.

However, despite this progress, the Bishop warned me that he will not countenance placing this particular parish in a bachelor's keeping, however enthusiastic or dedicated the incumbent.

He enquired after you. I hope you don't mind but I confided in him and told him of your father's opposition to our marriage. The Bishop kindly volunteered to approach your parents on our behalf. He thought a direct appeal might persuade Mr Evans to reconsider. I thanked him for his offer, but asked him not to do anything until I had written to you. Perhaps if you showed this letter to your parents they might consent to discuss the matter with us again, in the presence of the Bishop? Believe me, the Bishop is only thinking of our future and welfare.

Please, dearest, write to me by return to let me know your thoughts.
God keep and bless you,
I am, and will always remain,
Your Peter Slater

Edyth returned the letter to its envelope, replaced it in her handbag and glanced at her wristwatch. Hopefully, her parents had reached the station in time to catch the six-thirty train. If they had missed it, there was another at seven-thirty and again at eight-thirty. To be on the safe side, she had decided that she should catch the eight-thirty.

That gave her plenty of time to walk down towards the

university buildings on the Mumbles Road, take the turning that led up the hill to the village of Uplands from where she could make her way through Cwmdonkin Park to the college.

All she had to do was order a taxi to meet her outside the gates at a quarter to eight, and the bursar would do that for her, after she had related the story she had prepared. She would ask for a driver who would be prepared to carry her luggage to the car and also on to the train.

She imagined the look on Peter's face when he opened the door to the vicarage later that evening and saw her standing in front of him. Or would he open it? Perhaps the housekeeper would, and when she did, she'd call to Peter and he would come running from his study, the look of shock on his face turning to a smile when he saw her. He would sweep her off her feet but he wouldn't kiss her. Not in front of the housekeeper. Perhaps later, when he showed her to the guest room that would hopefully be next door to his own bedroom, or just a few doors away on the landing.

She recalled what Bella had said. But Peter was a clergyman, not an artist like Toby, so she might have to wait until their wedding night to find out what it was like to make love to a man. Peter had been right. They would be man and wife, just as soon as her father realized how determined she was and the lengths she was prepared to go, simply to be with the man she loved.

Her father would have to give his consent to their marriage when he found out she had run away from college on the very day that he and her mother had taken her there. He would simply have to!

Edyth sat back on one of the upholstered benches in the empty first-class carriage the porter had found for her, and scanned the copy of the *Evening Post* she had bought from a vendor at Swansea station. There was no good news. Twenty-four people had died as a result of the heatwave. The temperature in London had reached 94 degrees that day and, according to the experts, there was no sign of the weather cooling. More than two million people had registered unemployed at the beginning of August and there was little hope of improvement. The only ray of hope was that the

Morris factory was producing a new car, but with the entire country locked into economic depression, she wondered who was going to buy it and what with.

Then she realized that, angry as she was with her father, her reaction to the news was the direct result of the politics and sense of fair play he had instilled in her while she was growing up.

She drove all thoughts of him and her mother from her mind. She had told the bursar that her brother's wife was ill and she was needed at his farm in the Swansea Valley to look after her. And that on no account was the college to contact her parents, as they wanted to spare her father any worry because he had urgent parliamentary business in London. Fortunately for the flimsiness of her story, the bursar either didn't know, or didn't realize, that Parliament was in its summer recess.

She folded the paper and looked out of the window. The sun was low on the horizon; a blood-red ball hovering above a copse of trees like an illustration in a child's picture book. She picked up the paper and fanned herself. The guard had opened the narrow window, but the air in the carriage remained oppressive and uncomfortable.

The train slowed, they drew into a station. 'Bridgend' hung on the sign above the platform; they had only covered half the distance to Cardiff. She checked the time. Ten past nine. According to the timetable, she should arrive in Cardiff at a quarter to ten. Doors slammed along the length of the train, a whistle blew, the brakes hissed and they steamed forward. Just at the point when she braced herself for the train to gather speed, it juddered to a halt and she was jerked forward.

She sat back in her seat and waited. Carriage doors opened, and people ran up and down the train. After a quarter of an hour had passed, she slid back her door and looked out. A guard was standing further down the corridor engulfed by a mob of irate passengers.

'I'm sorry,' he shouted above their heads, 'a freight train has broken down on the tracks ahead. I am afraid there is going to be a delay.'

'For how long?' one man demanded, before Edyth had plucked up courage to ask the same question.

'I'm sorry, sir, ladies and gentlemen, but that is all I can tell you. Workmen and officials are doing all they can to free the line. I will keep you informed of progress. Now, if you'll excuse me, I have to inform the passengers in the third-class carriages about the delay.' The guard fought his way through the crowd and disappeared into the next carriage.

Disgruntled, muttering vague threats about letters to the press and Great Western Rail Company the passengers dispersed. A middle-aged man gave Edyth a lecherous smile. She returned to her carriage and slammed the door. The sun had sunk lower. It was bound to be dark by the time they reached Cardiff. Tiger Bay was supposed to be too rough an area for a young girl to visit alone, although it had seemed remarkably quiet on her one excursion to Bute Street. What if she couldn't find a taxi to take her there? What if she couldn't find a taxi at all?

Deciding the time to worry about that was when it happened, she pushed the thought from her mind. But no matter how she tried, the stories she had heard about Tiger Bay kept surfacing in her mind. And not the innocuous ones she had told her father and the members of the jazz band at her sister's wedding, but stories of fights, knifings and men attacking women.

She pulled out the address of the vicarage in Church Street that she had tucked into her handbag. No taxi driver would refuse to take a respectable-looking woman to a vicarage. Would they?

She rose to her feet and peered anxiously in the sliver of mirror above the seat opposite. Her hair was damp with perspiration and bedraggled beneath her straw hat. Her silk dress was creased and clung clammily to her body. She glanced at her trunk, suitcase and overnight bag on the rack above the seats, and resolved to leave everything except her overnight bag in left luggage at Cardiff station.

Peter had written that the Reverend Richards had a house-keeper. She pictured a respectable spinster or widow who lived in, and would chaperone her while she slept at the vicarage. Peter would help her collect her luggage in the morning – and then?

Then what? At that moment it dawned on her that she had thought no further than reaching Peter. They still wouldn't be able to marry without her father's written consent.

She would ask Peter to telephone her father in the morning. Her parents would finally see sense and allow them to marry. If they didn't, she would have made all this effort for nothing. No, not for nothing – her mouth curled into a smile. After the lies she had told the bursar, one thing was certain: the principal would not allow her back into the college.

# Chapter 8

'YOU'VE GOT TO BE JOKING. There's no way I'm taking a young girl down Tiger Bay at this time of night,' the taxi driver said vehemently. 'The last thing I need is a copper flagging me down and asking questions about my involvement in the white slave trade.'

'Come on, Stan,' the porter coaxed. 'The lady's asking to taken to the vicarage not a pub or one of the houses.'

'She's asking to be taken to Tiger Bay – and that's enough for me. The coppers will take one look at her sitting in the back of my cab in Bute Street and pull me over. I can't afford to lose time on the busiest night of the week.'

'She's a young girl. You've daughters of your own.'

'Who look as though butter wouldn't melt in their mouths, just like Little Miss Muffet here, but I know what they're like under those innocent expressions. Who's to say where she'll go after I drop her off in Church Street? The Glamorgan, The Peel, The Cardigan or Anna Hughes's. Well, I'll not be held responsible.' The driver pointed to the row of taxis lined up behind his. 'Ask one of the other boys if they fancy taking a young girl down the docks at this time of night.'

'Please?' Edyth added her plea to that of the porter. The driver was in his forties, looked trustworthy and reminded her of the miners who visited her father in their house.

'Sorry, miss, you might be respectable and then again you might not. I like to sleep nights and I won't if I drop you off in Tiger Bay after midnight on a Saturday night.'

Edyth was hot, grubby, exhausted and exasperated. The train had been delayed outside Bridgend for over two hours and, as if that hadn't been enough, they had been held up outside Cardiff station for another half an hour so the scheduled trains could keep to their timetables. All she wanted was to see Peter and soak in a cold bath before sleeping in a clean bed, and she was convinced all three waited for her at the vicarage. But that was little use if she couldn't find anyone to take her there.

The porter who had miraculously found the key to the left luggage room so she could stow her trunk and suitcase there after it had officially closed for the night, had given up on Stan and was talking to the other drivers. Edyth watched him work his way down the line of cabs. He waved her forward when he reached the seventh in the queue.

'Best I can do for you, miss. But Tom will charge double the usual fare. He can after midnight,' he warned.

'Thank you.' Edyth was too grateful to argue.

'Here you go then, miss.' The porter opened the back door, lifted in her overnight case and looked expectantly at Edyth.

'You have been very kind.' She opened her handbag and pulled out her purse, Unable to see in the darkness, she moved closer to a gas lamp and extracted a shilling.

She thought she was being generous but the porter merely pocketed the coin, touched his hat and walked off. She stepped into the taxi and closed the door. The driver opened the glass panel that separated him from the passengers.

'The people at the vicarage in Church Street are expecting you, miss?' he checked.

'I know Reverend Slater,' she replied cautiously.

'The new curate?'

'You know him, too?' she asked in excitement.

'My daughter goes to the church school. New curate's already been there taking religious assembly. He's keen by all accounts and full of new ideas. But he has the good sense to tread carefully and ask the locals what they want. The people in the Bay don't like charity unless they're the ones dishing it out. That's where the Reverend Richards and his missus fell short. Still, mustn't speak ill of the dead.'

'Reverend Richards is dead?' Edyth was shocked to think that the man Peter had written about only the day before had passed away.

'No, his missus. She was too hoity-toity for the Bay by half. But there you are. Do-gooders are always poking around the docks, trying to "improve" the residents. Those who live there don't like outsiders coming in and looking down their noses at them, but from what I've been told, they've taken to this new bloke. You been held up on the train coming in from Swansea?'

'Yes.' Elated by the driver's verdict on Peter's work, Edyth sat back in her seat and looked out of the window, eager to absorb every aspect of the place that she hoped would soon become her home.

They drove out of station yard and along the main street before turning under a railway bridge and on to a wide road. Back streets that looked reassuringly familiar opened from it on both sides, reminding her of the terraced houses of Pontypridd and the Rhondda.

The sky was deep, dark navy above lamps that shed pools of light on to pavements, and beneath them, even at this hour, people were sitting on kitchen chairs that had been carried outside, presumably in search of cooler and fresher air. Elderly and middle-aged women were nursing small children and babies on their laps. Older children who still had the energy to run around were skipping with ropes or playing tag. She wondered why they weren't in bed then remembered it was a Saturday night. Even so, her parents had always insisted on regular bedtimes, including the height of summer.

Men had gathered in groups outside pubs that should have closed at ten o'clock, yet many were holding full glasses in their hands. A group was crouched low over playing cards spread on the ground. Gambling was illegal and so was drinking in public after hours, but if she closed her eyes she wouldn't see it happening, then she wouldn't be able to tell anyone about it.

She leaned back and did just that . . . for a moment . . .

'You wanted the vicarage, miss?'

The taxi driver's announcement, accompanied by the slam of

brakes, catapulted Edyth into startled consciousness. She opened her eyes. He had parked alongside a church set behind railings in a wide, straight, lamp-lit street that stretched ahead as far as she could see. The man left his cab, walked to the back of the car, opened the door and lifted her overnight bag from the floor. 'I'll carry this to the porch for you, miss.'

'How much do I owe you?' She opened her handbag and felt for her purse.

'It's double after midnight.'

'The porter warned me.'

'That'll be five bob.'

'Five shillings!' She squinted at her watch, holding it up to the window so she could read the face. 'It's less than a quarter of an hour since we left the station.'

'It's the going rate, miss.'

Careful not to open her purse too wide lest she lose any money, she felt gingerly among the coins, extracted two florins and a shilling and handed them over.

The driver went down a lane alongside the church and was swiftly swallowed by the darkness. Disorientated and half asleep, Edyth stepped cautiously on to the pavement. Jazz music wafted faintly in the hot, close air, along with ghostly, disembodied shouts and laughter. She was so relieved when the driver reappeared without her bag she had to stop herself from embracing him.

'The vicarage is down there?' she asked.

'Behind the church, miss. I thought you said you knew the curate,' he commented suspiciously.

'I do, but I haven't been here before.'

'He *is* expecting you?'

She realized what the situation must look like to someone who didn't know her or Peter. She imagined the driver relating the tale to his friends in a pub: '*This young girl insisted I drive her to that new, good-looking young curate's house after midnight. And she'd never even been there before.*'

'I should have been here hours ago. The train was delayed.' She took comfort in the thought that it wasn't exactly a lie.

'Well, I've taken you to where you asked to go; you're

someone else's problem now.' The driver climbed back into his cab and drove off, leaving her standing on the pavement.

She looked up at the church. It was massive and imposing, with huge double doors set in a wide arch, and a peaked roof flanked by twin pyramid-capped towers. She had to step back into the road to see the whole building silhouetted against the moonlit sky. Peter's parish was certainly impressive if the church was anything to go by.

A lamp burned on the pavement in front of the railings that separated the church grounds from the street, but the lane the driver had walked down was in darkness. Ignoring a group of women clustered around the lamps on the opposite side of the road, she steeled herself and braved the shadows. The high walls of the church on one side and the alleyway on the other blotted out the moon and for a moment she couldn't see even a glimmer of light. Forced to feel her way along the wall, she suddenly regretted the impulse that had led her to set off for Cardiff as soon as her parents had left Swansea. It would have been more sensible to have waited a day and written to Peter to tell him she was coming. He could have met her train and helped with her luggage, and she wouldn't have had to go to all the expense of tipping porters and paying a taxi driver double the rate.

It was only then that she realized why she hadn't told Peter what she'd intended to do. The Church insisted on respectability above all else, and after seeing the reaction of the porter and the taxi driver, she knew a young girl who travelled to Butetown alone in the early hours of the morning would most certainly not be considered respectable by the Bishop or the Dean.

Peter would have done everything he could to dissuade her from coming to see him. He would have also pointed out that there was no guarantee that her parents would allow them to marry even if she left college. She'd risked her reputation by being out alone at night in an unsavoury area and – as another burst of raucous laughter resounded from the streets behind the walls – possibly worse.

A light shone ahead of her and the lane opened into a small yard. The high walls of an imposing three-storey house rose on her left; the light came from an outside lamp above the door. She walked towards it and saw her overnight case on the step. She reached up and pulled the bell. She had to tug on it twice more before footsteps resounded behind the door.

'Who's there?' a woman shouted in a thick Scottish brogue.

'My name is Edyth Evans. I am a friend of the Reverend Slater. I would like to see him.'

'At this hour of the night?' the woman shouted back suspiciously. 'Is someone ill in your house?'

'My train was delayed. If it hadn't been, I would have been here hours ago.'

'No decent woman would come calling at this time of night. Go away!' The footsteps retreated.

Edyth opened the letterbox and shouted, 'Please, I must see the Reverend Slater. If you tell him Edyth Evans is here, he will want to see me.'

'I can't tell Reverend Slater anything. He's out at a sick bed. And even if he wasn't, I wouldn't disturb his sleep for a mad woman.'

'Out?' Edyth repeated in bewilderment. That was one eventuality she hadn't prepared for. 'Please, will you tell me where he is?'

'I will not. Sick people need peace and quiet in the middle of the night, not callers. And don't touch that bell or shout through the letterbox again. The Reverend Richards is very ill.'

'At least let me wait in the hall or the kitchen until Reverend Slater comes back,' Edyth pleaded.

'As if I'd let a stranger in the house in the middle of the night. The minute I'd drop off you'd steal us out of house and home, or burn the place down over our heads. Go away.'

'Please, I don't know anyone else around here.'

'That is your problem,' the merciless voice snapped.

'At least tell me where I might find a hotel?'

'There are plenty around here and in Cardiff, but no decent place will take someone in this time of night, let alone a young girl who's up to no good.'

'Please,' Edyth begged.

'Go away, or I'll call the police. And I have a telephone here to do it.'

Edyth heard the ping of a telephone receiver being lifted off a cradle. She hesitated despite the threat.

'If you don't go away, the police will come and arrest you for disturbing the peace.'

Edyth picked up her overnight case and walked back down the lane to the church and Bute Street. She hadn't thought the case heavy when she'd left home that morning, but now it seemed to weigh as much as her trunk. She stopped outside the church and looked up and down the street. Lamps pooled the darkness at intervals, but the areas in between were black and sinister.

The heat of the day still hung heavily in the air, and nothing moved, but she could hear a party of drunks belting out an unmelodic version of the sentimental Irish ballad, 'I'll Take You Home Again, Kathleen'. Live music was being played in the distance, the vibrant, toe-tapping tones of 'Putting on the Ritz'.

She stood beneath the lamp in front of the church and dropped her case. The buildings around her were large and imposing, some with three and more storeys. A few of the windows on the upper floors had lace curtains and the drapes behind them were closed.

She imagined families sleeping in peaceful, orderly rooms, and wished she knew someone besides Peter in Tiger Bay. She could hardly go knocking on doors at this time of night to ask householders if they took in lodgers.

The music seemed to be coming from a large building opposite but the doors were closed and she wasn't sure if her ears were playing tricks. Desperately hoping that a taxi would pass – and pick her up – she continued to stand, looking up and down the street, all the while willing Peter to appear. He had said in his letters that he had assumed all of Reverend Richards's duties and the woman in the vicarage had told her he was at a sickbed.

How sick? Could he be at a deathbed? A deathbed vigil could last until dawn, and if there were relatives to comfort, Peter wouldn't leave until his services were no longer required.

She glanced over her shoulder at the church. Surely, like all churches, it would be open and if it was, she could sit in a pew. Glad to have made a decision that required action she stooped to pick up her case.

'What you doing on our patch?' A thickset woman with improbably dyed red hair loomed over her.

'I . . . ' Edyth looked around. While she'd been debating what to do, the group of women she'd seen earlier had crossed the road and surrounded her. 'I don't understand.' Intimidated, terrified, she retreated to the wall, only to have someone poke her painfully in the back.

'This is our patch!' the girl shouted.

Edyth summoned all her courage. 'This is a public street.'

'It's ours.' The woman thumped Edyth painfully in the chest. 'I want to go in the church—'

'Tell us a story, why don't you?' The girl lifted her hand and slapped Edyth soundly across the face. Her head jerked back and hit the railings. The crack of her skull resounded in the darkened street.

Dazed and disorientated, Edyth tried to regain her balance, but the women gathered around her, pulling her hair and slapping and kicking her.

She opened her mouth to scream but the only sound she could make was a barely audible squeak. If it hadn't been for the pain, she might have believed herself locked into a nightmare.

Jed King left Judy and his wife in the front parlour where his mother lay, finally still and peaceful. The doctor had warned them four hours ago that death was imminent, and he was finding the waiting an intolerable strain. He went into the back kitchen in search of tea. Not because he, Judy or his wife wanted any, but because he felt that he would go mad if he didn't do something.

The room was full of family and neighbours, who had gathered silently and respectfully to honour his mother. He stood in the doorway and reflected that no one was allowed privacy in Tiger Bay. As babies they were born into houses crowded with well-wishers eager to catch the first glimpse of the newest arrival and press silver into their tiny hands 'for luck'. And they drew their last breath surrounded by people anxious to ease their passing and comfort those left behind.

But there was one man, slumped, snoring and drunk, in his

mother's easy chair next to the range, who had no place in the house. Or indeed Tiger Bay. Jed wanted him out – now. He walked over to the chair and hauled him upright by his collar.

Joshua Hamilton woke with a start and glared balefully at Jed through pink-rimmed eyes. 'What the hell do you think you're doing, Jed?' he demanded.

'Throwing you out of my mother's house, which is what I should have done when you had the nerve to show your face back here.'

'Judy needs me.'

'Your daughter needed you eighteen years ago when you walked out on her after her mother died.'

'I love her,' Joshua protested.

'Which is why you came to see her every time you were ashore, and sent my mother money to keep her all these years – I don't think?' Jed mocked scornfully.

'Jed, you were a seaman,' Joshua whined. 'You know what it's like to go from ship's berth to ship's berth, country to country. It's not my fault it's taken me years to work my passage back to Cardiff. I came as soon as I could.'

'Destitute, broke and drunk. And you didn't even have the common courtesy to go to the doss house. Instead you came here to sponge off the flesh and blood you would have dumped in the workhouse if my mother hadn't taken her in.'

'Jed?' His wife opened the door. 'Your mother and Judy can hear the shouting,' she whispered.

'Don't worry, it's about to stop.' Jed clamped his hand over Joshua's mouth and nodded to Tony and Ron. The three brothers lifted Joshua between them and carried him out of the house and down the street. They dropped him a hundred yards from the front door.

Fuming, Jed clambered to his feet. 'I've a right to see my daughter.'

'But not to stay in my mother's house or pawn her belongings. You think my brothers and I are stupid?' Jed challenged. 'Didn't you realize that we would miss the china dogs that have stood in her fireplace for years?'

Joshua tossed out one last desperate lie. 'Judy asked me to hock them. She said she needed the money for medicine.'

'It was Judy who noticed they were missing,' Jed growled. 'Sober or drunk, don't come back, Joshua. Not if you want to live to a ripe old age.'

'Stay away, if you know what's good for you,' Tony shouted as Joshua shambled off.

The anger that sustained Jed was replaced by an overwhelming tide of grief. He put his hands on his brothers' shoulders. 'Now that we've put out the rubbish, let's go back and say goodbye to Mam.'

Born accident-prone, Edyth had broken both her legs, arms and skull at various times when she was growing up. She'd fallen off horses, down stairs, out of trees and, on one spectacular occasion, from the roof of her Uncle Victor's barn. But every injury had been self-inflicted and accidental. No one had ever hit her in anger and, for the first few moments of the attack, she simply couldn't believe it was actually happening.

She came to her senses when she heard the sound of her hair being torn out by the roots. She dropped her overnight case and handbag, lifted her arms over her head and tried to protect herself. After two barely audible croaks, she finally found her voice and screamed loudly, in the hope that someone would hear and help her. But her cries only resulted in the women intensifying their attack. Covering as much of her head and face as she could with her hands, she tried to escape. But no sooner did she elbow one woman out of the way and gain an inch of ground, than another closed in.

Fingers padlocked around her wrists and forced her downwards. She was hemmed in by a forest of bare legs and feet encased in high-heeled shoes. The kicking started the moment her knees hit the pavement, the toes and heels of the women's evening shoes connecting with her back, arms and thighs. Curled into the foetal position, she breathed in the sour stench of the women's sweat and smelled their breath, a rank mixture of beer, whisky and undigested food, the whole permeated by a mix of sickly sweet, cheap scent.

The sharp sound of cloth tearing rent the air. To her horror, she realized they were stripping her frock from her. She made one last valiant effort to free her wrists. When that failed, she lowered her head, sank her teeth into the nearest hand and bit down with all her strength.

A woman yelped and sprang back, tearing her dress even more. Edyth took full advantage of the momentary diversion, lifted her head and screamed with all her might. Even her blood ran cold, as her cry echoed hollowly down the street.

Her neck bones cricked when her head was yanked back by her hair. She stared up at the stars and full, bright moon. A hand closed into a fist in front of her eyes and pulled back in preparation to slam into her unprotected face. But miraculously it froze in mid-air.

'What you doing, Anna girl?' a man asked in a Caribbean accent. 'You don' want to kill no sister good-time girl, now do you?'

'Let me go, Sam.' The red-headed woman rounded soundly on the speaker, slapping his face with her free hand.

Edyth took advantage of the diversion and gasped for breath. For the first time she was conscious of hot, sticky blood running down her face and arms. She retched, but there was nothing in her stomach to vomit. A draught blew across her bare skin and she retched again.

An Irish woman cried out, 'Watch your frocks, girls, she's throwing up.'

The rest of the women stepped away from her. Edyth felt herself slipping into unconsciousness. It would be so easy to lie down on the pavement and close her eyes . . . She moved her hand in front of her face, and fought with what little strength remained to keep alert.

More shadowy figures materialized, merging with those of the women around her. There was a hubbub of angry conversation. A strongly muscled, bare black arm reached down to her.

'Come on, love, the pavement's no place for a young girl to sleep. That's it, ups-a-daisy, on your feet. Can you stand?'

Too shocked to think, let alone answer, she wrapped her arms around her rescuer's chest and clung to him.

'You all right, miss?'

Edyth stared blankly up into the face of a black man, who was looking down at her in concern.

'Here, miss, tie your dress together.' A handkerchief was pushed into her hand. She took it, but the dark mist continued to veil her eyes and she saw only segments of the scene around her, as though she were trapped inside a telescope.

Nailed boots rang out and a strong masculine voice rose above the hubbub. 'What's going on here?'

'New girl's working our patch, Murphy,' the red-head yelled angrily.

A wit shouted, 'The lady doesn't want to play with Anna and the girls, constable. And we don't think they should try to make her.' A burst of laughter followed the quip.

'They were slapping her around.'

'If we hadn't come along and stopped them, you'd have had a murder on your hands, copper.'

Constable Murphy stood in Edyth's line of vision and pushed his helmet to the back of his head. 'That's what I like to see, boys, public-spirited locals. I won't forget to tell the sergeant about your good deed.' He lifted his hand to his mouth and the piercing sound of a police whistle brought the thunder of more hobnailed boots. A dozen or more officers appeared. They turned to Edyth, who was still being held upright by the black man.

'Anna's been beating up a new girl,' Murphy shouted to his colleagues.

'Grab as many as you can, coppers,' one of the Negroes shouted, as the police ran around trying to round up the women, who were now charging off in different directions.

'They're slippery as eels and sting like wasps, especially in your wallet,' another yelled.

The crowd of men stood back, laughing and jeering, as the police officers continued to chase the women. Too quick for the constables, who were hampered by their thick uniforms and truncheons, most disappeared up dark alleyways. But a few fell prey. And every time one was caught, she screamed, reminding Edyth of the noise her Uncle Victor's pigs made at farrowing time.

'Here, miss.' The man who was holding her helped her back to the railings, but he continued to support her until the bizarre chase was over.

'I'd say you lost about three-quarters of them, coppers,' a cheery voice shouted from the crowd of onlookers.

'Jones, go down the station and get the Black Maria out. I'd say we've found a full night's work for the desk clerk,' Murphy ordered a handsome, fair-haired policeman, who looked considerably younger than his colleagues.

'Serve bloody Pugh right for organizing himself a cushy number,' another officer grumbled.

Holding the red-head called Anna in an arm-lock, Murphy turned to the crowd. 'We'll take it from here, boys. Thanks for your help.'

'Night, officers.' The men disappeared into the darkness between the lamps.

'The bitch was working our patch.' Anna kicked, clawed and bit Murphy, who was only just managing to hold her.

'Lay off, Anna,' he warned irritably, 'or you'll be facing a charge of grievous bodily harm as well as affray.'

'The bitch—'

'We take a dim view of murder, even of bitches, Anna, and there's nothing to indicate the lady is one,' another constable remarked, somewhat placidly given the circumstances.

Edyth wondered if someone had switched off the street lamp. Then it went on again. Then off. She continued to stare at the place where it had been. A shadow lifted and she realized the light hadn't gone out at all. It was simply the officers who were struggling to hold her attackers, moving and blocking the lamp from her view.

'You all right now, miss?' the man who was holding her asked.

She nodded, but when he released her, the street whirled around her. She grabbed the railings for support. Confused, feeling as though the women were still pulling her hair, she lifted her fingers to check, although she knew they couldn't possibly still be tugging at it. Her bodice flapped open and she grabbed the torn edges, holding them together with the handkerchief. Using it as cover, she pulled her bust-shaper back into position and gulped in air.

'You really all right, miss?' Murphy handed Anna over to another officer and handcuffed their wrists together.

She croaked, 'Yes.' Looking around, she saw that the man who had helped her had left. She was alone with the police officers and her assailants. Constables were fastening handcuffs to the other women's wrists but as she looked at them she realized they'd only caught four. At least a dozen had attacked her.

She swayed and Constable Murphy grabbed her arm. 'Don't go wandering off, miss. Not until I find out what's been going on here.'

'They attacked me,' Edyth murmured.

'Anna said you were working their patch. Were you?' Murphy demanded.

She looked at him in confusion. 'Patch? I don't understand . . .'

'Course she bloody understands, the bitch,' Anna shouted. 'Times are hard enough without bloody amateurs muscling in on our territory and taking our customers. We work hard—'

'Course you do, Anna,' yawned the constable who was cuffed to her.

'Here we go,' another said when the Black Maria pulled up alongside them in the street. 'A carriage for the hardworking madams.'

'She tried to steal from us . . .' Anna had to be dragged, still kicking, into the back of the police van.

'That didn't give you and the girls the right to try and kill her, Anna,' Murphy called out. He turned his attention to Edyth. 'Now, young lady.' He pulled her around in front of him. 'Perhaps you'd like to explain what you're doing out here half naked in the middle of the night?'

'I was waiting for someone,' she mumbled.

'At half past one in the morning?'

'Yes.' She suddenly realized just how ridiculous that sounded.

'And who exactly were you waiting for?' he persisted.

Shocked, upset and in pain, Edyth still had enough sense to know that she couldn't mention Peter. How would it look to the Bishop if he ever discovered that the future wife of the vicar of Tiger Bay had been mistaken for a streetwalker by a group of common prostitutes, and beaten up by them because they thought she was trying to take over their territory?

'I thought so,' Murphy drawled. 'You don't know the name of your friend because you haven't met him yet.'

'I travelled down here this evening from Swansea. The train was delayed. You can check if you don't believe me. The half past eight was held up by the derailment of a goods train outside Bridgend. If it hadn't been, I would have been here much earlier. As it was, I didn't arrive in Tiger Bay until after midnight. My friend was out. I decided to wait for him.'

'On Anna's territory.' Murphy whistled. 'Now that *was* a silly thing to do, miss.'

'Murphy, what's happening here?' An officer walked up to them. Even in her distressed state, Edyth recognized the sergeant's stripes on his tunic.

'Anna and the girls took a dislike to a newcomer muscling in. Fortunately for her, Sam and his boys came to the rescue before they stripped, scalped and killed her. Although, as you see, they made a start.'

'Good for Sam and his boys.'

'They're not a bad lot when they're not gambling in the street or drinking after hours.'

'Or flogging on stuff that's fallen out of a ship's container.' The sergeant slipped his fingers beneath Edyth's chin and turned her head to the street light. 'Bit young to be on the game, aren't you, miss?'

'I'm a respectable girl—' Edyth began hotly.

'Yes, well, we'll find out just how respectable down the station. Cuff her, Murphy.'

'And put her in the back of the van with the other girls, Sarge? She'll never reach Maria Street alive.'

'You can walk her there.'

'She's half dead.'

'It's only a ten-minute stroll. Carry her if you have to,' the sergeant said shortly. 'This is best sorted at the station and I'm dying for a cuppa. I haven't had a morsel since teatime. My stomach thinks my throat is cut.'

Panic-stricken, Edyth watched Murphy snap a handcuff on to one of his wrists and the second on to hers. 'I haven't done anything.'

'Then you've nothing to worry about, miss.' Murphy started walking. 'Come on, the station's only just down the road.'

Edyth looked around as she was jerked forward. 'My case! My handbag!'

Even the officers who were still loading the girls into the back of the van stopped and glanced up and down the street.

'I had an overnight case, a red plaid Gladstone, and a white leather handbag.'

'Nothing here, miss.' Murphy continued to move and she was forced to follow.

She tried to stand her ground. 'But I've been robbed. All my things, my purse . . . I had over five pounds in it, and my bank book . . .'

'A likely story,' the sergeant sneered.

'I *did*,' Edyth countered forcefully.

'Just tell me one thing: if you had a fiver, why aren't you tucked up safe and sound in a bed somewhere instead of working the street?' the sergeant asked.

'I told you, I wasn't trying to pick up anyone. I've been robbed. Aren't you even going to look for my case and bag?'

'I've looked and I'll look again.' The sergeant stared ostentatiously at the pavement beneath the lamp. 'I can tell you one thing, miss: if your bags ever existed outside of your imagination they're not here now. Come on, Murphy, the sooner we get to Maria Street the sooner we can get a cuppa.'

'And one of them jam doughnuts the missus made earlier, Sarge?'

'Mrs Murphy does us proud, Murphy. Keep two back for me, will you?'

# Chapter 9

BARELY ABLE TO WALK for the aching in her entire body, furious at being robbed and mistaken for a streetwalker, first by a group of common prostitutes and then by police officers, Edyth found herself being pushed through the doors of the largest police station she had ever seen. The reception area was dark and dingy. The walls were covered in sickly, yellow-green, brick-shaped tiles; above them the plastered walls were painted a nicotine yellow that might once have been white. The wood-block floor was scuffed and stained by things she'd rather not think about, and the stench was overwhelming – sweat, vomit and urine spiced with a hint of carbolic.

An officer was sitting on a high stool behind a reception desk chatting to three women, who were weighed down by cheap paste jewellery and plastered with more make-up than Edyth had seen anyone wearing, on or off stage.

The officers were propelling the girls they'd unloaded from the van through the doors, past the desk and down a corridor. All four fought every inch of the way. Edyth saw that two of the constables had lost their helmets, including the young one whom Murphy had called Jones. Despite her predicament she noticed that he was not only handsome but looked more like a choirboy than an officer of the law. He had deep scratches on his face and blushed crimson every time one of the women or his fellow officers shouted at him.

Murphy unlocked the cuff that fastened his wrist to hers, slipped it off and snapped it around an iron bar set in front of the desk.

'Book her in for me, Pugh?' he said to the desk clerk. 'I'm getting tea for the sergeant.' He disappeared down the corridor.

'Bastard! Locking us up, just for trying to earn an honest living,' Anna yelled at the top of her voice after him.

'I'll talk to you when you show me your tax bill marked "paid", Anna,' Murphy called back.

The officer behind the desk shook his head. 'Come on, Anna. Less of the name-calling. You know the drill. You play fair with us and we'll play fair with you.'

'Albert Pugh is right, Anna,' said one of the women at the desk.

'You shut your face, Lettie Marshall,' Anna screamed in temper.

'Common, that's what she is,' Lettie said to her companions. She looked back at Constable Pugh, lifted her skirt and kicked her leg in his direction before following her companions out of the door.

Pugh watched them go, then turned to Edyth. 'The boys tell me you're the cause of all this upset.' He opened a book, picked up a pencil, licked the end and tutted at her.

'I haven't done anything,' Edyth protested. 'Those women attacked me.'

'They wouldn't have done that without good reason, now would they?' he asked calmly.

'Bitch!' Anna flung a final insult at Edyth before she was bundled out of sight. Her face had turned a murky shade of green and Edyth wondered if she was ill or if the effect was down to the harsh light of the naked lightbulbs that hung from the ceiling.

Feeling faint, she leaned on the counter for support.

'Stand up straight, miss,' Pugh barked. 'Can't have prisoners lolling about making the place look untidy.'

A man appeared in the open doorway of an office next to the counter. Edyth was accustomed to seeing tall men. Her father, Harry and Uncle Joey were all over six feet, and her Uncle Victor was over six and a half feet. This man looked both taller and broader. He was in shirtsleeves but his stance and demeanour left her in no doubt that he was in command. The moment he appeared, all the officers who spotted him straightened to attention.

Pugh murmured, 'Inspector.'

The man glanced up the corridor. The women were still

shouting, but their noise was drowned out by the ringing of footsteps, the clang of metal doors slamming shut and keys turning in locks. He looked enquiringly at the desk clerk.

'Anna and her girls attacked this . . .' Pugh paused long enough to make the word sound like an insult, '*lady*' for touting for trade on their patch. Sam and his boys rescued her.'

'Magistrates job?'

'We haven't formally charged any of them yet, sir. We'll let Anna and her girls cool off in the cells. But I doubt this . . .' he eyed Edyth as if she were a stray dog, 'person will want to make a formal complaint.'

'If she was on Anna's patch, charge her with disturbing the peace. She looks fit enough to hear the standard caution. Empty her pockets. Take her stockings and anything that's left of her clothes that she could hang herself with.'

'Sir,' Pugh snapped to attention.

The Inspector flicked his gaze over Edyth's tattered dress. She lifted her free hand and clutched the handkerchief the Negro had given her even more tightly to her exposed bust-shaper.

'Find out who she is and where she's from, Pugh, then lock her up. There's no point in rousting out her relatives before morning, that's if she has any who'll own her.'

Murphy walked down the corridor carrying two mugs, a plate of doughnuts balanced on top of one of them. 'One of the boys just said that Anna told him the girl arrived at the church in a taxi. She walked down the alley past the church and came out about ten minutes later. Then she started touting.'

The Inspector stared at Edyth. 'Why go down the alley past the church, miss? There's no doss house down there.'

Edyth gathered together the ragged remains of her clothes and dignity. 'I wasn't looking for a doss house.'

'I can't wait for you to tell me what you were looking for in Bute Street this early in the morning,' he said.

He moved out of the doorway, caught hold of her chin and turned her head, first one way then another. 'The girls did a good job on you. You're covered in bites and scratches. All superficial but they could get infected if they're not swabbed. Want us to call out the police doctor, miss?'

'No.'

'There's not a lot left of her frock.' Murphy placed the mugs and plate of doughnuts on the desk.

The Inspector examined Edyth's scalp. 'There are a couple of bloody spots here where they pulled out her hair. Are you sure that you don't want us to call the doctor?'

'I am sure,' Edyth repeated.

'You'll have to sign a statement to the effect.'

'Give it to me and I will.' Edyth managed to keep her voice steady although she was quaking inside.

'Do you want to press charges of assault on Anna and the other girls?'

Edyth blanched when she thought of the trouble that would cause not only Peter, but her parents. Her mother would be upset and her father – she visualized the newspaper headlines: LABOUR MP'S DAUGHTER IN BRAWL WITH STREETWALKERS IN TIGER BAY.'

'No,' she said firmly.

'No to the doctor or no to pressing charges?' Pugh poised his pencil over the book on the desk.

'No to both,' Edyth answered.

'Your first time in Bute Street, miss – or is it madam?' the Inspector asked.

His inference was obvious. Edyth was furious but she sensed she had nothing to gain by offending him. 'No,' she answered coldly but not impolitely. 'The last time I was here I attended a party in Moore's shopping offices.'

'I'm surprised the old man let you in. He's particular about who walks through his doors – during office hours. His grandson's more open-minded. So I take it you visited Charlie Moore? Private party, was it?'

'I visited the shipping offices, not Charlie Moore.' Edyth recalled Charlie's attack on Judy Hamilton and guessed what kind of 'parties' he held in his rooms.

'So you know Charlie Moore. Were you waiting for him or just hanging about on the off-chance he'd appear?' The Inspector returned to the doorway, leaned against the post and crossed his arms over his barrel chest.

'I only know Charlie Moore socially. And I certainly wasn't waiting for him.'

'Only socially?' Murphy whistled derisively.

'There are plenty of opportunities for a young girl like you to make a living without resorting to streetwalking, so why do it?' the Inspector asked bluntly.

Edyth looked down. To her horror the handkerchief had slipped and she noticed that it wasn't just her frock that had been torn to the waist, but also her petticoat. She snatched at the edges of her dress and held them together.

The Inspector saw her scrabbling. 'Get her a shirt, Murphy.'

'Sir.' The officer immediately ran up a flight of stairs and through a door marked 'Private.'

Edyth continued to stand in silence. She was very aware of the men around her, and the noise coming from the unseen end of the corridor where the girls who'd attacked her were still shouting insults at the officers who'd locked them up.

Murphy eventually returned with a freshly laundered blue cotton collarless shirt. He thrust it at Edyth. 'I want it back. Washed and ironed.'

'Of course. Thank you.' Edyth took it gratefully and hugged it close, but she didn't risk exposing any more of herself by trying to put it on.

'We need your name and address, miss.' Pugh filched one of Murphy's doughnuts.

Edyth opened her mouth then shut it again. She couldn't possibly give the police her parents' names and address. Both of them would be furious with her for leaving Swansea so late in the day and that was without everything that had happened to her since, that she sensed they would quite rightly blame her for bringing on herself.

'Miss?' Pugh prompted.

'I haven't done anything other than stand in the street in front of the church,' she said earnestly.

'You're about to be charged with disturbing the peace.'

'All I was doing was standing on a pavement,' she repeated.

'At half past one in the morning on a streetwalkers' rabbit run.'

'I thought it was an ordinary road. I'm a decent, respectable girl.' Edyth was beginning to realize just how difficult it would be to prove that.

'I don't know many respectable young ladies eccentric enough to walk down Bute Street at one in the morning.' Murphy looked sceptically at her over the edge of his mug of tea.

'I am respectable,' she reiterated.

'Come on, love, don't make this any harder on yourself than it already is,' coaxed Pugh, who resembled a kindly grandfather more than an officer of the law. 'Let's have your story.'

'There is no story, only the truth. I was attacked,' Edyth insisted.

'Because you were touting for trade on another girl's patch,' Murphy reminded her.

'I most certainly was not. And that is insulting.' Edyth was trembling but she was determined not to break down in front of the officers.

'Let me guess,' the Inspector said in a conversational tone. 'You went into service and found yourself laid off because of the recession. Your money ran out and you didn't want to go home because things are hard enough there without one more mouth to feed, so you thought you'd try your luck down here?'

'I was never in service. I am respectable—'

'We're short-tempered at the best of times, love, and you're trying our patience.' Murphy rolled his eyes and looked up at the ceiling.

'It's the truth. Why won't you believe me?' Edyth demanded.

'You're a fair actress, you talk better than some on the game and you're easier on the eye than most. But we're not born yesterday.' Murphy finished his tea and wiped his moustache with the back of his hand.

Desperate, Edyth said the one thing she had been anxious to avoid. 'I am an acquaintance of Reverend Slater. If you talk to him he will vouch for me.'

'Reverend Richards's new curate?' Murphy asked in astonishment.

'He was out when I called at the vicarage. I intended to arrive there earlier but my train was held up for over two hours outside Bridgend. You can check that if you like. I didn't reach Cardiff station until after midnight. The woman who answered the door at the vicarage wouldn't let me in.'

'I'm not surprised. Lizzie Mack knows better than to let in trouble, especially after midnight.' Murphy pulled a packet of Senior Service cigarettes from his tunic pocket.

'That was why I was standing on the street,' Edyth insisted. 'And it was there the women attacked me.'

'You're a right comedienne, love.' Pugh dropped his pencil and leaned on his elbows.

'Why are you questioning me instead of trying to find my handbag and overnight case?'

'This is Bute Street. The bag and case will be in the dock by now,' Murphy declared flatly.

'Empty,' Pugh added philosophically.

'Come on, love, stop wasting our time.' Pugh's tone hardened. 'The sooner you give us your name and address, the sooner we can put you in a nice cosy cell.'

Edyth swayed on her feet.

'Get her a chair,' the Inspector ordered.

Murphy pushed a chair behind Edyth. Still clutching the shirt, she sat down, but she continued to meet the officers' stares.

'Right, let's try again.' Pugh picked up his pencil. 'Name? Address? Occupation?'

A constable burst through the doors shouldering a man whose head was swathed in bandages.

'Trouble, Smith?' the Inspector enquired laconically.

'Punch-up in the open-air casino outside the Packet. Pastor Holsten's patched up the minor casualties. We sent one major to the infirmary. This is the card sharp who started it. Apparently, he had two aces up his sleeve.'

'Any more coming in?' The Inspector filched one of Murphy's cigarettes and lit it.

'Only one. Pastor Holsten offered to bring him in so the rest of the boys on the beat can clear the street.'

'Good evening, officers, Sergeant.' A tall, spare man came in supporting another casualty.

'Pastor, I hear you're being a Good Samaritan again.' The Sergeant beckoned to Murphy to take the injured man from Micah Holsten.

Edyth blanched when she recognized the Pastor as one of the musicians who had played at Bella's wedding. From the look on his face, it was also obvious that he remembered her.

Micah Holsten thrust the man he was helping at Constable Murphy. As soon as his hands were free he tipped his hat. 'It's a fine night, Miss Evans.'

'You know this lady?'

'I do, Inspector Cummings.'

'Then you can tell us who she is.'

Edyth shook her head and he understood her instantly.

'She is a most respectable young lady. I had no idea you ever visited the docks, Miss Evans.'

'I came to see Reverend Slater. My train was held up in Bridgend. I didn't get into Cardiff until after midnight and then I was attacked by a crowd of women outside the church. These officers seem to think I did something to deserve it.'

'Surely not?' Micah Holsten turned to the Inspector.

'You can't blame us, Pastor. Bute Street after midnight is not the usual haunt of decent young ladies.'

'It appears there are extenuating circumstances, Inspector.' Micah brushed his hair out of his eyes.

'You can vouch for this girl?' the inspector asked.

'I can, and I believe Reverend Slater will be extremely displeased when he hears of her ordeal.' He rolled down his shirtsleeves. 'Mrs Brown is helping me at the mission this evening. She could chaperone Miss Evans until morning. Miss Evans *is* free to leave?'

Pugh looked to the Inspector, who shrugged his shoulders.

'It appears she is,' Pugh replied.

Edyth could see the officers were relieved to be rid of her. She rose to her feet. 'There is still the matter of my handbag and overnight case. You haven't even taken a description of them.'

'White leather handbag and red plaid Gladstone,' Murphy said to the clerk, and Edyth realized that he had listened to her after all.

'You'd better give me a list of the contents, Miss . . . Evans,' Pugh suggested. 'Just in case something does turn up. But don't hold out too much hope.'

'There was a five-pound note and some coins in a purse in the bag and a bank book.'

'Colour of purse?' Pugh didn't look up from the book.

'White leather, the same as the handbag. There was also a blue leather pocket diary, a bristle hair brush, American cloth cosmetic bag with a gold lipstick case and powder compact, a bottle of essence of violets and a pocket edition of Emily Bronte's *Wuthering Heights*.'

'And the contents of the overnight case?'

'A white cotton nightdress trimmed with lace, a matching white cotton robe, a green American cloth toilet bag with soap, toothpaste and face cream, and a pair of white slippers. A green cotton print frock, underwear and stockings.'

'Was the bag labelled?'

'Yes', Edyth hesitated. 'With my name and address. And my diary also had my address inside.'

'Any keys that fit locks at the address?'

'No.'

'We'd still better have it.'

Edyth hesitated.

'You won't contact the lady's parents until she has had an opportunity to do so first thing in the morning?' Micah Holsten asked.

'We won't.'

'You promise?' Edyth demanded.

'You have our word, miss.'

Edyth went to the desk, scribbled her name and address on the slip of paper Constable Pugh handed her and gave it back to him. He glanced at it. If he recognized her father's name he didn't comment.

'Put out a report to all the beat constables. Ask them to keep a look out for a white leather handbag and a red plaid Gladstone,' the Inspector ordered. 'If anything is handed in before morning, Miss Evans, where can we contact you?'

'The Norwegian mission before breakfast and afterwards the vicarage?' Micah looked to Edyth for confirmation.

'Yes, please.'

'Enjoy what's left of the night, Miss Evans. I trust it will be less eventful than it has proved so far.' Inspector Cummings walked into his office. 'Night, Pastor,' he called over his shoulder. 'Thanks for the help.'

'Any time, Inspector. Goodnight everyone.' Micah looked at Edyth. 'There's a lavatory down the corridor if you want to put that shirt on.'

'Thank you.' She darted self-consciously inside. After locking the door she examined her face in the mirror. There were bright red scratches down both cheeks and around her mouth and forehead. Her left eye was half-closed, red and swollen, and her arms were as bloody and battered as her face. Tearing a piece from her bodice, she wiped her face and arms. They hurt, but Constable Pugh was right, her injuries were superficial. The dizziness she was feeling had to be down to shock. Then she caught a glimpse of the right side of her head.

Holding the rag she'd torn from her frock under the tap, she soaked it and rubbed her scalp. There was an unmistakable bald spot.

'Miss Evans, are you all right?' Micah Holsten knocked the door.

'Fine, Mr Holsten, I'll be out in a minute.' She threw the rag into the toilet pan, flushed it and buttoned the shirt, which was far too large for her, over the ragged remains of her dress. She rolled up the sleeves and, feeling like a child in dressing-up clothes, returned to the reception area.

Micah did just what her brother, Harry, would have done under the circumstances: slipped his arm around her shoulders and led her outside, relinquishing his hold on her only to open the door of the police station. She walked past him, stepped into Maria Street, staggered, and would have fallen if he hadn't caught her.

'Are you up to walking?' Micah asked solicitously. 'If not, I could leave you here and fetch my van.' He wrapped his arm around her shoulders again.

'No, thank you. Please, I'm just stiff from sitting on that chair. I can walk.'

'You should see a doctor to get those cuts dressed.'

'No, thank you. I looked at them in the mirror. There are a few scratches and bruises but nothing serious.'

'Or more than fingernail deep?' he guessed.

'Frankly, Mr Holsten, my pride sustained the most serious injury. And my hair. A clump was torn out by the roots.'

'It will grow again.'

'I sincerely hope so.' She took a deep breath. The air was heavy and stale despite their proximity to the sea. Emotionally as well as physically drained by the train journeys, the effort it had taken to, if not exactly lie to her parents, mislead them, the women's assault on her, and her subsequent ordeal in the police station, it was as much as she could do simply to remain upright.

Although it had happened less than an hour before, the attack already seemed more nightmare than reality. She tried to push it, and the humiliating scene in the police station, from her mind. But guilt prevented her. She had been incredibly stupid to continue her journey to Tiger Bay so late at night. She should have either taken the last train to Pontypridd or booked into a hotel in Cardiff city centre. Now, when she thought of it, she didn't know why she hadn't done just that when she'd had enough money in her purse to rent a room for the night. Money, she suspected, she would never see again.

She was also confused by the cavalier way the Inspector had entrusted her to the care of a man with whom she had only the briefest acquaintanceship, not that she wasn't grateful to Micah Holsten for vouching for her. But then Micah Holsten was a Pastor, and – she smiled when an image of Peter rose in her mind, a smile that cost her dear when it opened a scratch on her face –

church ministers, of whatever denomination, were almost always considered respectable by people in authority.

'Are you absolutely certain that you are up to a ten-minute walk?' Micah intruded on her thoughts.

'Yes. I'm just a bit shaky.' She took the arm he offered her and forced herself to put one foot in front of the other.

'I'm not going too fast for you, am I?' Micah asked after a few minutes.

'Not at all.' She quickened her pace, not wanting to admit that was finding it difficult to keep up with his long-legged stride.

'The sooner we get to the mission the sooner I can see to those cuts on your face and the sooner you can rest.'

'I thought you were a pastor not a doctor.'

'I studied medicine for a while,' he informed her briefly in a tone that didn't invite further questioning. He propelled her down a double terrace of modest 'two-up two-down', which reminded her of the mineworkers' homes around the collieries in Pontypridd, before diving down a narrow, dark alleyway that separated back yards crammed with wooden outhouses, coal sheds and, judging by the smell, poultry coops.

Snatches of music rose to meet them, fading as they passed: the strains of a homesick violin playing an Irish air; a Spanish guitar strumming a flamenco that set her mind dancing, even though her body hurt too much to follow; brass instruments belting out American jazz; and voices – deep, resonant Negro baritones – that reminded her of the recordings of Spirituals her father bought despite his avowed aversion to all things religious; scurrilous comic songs delivered in the distinctive Welsh lilt; an Italian imitating Caruso's *Ave Maria*, and, in the distance, high-pitched, drunken caterwauling she failed to recognize as any language.

The hands on the clock in the police station had pointed to half past one when they'd left, yet the streets were as crowded as Pontypridd on market day. Micah continually tipped his white felt trilby; to women sitting in groups on chairs that they had carried out of their homes; to men rolling dice and playing cards on the pavements on street corners; and others who were simply loitering and gossiping.

Micah took Edyth's hand and, wrapping his fingers around hers as though she were a small child, led her across a large square. A Catholic priest in a cassock scurried towards a terrace that led off one corner. He was deep in conversation with a small boy at his side.

Micah released Edyth's hand, ran across the road and intercepted them. 'Mrs King?' he asked urgently.

The priest crossed himself. 'God bless and help her in her hour of need.'

'She's—'

'Clinging on, or so I understand from what the boy told me, but it won't be long now,' the priest murmured.

'Tell Jed, Ron, Tony and Judy I'm thinking of and praying for them and Pearl.'

'I will.'

'And if they need any earthly help they only have to send word.'

'I'll tell them, Micah, but they already know that.'

'My sister will call on Judy in the morning.'

'No doubt Judy has women with her. But she will be needing help with the funeral – and afterwards.'

'She'll get it,' Micah promised.

'Thank you for your charitable thoughts, Micah. You're a good friend to the family.'

'They're good friends to me, Father.'

An elderly matriarch was perched on the narrow window sill of a terrace house smoking a clay pipe. A crowd of younger women had gathered around her, a few of them nursing babies 'Welsh fashion' with shawls wrapped around them and their infants. They watched in silence as the priest and the boy entered the house. The door was open, and they didn't close it behind them.

'The Bay rarely sleeps, especially in times of sickness and death,' Micah said when he saw Edyth looking at the small terrace.

She hit the toe of her shoe on a kerb, stumbled and would have fallen if Micah hadn't saved her.

'Careful.' He slipped his arm below her elbow and steadied her.

'As you probably gathered from what my brother, Harry, told you, I'm naturally clumsy and have been all my life.'

'I'd rather you didn't break your neck when you're with me. Especially as we're almost at the mission.'

'I take it Mrs King is related to the King brothers and Judy Hamilton, who played at Bella's wedding?'

'The brothers' mother and Judy's grandmother.'

'I'm sorry.'

'Mrs King is very ill. Death will come as a release for her but a tragedy for Judy. Her mother, Pearl King's only daughter, died shortly after she was born, and her father abandoned her. She has her three uncles but they all have large families of their own and their houses are full to overflowing. Her grandmother's house is rented and the landlord's already found another family to put in it. But we have to bury the poor woman before thinking of Judy. And there's nothing any of us can do tonight except pray for Pearl King and her family.'

They crossed a second, more imposing square that bordered a fenced park ringed by four-and-five-storey late-Georgian and Victorian edifices, which would have graced the most fashionable areas of London. Beyond it was a bridge and Edyth cried out in surprise at the sight of a perfectly proportioned wooden Norwegian church that gleamed white in the darkness. It looked as though a giant had plucked it from a Scandinavian forest and dropped it incongruously on Cardiff docks.

'It's beautiful, just like the one in Swansea.'

'You'll find Norwegian seamen's mission churches in ports all over the world, and all built to the same design, Miss Evans. This one also happens to be my home. You're welcome to spend what's left of the night in my room.'

'I couldn't possibly deprive you of your bed,' she protested, embarrassed by the trouble she had caused him.

'If you're worried about your reputation, my sister is working tonight. She'll chaperon you,' he reassured her.

'She works for your church?'

'In a voluntary capacity. We have a lot of helpers, wives, widows, sisters, mothers, daughters and grandmothers of seamen who do all they can to ensure that the Norwegian sailors are well looked after when they're ashore, in the hope that someone will do the same for their men in a port elsewhere in the world. Not that we cater only for Norwegians – or Scandinavians. Our doors are open to everyone.'

'Even wayward girls,' she commented drily.

'Especially wayward girls.' He smiled. 'In my experience they are our most interesting guests. But in your case I'd say ill-advised is a more apt word than wayward.' He waited for her to walk up the steps that led to the main door.

'You hold services here?'

'We do.' He pushed open the door and they entered a small hall. 'But that's not the main purpose of the mission or why most of our visitors come here.'

The first thing that struck her was the hubbub of conversation and laughter echoing from the floor above. She breathed in deeply. 'There's the most gorgeous smell. Vanilla and cream and—'

'Waffles,' he informed her succinctly. 'The staple of all Scandinavian cooking and the principal attraction of every Norwegian mission. Every seaman knows he can get coffee, waffles, a welcome, a comfortable chair and all the books and magazines he can read in a mission. We try to make every one a home away from home. But as you hear from the noise, word has travelled and we don't cater exclusively for mariners.'

She glanced around. The floor was light, highly polished wood, shining and spotless. The planked walls were whitewashed. Four doors were set in the walls in front of her. Micah pointed to them in turn.

'The chapel, the disrobing room—'

'Disrobing!'

'Bad translation, it's a cloakroom where people hang up their coats. It's also the Bute Street Blues Band's rehearsal room.' He smiled in amusement and she coloured in embarrassment.

'The public room and my bedroom are upstairs. If you'll excuse me,' he walked ahead of her, 'my mother taught me that a gentleman always walks up the stairs before a lady so he can't look up her skirt.'

'And follows her downstairs.' A young woman, tall and slim,

with startlingly blue eyes and white hair like Micah's, stood at the top of the stairs. 'Was anyone seriously hurt in the fight, Micah?'

'Only one had to be sent to the Royal Infirmary. I patched up the others and they're sleeping it off in the cells.'

'Why do sailors always behave badly when they drink? But you, poor girl,' she turned her attention to Edyth, 'look as though you have been in the wars. And you're wearing a police shirt.'

'Miss Evans, my sister, Mrs Helga Brown,' Micah introduced them. 'Miss Evans's dress was torn so the police loaned her the shirt. As it was so late they thought she would be more comfortable with us than in the cells.'

'I should think so, too. Pleased to meet you.' She offered Edyth her hand.

'I'm very pleased to meet you, Mrs Brown.' Edyth shook the woman's hand.

'Come in. I'll get you something to eat and drink.' Helga Brown stepped back and indicated the door behind her.

'I'm not hungry but I am tired.' Edyth followed her into the large public room. She found it strange that Helga hadn't asked Micah to elaborate on his brief explanation for her presence, or questioned why she was in the police station in the middle of the night.

'Miss Evans can sleep in my room.' Micah loosened his collar and tie.

'For the little that's left of the night,' Helga commented. 'I'll change the sheets.'

'There is no need,' Edyth demurred, upset by the amount of work she was creating.

'It wouldn't be proper for a young girl to sleep in a bachelor's sheets. Waffles and coffee for Micah and our guest, Moody,' she called out to an African boy who was standing behind a counter that held an assortment of cups, saucers and plates.

'Miss Evans, please sit down.' Micah indicated a table and chairs set slightly apart from the rest. 'If you'll excuse me, I must talk to my sister for a moment about Mrs King.'

# Chapter 10

EDYTH STUDIED the spacious loft that had been built into the rafters of the church as its public room. It was furnished with low tables, open bookshelves and simple, wooden-framed chairs padded with calico-covered cushions. The effect was plain and rustic, yet she considered it charming. The clean lines of the bleached wood, whitewashed wooden walls and pale upholstery reminded her of a snowy winter's day, until she saw the tapestry that almost filled the longest wall. It was of a steep-sided, conifer-clad mountainside that tumbled down to a sheer grey cliff. Below it, the sea swirled in blue shades of satin stitch, punctured by stab-stitched rocky outcrops and French knots of white-crested foam.

'That is beautiful,' she complimented Micah when he returned.

'It was begun by my mother and finished by my sister. And now I think we should tend to your face and arms.'

'No, please—'

'I have antiseptic and plasters. Please, come down to the bathroom. My sister will accompany us,' he added.

She resigned herself to following him. Ten stinging, uncomfortable minutes later, she looked at herself in the mirror Helga handed her. Micah had bathed her wounds in iodine and put plasters on the deepest cut, which was next to her mouth.

'Your hair looked worse than it was.' Helga gently washed the area that had been scalped. 'The blood had dried. Now that I have dampened it, you can easily cover the spot and it will soon grow back.'

'Really?' Edyth asked hopefully.

'It will,' Helga said emphatically. 'And now, Micah, I'll take your jacket, if you please, before those stains set.'

'It's ruined.' Micah examined the white linen sports coat he had hung on the back of the chair. It was blotched with blood.

'It will be if *you* try to wash it.' She took it from Micah, folded it over her arm and left the room.

'Shall we go back upstairs, Miss Evans?'

'My name is Edyth and, given the circumstances, I think you should use it.'

'I will if you call me Micah.'

Edyth followed him back up the stairs into the public room and sank gratefully into a chair. The cushions billowed around her and she was tempted to close her eyes, but resisted, knowing that if she did she would go to sleep. Micah sat opposite her and Moody brought a tray that held two mugs of coffee, a jug of milk, a bowl of sugar and a stack of cutlery. He set it in front of them and returned a moment later with a wooden board heaped high with steaming waffles and saucers of butter and preserves.

'Thank you, Moody. Edyth, this is Moody Brown, Helga's brother-in-law and my brother by adoption.' He winked at the boy, who smiled and shyly offered Edyth his hand.

'Pleased to meet you, Moody.'

'This is just what the doctor – or should I say pastor? – ordered, Moody.' Micah placed a waffle on a plate and handed it to Edyth.

Edyth looked down at the waffle, which bore the imprint of two fishermen pulling in a net of hearts. 'This looks too pretty to eat.'

'The Holsten waffle iron.' Micah gave her the saucer of butter. 'Every family in Norway commissions their local blacksmith to make a waffle iron and emboss it with their particular symbol so no two are alike.'

'So this is a Micah Holsten waffle?'

'Not mine, but one branch of the Holsten family's. My grandfather created the design and had the village blacksmith cast it as a wedding present for my grandmother. He was a fisherman and, according to my father, he used to say that the best catch he ever made was my grandmother. I inherited it after the death of my parents.'

'I've never seen anything like it.'

'The preserves are lingonberries.' He sniffed them appreciatively before passing them over. 'The sailors bring them in for me from Norway when they're in season and my sister and the other women here make the preserves. Try them; I guarantee they're not like anything else you've tasted. A unique, bitter-sweet taste of the homeland I haven't seen in a quarter of a century.'

'You don't look that old,' she said thoughtlessly.

'My parents left the country to run the Norwegian mission church in Danzig six months after I was born. I've never been back.' He waited until she'd helped herself to the butter and preserves before taking the dishes and spreading liberal portions on to his own waffles.

Although he'd warned her that the preserves were bitter-sweet, the first mouthful was more tart than she'd expected. She saw him watching her and said, 'It's good.'

'Warming on a cold stomach and quick and easy to make, for an ambitious boy like Moody, who has hopes of becoming a ship's cook.' He waved to the young boy, who was busy making more waffles for a crowd of men who'd commandeered the largest table. 'Which is why you'll find waffles being served in every Norwegian mission from here to Bombay and Sydney.' He finished one waffle and helped himself to another. 'Does anyone know you're here?' His tone was conversational, but it didn't fool her. He was obviously trying to find out just how much responsibility he had taken on when he had vouched for her at the police station.

'Not here in the mission, apart from the police, that is,' she replied guardedly, trying not to picture her parents' reaction if they could see her now, eating waffles in a Norwegian seaman's mission on Cardiff docks in the early hours of the morning with a pastor and jazz musician, after being attacked, robbed and mistaken for a prostitute.

'Do you want to get a message to anyone?'

'I told the police the truth. I came to Butetown to see Reverend Slater. I intended to arrive much earlier in the evening but the train was delayed for hours.'

'The vicarage has a telephone. I know it's late but church ministers are used to being disturbed in the early hours. Peter Slater wouldn't have minded you calling him.'

'I didn't think of it until I reached Cardiff and all I could think of then was reaching him. But there's no point in trying to get a message to him now. He wasn't expecting me, and the housekeeper at the vicarage told me he's visiting a sick parishioner.'

'So, Peter didn't know you were coming to see him?'

She sensed condemnation and looked into his blue eyes. They were cold, probing, and she felt the need to offer more of an explanation. 'Peter asked me to marry him.'

'And you said yes?' There was a peculiar expression on his face she was too tired to decipher.

'My parents refused to give their permission.'

'That's hardly surprising.' He cut into his second waffle. 'You are very young.'

'Eighteen,' she retorted defensively. 'Bella's married and she's only eighteen months older than me.'

'Someone mentioned at the wedding that she'd known her fiancé for some years.'

'What have years got to do with it?' she retorted, exhaustion making her irritable. 'I may have only met Peter a few weeks ago, but I know him as well as I know myself.'

'You do?' His sceptical lift of the eyebrow tipped her impatience into anger.

'I love Peter, and he loves me. He asked my parents if we could marry, they refused. They took me to Swansea today and left me in the teacher training college . . .' She fell silent when she realized she was arguing with him exactly as she would with her father.

'Didn't you want to go to college?' He scooped more butter on to his waffle.

'I did – before I met Peter.'

'Peter changed your mind about going?' he enquired mildly.

'A college place is wasted on a woman who intends to marry. Even if I had stayed in Swansea, worked hard for three years and qualified as a teacher at the end of it, I wouldn't be allowed to teach – not after we were married.'

'Do you really believe a woman shouldn't be educated?' he challenged.

'In my case, yes,' she affirmed, conscious that she was reiterating Peter's arguments not her own.

'So, the minute your parents left you safe and sound, or so they thought, in Swansea, you caught the train to Cardiff to join Peter Slater?'

'Yes,' she said defiantly.

'I know you said you were delayed but, given the distance between Pontypridd and Swansea, you must have left Swansea in the afternoon.'

'Early evening.'

'Couldn't you have waited until morning?'

It was the same question she had asked herself earlier, but his directness annoyed her. 'I needed to talk to Peter right away.'

'If it was that urgent, you could have telephoned him. Presumably there was a public one that you could have used in the college?'

'I wanted him to see that I had decided not to go to college for the right reasons. And, as you heard me tell the police, the housekeeper wouldn't let me wait in the vicarage, so I decided to sit in the church. It was then that those women attacked me.'

Micah finished his third waffle, set his knife and fork on his plate, and pushed it aside. 'First thing tomorrow morning you must telephone the college, Peter Slater and your parents to let them know you are safe.'

'I told the college I was going to my brother Harry's house in the Swansea Valley. He lives on a farm there.' She couldn't bring herself to repeat her lie to the bursar that Harry's wife was ill. 'My parents think I am still in Swansea and Peter doesn't know I'm here.' When Micah didn't comment, she felt that he considered her a foolish, spoiled brat, and what was worse, with good reason.

He glanced at his watch. 'If you're absolutely certain no one is worried about you, there's no point in disturbing anyone now. But you'll have to contact all of them in the morning.'

'Peter certainly,' she agreed.

'And your parents,' he added.

'I told you, they don't know I've left Swansea.'

'And if the bursar telephones your brother to find out if you

160

arrived safely at his farm?' He continued to look at her intently. 'Harry does have a telephone?'

'Yes,' she conceded.

'As do your parents. I saw one in the hall of your house.' He stacked his mug on top of his plate. 'You can use the telephone here.'

'I'll pay for the calls, just as soon as I am able to draw money from my bank account.'

'Thank you. The mission pays the bills, but our only income comes from charitable donations made through the Lutheran Church.' He glanced up as Helga rejoined them.

'The bed's made up for Miss Evans.'

'Thank you, Helga. Edyth, is it all right if I ask Helga to wake you at seven so you can make those calls? It will mean that you'll only get four hours sleep but you can catch up later in the day.'

'Yes, of course. I'm very sorry to put both of you to so much trouble.'

'I'll show you the washroom.' Helga led Edyth back down the stairs and opened the door on a small room furnished with a toilet and sink. She handed her a clean towel, but Edyth was too tired to do more than wash her hands. Micah had warned her not to touch her face. When she'd finished Helga took her back upstairs to a tiny room no more than seven feet square.

White-walled and wood-floored, it held a narrow wooden bed made up with a crisp white cotton eiderdown and sheets. The curtains were also plain white cotton. There was a small chest of drawers, with a simple wooden-framed mirror fixed to the wall above it. An aluminium portable washstand with basin, water jug and slop pail, and an open rail with a man's dark suit and three shirts completed the furniture. The only decoration was a plain wooden cross above the bed. If it had been a crucifix, the room could have passed as a monk's cell.

Helga took a man's striped nightshirt from a chest of drawers and handed it to Edyth. 'See you in the morning, Miss Evans.'

'Edyth, please, Mrs Brown.'

'And I'm Helga. Sleep well. If you need anything during the night I'll be just outside.' She closed the door behind her.

Edyth changed quickly. The bed was narrow and the mattress hard, but the quilt that covered it was thick and soft, and the coarsely woven cotton cover was freshly laundered. The cool, clean sensation of it lying against her bare legs only just had time to register before she plunged headlong into sleep.

A gentle knock shattered Edyth's dreams. She opened her eyes and was almost blinded by the sunlight streaming in through the translucent cotton that covered the window. She looked around in confusion, before recalling the events of the previous night. A second knock followed.

'Miss Evans – Edyth?'

'Please come in, Helga.' Her voice was hoarse, thick and sluggish. She sat up in bed and ran her fingers through her short, waved hair, brushing it back from her face. To her dismay she could feel the bald patch. Helga opened the door and carried in the white handbag and plaid overnight case that had disappeared from outside the church the night before.

'My bag – my case.' Edyth swung her legs out of bed and knelt beside them. 'The police found them?'

'Let's just say they found their way back to their owner. Micah telephoned the police station when they were delivered an hour ago, and they insisted on sending a constable down to check the contents against the list you gave them. It all seems to be there, even your purse. I'm sorry, but it's empty.'

Edyth opened her purse and shook it. There was nothing in it, but her bank book was still in her handbag. She opened it to reassure herself that the balance was the same, although there hadn't been time for anyone to withdraw any money from the account. She turned from her handbag to the overnight case. The nightgown, spare dress and underclothes she had packed were rumpled, but at least she had a frock to replace the one that had been torn to shreds, and the use of her own toilet bag.

'Thank you so much,' she said sincerely.

'Thank Micah, not me. He has a way of pricking the conscience of the most hardened sinner, but as you see,' Helga glanced at the empty purse, 'with limited success. When you've washed and dressed you'll find Micah in the office. It's the door facing you at the foot of the stairs. In the meantime, I'll make a start on breakfast. You'll eat bacon, eggs and waffles with us?'

'Just toast will be fine, thank you.'

'Are you saying that because you're not hungry, or because you don't want to put us to any trouble? I thought so,' Helga continued without giving Edyth time to answer. 'Don't worry about the trouble. You can earn your supper and breakfast by washing and drying the dishes while Moody and I prepare the church for service.'

It was only then Edyth realized that she was going to turn up on Peter's doorstep on the worse possible day of his week – Sunday.

Edyth washed and dressed as quickly as she could, given the confines of the small room, and the fact that she had to root in her bag for everything she needed. She tried not to look in the mirror. The scratches had become raised, yellowed, iodine-tinted welts, her face, arms, legs and as much as she could see of her back were black and blue, and she could barely open her right eye. Her scalp was tender to the touch and even a quick comb-through of her waves was agonizing.

The frock and petticoat she'd worn the day before were beyond repair. She stuffed both into the bottom of her laundry bag along with her stockings and underclothes, before bundling it into her overnight case. Whatever happened, she couldn't allow her mother or Mari to see the frock. If they did, she suspected there'd never be an end to their lecturing. She also put the police shirt in the bag. Its presence would take some explaining but she could hardly send it back unlaundered and she had all day to think of a suitable covering story.

She carried her bag and handbag to the corner nearest the door and stripped the bed. The bottom sheet and pillow case proved no problem, but it took her several minutes to wrestle the eiderdown from its cover. Setting the bundle of linen next to her overnight case, she folded the eiderdown neatly on the bed, left the bedroom and, ignoring the appetizing smell of frying bacon, walked down the stairs. The office door was open. Micah was sitting at an unvarnished pine desk, writing. He looked up when he heard her step.

'Good morning. Did you sleep well for what was left of the night?'

'Very well thank you,' she replied. 'I was too tired to thank you properly last night, but it was kind of you to rescue me from the police station. I wouldn't have liked to have spent a night in the cells.'

'You wouldn't have had much sleep there on a Saturday night after they'd finished collecting the drunks from the street. And Anna and her girls know how to keep the duty officers awake,' he added wryly. He held up a black ceramic pot. 'Coffee?'

'Please.'

'Sit down.'

She sat on the wooden chair in front of his desk. He filled a mug that matched the pot, and pushed a sugar bowl and cream jug towards her. 'From the look of the shadows beneath your eyes I'd say you had about half of the recommended eight hours.'

'Which would be more than you.' She poured cream into her coffee.

'I am used to missing a night's sleep, you are not.' He sat back in his chair and watched her stir a spoonful of sugar into her mug. 'I telephoned Peter in the hope I'd catch him before morning service. It's just as well I did. News travels fast around Tiger Bay. He had already been given an account – with embellishments – of the attack on a young girl in front of his church during the early hours. He will be here as soon as he has finished conducting early communion.'

'Did you tell him everything that happened?'

'Everything you told me.'

'Did he give you any message for me?' She took care to keep her voice steady but her hand shook as she lifted the spoon from her mug.

'Only that he would be here as soon as he could.' Micah lifted the telephone from beside his elbow and, holding the lead carefully so it wouldn't catch in the coffee mugs, handed it to her. 'Your parents?'

She hesitated for a fraction of a second before glancing at the clock on the wall behind him. Twenty minutes past seven. Mari would be in the kitchen preparing breakfast. With any luck her mother and father would still be in bed. If her sisters had been to a party or visited the Town Hall the night before, they would almost certainly be sleeping. Glyn would be awake, but he would be playing in his room . . . What could she say to Mari? *'Hello Mari, it's Edyth. I've left Swansea and I'm in Cardiff but I'm absolutely fine. Could you please ask Mam or Dad to telephone this number when they get up? I'll explain everything to them then.'*

She'd have to be quick hanging up.

'You promised to telephone them first thing,' Micah reminded her.

'I was looking for your number in case they're still in bed and have to telephone back,' she lied.

'It's on the dial.'

'So it is.' Furious with herself because she couldn't think of a single solitary reason to delay, she lifted the receiver to her ear. She avoided meeting Micah's eye while she spoke to the operator, recited her home number and waited to be connected. However, he made no effort to leave the room, which left her in no doubt that he didn't trust her keep her word.

'Lloyd Evans.'

Edyth's heart sank. Her father frequently worked early in the morning on weekends in order to free a few hours to spend with the family later in the day.

'Dad, it's me.'

'Edyth? Has something happened?'

'I'm fine.' She was acutely aware that it was the first time she had spoken to her father since the day he had refused to give her permission to marry Peter.

'You're not in Swansea.' It wasn't a question.

'No.'

'When did you leave?'

'Yesterday afternoon.'

'After your mother and I returned home?' There was pain in her father's voice, pain and concern – no anger.

Edyth had a flashback to childhood. Their Auntie Rhian had made Bella a beautiful pink organdie frock to wear on her fifth birthday. She could still feel the stomach-churning jealousy that had driven her to tell Bella that a duck had hatched a brood on the edge of the ornamental pond in the garden of their old home. Trusting her story, Bella had followed her to the edge of the water and she had pushed her in.

The memory of her sister howling at the top of her voice as she clambered to her knees in the shallow water, her glossy black ringlets wet and bedraggled, dripping with green slime, her party frock blotched with clumps of foul-smelling, stagnant black weed, still had the power to make her squirm.

Instead of the punishment she had expected, her father had sat her on his knee while Mari and her mother had cleaned up Bella, and explained how everyone, even him, occasionally felt jealous when others were the centre of attention. But there was no need to be envious because every single person in the world had their moment of glory. And he was sure that when her birthday came she'd have a frock, if not exactly like Bella's, equally pretty.

Afterwards she had apologized to Bella — probably her first ever sincere 'sorry' and, as though events had conspired to make her feel even more guilty, their Auntie Rhian had presented her and Maggie — it had happened before Beth and Susie had been born — with similar pink fairytale frocks to Bella's as 'the sister of the birthday girl gifts.'

'Where are you, Edie?'

Her father's question brought her sharply back to the present. 'The Norwegian mission church in Tiger Bay with Mr Holsten and his sister.' Her voice cracked with the emotion that she had managed to keep in check until that moment.

'Is Mr Holsten there?'

'Yes.' She choked on the word.

'Edyth? Edyth — are you still there?'

'Yes,' she whispered.

'Hand him the receiver.'

Edyth did as her father asked before delving in her pocket for her handkerchief. It was difficult to make out the conversation from hearing only one side, but from Micah's repeateds, 'It was no trouble, Mr Evans', 'of course', and 'look forward to seeing you', she guessed that her father was making arrangements to fetch her.

Micah returned the telephone to its original position on the desk. 'Your parents will be here as soon as they can.'

'To take me home?'

'You'd like to go somewhere else?' His lips curved in a ghost of a smile.

She blew her nose. 'I suppose you think I've behaved like a fool?'

'What is it the Americans say? "I'd rather not answer that question on the grounds that it might incriminate me."' He pushed his notepad aside and rose to his feet. 'Let's have breakfast before Peter and your father and mother arrive, Edyth. I've no doubt they'll have enough to say to you without me putting in my two pennies worth.'

Edyth had cause to remember Micah Holsten's words when Peter arrived at the mission just after nine o'clock. He was bareheaded, red-faced and breathless, and had obviously run straight from the church. He hadn't even taken the time to remove his surplice. She just finished washing the dishes in the small kitchen upstairs after breakfasting with Micah, Helga and Moody in a corner of the public sitting room. Not that she'd eaten much. The thought of seeing her father after their brief telephone conversation and the events of the previous night, had prevented her from swallowing more than a couple of mouthfuls. And even those had stuck in her throat.

Peter burst through the door, startling three seamen who were reading the Sunday papers over coffee. She knew he was angry with her when he barely nodded in her direction. Micah calmly shook Peter's hand, escorted both of them downstairs and showed them into his office. He closed the door to give them privacy, in contrast to his behaviour earlier, when he had sat and watched her speak to her father on the telephone.

She didn't dare look into Peter's face until they were alone. But her hopes for a welcoming smile were dashed when he glared at her, his eyes cold, hard and intractable.

'What on earth possessed you to visit me so late at night?' he demanded without any preliminaries. 'You're the talk of the Bay. Do you know what those women are? The police assumed you were one of them. My fiancée a—'

'They made it obvious what they thought I was,' she interrupted. His anger hit her with the force of a body blow and she leaned on the back of a chair for support.

'Given the time of night that they picked up you in Bute Street, can you blame them?'

'It wasn't that late when I left Swansea. I should have arrived at the vicarage before ten o'clock but my train was held up outside Bridgend.'

'If you had written or telephoned I would have talked you out of rushing down here. I simply can't understand what you hoped to accomplish by doing something so stupid.' He finally turned and looked her in the eye. 'Given your injuries there's no chance that we'll manage to keep this quiet. One look at your face and everyone who has heard the gossip will know that it was you brawling with those women at two in the morning.'

'It wasn't that long after midnight.'

'It was late and that's what matters. Didn't you think how it would look? You knocking on my door at that hour of the night? We're not even officially engaged, Edyth. And even if you had arrived earlier, you hadn't made any arrangements to rent a room or stay anywhere respectable.'

'You said in your letters that the Reverend Richards had a housekeeper. I assumed she lived in.'

'She does,' he concurred irritably. 'But she is an elderly widow. It's one thing for her to sleep in a bachelor household, quite another for a young girl like yourself.'

'She could have chaperoned me. I needed to see you, Peter.' She softened her voice in an attempt to diffuse his anger.

'You had the telephone number of the vicarage. You could have spoken to me any time you wanted. You haven't telephoned me once since I've been here,' he reproached. 'And then to come down here on a whim and get yourself arrested—'

'It wasn't easy to talk to you on the telephone at home. My parents and my sisters were always around, I didn't want them listening in on our conversation. Besides, I wanted to tell you face to face that I had decided not to take the place I'd been offered at college.'

'For pity's sake, Edyth, I knew you didn't want to go to college. We'd discussed it before I left Pontypridd and in our letters since.' He closed his hand into a fist and placed it over his mouth as though he were trying to keep his exasperation in check.

'But you didn't know that I was prepared to defy my parents to help you get your own parish.'

'Well, you're not in a position to help me, or anyone else, now that your reputation is ruined.'

'Hardly ruined, Peter,' she remonstrated.

'No?' he queried angrily. 'I hadn't even returned to the vicarage this morning from Mr Marchant's deathbed when I heard that a young woman had knocked the door after midnight last night asking for me. And when the housekeeper, quite rightly, refused to admit her, she started . . . started . . .'

'Started what, Peter?' she enquired coldly, furious at his insistence that her reputation was ruined.

'Accosting men in the street.'

'That is not true.'

'No?' he questioned acidly.

'No,' she reiterated forcefully. 'After your housekeeper refused to let me into the vicarage, I decided to sit and wait for you in the church. But before I could reach the door those women attacked me.'

'Because they mistook you for one of them,' he snapped. 'A woman prepared to sell herself to any man prepared to pay for an hour or two of her favours. A woman with no morals or modesty. And, a reasonable mistake to make on their part, given that you were out alone at that time in the morning, talking to Negroes.'

'I was not talking to them, leastways, not until after they rescued me. They pulled the women off me. The police didn't come until later,' she explained. But Peter was in no mood to listen to her account of events.

'After hearing what happened from some of my parishioners this morning, you certainly appeared to have behaved like a loose woman, talking to strange men, brawling with strumpets—'

'All I'm guilty of is standing in the street after midnight. Any "brawling", as you put it, that I did was a useless attempt to defend myself. As you see from the state of my face and arms, I made a pathetic job of it. And the only men I spoke to were the ones who pulled the women off me. Not surprisingly, I thanked them. But what hurts more – much, much more than my injuries – is that you prefer to believe gossip rather than me.'

He ran his hands through his hair. 'Edyth, you don't seem to understand the gravity of what you've done.'

'Peter, you said that you love me.' She paused for a moment, hoping that he would tell her again. When he didn't, she continued. 'If you didn't, you wouldn't have asked me to marry you. So why do you give a damn what people say about me?'

'There is no need to resort to crude language,' he reprimanded.

'Oh yes, there is, if it's the only way I can make myself heard,' she contradicted. 'My parents wouldn't listen when I told them that I didn't want to take the place I'd been offered in college. I thought that if I came to see you, you'd understand and . . .' She turned away, unable to meet his steady gaze.

'And?' he questioned.

She tightened her grip on the chair. With hindsight she realized she'd been stupidly naive to believe that her father would change his mind and consent to her marriage to Peter after the way she'd left Swansea. If anything, it would only confirm his conviction that she was too immature to make any serious decisions about her future.

'You don't seem to understand how important it is for a woman to have an unblemished reputation, Edyth,' Peter lectured as though he were in a pulpit. 'Especially down here in the Bay. Respectability is everything, and doubly so for the wife of a vicar. Last night you were arrested by the police—'

'Not arrested, Peter,' she corrected. 'I was the victim of an attack.'

'But you were taken to the police station in the company of known streetwalkers,' he emphasized. 'I don't seem to be able to make you understand how serious that is.'

'I understand perfectly.' She was livid at his greater concern for her reputation than her safety 'I was the one who was kicked, scratched, scalped and beaten by those women. I dread to think what would have happened to me if those men hadn't happened along when they did. Then I was hauled off by the police, who would have put me in the cells if Mr Holsten hadn't vouched for me.'

Peter lowered his voice. 'Mr Holsten is hardly the most respectable person on the docks.'

She stared at him in astonishment. 'He is a pastor.'

'He is renowned for having some less than savoury friends. And you spent the night with him in his private accommodation.'

'Chaperoned by his sister.'

'Mrs Brown is married to a coloured man.'

'There is no need to state the obvious, Peter. I met her brother-in-law.' Taught by her father to deplore racial and religious prejudice she raised her voice. 'Isn't it your Bible that teaches us all men – and presumably women – are born equal?'

'Isn't it your Bible, too?' He threw the question back at her.

They stared at one another for what seemed like an eternity to Edyth who was light-headed from lack of sleep. Finally her anger was supplanted by sheer weariness. 'What do you expect me to do now?'

'Do?' he repeated. 'I rather think that you've done enough for one day and night, don't you?'

'One thing's certain,' she murmured flatly, only just beginning to realize the finality of the decision she had made the previous day, 'they won't take me back in college, not after the way I left.'

'Did you tell them that you were coming to see me?' He sat on the edge of the desk and looked at her in alarm.

'I told the bursar that Harry's wife was ill and I was needed to look after her.'

'You lied?' he gasped. 'On top of everything else, you actually told a lie?'

'Yes, I lied!' she confirmed. 'I wanted to see you.' She knew she was repeating herself but she couldn't think of anything else to say. Dizzy, shocked by his anger, she suddenly had the oddest feeling that she was standing outside of herself.

For the first time she saw Peter objectively and began to wonder if it was possible that he truly considered propriety and respectability and other people's opinions more important than her? She pushed the idea from her mind. Not Peter, not even now when they were arguing and he was angry with her. He loved her. Hadn't he told her so?

And she loved him – no amount of quarrelling could change that. Given her upbringing and her father's aversion to organized religion, she wasn't used to Peter's dogmatic way of thinking. That was all.

On his own admission his parents had been middle-aged when he was born. They had probably instilled Victorian values in him that they had been brought up to regard as sacrosanct. Once she'd convinced him that she'd left Swansea solely because she'd wanted to help him realize his dream to run his own parish, he would forgive her.

But when he continued to glare at her, she wasn't so sure.

# Chapter 11

PETER'S VOICE, loud in anger, resounded up the stairs of the Norwegian church into the public sitting room. Micah listened for a moment before folding and setting aside the copy of the *Sunday Pictorial* he was reading; because it had been the only newspaper left in the rack. He left his chair, went to the counter, lifted a tray from the stack set neatly to one side, and laid two mugs, a sugar bowl, milk jug and coffee pot on it. Then he picked up the coffee-grinder, filled it with beans, closed it and turned the handle.

'What are you doing, Micah?' Helga dumped the tray of dishes she had collected on to an empty table and watched him.

'What does it look like I'm doing, Helga?' he answered mildly.

'Making coffee for two?' she suggested.

'Then that's what I'm doing.'

'You're asking for trouble. No man should walk in on an argument between lovers. If that's what they are,' she qualified in a whisper that didn't go any further than his ears.

'That poor girl has been through enough in the last twelve hours without Peter Slater screaming at her for losing her reputation.'

'You've been listening hard,' Helga commented.

'When someone is shouting that loud, it's difficult not to hear what they're saying.'

'Apparently not.' She couldn't resist adding, 'Especially when you're determined to listen.' She pulled a stool close to the counter and sat down. 'If I were you, I wouldn't interfere in things that don't concern you.'

'I'm not you.' He tipped the coffee he'd ground into the pot, and turned up the electric hotplate, setting the water boiling.

173

'You must have heard what people are saying about Peter Slater.'

'There's always gossip going around the Bay.'

'Gossip – but not the kind of things I've heard.' She picked up a tea towel and folded it.

The kettle began to hiss steam. Micah took it off the plate and poured it on top of the grounds.

'Hasn't it occurred to you that Edyth might be better off without him?' she asked.

'It has. In general, vicars' wives lead miserable lives, subservient not only to their husbands but to their parishes, parishioners and bishops.'

'Then why are you trying to get them together?'

'Who says I am?'

'You're obviously intent on playing the mediator.'

'All I'm trying to do is save Edyth Evans from a dressing-down she doesn't deserve.' He checked the tray, picked it up and headed for the stairs.

Peter answered the knock on the office door.

'My sister thought you'd like coffee.' Micah Holsten breezed in and laid the tray on the desk. Edyth noticed there were only two cups and wished he would stay. Ever aware of propriety and other people's opinions, Peter would never argue with her in front of Micah.

'Thank you,' she murmured.

'Glad to see your fiancée safe and sound, if a little scratched and bruised, Peter?' Micah surprised Edyth with the familiarity with which he used Peter's Christian name.

'It would have better if she hadn't ventured into the Bay so late at night in the first place,' Peter answered tartly.

'There's no harm done. Edyth only gave the officers her name and address in relation to her stolen property – which has now been recovered.' Micah gave Edyth an encouraging smile and she suspected that he'd heard Peter arguing with her. 'No charges have been made against her and no official complaints. The officer who came down here first thing this morning to check the contents of

Edyth's handbag and suitcase against the list she gave them last night, told me that all the women had been released without charge or caution – at Edyth's instigation. To them it's just one more fracas in the Bay. It will be forgotten by the end of the week if not tomorrow.'

'You weren't charged with anything?' Peter looked to Edyth for confirmation.

'If you'd listened to what I've been trying to tell you, you'd know that I wasn't,' she snapped irritably, angry with him for believing Micah before her.

'Are you sure?' he pressed.

'The police wouldn't have allowed me to take Edyth out of the station last night if she had been charged with an offence.' Micah poured the coffee. 'Frankly, from what the officer told me this morning, I think the Inspector is relieved that Edyth chose not to press charges against the women. In fact, he mentioned that the Inspector had commented on her common sense. A less mature person might have wanted revenge for a totally unprovoked attack by strangers. As it is, there's no police report – and no paperwork – to connect Edyth to any event, other than, of course, her stolen handbag and suitcase.'

'That does put a different complexion on things.'

Edyth wished Peter didn't sound quite so relieved. It only confirmed her suspicions that he thought more of propriety than of her.

'I told the officers that Edyth's character is beyond reproach. They won't be so ungentlemanly as to bring up the incident again. You have my word on that.' Micah was so emphatic that Edyth wondered what exactly he had told the officer who had called that morning when she'd been asleep. 'You take sugar in your coffee, don't you, Edyth?' He held the spoon above the sugar bowl.

'One please.' Edyth gave him a small smile of gratitude.

'Miss Evans telephoned her parents after I contacted you this morning. They are on their way. You're welcome to wait for them here,' Micah offered. 'I have to conduct a service in twenty minutes.'

'I must return to the vicarage. Reverend Richards took a turn for the worse this morning before I left for church. Mrs Mack sent for the doctor and I would like to speak to him.'

Edyth summoned her courage. 'Would you like me to come with you, Peter?'

'I think you've trespassed on Micah's hospitality quite long enough, Edyth,' he replied evasively.

'Not at all,' Micah interposed. 'Feel free to pay us a visit any time you like, Edyth, you'd be most welcome. Shall I ask Mr and Mrs Evans to call at the vicarage when they arrive?' Micah finished pouring and sugaring Edyth's coffee and handed it to her.

'If you would, please.' Peter took the cup Micah gave him.

The coffee was hot and burned Edyth's throat, but she drank it quickly and in silence. As did Peter. Micah brought down her overnight case and handbag from upstairs and showed them to the door. Edyth shook his hand, thanked him again and asked him to remember her to his sister and to Moody.

Peter offered her his arm when they reached the street, but any hope she had that it was a conciliatory gesture ended when he walked her to the vicarage without saying a single word. It didn't help that he chose a route that took them through all the back lanes. She couldn't help feeling that, despite Micah's spirited defence, Peter regarded her as being 'in disgrace' and was ashamed of her and her tell-tale cuts and bruises.

The lanes weren't totally deserted. Children and adults ran in and out of back gates, calling on family and friends, and Edyth and Peter encountered a few groups walking purposefully towards the main thoroughfares dressed in their Sunday best, talking, laughing and smiling as they made their way to church, chapel, Sunday school, or to visit friends and relations.

Peter said hello to a few people but only after they had greeted him. He was clearly embarrassed by her because he didn't attempt to introduce her to anyone. He also kept lifting his hand to his head to raise the hat he had left in his church vestry in his haste to get to the Norwegian mission.

They saw a police constable talking to some Chinese men outside a cafe, but Edyth didn't recognize him from the previous night and, to her relief, if he remembered her, he was diplomatic enough to ignore her.

The lane that led around the church to the vicarage was as narrow as she remembered, but nowhere near as sinister in broad daylight. The front door of the vicarage was unlocked. Peter opened it and called out, 'I'm back, Mrs Mack.'

A skeletally thin, elderly woman came down the passage to meet them. Her grey eyes were watery and swollen.

'Reverend Slater, the doctor says Reverend Richards has to go to the Infirmary. He's . . .' She stopped and stared at Edyth when she saw her standing behind Peter.

'This is my fiancée, Miss Evans, Mrs Mack. As you can see from her face, she has met with a slight accident.'

Edyth's spirits rose at Peter's introduction. Only a few minutes before he had reminded her that they weren't even officially engaged, now he was introducing her as his fiancée. Surely that meant that he had forgiven her for dashing up from Swansea to see him and getting embroiled with the police?

'Pleased to meet you, Miss Evans. I hope those cuts and bruises on your face will soon heal.' She wrinkled her nose suspiciously. The woman spoke oddly, slurring her words.

Edyth presumed that grief at Reverend Richards's condition was making it difficult for her to talk. 'I'm sure they will, Mrs Mack.' Hoping the housekeeper wouldn't recognize her voice from the night before, Edyth said, 'And I'm very pleased to meet you, too. Reverend Slater has written to me about you.' She held out her hand but Mrs Mack bobbed an old-fashioned curtsy.

Peter glanced up the stairs. 'Is the doctor still here?

'Doctor Williams arrived an hour ago. He took one look at Reverend Richards, picked up the phone and called for an ambulance.' She pulled a handkerchief from her sleeve and noisily blew her nose. 'The doctor said he'd wait with the Reverend until it arrived. It's bad, Reverend Slater. When he was talking to the hospital I heard him say,' she dropped her voice until it was barely audible, 'pneumonia.'

'I'll go up and see if there's anything that I can do for the

Reverend Richards or the doctor, Mrs Mack. Please show Miss Evans into the drawing room.' Peter ran up the stairs.

Feeling very much in Peter's and Mrs Mack's way, Edyth followed the housekeeper into a dismal, cheerless room. It was larger than the sitting room in her parents' house, but the only window overlooked the high wall of the church barely six feet away. And the furniture did nothing to lighten the gloom. The sofa and chairs were covered in a slippery, shiny, bottle-green rexine. The blue and gold patterned Persian rug, which covered most of the dark wood floor, clashed with the suite and the green and red wallpaper. The sofa table and bureau bookcase were of age-stained mahogany. Every available inch of mantelpiece and table was covered with china dogs and cats of varying shapes and sizes. In pride of place on the chimney breast, above the massive slate fireplace, was an oil painting of Scottish cattle. It either hadn't been cleaned in decades or else had been painted in a thick and dirty mist. The general effect was that of a freezing, musty-smelling junk shop crammed with unwanted Victoriana.

Mrs Mack was tearful but she remembered her manners. 'Sit down and make yourself comfortable, Miss Evans.'

Edyth moved a solid cross-stitch cushion that might have made a more serviceable hassock, and perched on one of the hard, rexine chairs. After the comforts of the Norwegian mission she found the room cold and unwelcoming. There were sticks and coals in the brass settles in the hearth, but from the chill in the air, which had surprisingly survived the summer heat, she surmised that it had been a long time since a fire had been lit in the room.

'Would you like a cup of tea, Miss Evans?'

Having drunk more than double her normal quota of coffee that morning, Edyth shook her head. 'I've only just had breakfast, but thank you for offering, Mrs Mack.'

'If you'll excuse me, I have Sunday dinner cooking. The Reverend Richards is fond of his midday meal on the Sabbath. Perhaps the ambulance will be late and he'll have time to eat before he is carried away . . . although his appetite is quite gone these days . . . he eats next to nothing . . . nothing at all . . .' She lifted her handkerchief to her eyes.

'Can I do anything to help you in the kitchen, Mrs Mack?' Edyth jumped to her feet when the old woman started sobbing.

'The old Reverend would be angry if he heard me say this,' Mrs Mack gulped out between wails. 'But someone has to, Miss Evans.' The housekeeper straightened her back and her eyes flashed in anger. 'You might be the young Reverend's fiancée, but that doesn't give you the right to be here. Not with the Reverend Richards lying ill upstairs. It's as though you and the young Reverend are moving in, and taking over before the old Reverend is cold.'

'It's not like that at all.'

'Then why are you here?'

'The Bishop sent Reverend Slater here to help, because he knew Reverend Richards wasn't well and he was concerned about him,' Edyth explained.

'And now the old Reverend's going to the Infirmary. He'll die there and I'll be thrown out on the street,' she cried despairingly. 'I'll have nowhere to go and no one will care whether I have a roof over my head or not. Or even if I live or die. That's all the thanks I'll get for taking care of the Reverend and Mrs Richards for over forty years. And when she passed into God's glory, God and all the saints rest her soul, I looked after the Reverend's every need. Cooking and washing and cleaning for him and chivvying him to eat when he said he wasn't hungry. He would have starved to death after Mrs Richards went if it wasn't for me, Miss Evans. And that's God's own truth.'

'I believe you.' Edyth wouldn't have dared say otherwise.

'I've looked after the old Reverend like he was my own father . . .' The rest of her words were lost in a bout of incomprehensible howls.

'The doctor wouldn't send the Reverend Richards to the Infirmary if there was any alternative, Mrs Mack. But I'm sure the Church,' Edyth hoped that she wasn't taking too much upon herself, 'won't see you thrown out on the street.'

'You and the young Reverend will need a housekeeper, and as I'm already here and know the house, it would make sense to keep me on.' Mrs Mack dropped her handkerchief and stared hopefully at Edyth.

'Reverend Slater may not be the next vicar here, Mrs Mack,' Edyth replied, noticing that Mrs Mack's tears had miraculously dried.

'Of course he will. Everyone in the Bay says so,' the old woman dismissed. 'And you're his *fiancée*. Now the old Reverend is sick you'll marry Reverend Slater and live here.'

Edyth looked around the dismal, cold dark room. Live here? If she was going to be mistress of this vicarage there was a lot of work to do, and not only in the parish. Peter had warned her they wouldn't be rich, which presumably meant there'd be little, if any money for new furniture. But she had some savings. There was no way that she could live in this dreary room, not with this wallpaper . . .

The doorbell rang, shattering her vision of light distempered walls and elegant, art deco furniture.

'That'll be the ambulance. I couldn't bring myself to watch them carry out the old Reverend – not if you paid me.' Mrs Mack collapsed on the sofa.

'I'll answer it.' Edyth walked down the tiled passageway. The only light came from a skylight and a window halfway up the stairs, but the area was brighter and warmer than the sitting room. The floor and wall tiles were scuffed and in dire need of a good clean and polish. But then, she reflected, she wasn't mistress of the vicarage yet, and given her father's opposition towards her marriage to Peter, might never be.

She opened the door. Her parents were standing on the doorstep. Her mother looked uneasy, her father sombre.

For the first time in her life, she was afraid to face them and she didn't like the way it made her feel. Not one little bit.

Lloyd made the first move. 'May we come in?' he asked gruffly.

'Of course, I'm sorry.' Edyth stepped back and held the door open. 'I wasn't expecting you so soon. The housekeeper thought it would be the ambulance.'

'Your face . . .' Sali stammered, when the light fell on Edyth.

'It's not coming for me. I'm fine. These are just a few scratches.'

'Then someone else is ill,' Sali said in concern. 'Peter?'

'It's for Reverend Richards. The doctor has sent for an ambulance to take him to the Infirmary. Peter is upstairs with him now.'

'We've heard it from Mr Holsten but I'd like to hear it from you, Edyth. How did you get those injuries?' Her father removed his hat and followed her mother into the hall.

'A woman mistook me for someone else last night, but I'm fine, I really am. It's nothing.' Sensing that she was protesting too much, she fell silent.

Lloyd looked around the hall. 'So, you haven't taken up residence yet?'

'You know she hasn't, Lloyd,' Sali rebuked. She kissed Edyth's cheek. 'Mr Holsten said that you'd been attacked by some women last night who mistook you for someone else. He warned us that you'd been slightly hurt, although I must say after seeing you, it looks a great deal worse than that.'

'He said he recognized you in the police station, after the police had taken the women into custody. Who did they mistake you for?' Lloyd asked.

Edyth blessed Micah's tact. 'I have no idea. They didn't want to talk, only fight.'

'You poor darling.' Sali stroked Edyth's face.

'I know I look dreadful but I really am perfectly well. Mr Holsten and his sister put iodine on the cuts. That always makes them look worse.' Edyth knew she was being unfair, but her mother's concern irritated her more than her father's suspicions and direct questioning.

'Mr Holsten mentioned that you spent last night with him and his sister in the mission,' Sali continued.

'I did.' Edyth explained about the train being held up outside Bridgend but she stopped short of telling her parents that the women who attacked her were prostitutes, or that they'd torn her frock. And she also kept the theft of money from her purse to herself. She took her parents through the house and into the cheerless sitting room. As soon as the housekeeper saw them she left her chair and curtsied.

'Mrs Mack, these are my parents, Mr and Mrs Lloyd Evans. Mam, Dad, this is the Reverend Richards's housekeeper, Mrs Mack.'

'Pleased to meet you.' Sali extended her hand but Mrs Mack bobbed another curtsy. Lloyd however, gripped her hand and shook it firmly.

'Pleased to meet you, Mrs Mack.'

'Would you like some tea, madam, sir?'

'No, thank you,' Lloyd replied at the same time as Sali said, 'That would be nice, thank you, Mrs Mack.'

'I'll make some anyway. Like as not, the Reverend Richards will be able to manage a cup. He's fonder of his tea than he is of his Sunday dinner.' The housekeeper shuffled out of the room, still dabbing at her nose with her handkerchief.

'She's upset about the Reverend Richards,' Edyth explained superfluously. 'She was telling me before you came that she has been his housekeeper for over forty years and she's afraid that if anything happens to him she'll lose her home as well as her job.'

'That's the Church for you. Use people and then abandon them to the workhouse when they reach old age.' Lloyd went to the window and stared at the church wall.

'Micah Holsten told us that Peter came to fetch you from the Norwegian mission this morning.' Sali sat on the sofa.

'He telephoned Peter first thing.' Edyth was aware that her mother was only talking in the hope of ending her father's tirade against the Church by drawing him into conversation.

'Peter wasn't here when you arrived last night?'

'He was out visiting a sick parishioner. After I called here, I was involved in the scuffle Mr Holsten told you about . . .'

'Just who did those women think you were, Edyth?' Lloyd repeated. He turned and looked her in the eye.

'One of their acquaintances, I assume,' she answered evasively, but he wasn't to be put off so easily.

'They thought you were a prostitute?'

'I didn't have chance to talk to them. The police came along,

182

arrested them and took me to the police station as well, to make sure that I was all right, which as you can see, I am.'

'What time was this?'

'It was after midnight when Micah Holsten saw me in the police station and suggested that I spend the night with his sister.' Edyth omitted all mention of how she had arrived at the police station, hoping that was one piece of information her parents would never hear.

'It's just as well that Micah was there. I've never hit one of my children, but I don't mind telling you that I don't know whether to hug or spank you at this moment. What possessed you to walk around Bute Street so late at night?'

'I was supposed to arrive early in the evening. The train was delayed . . .' A lump rose in Edyth's throat and her voice tailed into silence.

'What's important is that you're safe and well now, Edie.' Sali jumped up and hugged her.

Lloyd turned from the window and looked at them both. 'Have you anything to say to us, young lady?'

'I'm very sorry, Dad. I should never have left Swansea the way I did.'

'It's you we're thinking of, darling.' Sali led Edyth to the sofa. 'Anything could have happened to you while you were wandering around the dock area alone at that time of night. It simply doesn't bear thinking about.'

Lloyd was more direct. 'Sailors leave ships with two things on their mind: getting drunk and having a good time. And when drunk, most men aren't responsible for their actions. Just be very grateful that you were attacked by women, not men.'

'I really am very sorry. I know I shouldn't have come down here so late. It would have been better if I'd caught the last train back to Pontypridd when I reached Cardiff station.'

'You had no right to leave Swansea in the first place,' Lloyd snapped.

'Hindsight's a wonderful thing,' Sali said soberly.

'Did you just leave the college, or did you tell them you were going?' Lloyd finally left the window and sat on one of the chairs.

Edyth loathed admitting that she'd lied to the bursar but, as she would have to contact the college to let them know she wasn't returning, she didn't doubt her father would find out what she'd done sooner or later. 'I said Harry needed me,' she admitted in a small voice.

'Why would your brother need you?' Lloyd delved in his pocket in search of his pipe.

'I said Mary was ill.'

'So you told lies as well.'

'What's done is done, Lloyd.' Sali kept a grip on Edyth's hand. 'We both agreed on the journey down here that there's no point in forcing Edyth to go to college when she doesn't want to be there.'

The doorbell rang; they heard Mrs Mack speak to someone. Footsteps echoed up and down the hall and stairs.

'That must be the ambulance.' Edyth rose to her feet.

'Reverend Richards won't want strange women fussing around him while he's being carried out of his home. You stay with your mother. I'll see if they need help.' Lloyd left the room.

'I've made the most awful mess of things, haven't I, Mam?' Edyth crossed her fingers under cover of her skirt in the hope that her mother would contradict her.

'I can't understand what you hoped to accomplish by coming here,' Sali answered frankly.

'I wanted you and Dad to take me seriously. Did he say anything to you about me?'

'As I just said, we agreed on the journey down here that there's no point in forcing you to go to college.'

'Nothing else?' Edyth pressed.

'No.'

'I see.'

'Nothing, that is, until we saw Mr Holsten, then your father said he was relieved that you were all right.'

'Mam—'

'I know you want to talk about Peter but I don't, Edyth,' Sali said firmly. 'Not until your father returns.'

They sat in silence for ten minutes, then the front door slammed and an engine started up outside. The door opened and Lloyd walked in followed by Peter. It was obvious the atmosphere between them was cool. Peter immediately walked up to Sali and offered her his hand.

'Mrs Evans, I'm sorry, you've caught me at a bad time.'

'I rather think that Edyth chose the time not you, Reverend Slater.' Sali took his hand and shook it.

'I didn't realize that you were here until Mr Evans came to see if he could help carry Reverend Richards downstairs.'

'You didn't think we'd come to fetch our daughter home, Slater?' Lloyd enquired acidly.

'I knew you would come, sir. But I wasn't expecting you to arrive so soon.' Peter hovered awkwardly in front of the fireplace. 'Please, do sit down. I'll call Mrs Mack. Would you like tea or coffee?'

'Mrs Mack did say she was going to make tea but with all this upset she's probably forgotten,' Edyth said quietly.

'I'll remind her.'

'Please, don't bother, Slater, we'll be leaving in a few minutes,' Lloyd said curtly.

'How is Reverend Richards, Peter?' Sali enquired.

'Very ill,' Peter murmured.

'Which, from what you told us, doesn't suit you or the Bishop at all,' Lloyd observed. 'You were hoping to be a curate here for six months, weren't you?'

'That was the Bishop's original plan, yes, sir,' Peter conceded.

'So the Bishop will appoint someone else vicar here?' Lloyd persisted.

'That is for the Bishop to decide, sir, not me,' Peter answered uneasily.

'I know what you're thinking, Dad,' Edyth interrupted. 'And you couldn't be more wrong. Peter didn't know that I intended to leave college or that I was coming here yesterday.'

'Is that the truth?' Lloyd eyed Peter sternly.

'Yes, sir. If I had known what Edyth intended to do, I would have done everything in my power to dissuade her from behaving so recklessly.'

There was such sincerity in Peter's voice, Lloyd believed him. 'Then this whole harebrained scheme was all your doing, Edyth?'

'I tried to tell you that I didn't want to go to college,' Edyth protested defensively. 'You wouldn't listen to me. I can see now that I behaved like an idiot charging up here from Swansea yesterday, but all I could think of after you left was reaching Peter. I knew Reverend Richards was ill and Peter had no chance of being appointed vicar here if he wasn't married—'

'And you thought if you came here and spent the night with him I'd have no choice but to allow you to get married?'

'No,' Edyth gasped, smarting at the inference that she would stoop to using such a blackmailing ploy.

'Then what?'

'I didn't think any further than getting here and talking to Peter. And that is the truth. No matter how many times Peter and I asked for permission to marry, you refused. You wouldn't even talk to us about it,' she reproached. 'All the time I was growing up, you used to say to me and the others that no matter what our problems were, you'd always try to help. But my problem was that you refused to discuss my future or what I wanted to do with my life with me. I know what I did was wrong, but when you stopped listening to me I simply didn't know what else to do.'

Lloyd sat back, crossed his arms and looked from Peter to Edyth. 'Well, one thing is certain: Your mother and I have lost control over you. This is not the way that I hoped to see any daughter of mine married, and certainly not under the age of twenty-one. But given the circumstances I feel that you – both of you – have left me no choice but to consent to your marriage. I can see that if I don't, I may well lose you permanently.'

'Do you mean that, Dad? You will give us your consent?' Edyth asked eagerly.

'If Peter and this parish are more important to you than your education, your independence, and your parents' advice and wishes, Edyth, you'd better have them. I only hope that you won't live to regret your choice. If you do, it might console you to know that the money I will save on your education should just about fund a divorce,' he added caustically.

'Sir . . .' Peter saw the look of abject misery on Edyth's face and the protest he'd been about to make, died in his throat. Silence fell over the room. Edyth reflected that she had won the battle, but at the cost of losing her father's respect. It was a price she was loath to pay.

'If you are serious about allowing me to marry Edyth, sir, I have no doubt that the Bishop will give me this parish. And that means I will be able to support your daughter,' Peter ventured courageously.

'How soon do you want the wedding?'

Edyth felt now that her father had finally given his consent he couldn't wait to be rid of her.

'As soon as possible, sir.' Peter smiled at Edyth but she was too devastated to react.

'It took us over a year to arrange Bella's wedding,' Sali said thoughtfully.

'Edyth and I wouldn't want anything as elaborate as your eldest daughter's wedding, Mrs Evans,' Peter said swiftly.

'You're speaking for Edyth already, Slater.' Lloyd pushed his pipe into his mouth but he didn't attempt to light it.

'We just want to be married so Peter can have the parish, Dad,' Edyth said quietly.

'The church service will be the most important part of the proceedings and I hope the Bishop will consent to officiate. But the guest list will be small. My only relatives are my mother and my aunt, although I would like to invite the wives of the Bishop, Dean and Reverend Price,' Peter added.

'As you are aware, our family is large and Edyth couldn't possibly get married without all her brothers and sisters present. And then there are my brothers, their wives and children, and all our friends, who will expect to be invited just as they were to Bella and Toby's wedding. If we do any less for Edyth than we did for Bella, people will assume that we disapprove of her choice of husband,' Lloyd said shortly, leaving 'with some justification' hanging unspoken in the air.

'Yes, sir.' Peter knew he'd been rebuked and looked suitably humbled. Edyth could have hugged him for not arguing.

'We'll ask some of our friends to move over to your side of the church so it doesn't look too lop-sided, as we did in Bella and Toby's wedding.' Sali began to concentrate on the practical aspects of the arrangements because they were easier to cope with than the emotional damage to Lloyd and, she suspected, Edyth. 'First we need to set a date. Do you want the ceremony to take place in St Catherine's?'

'As it's Edyth's local church it would be the most suitable,' Peter concurred. 'The banns will have to be called and they take three weeks. We could set a date for a month from now.'

'That won't give us much time to order clothes and a cake. And that will take us into October.' Sali frowned. 'It will be cold in a marquee and the house isn't large enough for everyone.'

'We'll hold the wedding breakfast in the New Inn, or, if it is booked, the Park Hotel,' Lloyd said.

'Won't that be very expensive, sir?' Peter ventured.

'That is my concern as the father of the bride.'

'As Lloyd said, we can't do any less for you and Edyth than we did for Bella and Toby.' Sali attempted to soften Lloyd's harshness.

'Just one thing, sir. I would prefer not to have a jazz band, if you don't mind.'

Edyth was mortified. She felt that in that one request Peter had emphasized the divide between himself and her family. And when she heard her father's reply, she wished the ground would swallow her up.

'Which would you prefer, Slater: a church organ recital, or a hymn-singing choir?'

# Chapter 12

JUDY HAMILTON sat in the centre of the upstairs sitting room of the Norwegian church, surrounded by most of the residents of the Bay. Practically everyone she knew was there – her uncles, aunts, cousins, friends and neighbours – yet she had never felt more alone.

People were talking about her grandmother as if she had been dead for years not days. Then she realized from the shouts of laughter from her grandmother's elderly friends as they exchanged amusing anecdotes about the young, newly married Pearl King and her dashing West Indian husband, the past was the land of preference for old people.

Her young cousins sat rapt, listening in silence, wary of making a noise lest someone notice them and shoo them out of earshot of the 'grown-up' conversation. Her Uncle Tony began to weave a story that described how twelve-year-old Pearl Plummer had left her parents and nine brothers in the house of her birth in the mining village of Bedwas, because ten miners in one house – whom she had to help her mother wash, cook, clean and get baths for – were nine too many. He painted the many and varied adventures that had led her down to Tiger Bay, in terms that would have done credit to the brothers Grimm.

' . . . You've seen the house in Loudon Square where she worked. Seen it, but not gone inside or counted all the marble fireplaces that she had to clean out every morning, scrub, polish and lay and light fires in. She had to make twelve trips out to the bins behind the basement kitchen just to dump the ash.

'The mistress was very particular, the cook and housekeeper even more so. They wouldn't tolerate a speck of coal on the carpets or a hint of dust. But every other Wednesday,' he dropped his voice to a whisper, 'young Pearl had two whole hours off. From seven until nine in the evening. And being Pearl, and always looking to help others, she used to go down to the John Cory Sailors and Soldiers Rest Home where she served tea and coffee and handed out library books. And there, one freezing cold winter's night, a handsome young West Indian seaman called Jeremiah King walked in, took one look at her . . . ' Tony raised his eyebrows, 'and knowing a good thing when he saw it, carried her off and married her in less than a week because he'd already signed up for another voyage to the Caribbean. And he wasn't prepared to run the risk of a rival stepping in and taking the love of his life. On their wedding day she wore a dress of pure French lace embroidered with real pearls . . . '

'One day those little ones will be telling that story to their grandchildren, to explain the colour of their skin.' Micah Holsten perched on the arm of Judy's chair.

'Uncle Tony makes me wish I'd never said, "Oh no, Gran, please not that old tale again."'

'We're all guilty of not listening enough to our parents. We never appreciate them until they've gone.' Micah spoke from the heart – and bitter experience. He handed her a plate containing two sandwiches and a slice of homemade sponge.

'Thank you, I'm not hungry,' she said politely.

'You have to eat.'

'I will. Just not bloater paste sandwiches and quince jam sponge.' She gave him a small smile. After days of grief and misery her face muscles felt stiff and strange.

'Don't let Mrs George catch you saying that, she made them,' he warned. 'In fact, just about everyone in the Bay brought one or two plates around this morning for the funeral tea. I only hope they recognize their crockery when this finishes. Our cupboards will never hold the extra.'

'I had no idea Gran knew so many people.'

'She knew everyone, rich, poor, respectable and less so.' He nodded to Anna Hughes, who was setting out a tray of shop-bought pasties on the buffet table. 'There can't be a soul left in a house or on the streets in the whole of the Bay. And I've never seen so many flowers covering a coffin, which says a great deal about the love and respect everyone had for your grandmother.' He looked keenly at her. 'I wish I could say something to comfort you.'

'Thank you for trying, Mr Holsten. But at the moment I just feel numb. Then occasionally it hits me that she's gone and I'll never see her again, and I start crying.'

'I remember how I felt when my father and mother died within two weeks of one another of diphtheria. I believed my world had come to an end. It took me a long time to develop an interest in life again.'

'You were lucky to know your parents.'

'I was, and you were lucky to have your gran.' Micah deliberately changed the subject. 'Jed tells me that you're moving in with him and his family.'

'Gran's cleaning jobs in the pubs paid the rent and my money bought us food. I'll never manage to keep the house going on my own, and the landlord knows it. He already had someone interested in taking it, and at a higher rent than we were paying. It's good of Uncle Jed to take me in.'

'He loves you like a daughter.'

'He has a houseful of children of his own,' she said pointedly.

Micah allowed the comment to pass. Judy and her grandmother had enjoyed the luxury of space, which was a rare commodity on the Bay. Jed and his wife had six children – four girls and two boys – and another on the way. It was anyone's guess where Judy would sleep in their small three-bedroomed terrace.

'I know that my uncles and their families are grieving as much as I am,' Judy murmured, 'although they didn't live with her. They were only a few doors away but it's not the same as living in a house with someone. I'm not just losing the only parent I've ever known, Mr Holsten, but my home. I'm not ungrateful, and it's not that I don't love Uncle Jed and his family, but it won't be like living with Gran. The evenings we spent together were so special. She was always rushing around working in the day but after tea in winter we'd sit in front of the range and in summer we'd carry our chairs out into the street.'

'I often saw the two of you. And your hands were never still.'

'Gran was always making something: stitching quilts or knitting pullovers for the boys, or making dresses for the girls. Sometimes we'd talk, sometimes it was good just to sit together and not say a word.'

'You all right, Judy?' Jed stood behind them and leaned over Judy's chair.

'Yes, thank you, Uncle Jed.'

'If you pack your things this afternoon, I'll carry them round to our house. The rent's paid until the end of the week but it's probably going to take us that long to clear and clean the house. You do know that Mam left you all her jewellery and china?'

'It should be shared.'

'Your mother was Mam's only daughter so it's fitting it goes to you, Judy,' he said decisively. 'I want to thank you and Helga, Micah, for laying on this spread.'

'I was just telling Judy, we didn't. All we did was put up the tables; they filled themselves.'

'It'll still be a lot of work to clear up after this lot.' Jed looked at the children running around with slices of cake in their hands, oblivious to the crumbs they were scattering in their wake.

'Mr King . . . Mr King . . . ' Patterson's butcher's boy ran up the stairs and looked around frantically for Jed. He was red-faced, and puffing and panting so much he couldn't get another word out.

'Come on, boy, what is it?' Tony was annoyed at the interruption that had diverted the attention of his audience from the tale of the thieving African monkey his father had brought home from one of his voyages.

'Mr Patterson said I was to get you and that you were to come at once. He was delivering meat to your street when he saw it outside Mrs King's house. Mrs King that was . . . ' He gave Jed's wife a sideways glance.

'Saw what?' Tony demanded.

'A lorry. They'd loaded up all her all furniture and everything . . .'

192

Jed, Tony and Ron didn't wait to hear any more. They dashed out through the door, their boots clattering a staccato drumbeat on the wooden staircase. Judy charged after them. Micah caught up with her, took her hand and ran after the brothers.

'I tried arguing with them.' Brian Patterson pushed his cap to the back of his head and faced the three King brothers. 'But they had a legal bill of sale, signed by your brother-in-law, Joshua Hamilton. I told them straight that the house contents weren't his to sell. Even sent the boy to get the police. But they'd finished stripping the house before I arrived and they drove off before the boy even reached the end of the street. Not that it would have made any difference. Constable Jones came round on patrol five minutes after they'd left, and he said it would be a matter for the courts.'

'You seen the lorry driver before, Brian?' Jed asked.

'Never set eyes on him. Nasty piece of work, gave the impression that he was looking for trouble and didn't care where he found it. He said his boss had paid for the goods, fair and square. He'd been ordered to pick them up, and pick them up he would. I would have tried to keep him here until you came, but he had five other men with him. Great big hulking brutes they were, too. Looked like bailiffs. And they'd just about cleared the place by the time I got here.'

'Did he say anything else that you can recall?' Jed pressed.

'The driver said the man who'd sold the contents to his boss was most particular about the time they had to be picked up. Today between ten and eleven in the morning. Any other time and the deal was off.'

'When we were in the cemetery burying Mam.' Jed clenched his fists impotently.

'The bastard,' Tony swore, forgetting his niece's presence. 'We told him to stay away but it wouldn't have taken much asking around for him to find out the time of the funeral.'

'When I find Joshua Hamilton, I'll kill him.' Ron, the quietest of the brothers, was vehement.

'The milkman said he sailed out on the *Sukhov* last night, bound for Russia.'

Judy walked past her uncles and went into the house. The parlour had been stripped of everything except the linoleum on the floor and the wallpaper. She turned away, not wanting to see the lighter squares where her grandmother's precious family photographs had hung, protecting the walls from the smoke of the occasional rare fire that had been lit in the room.

The bed her grandmother had bought as a bride, in which she had given birth to all her children, and died, her furniture, linen, even her clothes had gone. Nothing remained. Judy ran upstairs. The doors to all three bedrooms were open. The only object left in her room was a single hairclip lying on the bare floorboards.

Micah Holsten followed her. When he saw her shoulders shaking he held out his arms. She went to him, buried her head in his chest and started crying. Not the resigned, silent tears she had shed over her grandmother's death but sobs that shook her entire body. 'I have nothing left. Nothing! Just this black dress. There was six shillings in the box on the mantelpiece: it's gone. Everything's gone. Our dishes . . . the family photographs . . . her clothes . . . all the ornaments . . . the family Bible . . . her jewellery . . . all gone . . . '

Micah knew it wasn't the few shillings or even her grandmother's things that Judy was crying for, but the way of life that had suddenly been taken from her. And she didn't even have a single keepsake left to remember it by.

Jed came up the stairs, Tony and Ron behind him.

'Two quid. Two bloody quid!' Tony's voice was hoarse from shock. 'He sold Mam's entire life for two quid.'

'We could try to buy it back,' Ron suggested.

'With what?' Tony asked.

'We could borrow the money if we have to,' Jed said. 'But Brian Patterson said the driver and all the men were outsiders. They could have come from anywhere – Swansea, Newport, Bridgend. Our mam's things could be lying in a warehouse or on a market stall right now. We'll never find them.'

'I'll go to the police and find out if there's anything we can do,' Ron muttered.

'Tony, go with him,' Jed ordered. He looked in what had been Judy's bedroom and Micah pushed his niece gently towards him.

'I'll ask round the Bay. Perhaps one of the other delivery boys saw something,' Micah said.

'It'll probably be a waste of time,' Jed said flatly.

'Judy needs clothes and things. I'll ask my sister to see what she can do.' Micah clasped Jed's shoulder and walked back down the stairs.

The month of September and early October passed in a surreal whirl of preparations for Edyth. Her arm turned blue from the number of times she pinched herself to prove she wasn't dreaming. Most days she felt as though she were in a theatre watching a play unfold on stage rather than one of the principal participants in an actual event.

Almost by default the decision had been made. She was to marry Peter. It was what she wanted – wasn't it? It was the reason she had run away from college. But she tried not to think too hard about the life beyond the wedding ceremony that had been suddenly mapped out for her, especially at night when she couldn't sleep. Instead she concentrated on her love for Peter, his for her, and the practical decisions that had to be made. Like what flowers she should have in her bouquet and the menu for the wedding breakfast.

Her parents ignored her repeated assertions that she would be happy to marry Peter in sackcloth, and continued to insist that they couldn't do any less for her than they had for Bella. So, her mother and younger sisters threw themselves into planning the day, but Edyth knew, as did her father, that her mother was simply keeping busy to conceal her misgivings about the way she'd forced them to give their consent to her marriage.

Her father was uncharacteristically silent and taciturn, especially in her presence, but although their relationship had been irrevocably damaged by her flight from college, he signed the bills her mother left on his desk without a murmur about extravagance or expense.

Edyth only wished that she could have enjoyed the excitement of preparing for her wedding as Bella had done less than two months before, but the knowledge that her parents, and especially her beloved father, disapproved of her choice of husband blighted any happiness she might have felt. Not that either of them gave her any cause for reproach. Her father attended the discussions over menu and decorations at the New Inn Hotel, her mother oversaw her dress fittings at Gwilym James and helped her pick out her sisters' bridesmaids' dresses, but both of them constantly deferred to her, reminding her that it was 'her and Peter's day' not the family's, a phrase she couldn't remember ever hearing when Bella's wedding had been at the planning stage.

In addition to paying for the wedding, they bought her and Peter a bedroom suite but left the selection to her and, when Sali abdicated all choice of music and hymns in favour of Peter's preferences, Edyth took it as an indication that her parents couldn't care less about the ceremony.

She only saw Peter once during the month, when he visited Pontypridd to discuss the arrangements for the church service over lunch with the Reverend Price and the Bishop, thankfully for their stomachs, at the Bishop's invitation in the Park Hotel. The Bishop asked her parents to join them but they refused, citing a long-standing engagement with the committee of the miners' welfare fund. And if, as Edyth suspected, it was a tactical engagement, neither Peter, Reverend Price nor the Bishop questioned their absence.

Apart from that one brief day with Peter, when they met in the jeweller's in Market Square so she could select her wedding and engagement rings from a tray he had arranged for the assistant to show her, most of her waking hours were spent in Gwilym James department store in Pontypridd.

Even after she had chosen her wedding dress, there were endless fittings and accessories to be chosen, both for herself and the bridesmaids. And for her new home, cutlery and china patterns, bed and table linen, and kitchen utensils to be picked out and decided on. But Peter insisted that they defer the actual buying until after they had received their wedding presents.

Peter was so busy with parish affairs that he couldn't spare another day to visit her in Pontypridd, but he did manage to steal enough time to make occasional visits to Gwilym James's sister store in Cardiff to view her choices. To her surprise, unlike Harry and her father, who left all domestic decisions to Mary and her mother, she discovered that Peter had very definite ideas on tableware, ornaments, linen and even bridal accessories and her trousseau.

He sent her daily epistles, relating details of the new church societies he was setting up, improvements he had made to the old ones, happenings at the weekly meetings of the parish council and descriptions of the friends he was making – friends, he reminded her, that would soon be hers. And, at the end of every letter, he outlined the improvements the builders and decorators, employed by the Church at the behest of the Bishop, were making to the vicarage in Cardiff Docks.

His letters were more practical and informative than the romantic love letters she had dreamed of receiving when she was growing up, but what they lacked in passion they made up for in plans for their future together.

Affected by the strain of trying to pretend that her relationship with her parents was as close as it had ever been, she retreated to her room as often as she could during her last month at home. She packed boxes of personal possessions to be sent on to the vicarage by carrier to await her arrival after her honeymoon. And she looked for clues in Peter's letters that would help her to visualize the new life that awaited her in Cardiff docks.

. . . *In addition to redecorating every room in the vicarage, the Bishop has ordered the builders to modernize the bathroom and the kitchen. To Mrs Mack's delight they have already installed a new kitchen sink, stove and bathroom suite. I don't think you saw either room on your short visit here. They certainly needed updating. The enamel on the sinks and the bath was crazed with black lines that Mrs Mack insisted no amount of scouring with* Vim *would remove. We will also have constant hot water available from the very latest design in gas boilers.*

*You have probably received a letter from my mother, if not, she intends to write to you very soon to tell you how delighted she is with our news. She has offered us her furniture, which was placed in storage after my father's death. Most of it is antique Regency which my father inherited from his grandmother. She realizes that it may not be to your taste, and she won't be in the least offended if you decide to refuse it. However, as the Reverend Richards has given his furniture to his brother who runs a boarding house in Porthcawl, I won't need to remind you that we are in need of all the help we can get in setting up home.*

*I confess, Edyth, I rather like the idea of being surrounded by the trappings of my childhood. As Mother pointed out, the pieces are only deteriorating in storage and if you really don't like them we can discard them as soon as we can afford to replace them with new, although I warn you that is not likely to be very soon.*

*I am sorry I was so angry when you came to see me on the spur of the moment in Cardiff. I understand now that you only had my interests at heart and I regret that I wasn't more sympathetic on hearing about your ordeal. Just as Micah Holsten said it would, the fracas has been forgotten and I doubt that anyone will connect you with the girl who was attacked outside the church in the early hours of the morning.*

She didn't believe for one minute that Anna and the other women who had kicked and thumped her would forget it – and nor would the police.

*After checking with the Bishop I have decided to ask Micah Holsten to be our best man, although he is a Lutheran. It seems fitting as he rescued you that night. I trust you will approve. As the saying goes, things have worked out for the best. God truly does move in mysterious ways. I only hope that I will be deserving of your unselfish love.*

*All my love, now and always,*
    *your Peter*

Edyth set down the letter. Carried away by the excitement of setting up her own home with Peter, she had been happy to go along with all his suggestions. She had already furnished the vicarage in her mind's eye with tasteful Regency pieces, even going so far as to seek out complementary fabrics for curtains and cushions in Gwilym James and earmarking them for future purchase.

The telephone rang in the hall but, unable to decide between an imaginary green and gold Turkish rug and a red and dark blue Bokhara for the sitting room, the sound barely registered until Maggie shouted up the stairs, 'Edyth, it's for you.'

She walked out on to the landing. Maggie was standing at the bottom of the stairs with her lips puckered. She made a theatrical sucking noise. 'It's Lo-ve-er Boy.'

'Why so childish, Mags?' Edyth ran down the stairs and snatched the receiver from her sister.

'Ooh, we mustn't tease the vicar or his fiancée, must we, Edyth?' Maggie chanted in a sing-song voice.

Edyth covered the receiver with her hand. 'When are you going to grow up?'

'When I go to college, which is more than you'll ever do, Miss Forget the Promise You Made to our Father,' Maggie goaded.

Edyth took a deep breath in an effort to contain her temper. 'Privacy, please,' she snapped, an expression Bella had used when she had been courting Toby. Turning her face to the wall so she wouldn't have to look at Maggie, she spoke into the telephone. 'Hello, Peter.'

'Hello, Edyth. That, I take it, was Maggie.'

A lump rose in Edyth's throat. Peter sounded so close she felt that he could almost have been in the next room. 'You're right, it was.' She glanced in the mirror. Her sister was hovering in the hall, rearranging the dahlias their mother had cut that morning. She placed her hand over the receiver again and hissed, 'Clear off.'

'Pardon me for living.' Maggie flounced into the sitting room, only to turn at the last moment and seize the receiver from her sister. 'We're all *so* looking forward to the wedding tomorrow, Peter. I can't wait to have another brother. And Edyth's positively *dying* for the honeymoon . . .'

Edyth grabbed Maggie's arm and twisted it until she dropped the receiver, then pushed her through the sitting-room door. Maggie slammed it behind her. She heard Maggie's voice loud in complaint and her mother's softer tones.

'Sorry about that, Peter,' she apologized. 'How are you?' She lowered her voice when she heard a door open upstairs.

'You'll be pleased to hear that I've finally settled in the locum curate so I can look forward to tomorrow with a clear conscience. You?'

'Missing you.' Just hearing his voice had given rise to an overwhelming wave of longing. 'For two pins I would grab my hat and coat and run down to the vicarage . . . you are with Reverend and Mrs Price?'

'Not yet. I've been held up on church business. But please don't run down to the Bay, not after what happened last time.'

'I didn't intend for things to turn out that way.'

'Edyth, that was a joke,' he broke in swiftly.

The slight misunderstanding made her realize just how little time they had spent together. In some ways she felt as though she had known Peter all her life; in others – especially his church ways – she didn't know him well enough to sense when he was being serious or not. Her knees trembled. She lifted the telephone from the table, sank down on the stairs and cradled it in her lap. In less than twenty-four hours they would be married. *Married*. She continued to shake at the enormity of the step she was taking while Peter talked.

' . . . I'm sorry. After what happened, that was in bad taste. I wish it had been possible for us to have spent more time together this last month. I would give a great deal to be with you right now, but it would have been impossible for me to take even a week off for our honeymoon if I hadn't concentrated on the parish. With Reverend Richards in hospital it's been a nightmare to sort out the most basic things and then there's all the work on the vicarage. The builders needed constant supervision—'

'How is the Reverend Richards?' Edyth interrupted, feeling the need to say something before Peter noticed her silence.

She was nervous – that was all. Didn't every bride feel nervous? Even Bella had complained about leaving her reception early and, unlike her and Peter, she and Toby had already made love.

There were so many things to think about, so many adjustments to be made . . .

'The doctor told me that if Reverend Richards continues to improve, they will move him to the convalescent home at the end of next month.'

'That is good news.' Edyth tried to concentrate on what Peter was saying, but she found it difficult to sound enthusiastic about the recovery of a man she had never met. Particularly in view of the fact that if he hadn't suffered from ill-health, Peter would never have been given his own parish.

'I'd like you to meet him, Edyth. Perhaps we could visit him after he has moved out of the hospital. He and his wife never had children and he has no close family left, only a distant cousin in England and another in Australia, and they hardly ever write. The parish was everything to him and he put every ounce of energy he possessed into it for over forty years.'

'We'll call on him as soon as he is settled in the convalescent home.' She found it hard to understand why she was still shaking when she had fought so hard for her parents' permission to marry Peter.

'Ask me about the vicarage.'

They were perfect for one another. Hadn't Peter said so? And he loved her. Why couldn't she quell her feeling of unease?

'Didn't you hear me, Edyth? I said, ask me about the vicarage.'

'Is it ready for our return?'

'That would be telling,' he teased.

She turned around when she sensed someone behind her. But it was only Mari carrying a tray into her father's study. 'Did the furniture arrive?'

'It did.'

'And you've arranged it?'

'Not so it can't be moved.'

'I'm longing to see it.' She tried to envisage the gloomy sitting room, gloomy no longer but bright and cheerful with new wallpaper and light-coloured paint. But as Peter had refused to disclose the colour schemes the Bishop had allowed him to pick out, she found it impossible.

'Then I'll cancel the honeymoon, shall I?'

'Now I know you're joking.' She lowered her voice, when she heard Mari and her father talking.

'I can't wait to see your travelling outfit. Did you find that pleated purple coat and bronze-green dress in Gwilym James in Pontypridd?'

'You expect me to tell you that when you won't even give me a hint about the changes that have been made to the vicarage and the colour schemes I'll be expected to live with for years?' She heard the doorbell ring on the other end of the line and Mrs Mack's strong Scottish accent.

'I'm sorry, Edyth. That is the secretary of the church council. I've called a meeting. I know I'll only be away for a week but there are a few things to put in place. Don't worry; I'll be on the eight o'clock train out of Cardiff tonight and at the church bright and early in the morning.'

'You just wanted someone other than Mrs Price to cook your dinner,' she suggested mischievously.

'I've already eaten. Micah Holsten and his sister invited me to share beetroot soup, roast duck and peach preserve with them. Be grateful, the Reverend Price wanted to invite both of us to dinner this evening, but I told him that you'd be busy with your family.'

'Mam and Dad have invited all the cousins and aunts as they did before Bella's wedding, to help with the flowers and the last-minute things.'

'I have written to you today. Hopefully it will be the last letter I will have to send to you. It will certainly be the last time I will write "Miss Edyth Evans".'

'Thank you, that was a lovely thought. I'll treasure it.'

'You don't know what's in it yet. Sorry, the secretary of the church council is waiting; I am going to have to go. Until tomorrow.'

'Edyth, I'm waiting for a telephone call.' Maggie stuck her head around the sitting-room door.

'You can wait.' Edyth turned her back and plugged her free ear with her thumb but she could still see Maggie in the hall mirror. Her sister made no attempt to move and, unaware that her reflection could be seen in the mirror, stuck her fingers in her ears and wiggled them at Edyth.

'You watch the wind doesn't blow and fix you like that permanently, Miss Maggie,' Mari warned, catching sight of her when she left Lloyd's study.

Maggie retreated back into the sitting room. She clutched the door until the last moment and Edyth braced herself for a slam, but her sister knew better with Mari watching. She closed it quietly. Mari shook her head and carried on down the passage to the kitchen.

'It sounds like your house is busy.'

'It is. And we're expecting Harry to arrive any minute, and Bella and Toby are coming in on the five o'clock train.' After a quick glance up and down the passageway to make sure it was empty, she whispered, 'Love you.'

He muttered, 'Likewise,' and she suspected that his visitor was close by. 'See you in church.'

Edyth replaced the receiver and opened the sitting-room door. Maggie was sitting on the sofa, a picture of innocence, reading an article entitled 'To Marry or Not to Marry' in a copy of *Good Housekeeping*.

'The telephone's free for your important call, Maggie.' Edyth knelt on the window seat in the bay and looked out of the window.

'I didn't know that you were waiting for an important telephone call, Maggie,' Sali said from her chair next to the fireplace where she was stitching together the pressed pieces of the baby's layette she had finished knitting.

'One of the girls in school said she was going to telephone me about homework,' Maggie replied.

'When are you going to stop annoying Edyth?' Sali asked evenly.

'I don't annoy her,' Maggie snapped.

'You never stop,' Edyth bit back, angry because she couldn't stop shaking at the thought of what was going to happen in less than twenty-four hours.

'Do you know what your trouble is, Miss Goody Two Shoes? Or should it be Mrs Vicar Goody Two Shoes? You're oversensitive,' Maggie crowed.

'I do wish you two would stop squabbling.' For once Sali allowed her own irritation to show.

'Considering we'll be living in different houses, we will after tomorrow,' Edyth said quietly. She left the room. Before she closed the door she heard her mother say to Maggie, 'Now look what you've done.'

But she knew that her arguments with her sister were only a symptom of the blight that had hung over the house since her parents had brought her back from Cardiff after her flight from college. No one in the family liked Peter, and try as she may, not even her love for him, his for her, and the thought of the new life they would make for themselves down in Tiger Bay could entirely make her forget their disapproval.

# Chapter 13

'CAN YOU BELIEVE IT, our taxi turned in the drive at the exact same moment as Harry's car . . .'

The sound of Bella's voice in the hall brought Edyth running down the stairs, Sali, Maggie, Beth and Susie out of the sitting room, and Lloyd from his study.

'Belle, I couldn't believe it when you wrote that you and Toby would come back in time for my wedding.' Edyth flung her arms around her sister's neck.

'You didn't think Toby and I would have stayed in America and missed it, do you? Besides, we only had to cut our visit short by a week and by then even Toby was sick of New York. The sights are wonderful and the museums and art galleries heavenly, but it's so big and noisy. We hardly slept a wink.'

'Really, sis?' Harry lifted one eyebrow suggestively after dropping two suitcases at the foot of the staircase.

'Because of the traffic.' Bella's cheeks flamed crimson, but Toby laughed.

'Don't you dare lift a single thing out of that car except yourself, Mary Evans,' Harry shouted to his wife over his shoulder. 'Davy, help your sister in here this minute. I warned you, that you could only go to Edyth's wedding if you promised to behave yourself and not lift a finger more than necessary.'

'I'm having a baby, not knocking on death's door, Harry.' Mary hugged Sali, Edyth and Bella in turn.

'You're huge, Mary. The baby looks as though it's about to arrive any minute,' Bella said tactlessly.

'Mary, sit down before I have a heart attack,' Harry ordered, stepping out of the way when his two young brothers-in-law galloped through the hall to the kitchen in search of Mari, or what was more likely, orange juice and biscuits.

'Come into the sitting room and sit down out of this crush.' Sali slipped her arm around Mary's shoulders and led her out of the hall. 'You must be parched after that long journey. I'll get us some tea.'

'I'll go next door with the taxi driver and drop off our luggage, Mrs Ross.' Toby kissed Bella's cheek.

'Don't forget to leave Edyth's wedding present here.' Bella hugged Edyth again. 'I can't wait to see your gown.'

'Edyth, where are you displaying your presents?' Harry asked when David walked in from the car carrying a large and by the look of strain on his face, heavy box.

'They're in the conservatory.'

'Congratulations, Edyth.' David said flatly. 'The vicar's a lucky fellow.'

'Thank you, Davy.' He looked so devastated Edyth was glad to follow Bella up the stairs and into her bedroom. Negotiating the packing cases that littered the floor, she closed the door and pointed to the gown hooked on to the outside of her wardrobe.

Bella unbuttoned the calico cover. 'Oh my, it's velvet.'

'Just as well the weather's gone cold. It was horribly expensive, but Mam said it cost about the same as yours, and she kept insisting she couldn't treat any of us differently to the others.'

'You're wearing Grandmother's veil and tiara.' Bella picked them up from the dressing table.

'Do you mind?'

'Not at all. I think it's lovely. I hope all the others wear them, too. It's the something old and the something borrowed, as well as a bit of Granddad and Grandma carrying on down the family. A new family tradition that started with us.'

'With you,' Edyth corrected. 'You were the one who found them when we cleared Granddad's house.'

'Just think, around twenty years from now our daughters could be wearing them on their wedding day. And in between there's Uncle Joey and Auntie Rhian's girls as well as the rest of our lot.' Bella replaced them on the table. She sat on Edyth's bed, wrapped her arms around her legs and rested her chin on her knees. 'When I read your letter telling us that you were getting married – and to a vicar – I checked my diary to make sure it wasn't April Fool's Day. When we left, you were set on going to college.'

'The Bishop told Peter he would only be given the parish on Cardiff docks if he was married,' Edyth interrupted. Not wanting to discuss the events that had led to so much upset and argument, she picked up the tiara and polished it absently with her handkerchief.

'But you do love Peter?' Bella asked.

'Very much,' Edyth said seriously. 'And I'm certain that he loves me.'

'That's all right, then,' Bella returned her smile. 'And,' she added archly, 'you can't keep your hands off one another?'

'Peter's a vicar—'

'Don't tell me he prays first?' Bella joked.

'I've only seen him once in the last month. He's been so busy in the parish. The last vicar has been ill . . .'

The sound of footsteps thundering up the stairs interrupted them. 'Belle, where are you?' Toby shouted.

'In Edyth's room and she's dressed, so it's safe to come in,' Bella called back.

'Which door is it? There's a whole pile of them out here.'

'Making me move just when I was comfortable,' Bella grumbled, but she left the bed. Toby was standing in the middle of the landing.

'There are two parcels with Edyth and Peter's name on them. Are they both supposed to go with the wedding presents?'

'That's men for you,' Bella sighed dramatically. 'They can't do a thing without you giving them precise and exact instructions. Be warned, you'll have to run around after Peter from morning till night.'

'That's charming, Belle; you make us sound like untrained dogs.'

'Aren't you?' Bella asked innocently. 'Of course both parcels are for Edyth and Peter, darling. If they weren't, I wouldn't have written their names on them.'

'I'll put them in the conservatory. David's helping Mari to carry in more trestle tables. Looking at the size of the pile waiting to be unwrapped I do hope that Peter has been given a large vicarage, Edyth. Must go, the taxi driver's waiting.' He ran off whistling 'Ten cents a dance.'

'I hate that song and everyone in America seemed to be singing it all the time, not just on the radio but even the doorman at the hotel and the elevator boy. Listen to me – I even sound like an American. Oh, it is good to be back in Ponty!' she exclaimed fervently. 'I've missed all of you and I can't wait to move into the new house and get it exactly as I want it. Toby's looking forward to working in his studio, too. It will be the first he's designed from scratch.' Bella went to the window and looked down on her husband who was climbing into the taxi. 'Is it big?'

'What?' Edyth was engrossed in buttoning the calico cover back on to her dress.

'Your vicarage? Is it big?'

'I've only seen it once but it seemed huge. It's been redecorated and builders have installed new kitchen and bathroom fittings. As soon as we're settled, you and Toby must come and stay.'

'I read between the lines of your letters, Edie. I know that you must have had a difficult time persuading Mam and Dad to let you give up college to get married. I didn't make it easy for you. They were horribly disappointed when I insisted on marrying Toby instead of completing my education.'

'Worst of all was knowing how much I was upsetting Dad,' Edyth confessed.

'But you love Peter and loving someone is everything. Dad only wants the best for us, but sometimes I think he's forgotten what it's like to be young and in love.' Bella turned to the door. 'Come downstairs and see what we bought you in New York. I hope you like them.'

'Them?' Edyth asked warily.

'Toby and I had such fun choosing them.'

'China figurines?'

Bella laughed. 'Your taste was just like mine when we were small.'

'Only because you hit me every time I tried to disagree with you,' Edyth reminded her.

'Never that hard.'

'That is debatable.'

'I suppose it depends on whether you were on the giving or receiving end of the blows. But this time there isn't a china figurine in sight. And I won't hit you, even if you don't like our presents; I'll keep them for myself.'

Much as Edyth adored her father's brothers and their wives, she occasionally found her cousins, especially the younger boys, exasperating. And when the entire extended family of uncles and aunts and their children descended on the house that evening, along with a few of her parents' closest friends, she found herself longing – somewhat guiltily and ungratefully – for the peace and solitude of her own room.

Everyone had come out of kindness and a desire to help with the last-minute preparations, and they all brought embarrassingly generous wedding gifts along with their congratulations and good wishes for her and Peter's future. The gifts were so numerous it took the combined efforts of her, Bella, Mari and her mother to arrange them for viewing in the conservatory.

Supper was a long and noisy affair. Afterwards her father, his brothers, Harry and Toby retreated into the study, ostensibly to smoke, although the clink of glasses soon echoed from behind the closed door. Wishing for peace and quiet more than ever, Edyth helped Mari and her sisters to clear the table and carry in the trays of greenery and boxes of white carnations that Sali had ordered from the florist.

They set to work making buttonholes and Edyth recalled the evening before Bella's wedding when they had done the selfsame thing. She wondered if it were her imagination, or if they really had been happier then? The only emotion she felt when the last carnation and sprig of fern had been twisted into silver paper was relief. Her mother must have sensed her mood, because she reminded her that she would have to be up early the following morning.

Edyth kissed her aunts and cousins goodnight, hugged Bella and exacted a promise from her to arrive early the next morning to help her dress, shouted a 'goodnight' through her father's study door and climbed the stairs.

She undressed, climbed into bed, switched off the bedside lamp and waited, but sleep eluded her. She continued to lie tossing and turning on the mattress, physically and emotionally exhausted, yet unable to stop her mind from racing as she listened to the distant hum of conversation emanating from downstairs. The sound was too faint for her to make out individual voices, except for the occasional eruption of laughter, and there were more of those from the study than the sitting room.

It seemed odd to hear Harry and Toby's laughter join that of her father and uncles, and she realized that whereas marriage had elevated them to the world of male adulthood, there was no such marked distinction for women. Bella still sat with their mother, aunts, younger sisters and cousins just as she'd always done at family gatherings. She was still wondering why that should be, when she heard the front door open and Toby and Bella calling, 'Goodnight.'

Shortly afterwards the hubbub intensified, the door opened again and her Uncle Joey's and Uncle Victor's cars roared into life in the drive below her window. There were more shouts of 'Goodnight', they drove away and the family began to troop up the stairs in twos and threes. She heard Harry whisper in concern as he helped Mary; and David hush his younger brothers as they piled into Bella's old room. Martha and Susie ran up giggling, and from the length of time that elapsed before they turned off the light in Susie's room, she guessed they'd tried on their bridesmaids' dresses before they went to bed.

She turned on her side and watched the hands move round the radium dial of the travelling alarm clock her Uncle Joey and Aunt Rhian had bought her as a congratulatory present when she had passed her matriculation. One o'clock came and went. Shortly afterwards she recognized the light tread of her father on the stairs. He was always the last in the house to go to bed. She heard the click as he closed her parents' bedroom door.

Half past one . . . two o'clock . . . half-past two . . .

She remembered Bella's wedding, how tears had come to her eyes when Bella had taken her vows.

*. . . To have and to hold from this day forward, for better for worse, for richer for poorer, in sickness and in health, to love, cherish, and to obey, till death us do part . . .*

*Till death us do part.* Marriage was such a serious and important milestone in life. Were her parents right? Was she too young to be taking such a momentous step? Was she doing the right thing in marrying Peter? Did he really love her or was he just saying that to get a parish?

She hated herself for even giving that thought consideration.

Peter had fallen in love with her the first moment he'd looked at her. He'd told her so, time and again. It had to be the truth. It simply had to be.

Unable to bear the doubts crowding in her mind a moment longer, she sat up, switched on her bedside lamp and looked at the framed photograph of Peter that he had given her the day after he'd asked her father if they could 'court formally'. Of course he loved her. How could she even think otherwise? She was simply suffering from pre-wedding nerves, just as she'd done earlier when she had spoken to him on the telephone.

Restless, she decided to go downstairs and make herself a cup of hot milk – and not just milk, she'd put chocolate in it. And she'd investigate Mari's tins to see if any of the macaroons or jumble biscuits the housekeeper had baked for the visitors that morning were left.

Glad to have a plan of action, she swung her legs out of bed and reached for her robe. She tied it around her waist, muffled the lock on her door with her fingers and stole out on the landing.

Wary of switching on the lights lest she disturb anyone, she felt her way down the stairs and along the passage into the kitchen. She closed the door behind her before turning on the lamp. Blinking hard to adjust to the glare, she stumbled, light-headed from sheer weariness. She filled the milk saucepan from the churn on the marble slab in the pantry, set it on the stove and lit the gas. While it was heating, she blended chocolate powder, sugar and cold milk into a paste in a cup. When the milk began to simmer, she poured it on to the chocolate mixture and carried it into the conservatory.

Even in the half-light that came from the kitchen she could see the trestle tables were groaning with gifts. Peter had been right to warn her to wait before buying anything for their home. Her parents had been generous with the wedding reception and bedroom suite. Her Uncle Victor and Auntie Megan had presented her with all the bed linen she and Peter were likely to need for the next twenty years, including two beautifully hand-crocheted double bedspreads and patchwork eiderdowns she recognized as her aunt's handiwork.

She fingered the delicate stitches before moving on to her Uncle Joey and Auntie Rhian's present: ten embroidered Irish linen tablecloths, each with a dozen matching napkins. The family solicitor's present was a mahogany-cased radio gramophone. Harry and Mary had given them sturdy, everyday sets of china tableware and pressed glassware, then added a delicate and, she suspected, horrendously expensive, twelve-place porcelain dinner and tea service complete with full sets of cut glasses, decanters, fruit bowls and sweet dishes for best, as well as a canteen of silver cutlery.

Bella and Toby had bought them silver trays, serving dishes, coffee pots and teapots, sugar bowls and cream jugs in Tiffany's. Even Maggie had chosen her gift with care, selecting a bound set of the complete works of the Brontës, knowing they were her favourite authors.

Father Kelly, an old family friend, had given them towels, and Mari had thoughtfully bought them all the baking tins they could possibly need – or want.

'Who's a lucky girl, then?'

Edyth whirled around, splashing chocolate on to her wrist. She cried out in pain.

'I didn't mean to startle you. Here, let me, sis.' Harry ran into the kitchen, soaked a tea towel under the tap, brought it back and wrapped it around her arm. 'I've never known anyone like you, Edie. If there was a single matchstick in the whole of the Sahara and you were lost there, I'd guarantee you'd trip over it. But,' he studied the pink mark on her arm, 'fortunately for you, considering what you have planned for tomorrow, that doesn't look bad.'

'It's not.' She took the towel from him. 'Can't you sleep?'

'No more than you, by the look of it, and I have a better excuse for leaving my bed.' He returned to the kitchen and filled the kettle.

'What excuse?' She followed him and sat at the table.

'Sleeping next to Mary is like sleeping next to a bomb that's about to explode. Every time she moves I expect her to go into labour.'

His blond hair shone like a halo in the lamplight but there were dark circles beneath his blue eyes. 'You look terrible,' she said cheerfully.

'So Mary keeps telling me.'

'I don't remember you being this nervous when Mary was having Ruth.'

'I didn't know what to expect then; I do now. I don't know how women can go through it once, much less a second time. If it was up to us men, the human race would become extinct.'

'But you did want this baby?'

'Of course I want the baby. Or at least, I wanted it at the time, when I wasn't thinking further than the moment and another gorgeous toddler like Ruth running around the house.' He tipped some hot water from the kettle into the pot, swirled it around and warmed it.

'Make it as strong as that and you won't be sleeping for the rest of the night,' she warned when he heaped four spoonfuls into the pot.

'Don't you want any?'

She held up her cup. 'I have chocolate.'

'I need sustenance.' He started opening cupboard doors. 'Some of Mari's Parkin biscuits or ginger snaps.'

'There should be macaroons and jumbles. I meant to get some.'

'They'll do.'

He foraged in the tins and set a selection on a plate before sitting opposite her. 'It's years since we had a midnight feast.'

'Last time was in the old house. It was so big and draughty Mam used to buy us thick flannel dressing gowns, do you remember?'

'I'll never forget how they itched. The Romans had the right idea; central heating makes a big difference to a house. Look at us now – me in cotton, you in silk – and it's autumn. Cigarette?' He pulled a packet of Players and his lighter from his pocket, and looked around for an ashtray.

'I shouldn't. Peter doesn't approve of women smoking.'

'He stops you?' He took an ashtray from beside the sink and set it on the table in front of him.

'No, just mentioned it in passing,' she murmured, seeing indignation burning in Harry's eye.

'Typical vicar.'

'Harry—'

'I wasn't going to say anything, but damn it all, Edie, someone has to,' he cut in irritably. 'Dad told me how you ran off from college.'

'I tried to tell him and Mam that I didn't want to go to Swansea. They wouldn't listen.'

'So I gathered. But that didn't mean you had to rush off and marry the first man who asked you.' He flicked his lighter and lit his cigarette, before. pushing both packet and lighter across the table to her.

'You make it sound as if I am still a child. I'm not, I'm a woman. Peter loves me and I love him.' She spoke fiercely, daring him to contradict her.

'He loves you?' he asked softly. 'Or the idea of having a wife that will get him a parish?'

'That is a horrible thing to say, Harry.' She was so furious with him for voicing her own doubts that she took a cigarette from the packet and lit it without thinking.

'Can't you see it's what we're all thinking, Edie? I've never known everyone in this house be so overly polite as to keep their thoughts to themselves before.'

'Peter fell in love with me the moment he saw me—'

'At Bella's wedding. I watched the pair of you at the reception.'

He leaned back in his chair and shook his head. 'I should have warned you then.'

'Warned me? About what?' She drew heavily and inexpertly on the cigarette then flicked it into the ashtray although it hadn't burned down enough to create ash.

'That some men aren't the marrying kind.'

'What do you mean? Peter's good, kind—'

'I have no doubt he is all of those things, sis,' he interrupted her again. 'But some men don't make good husbands and I have a feeling Peter Slater may be one of them. Don't ask me to explain, Edie, because I can't.'

'Of course you can't, because you're just being ridiculous!' she cut in acidly.

'The last thing I want to do is quarrel with you or make you angry, Edie, especially tonight of all nights. I've loved you since the day you were born, through all the frights, scares and grey hairs you gave us when you broke your bones and fractured your skull falling down the stairs in the old house. What I'm trying to say, and badly, is that it's not too late to change your mind and call off the wedding.'

'Have you gone mad? The church and choir are booked. The Bishop, the Dean and Reverend Price are conducting the service. The reception is organized in the New Inn. We've had acceptances from all the guests—'

'Who can still enjoy a party in the New Inn if you call it off. But if you go ahead and marry Peter, it will be for the rest of your life, Edie.'

She had barely smoked a quarter of the cigarette but she ground it to dust in the ashtray. 'Did Dad ask you to talk to me?'

'No, but I can tell how upset he is with your choice of husband.'

'He's only upset because Peter's a vicar.'

'You marrying Peter has nothing to do with Dad's attitude to organized religion and everything to do with Peter himself.'

'That's nonsense,' she said dismissively. 'You know how he hates churches and all preachers, vicars and ministers.'

'Believe me, Edie, that's not the case with Peter. You know as well as I do that if Dad liked him he'd rag him about his job, just as he's always ragging Toby about making his living from painting. He's concerned because, like me, he doesn't think that Peter Slater can make you happy.' He offered her the plate of biscuits.

Suddenly nauseous she shook her head. 'Peter is the only man who can make me happy.'

'I hope you're right for your sake.' He stared at a jumble before biting into it. 'I wasn't going to say anything until I saw you in the conservatory looking at your presents just now. There was the oddest look on your face, Edie, and before you ask, I don't know what it was, but I can tell you what it wasn't. It wasn't the happy bride look, because I've seen that many times. On Auntie Rhian and Auntie's Megan's faces on their wedding days, and on Bella's and Mary's. I'm too fond of you to let you make what I think will be the biggest mistake of your life and not say a word to try to stop you.'

'Peter's not like you or Dad, or the uncles or cousins, he's quieter.'

'Come on, Edyth, you can't get anyone quieter than Uncle Victor.'

'Peter's a vicar,' she persisted. 'No one in this family understands him.'

'We understand Father Kelly,' he pointed out mildly. The Catholic priest had been their grandfather's best friend, and had remained close to their father and uncles in the years that followed Billy Evans's death.

'That's because we grew up knowing Father Kelly, and he's known Dad and the uncles since they were boys.'

Harry left the table. 'I can see that I'm not going to change your mind, Edie. Just two more things before I shut up for good. If ever you need me, you know where to find me. And I wish you well, I really do. And now, I'm for bed.'

She watched him empty the ashtray and teapot, clear his cup and saucer into the sink, and replace the uneaten biscuits in the tins.

'You'll switch off the light?'

'I will, Harry.'

'You might not like everything that Mam, Dad and the rest of us have said, Edie, but don't forget, we only said it because we love you.'

She grasped the hand he'd laid on her shoulder. 'I know that, Harry.'

He closed the door behind him. She continued to sit in the lamplight, wishing that she could dismiss Harry's warnings and concerns. But how could she, when they were also hers?

After all the noise, bustle and excitement of dressing with her sisters in her bedroom, Edyth felt positively abandoned when they left with their mother to wait for her at the church. She couldn't recall the last time the house had been so quiet. She was also very aware of her father waiting for her downstairs. But she continued to linger in her room, scarcely daring to breathe, let alone move, lest she disturb the veil that Bella had so carefully arranged over her face, head and shoulders.

Just as Bella had done on her wedding morning, she gazed at her reflection in her mirror. She found it difficult to believe that she was looking at herself and not one of the illustrations in the books of fairytales that she and Bella had so eagerly poured over when they had been children.

She could have been the bride in a 'Happily Ever After' picture of Cinderella or Snow White. And the veil added to the sensation of fantasy. It was as though a thick mist had fallen over the world, intensifying the peculiar, dreamlike sensation that had beset her since her alarm clock had roused her at seven. A feeling she attributed to lack of sleep.

She had lain in bed watching the hands move around the face of the clock until half past four, and when she had finally slept, it had been fitful and nightmare-ridden. She had dreamed that she'd been running through the town to St Catherine's church dressed in her wedding finery, all the while knowing she was late, and terrified that Peter and all the guests would think that she wasn't coming and leave before she reached there.

She had still been running when the alarm had sounded. The result was dark shadows beneath her eyes which Bella had shaken her head at before concealing with layers of foundation cream. But now, as she stared into the mirror, she was as perfect as artifice and Bella could make her.

The moment that she had been waiting for and planning for weeks had actually arrived. She was about to marry Peter Slater. She repeated the name that would shortly be hers: 'Mrs Peter Slater . . . The Reverend and Mrs Slater . . . Mrs Peter Slater . . .'

It was about to happen and she still couldn't believe it. A silver-topped perfume atomiser stood on her dressing table. She picked it up and, walking slowly and carefully so as not to disarrange her veil, carried it over to the bed and dropped it into the open suitcase she was taking on her honeymoon. For the first time in over two weeks the floor was clear. Harry had carried all her packing cases into the box room after breakfast to make room for her and her bridesmaids to dress.

Her wardrobe door was open. The only garments hanging in it were her going away outfit of a pleated purple silk coat and bronze-green silk dress. Matching green crossbar shoes were neatly laid out beneath it, and her new green handbag and silk beret lay on her chest of drawers. Otherwise the room was bare. Stripped of her clutter it had taken on an impersonal air, as if the walls knew that she would never sleep within them again.

Her blood ran cold at the thought. A huge part of her life was over and the next was about to begin. What would it bring?

She glanced at her wrist before remembering that she had decided not to wear her watch. Her travelling clock was in her suitcase and she was loath to dig down to find it. Her mother had told her to go downstairs in ten minutes. Had ten minutes elapsed since then?

She heard footsteps on the landing and tensed herself. Would her father tell her, as Harry had done, that it wasn't too late to call off the wedding? And if he did, how would she answer?

She started at his knock although she had been expecting it.

'Edyth, can I come in?'

'Yes, Dad.'

He opened the door and they gazed at one another wordlessly for a moment. Her father had been handsome as a young man, and although he was now in his early fifties, his figure was still slim and upright. His black hair was heavily streaked with grey and the lines around his eyes and mouth had deepened. But somehow the signs of aging only made him look more distinguished, especially when dressed in his morning suit.

'You look very beautiful, my sweet.'

'Thank you, Dad.' A lump rose in her throat. 'You look very handsome.'

'So your mother told me but it's always nice to hear it from someone else.' He walked into the room. 'I'm sorry about all the arguments. But whatever was said was the result of your mother and me wanting the very best for you. We love you very much, Edie.'

'I know, Dad.'

'Remember, no matter what happens, this will always be your home.'

Forgetting her veil and dress, she ran to him, intending to hug him, but he held her at arm's length. 'Belle will never forgive me if I crease the apparition she's created. But I won't forget that you owe me a hug. I'll have it after the ceremony.'

'I'll remember.'

'See that you do.' He held out his arm, she took it and he led her down the stairs. Through the open front door, she could see the Bentley hired to take them to the church. The driver was standing, holding open the back door. He tipped his chauffeur's hat.

'Good luck, Miss Evans. Reverend Slater is a lucky man.'

'Thank you.'

'And that is probably the last time anyone will call you Miss Evans.' Her father lifted her veil and held it carefully when he helped her into the back of the car. When she was sitting down he folded it and the skirt of her long dress around her legs, away from the door.

'I'll always be your girl and I'm sorry for disappointing you, Dad,' she whispered when he sat behind her.

'You didn't disappoint me, Edie. I disappointed myself. Your mother made me see that the dreams of college were mine, not yours.' He took her right hand in his. 'I wish you and Peter every happiness. Let's make this day a new beginning for both of us.'

Choked by emotion, she could barely whisper, 'Thank you.'

'No tears, they'll spoil your make-up, and your mother and sisters will think we've been quarrelling again. And that's something I don't want to do, ever again.'

'Me neither, Dad.'

He looked at the gate and laughed. 'You're about to find out what it feels like to be royalty. I think everyone we know in the town who isn't actually sitting in St Catherine's has walked up the hill hoping to catch a glimpse of you. You'd better wave as we drive past.'

All the doubts and concerns that had troubled Edyth for the past few days dissipated when she walked down the aisle holding on to her father's arm, with her pageboys, flower-girl and bridesmaids walking behind her, because standing in front of the altar, his arm outstretched towards her, was Peter.

She recalled the wish she'd made at her sister's wedding, just a few short weeks before; that one day a man would look at her with the exact same look of love and adoration that Toby had Bella. And now it was actually happening.

She and Peter were going to be happy – she just knew they were. Maggie took her bouquet, she relinquished her hold on her father's arm, stepped up and stood beside Peter, hoping he could see the smile beneath her veil.

The Bishop moved in front of her, Peter and the congregation, but she only had eyes for the man she loved and, afterwards, the only words she remembered hearing were Peter's vows.

# Chapter 14

'MOTHER, AUNT FLORENCE, this is my,' Peter smiled self-consciously, 'wife, your daughter-in-law and niece, Mrs Peter Slater – Edyth.'

Edyth had to squeeze past Micah Holsten and her sisters to greet Peter's mother and aunt. The wedding party had retired to the vestry to sign the register, but the room was far too small to accommodate the three officiating clergymen, four bridesmaids, matron of honour, best man, groomsmen, immediate family and three small children who felt they had been good pageboys and flower-girl for quite long enough and it was time to play hide and seek between the grown-ups' legs, even if it did mean tripping them up.

'I am so very pleased to meet you at last, Mrs Slater, Mrs Beynon.' Edyth had exchanged letters with Peter's mother during her brief engagement. And, after answering a congratulatory note from his aunt, they had also entered into a short correspondence. Peter had told her that Alice Beynon was six years older than his mother. She had married a wholesale butcher who had died of a heart attack on his fortieth birthday. Before he had gone to an early grave he had amassed a considerable fortune that he had wisely invested in commercial and residential property in Swansea, and the rents enabled his widow – and the sister she had taken into her home – to live in luxury.

He also mentioned that his aunt was childless, and had no relations other than him and his mother on whom to lavish her love, attention and money.

'Peter has told me so much about both of you.' Edyth wished Peter had taken the trouble to differentiate between them. Both

221

were elderly, but she found it impossible to decide which was older. And, although they were sisters, there was little resemblance between them.

One was taller than her. Broomstick thin, with a hooked nose and piercing brown eyes, she looked severe, and unsmiling, with iron-grey hair scraped back in an old-fashioned bun at the nape of her neck. The only concession she made to her age was a silver-topped walking stick, and she stood determinedly, almost painfully, upright. Her wide-brimmed, black silk hat had been fastened low on her forehead with jet-headed hairpins to accommodate her hairstyle and she was wearing an ankle-length, black silk dress, which had probably been the height of fashion thirty years ago. She looked formidable and intimidating, and it didn't help that Edyth's most disliked teacher at school could have been her twin.

But she was undeniably and instantly recognizable as a 'lady'. Edyth knew the type. They never went further than the garden gate without being correctly dressed, and that included hat, gloves and handbag. Dozens of them lived in and around Pontypridd, the wives and widows of men they were careful to describe as 'office workers', instantly placing themselves in a class above that of the miners and their families.

To mark their superiority they wore expensive if unfashionable clothes to church on Sundays and for their 'constitutional' in Ynysangharad Park afterwards. They also met in flocks to drink morning and afternoon tea — with scones — in the rarefied atmosphere of St Catherine's café in Pontypridd Co-op arcade.

'Edyth, as you said, at last we meet.' She proffered a pale, dry, cheek, as wrinkled as a prune. Edyth kissed her and breathed in a peculiar mix of lavender water, carbolic soap and mothballs.

'We were so excited when Peter wrote and told us that he had fallen in love with the girl of his dreams. You are exactly how I imagined. Pretty as a picture, and fresh as a daisy. And only eighteen. Welcome to the family, my dear. Oh look at me!' The second lady dabbed her eyes with a scrap of handkerchief that was more lace than cotton. 'Crying like a baby. But then, what's a wedding without a few tears? That's what I always say.'

She was a full head shorter than her sister, plump and overdressed in a bright blue satin gown and matching coat and hat. Far too young a style for her, it showed every bulge of her tightly corseted body. Her make-up was thick and inexpertly applied, especially her rosy cheeks, one of which was lower than other. Her perfume was exotic, oriental and too heavy for day wear, and her blue-black hair, which clearly owed its colour more to artifice than nature, was permanently waved in an elaborate style Edyth had seen the Hollywood star Lillian Gish wearing on-screen. To complete her ensemble she wore so many rings, bracelets and brooches that she shimmered like a tinselled Christmas angel.

She was the embodiment of the proverbial mutton dressed as lamb, but her brown eyes sparkled with undisguised warmth, her wide smile was sincere and her good humour and determination to be pleased with everyone and everything around her infectious.

Edyth kissed the cheek of the shorter woman. Hoping she'd made the correct choice on the flimsy grounds that she suspected it would be easier to make friends with her than the tall, frigidly polite lady, she said, 'Thank you so much for all your letters, and generous wedding present. I haven't seen the furniture yet, but Peter told me that it has been delivered to the vicarage.'

Peter caught her elbow. 'Edyth, this is Aunt Alice, not my mother.'

'Did you hear that, Flo?' Alice dug her sister in the ribs and cackled loudly. 'She thinks I'm you.'

Peter's mother screwed up her mouth as through she were sucking a slice of lemon.

'I am sorry, Mrs Slater,' Edyth apologized. 'Peter did show me a photograph of you, but it was only a snapshot.'

'If it was the one that was taken when he was three years old, I can understand your mistake.' Her voice was soft, carefully modulated, with no trace of the Welsh lilt. It reminded Edyth of the elocution teacher who had visited the Grammar School twice a week to give the sixth formers lessons designed to 'Anglicize' their speech and make it more acceptable to English colleges.

Failing to detect a hint of warmth or proffered friendship in the comment, Edyth's heart sank. She had desperately wanted to make a friend of Peter's mother.

'That was the snapshot, Mother,' Peter confirmed. 'It's the only one that was taken of all three of us together. You, me and father, remember?'

'I remember, Peter.' Florence Slater studied Edyth, making her feel as though she were goods on sale in a shop, and shoddy goods at that. 'I'm sorry we didn't have time to get acquainted before the wedding, but Peter's career has to take precedence over family and social life. He is dedicated to his vocation, just as his father was before him.'

'I know.' Determined to give Peter's mother no cause for complaint, Edyth forced a smile. 'I helped Peter with the drama society and youth club when he was curate of St Catherine's—'

'So both you and Peter wrote me,' she cut in.

'I do hope that we will become good friends as well as mother-in-law and daughter-in-law,' Edyth added.

'We will.' She gazed adoringly at her son. 'After all, we both love Peter and want the best for him.'

'We are so glad that you decided to honeymoon in Swansea,' Alice said enthusiastically, taking advantage of the momentary lapse in conversation.

'It was very generous of you to make the booking in the Caswell Bay Hotel and meet our expenses,' Edyth said gratefully.

'Hopefully, it will be a wedding present you will remember for many years to come. When are you leaving?'

'On the three-thirty train out of Pontypridd,' Peter answered.

'You must come and see us the moment you can spare some time. We breakfast at eight take tea at eleven, lunch at one, take tea again at four and dine at seven. Cook always makes plenty so don't feel that you have to stand on ceremony. Drop in anytime, anytime at all.' She shook in unsuppressed excitement, sending her bracelets and bangles jingling. 'I simply *love* having young people around my barn of a house.'

'And we'd love to visit. Thank you so much for inviting us, Mrs Beynon,' Edyth smiled.

'Call me Aunt Alice, like Peter.' She stood on tiptoe, planted a damp kiss on Edyth's cheek and immediately scrubbed it with her handkerchief. 'Now look what I've done; I've covered you with lipstick. There, it's all off now.'

'Thank you.'

She grabbed Edyth's hand, looked at her wedding ring and giggled like a schoolgirl. 'Aren't weddings thrilling? Yours reminded me so much of my own. We are going to be great friends, Edyth. I can feel it.'

'Edyth, Peter, you're needed to sign the register,' Micah Holsten called over a sea of heads.

'You, too, Mother,' Peter reminded. 'We decided that Edyth's father and you would be the most suitable witnesses, remember? I wrote to you about it.'

'So you did.' She smiled at Peter but when she turned to Edyth her eyes were glazed with frost. 'Edyth, you must call me Mother, as Peter does.'

'Thank you — Mother.' Edyth couldn't help feeling that Florence Slater wouldn't have made the invitation if it hadn't been for her sister's insistence that Edyth address her as Aunt Alice.

'Go on, they need you to sign your independence away.' Alice pushed Edyth gently forward. 'This is your and Peter's day, we won't monopolize any more of it. We have all of next week to get acquainted.'

'Mother?' Peter offered his mother his arm.

Edyth stood back and watched her husband escort her mother-in-law to the table where Reverend Price had laid the parish register on a drawn threadwork, linen cloth that must have taken many hours of Mrs Price's life. Peter patted the hand his mother had hooked into his elbow, and leaned towards her to catch what she was saying. She smoothed his hair away from his face. Her touch was intimate, possessive, and Edyth felt not only slighted, but uneasy.

It was as though Peter's mother was deliberately trying to exclude her from the family circle. Surely she couldn't be jealous of her own mother-in-law? If so, that was mean and ridiculous of her. Peter had told her that he and his mother were close. It was only natural they should be, considering how young Peter had been when his father had died.

'Edyth?' Peter called to her over his shoulder. 'You have to sign the register, too.'

'It's too late to change your mind,' Micah Holsten quipped. 'The Bishop has declared you man and wife. There's no breaking the contract now.'

Edyth joined in the laughter that followed. But when Peter's mother continued to hover next to him, separating her either by accident or design from her new husband, Edyth was very glad that Florence Slater lived in Swansea, a good forty miles from the vicarage in Tiger Bay, and that the demands Peter's parish would make on both of them wouldn't allow for frequent visits – either way.

Micah Holsten finished his best man's speech, looked along the flower-decked top table to where Edyth's younger sisters and Harry's sister-in-law Martha were sitting, raised his glass and toasted, 'The bridesmaids.'

Chairs scraped back over the wooden floor of the blue and silver dining room of the New Inn. The guests rose to their feet and lifted their drinks. The toast echoed. Then Mary reeled and Harry dropped his glass. It bounced twice before shattering into shards alongside his chair. He fell to his knees, catching Mary just before she would have hit the floor. Toby left Bella's side and ran to open the door so Harry could carry his wife out of the room.

David picked up Ruth and diverted her with a sip from his glass of champagne while Sali and Lloyd rushed outside only just ahead of Bella and Edyth.

'Go back inside, Edie, you can't leave your guests on your wedding day,' Harry ordered abruptly when he saw her dash out behind Bella on to the first-floor landing.

'But Mary—'

'I'm fine,' Mary murmured vacantly, although she was clearly anything but.

'You are not fine,' Harry snapped, concern making him terse.

'My car's parked in the yard at the back. Give me two minutes and I'll drive it around to the front door.' Toby hurtled down the magnificent antique staircase, startling two elderly matrons who were heading for the residents' sitting room on the ground floor.

'Lloyd, fetch my handbag and make my apologies for me, please. I'll go back to the house with Harry and Mary and telephone the doctor.' Sali hovered over Mary who was lying in Harry's arms. 'Shall I ask one of the waiters to get you a glass of water, darling?'

'No, Mam.' Mary opened her eyes and tried to focus on Sali. 'That was a stupid thing to do. The room was hot, that was all. I'll be fine. And please, don't come with us. Stay and look after Ruth. She loves parties and her cousins. She doesn't often get the chance to be with other children.'

'You don't have to worry about Ruth, Mary. People are fighting to look after her. So far your brother David has won the battle.' Megan had slipped out of the room and joined them.

'But Joey's making plans to kidnap her.' Rhian, who had followed Megan outside, glanced from Sali to Harry. She couldn't decide who looked the most concerned. 'What can we do?'

'Go back in,' Mary begged. 'Please, the way things are going there'll be more people out here than in the dining room and there's nothing any of you can do that Harry can't. There's no need to telephone the doctor. Just the midwife.'

'You're in labour?' Harry exclaimed.

'It's the early stages and you know how long it took for Ruth to put in an appearance. Harry, put me down, I'm fine now.' She grimaced in pain.

'I will not.' Harry tightened his grip.

'Please, all of you,' Mary reached for Edyth's hand, 'go back inside. I'll never forgive myself if you allow me to spoil your wedding day. Put me down, Harry,' she repeated irritably in a stronger voice when the pain receded. 'I'd much rather walk down the stairs than risk you tripping and falling on top of me and the baby.'

'She's right, Harry,' Sali said quietly. 'Come on, I'll help you take her down to Toby's car.'

'And then you go back to the reception, Mam,' Mary insisted.

'Please, I wouldn't be happy if you left here to come back to the house with us.'

'If you insist,' Sali agreed reluctantly.

'I'll call in and see you when I go back to the house to change.' Edyth gripped Mary's hand.

'If she's fit to be seen.' Harry was paler than his wife.

'Enjoy the rest of your day. I'm only sorry I won't be there to see it.' Mary gasped as another pain tore through her. After it ebbed, she smiled at Harry, who remained grim-faced. 'It's wonderful to have wedding memories to look back on.'

'We're making a different kind of memory right now, and one that I'm not likely to forget in a hurry.' Harry lowered her gingerly to the floor. He waited until Sali took Mary's left arm, he took her right, and they proceeded slowly down the stairs.

The photographer Lloyd had hired to record the wedding proved exacting and fussy, and Edyth was glad when he finally allowed her and Peter to finish posing and make the first real cut in the wedding cake. While he cleared away his flash lights and camera, a waiter carried the cake into the kitchen so the bottom tier could be sliced for the guests, and the waitresses began serving coffee, brandy and petits fours.

Peter glanced at his watch when he and Edyth returned to their places at the head of the table. 'If we are going to make the three-thirty train we will have to leave in the next ten minutes to change, especially if you want to come back here to say goodbye to everyone.'

'Will we see you for lunch tomorrow?' His mother asked when Edyth sat next to her.

'Of course they won't, Florence.' Alice leaned back in her seat so the waiter could refill her wine glass. 'You can't expect them to come and see a couple of old crocks like us on the first day of their honeymoon.'

'You'll never be old, Aunt Alice, not if you live to be a hundred.' Peter handed her one of the carnations from the vase in front of them.

'Thank you, gallant sir.' Alice simpered like a young girl, but the gesture was so theatrical that people laughed in amusement, which was exactly what Alice had intended.

'When *will* you visit us?' Peter's mother didn't raise her voice, but there was steel beneath the sugar coating and Edyth knew it was a demand.

'Soon, Mother,' Peter replied.

'We have a lot of things to discuss, Peter.'

'I know, Mother. I promise you, Edyth and I will come to see you at the beginning of next week.'

'The children can telephone us from their hotel to let us know when they're coming, Flo. That's if you're worried about laying on a good spread for them,' Alice consoled.

'I'm not worried about food, Alice. Your cook has proved herself perfectly capable of coping with any number of unexpected guests.'

Lloyd leaned towards them. 'Sali and I would be delighted if you would both come back to our house after the reception. You'd be most welcome to stay the night, Mrs Slater, Mrs Beynon.'

'Edyth did pass on your kind invitation, Mr Evans, but my sister and I are of an age where we prefer to sleep in our own beds,' Florence Slater said.

'Speak for yourself, Flo.' Alice dug her elbow into her sister's ribs and rolled her eyes suggestively.

'But both of you will come back to the house after we have seen Peter and Edyth off at the station?' Lloyd pressed. 'I will drive you to the station myself afterwards, to make sure that you catch your train.'

'We're booked on the half past six train out of Pontypridd,' Mrs Slater answered.

'But we can always catch a later one if it suits. I hate to miss a good party. Be warned, Mr Evans, you don't get that many invites in old age.' Alice was loud, tipsy, and looked ready to stay the week if Lloyd asked her.

'I don't believe that of you, Mrs Beynon,' Lloyd complimented.

'Appearances can be deceptive, although I do have my moments, even now.' She gave him a scurrilous wink. 'Flo wanted to return to Swansea on the same train as the honeymooners, but I told her straight, mother or no mother, there's no muscling in on young lovers. They need their privacy, don't they, Edyth?' She gave Edyth a wink all of her own. Edyth blushed, but she caught sight of herself in the mirror on the wall and noticed that Peter had turned a deeper shade of crimson than her.

'Are you ready to go to the house to change, Edyth?' Embarrassed by his aunt's innuendo and over-familiarity with Lloyd, Peter rose to his feet.

'I am but Harry was to have driven me to the house and he's not here. I can hardly walk through town dressed like this.' She held out the skirt of her wedding dress.

'You might start a new fashion, Edyth.' Bella waved to Toby when she caught sight of him walking through the door. He made a bee-line for Edyth.

'Harry told me he promised to drive you to the house to change, and back down here afterwards to say goodbye to everyone before taking you to the station. But, as he's otherwise occupied, I told him that brother-in-law Toby will step in and save the day. Just tell me when you're ready to go.' He set his hands on Edyth's shoulders as he made his way to his seat next to Bella.

'How is Mary?' Edyth, Bella and Sali cried in unison.

'In labour,' Toby said shortly. 'Harry was in such a state I thought I'd better fetch the midwife from Hopkinstown myself. If I hadn't, I don't think he would have survived the time it would have taken her to bicycle to the house. I left the maid boiling water and Harry running up and down stairs like a demented dervish. But the midwife seems a capable soul. I'm sure she can cope with both the maid and Harry.'

'Mrs Morris?' Sali asked.

'That was her name.'

'I told you Mary would be in good hands,' Lloyd said to Sali. 'She delivered Glyn and three of the girls,' he explained to Toby.

'I think I'll go up to the house with you. As Mari's here, the maid may need help.' Sali rose to her feet.

'Could you drop me off at the vicarage on your way, please, Toby?' Peter asked. 'It will only take me a few minutes to change out of this morning suit. It's bound to take Edyth longer, so I'll pick up my suitcase and walk on up to the house and meet you there. That way Edyth and I can travel back down here together to say our goodbyes and thank everyone for coming.'

'What do you mean, "it's bound to take Edyth longer"?' Edyth demanded in mock indignation.

'I can see Harry and I are going to have to give you a few tips on handling women, or more specifically wives, Peter.' Toby filched a piece of wedding cake from Bella's plate.

'Really, darling?' Bella drawled sceptically. 'Tell me, just who has given you the tips to pass on?'

'We have no time to spare if Peter and Edyth want to return here before catching the train.' Toby reached into his pocket for his car keys.

'Men!' Bella looked at Edyth. 'They don't understand the art of having a good quarrel. Particularly if they grew up as only children, like Toby – and Peter – or so I hear.'

'Peter may have been an only child, Mrs . . .'

'Ross.' Bella smiled at Peter's mother but the gesture wasn't returned.

'But I can assure you, he certainly wasn't spoiled or indulged as a child.'

'Certainly not by you, Flo.' Alice drained her glass.

'For the life of me I can't see the fun in quarrelling,' Toby observed.

'The fun is in the making up,' Bella said archly, with a sly glance at Edyth. 'If you are very good, darling, I may teach you how to do that later on tonight.'

'You'll be back, Peter?' His mother laid her hand over his when he pushed his chair under the table.

'Yes, Mother.'

'Stop fussing, Flo. Your little boy's grown up and he'll soon have little ones of his own. See you later, lovebirds.' Alice picked up her empty wine glass and waved it at the waiter.

Peter bent his head and kissed his mother.

'Edyth?' Florence Slater prompted.

'See you shortly, Mother,' Edyth kissed her mother-in-law's cheek, but she was very glad to follow Peter out through the door.

Toby parked his car by the front door of the Evanses' house. Before he had time to switch off the ignition, Sali was out of her seat and in through the door. It took a few minutes and the combined efforts of Toby and Bella to help Edyth, who was terrified of tearing the veil or her dress, out of the back seat. They went into the hall to find Harry sitting on the bottom step of the stairs, his head in his hands, talking to Sali. He looked up and gave them a tired but triumphant smile.

'Are you ready to be introduced to the newest Evans?'

'Mary has already had the baby?' Edyth cried out in surprise.

'Less than an hour after she left the New Inn. And that's the last time I'll listen to her when she tells me she only fainted because the room was warm.'

'How many more do you intend to have so she can fool you?' Bella questioned in amusement.

'That's not up for discussion until I've recovered from the strain of having this one.'

'*You've* recovered?' Bella exclaimed.

'How are they both? What is it? How much did it weigh? Have you given the baby a name yet?' Edyth demanded impatiently.

'One question at a time.' Harry smiled at his mother. 'It's a boy and we've decided to call him William Lloyd Evans, after Granddad and Dad, but because Billy is too much of a name to live up to in this family, we've decided to call him Will. And both of them are in better shape than me.'

'They couldn't be in worse.' Toby reached into his pocket. 'Have a cigar. I bought them to celebrate Edyth's wedding but now they'll come in doubly handy. You deserve one.'

'What for?' Bella asked. 'Mopping Mary's brow when she was in pain?'

'And braving the midwife,' Harry added. 'Mary insisted she wanted me there. We both told her that I held Mary's hand when Ruth was born, but she kept muttering, "it's disgraceful to have a man cluttering up the room at such a time."'

'Is it all right if we go up and see them?' Edyth stepped on the stair that Harry was sitting on.

'Go ahead. The midwife's in the kitchen having a cup of tea. I said I'd get one for Mary.'

'I'll make it, Harry,' Sali offered. 'You go on back up with the girls; Edyth only has a few minutes to see her new nephew.'

Mary was lying in the middle of Harry's double bed, looking down at a bundle wrapped in a shawl next to her.

Bella leaned over and stroked the baby's cheek gently with the back of her finger. 'He is gorgeous, Mary,' she complimented with a slight trace of envy.

'Isn't he just?' Mary pulled back the shawl that covered the baby's head. 'He has blond hair, like Harry.'

'But it's curly like yours, and I suspect that it will grow darker as he gets older, just as Ruth's has done.' Harry sat on the bed next to his wife, slipped his arm around her shoulders and pushed his little finger into the baby's hand. 'Aren't we clever?' He kissed her cheek.

' "We", indeed! Anyone would think you did all the hard work, Harry. Be careful, Mary. Any minute now he's going to burst with pride,' Bella warned.

'I'm only glad he's calmed down. The midwife was more worried about him than me during the birth. It's as well that I packed a holdall with baby clothes and nappies – just in case.'

'We would have managed if you hadn't. I still have some of the girls' baby things as well as Glyn's. Here you go, two cups of tea for the proud parents.' Sali brought in a tray. 'The midwife said she will be up to see you again before she goes, Mary. She also told me she's never attended such an easy or quick birth.'

'If that was easy don't give me difficult.' Harry took the teas from the tray and set them on the bedside table.

'Was he any help at all, Mary? The truth mind,' Bella probed.

'He held my hand.' She looked sheepishly at Edyth. 'Sorry I interrupted your wedding.'

'For the best possible reason.' Edyth held out her arms. 'Can I have a cuddle?'

'In that velvet frock?' Harry exclaimed. 'Is Glyn so grown-up now you've forgotten what a mess babies make?'

'Oh . . . . Vladivostock! Look at the time.' Edyth used the word her teachers had hated, because every time they heard her shouting it they assumed she was swearing.

'Careful, sis, you're married to a vicar now,' Harry teased. 'Can't have the Bishop hearing you say something that sounds naughty, even if it isn't.'

Bella saw her panicking and said, 'It's all right. You're all packed and I'll help you change.'

'Here, get acquainted with your grandson, Mam.' Harry handed his son to his mother. 'I'll drive you and Peter back to the New Inn to say your goodbyes, sis.'

'No, you will not,' Bella contradicted. 'The last thing Edyth and Peter need is a delicate man fainting when he's driving them down the hill.'

'I want to announce our good news to everyone,' Harry protested.

'Then you can squash in the back with Edyth and Peter. Edyth, if you want to make that train, start changing. Now!' Bella opened the door.

'Marriage has made you bossier than ever, Belle. Or does Toby like you that way?'

'That question is not worth answering, Harry Evans.'

Edyth went to the door. 'Peter's walking up from the vicarage to meet me here. Can I show him the baby, please, Mary?'

'Of course.' Mary couldn't tear her gaze away from her sleeping child.

'Change, madam, or you'll miss your train and have to spend your wedding night in a house crowded with people, children and a crying baby.' Bella shooed Edyth through the door.

'He's not going to cry,' Harry called after her. 'We're going to train him to be good.'

'Just like you did Ruth.' Mary lifted his hand from her shoulder and kissed it. 'I don't know how we're going to manage when the two of them climb into our bed every night. When Ruth lies sideways there's no room for us now.'

'I'll be firm with him,' Harry said decisively.

'That I can't wait to see.' Sali saw Mary staring at the baby and handed him back to her.

'Watch out, Will, you're in for a harsh, disciplined life,' Bella mocked playfully, before following Edyth into her bedroom.

'Some hope, when Harry's as soft as all the other Evans men,' Sali laughed.

'I can't wait to have a baby.' Bella unclipped the veil from Edyth's head and laid it on the tissue paper she'd spread out on the bed. 'Toby and I have talked about it, and we've decided we want at least half a dozen.'

'You talked about it?' Edyth recalled Peter's embarrassment whenever the subject of babies or sex was touched upon.

'At length. I know Toby's always making jokes about how many of us there are, and acts as though we're a tribe of barbarians, but he told me that he loves being one of a large family, even if it is only through marriage. Having lost his parents when he was young and then his uncle, he is determined that our children will never be as alone as he was.'

'And you're . . .' Edyth looked at her sister's waist, which was as slender as ever.

'Not yet. At least, not that I know about. Here, give me that frock, I'll lay it on the bed for now and pack it away later. Don't worry,' she reassured when she saw Edyth frown. 'I'll do it properly so your daughters can wear it when they get married – that's if they want to. The way fashion is going, it's anyone's guess what women will be wearing in twenty years' time. Feathers in our hair and hula-hula skirts comes to mind after seeing some of the musical shows on Broadway.' Bella took the dress from Edyth and draped it over the bed. 'Sit down; I'll take out the tiara. All your hair will need is a quick comb-through before you put your beret on.'

Edyth wriggled out of the long petticoat that she had worn beneath her wedding gown and slipped the simply cut bronze-green silk frock with its bias-cut skirt over her silk cami-knickers. The purple pleated silk jacket had no fastenings. She draped it over her shoulders, took the comb Bella handed her, and pulled it through her waved hair.

'You look perfect, apart from one thing.'

'What?' Edyth looked anxiously at Bella.

'Shoes?' Bella picked them up from the floor of the wardrobe and handed them to her. 'You may be married to a vicar, but I don't think the church will make you walk barefoot like a penitent. Not yet at any rate.'

Peter arrived at the house three-quarters of an hour before their train left the station, so they could barely spare five minutes to visit Mary and baby, but even in that short time Edyth sensed that Peter was ill at ease. She had assumed that he would be used to visiting women in their bedrooms; after all, he had administered the sacrament to Mrs Hopkins almost daily when he had been the Reverend Price's curate, but he was clearly perturbed at seeing Mary in bed.

Hoping no one else had noticed, she was glad when Toby chivvied them into his car. He drove them to the New Inn, where the family showered them with confetti when they walked back into the ballroom. But, by the time Harry had finished announcing the birth of his son, they had to leave.

Mrs Slater kissed Peter a tearful goodbye and complained bitterly at their having to rush off, but she declined to accompany them to the station with the other guests, although it was only a short walk away.

What seemed like a hundred kisses and a thrown bouquet later, which Alice Beynon caught, Edyth found herself sitting opposite Peter in a first-class carriage heading for Cardiff where they would have to change trains for Swansea.

'Well, Mrs Slater?' Peter asked. 'Happy?'

'Very.' She returned his smile. 'You?'

'Ecstatic.'

She turned aside and looked out of the window as they drew into Treforest station. 'It all happened so fast I still can't quite believe that we're actually married.'

'I have the certificate and the whole of our future to convince you.'

'That sounds wonderful. The whole of our future. It makes me think of one of the huge blank canvases in Toby's studio. You can imagine all sorts of things being painted on it.' She looked up at him. 'Happy things, if we're lucky. Children, home, family, Christmases with trees – and carol concerts and church services.' She added the last two for his benefit.

'A good life of hard work and Christian duty.'

'And love?'

'Yes, Edyth.' He pulled the blind on the corridor before moving across to her seat. 'I promise you love.' And then he kissed her.

# Chapter 15

'REVEREND AND MRS SLATER, on behalf of the management and staff, may I welcome you to the Caswell Bay Hotel.' The clerk left the desk and grandly, and rather ostentatiously, greeted Peter and Edyth as they walked into reception.

'Thank you,' Peter replied warily. He, like Edyth, had noticed that the man had recognized them the moment they'd stepped inside the hotel and hadn't needed to refer to the register to check their details.

'Large double with sea view, all expenses to be billed to Mrs Beynon's account.' The clerk flourished a pen in front of Peter. 'A valued and popular customer, Mrs Beynon. She frequently dines and hosts bridge parties here. I understand that you are her nephew, sir?'

'That is correct.' Peter dipped the pen in the inkwell and signed the register.

The clerk lifted a key from a row of numbered hooks on the board and smirked at the porter. 'Bags to be carried up to *eighteen*, Davies. Mrs Slater, Reverend, rest assured we will do everything in our power to ensure that you have a pleasant stay with us.'

'Thank you,' Edyth replied when she realized that Peter had no intention of answering the man.

'Eighteen,' the boy repeated. He stared at Edyth, but turned aside when he saw her looking back at him.

Peter's Aunt Alice had not only made the booking and arranged to pay their hotel bill as a wedding present, but also given them a generous cheque on the understanding that 'it was to be spent on nothing sensible'. After meeting Alice Beynon, and witnessing the staff's reaction to their arrival, Edyth didn't doubt that Peter's aunt had also informed the hotel staff that they were honeymooners.

'Breakfast is served from seven to nine, luncheon from twelve to two, and dinner from eight until nine-thirty in the evening, sir, madam. All meals are taken in the dining room, unless, that is, you'd prefer to eat in the privacy of your room.' His smile turned to a leer.

'No, thank you. We'll eat in the dining room.' Peter answered without consulting Edyth.

'Would you like an early-morning call, sir, madam?'

Peter looked enquiringly at Edyth.

'I've packed my alarm clock.'

'No, thank you,' Peter said.

'Should there be anything – anything at all – that we can do to make your stay with us more comfortable, please don't hesitate to ask.'

'We will.' Peter offered Edyth his arm, and they followed the porter up the stairs. They passed two maids in the corridor. Both dived into a walk-in linen cupboard the moment they saw them. Edyth heard giggling and suspected their odd behaviour wasn't anything to do with a directive about cleaning staff not being seen by guests, and everything to do with knowing that she and Peter were honeymooners.

She noticed the back of Peter's neck had turned bright pink above his collar, and she was surprised that he was more embarrassed by the overdose of innuendo in their welcome than she was.

'Your room, madam, sir.' The boy opened the door, carried their cases inside and lifted them on to a pair of canvas webbed trestles set at the foot of the double bed. 'Shall I send for a maid to unpack for you, sir, madam?'

'No, thank you.'

Edyth wondered if that was how Peter intended to respond to every enquiry the staff made of them during the week. He tipped the boy sixpence and closed the door before going to the window and opening it wide.

Edyth joined him and they gazed down the hill to Caswell Bay cove. The tide was in, lapping at the rocks and pebbles high on the foreshore. The sea was shimmering, gleaming, cold pewter in the clear October air. The moon had already risen although the sun hadn't set, and it hung, a pale silver crescent in the greying sky.

'What a wonderful view,' Edyth cried enthusiastically. 'I've always loved Caswell Bay. It's one of the best – after Langland and Oxwich – for bathing.'

'I keep forgetting that you've holidayed in Swansea and on the Gower.' Peter pushed aside the curtains and a fresh, chill breeze blew into the room. 'I was hoping to introduce you to my favourite places, but it seems you're as well acquainted with them as I am.'

'We've seen them through different eyes.'

'That's a tactful statement if ever I heard one. Did you holiday on the Gower every year?'

'Every year I can remember when I was growing up. First in my great-aunt's cottage in Port Eynon then, after she died, mostly, but not always, in a house at Horton that belonged to a friend of hers. The last two years we've stayed at the Mermaid in Mumbles. Mam wouldn't allow Dad to book us in there until Glyn reached what she called "a civilized age". She says hotels and small children don't mix.'

'She's probably right.' Peter sat on the window sill. 'Which is your favourite Gower bay?'

'That's a hard one.' She sat on the opposite end of the sill to his and leaned against the window recess behind the curtains. 'Rhossili is the most impressive.' She had chosen the bay at the end of the Gower Peninsula. Below its treacherously high and steep cliffs lay miles of clear sandy beach.

'Beautiful, but a long walk down to the sea,' he observed.

'Does that mean you're too lazy to want to visit there this week?'

'We'll see.' His hand shook when he loosened his tie.

'It's strange to think that all the time I holidayed here as a girl with my family you were living in Mumbles. We could have passed one another in the village, or on a clifftop walk. We could have even swum off the same beach, fished in the same rock pool or bought ice-creams from the same cart.'

'I went to boarding school when I was fourteen and you were four.' He turned away from her and studied the view.

'But you returned here for the holidays.'

'True,' he granted, 'but I rarely ventured very far down the Gower after Mother and I moved in with Aunt Alice. Her chauffeur always seemed strangely reluctant to drive us further than Mumbles and Langland. Possibly because he had sisters living in both villages and could be assured of a cup of tea after he dropped us off.'

'Aunt Alice is nice. And not just because she's paying for all this,' she added, lest he think her mercenary.

'Nicer than my mother?'

'What a peculiar question.' She was taken aback.

'Aunt Alice *is* very different from my mother.'

'It's hard to believe they are sisters,' she conceded.

'You may not have noticed in the short time you were in their company, but they don't get on.'

'They are certainly opposites,' she agreed tactfully.

'Aunt Alice means well and she's very generous with her money and hospitality, but Mother is more of a thinker and Aunt Alice, well, she's more of a . . .'

'Doer who likes a good time,' Edyth suggested when words failed him.

'You noticed that much on a brief acquaintance?'

'Your aunt seemed determined to enjoy our wedding.'

'Mother told me that although Aunt Alice is older than her, she has always been adolescent in her attitude towards life. As a young girl she never thought further than the next ball, party, picnic or good time, and she didn't change when she married or, I'm afraid to say, when she lost her husband.'

'Perhaps her determination to make the best of things is a reaction to losing her husband at such a young age,' Edyth suggested. 'Many widows adopt the philosophy of enjoying every moment to the full, while they still have them. It doesn't mean that they loved their husbands any less than the widows who observe

241

strict mourning.' Edyth surprised herself when she sprang to Alice Beynon's defence. But she had taken a liking to her warmth and spontaneity, if only because it proved, after the cool reception Peter's mother had given her, that someone in her husband's family was prepared to like her.

'Which is all well and good if you subscribe to the philosophy that this life is all there is.'

'Please don't let's quarrel about my father's beliefs, not on our honeymoon, Peter,' she pleaded.

He gave her one of his winsome smiles. 'I wasn't thinking of your father but Mother and Aunt Alice. Mother takes life far more seriously than her sister. She sees it as an opportunity for spiritual preparation for the hereafter.'

'I see.' Edyth did. She suddenly understood Peter's mother perfectly. Her interpretation of religion was the one her father had railed against all his life. Florence Slater equated godliness with a grim Victorian solemnity bordering on misery and, from what little she'd seen of her at the wedding breakfast, probably regarded anything enjoyable as the devil's work. But she was also her mother-in-law. Much as she didn't relish the task, it was up to her to make the best of the situation because she had a feeling that Florence Slater wouldn't be making any allowances for her. Time and patience would hopefully win her around. Perhaps when she and Peter had children . . .

She pictured Mary lying in bed with tiny Will at her side and imagined herself in the same situation, with Peter sitting on the bed beside her, a small bundle between them . . .

'Edyth?'

She focused on her husband. 'Sorry, Peter, I was miles away. Did you say something?'

'I was talking about Aunt Alice and Mother but it can wait. It's half past seven. We have time for a short walk before dinner or a longer walk afterwards. Which would you prefer?'

Edyth knew exactly what she would have preferred; a quiet romantic dinner in their room with a bottle of champagne. And afterwards making love with the curtains and window open so they could see the night sky and hear the sea . . .

'Edyth?' he prompted again.

'You choose.'

'You're proving to be a very accommodating wife.' He left the window sill and kissed her forehead.

She debated whether or not to wrap her arms around his neck and encourage him to kiss a whole lot more of her but he moved away while she was still wondering how he'd react. 'I promise you, Peter; I'll try to be just that, always.'

'I love you, Edyth Slater,' he said huskily. 'Never forget it.'

'I love you, too, Reverend Slater.'

He opened his suitcase and removed a linen suit bag. 'I think we should change for dinner now and go for a walk afterwards. It's always best to exercise before bed. I'll go to the bathroom and change.'

'I'll unpack,' she said brightly, forcing the disappointment from her voice. 'Would you like me to unpack for you?'

'No.' His reply was too sharp, too finite, and he realized it. 'I'm a bit of fusspot when it comes to my clothes and personal things. I'll put them away myself when you change. Did you see a bathroom when we came up the stairs?'

'There's one next door.'

'Then Aunt Alice probably asked for us to be put in this room. You can always trust her to think of the practical things and comforts of life.' He took a leather toilet bag from the top of his case.

'That's a very good characteristic for an aunt to have.' She lifted her feet on to the sill and rested her head on her knees.

'You're determined to like her.'

'I'm determined to love, not like, your aunt *and* your mother, Peter.'

'I won't be long.'

Edyth continued to sit on the window sill looking out at the Bay for a few minutes after Peter left. The tide was receding. Gradually the strip of sand below the pebbles widened, but she saw neither the sand, sea, gulls, old men preparing to dig for lugworm, nor the boy and girl walking a pair of red setters. She had imagined the moment when she and Peter would finally be alone together in a bedroom ever since he'd asked if he could 'court her with a view to an engagement'. She'd assumed that he would take her in his arms . . . kiss her . . . undress her . . .

But Peter was a vicar. That set him apart from most men. And he'd warned her, when he'd asked her to court him, that he was cautious by nature and experience. Different men loved in different ways. Bella's Toby was passionate and demonstrative – Peter wasn't. And, after meeting his mother, she could understand why he found it difficult to express his feelings.

She recalled the first time he had told her he loved her. What he lacked in passion he compensated for in dedication. She had always wanted the kind of relationship her parents had: a love that would last through bad as well as good times. And, in Peter she would find that, if only she could quell the tiny niggling doubts.

She climbed down from the sill, reached into her pocket for her keys, unlocked her suitcase and began to unpack, setting aside one of the most expensive gowns in her trousseau; a long-sleeved, russet satin evening frock that brought out the highlights in her hair. And when she placed piles of stockings and underclothes in the dressing-table drawers, she tried not to anticipate what was going to happen in that room that night. Because she was beginning to discover that too much anticipation led to a sense of anti-climax.

It was her over-active imagination that had led to – not disappointment exactly, she could never be disappointed with Peter – more like the end of expectation. But hadn't that been the case with almost everything in her life so far? Looking forward to an event was often so much more enjoyable better than the actual occasion.


David said goodnight to Harry's family, and goodbye to Lloyd's brothers and their wives and children, who were leaving, and climbed the stairs to Bella's old room. His two younger brothers, five-year-old Luke and ten-year-old Matthew, were already asleep, worn out by the excitement of the wedding and the impromptu party in Lloyd and Sali's house that had followed Will's birth and the departure of the newlyweds.

Luke was curled in a tight ball in the truckle bed beneath the window, in contrast to Matthew who was sprawled out, arms and legs extended, in the centre of the double bed.

Avoiding Matthew, David sank down on the side of the bed, lifted his ankle on to his knee and began to unlace his shoe. An image of Edyth came to mind. She was undressing, slowly, tantalizingly, in a luxuriously furnished hotel bedroom that gleamed with all the satin and silk drapes he'd seen in the Hollywood films Harry had taken him to see in Pontardawe. Peter was sitting in an easy chair, glass of brandy in hand, his shirt collar hanging loose by one stud as he watched her – and smiled. She returned his smile and moved closer . . . set her hand on his shoulder . . .

David shuddered and blinked hard, but the picture remained, searing agonizingly and unbearably on to his consciousness.

How could Edyth – his Edyth, – as he had thought of her until that day – reject him and marry a wet fish of a vicar like Peter? If he had lived nearer to her, or at least within riding or driving distance, he could have visited her, if not every day then a few evenings a week.

He would have courted her, persuaded her that he really loved her and then she would have married him not the stupid vicar. If only he lived anywhere but the farm. A girl like Edyth wanted to see life, not be buried in the middle of nowhere where the most exciting event of the day was the appearance of the lorry that picked up the milk churns from their stand at the side of the road.

Restless, he left the bed and walked out on to the landing. He could hear the new baby mewling and Harry and Mary whispering behind the door of their bedroom. For the first life in his life, he felt a pang of jealousy for his sister's happiness.

He went downstairs. The maids were talking in the kitchen. But the rest of the house was quiet. Taking his hat and coat from the stand, he unlocked the front door as quietly as he could and stepped outside.

The sky was clear. A sliver of new moon shone down amongst a bevy of glittering stars and he remembered his long-dead father telling him always to start a new enterprise on a waxing moon. Had Edyth heard that saying and fixed her wedding date accordingly? Or was it simply luck that she and Peter had picked that day? Either way, it was Peter Slater, not him, who had won both Edyth and the luck that came with a new moon. And the girl he loved was as lost to him in her vicarage in Cardiff as if she had moved to the other side of the world.

Wanting to get as far away from the house, and everyone and everything connected to Edyth, as he could, he started walking, neither knowing, nor caring in what direction he was headed.

'So if you take over the temperance society and the youth club—'

'Peter?' Edyth interrupted, allowing her exasperation to show for the first time that evening.

'What?' He unlocked the door and stood back so she could precede him into their room.

They were returning after an excellent dinner accompanied by a bottle of the vintage champagne that Alice Beynon had ordered to be sent to their table, not only on their first night at the hotel, but every night of their stay. They had finished with coffee and brandy and a walk on the terrace, which Edyth could have quite cheerfully forgone but Peter had insisted on taking. Apart from complimenting her on her gown and hair, he hadn't said one single word of romance all evening.

'It's our wedding night,' she reminded him tersely. 'And all you've talked about is your plans for the parish. I know it's important to you – to both of us,' she amended diplomatically, 'but the whole point of a honeymoon is to get to know one another away from everyday work and domesticity.'

'Sorry, Edyth.' He smiled sheepishly. 'I suppose I have talked rather a lot about parish business tonight.'

'Only all through dinner, the walk in the garden and up the stairs.' She made a poor attempt to turn her complaint into a joke.

'Sorry. It's just that I can't stop thinking about it.'

'It will be there next Saturday and so will we.'

'I know.' He moved a chair in front of the window.

'You want to sit up?'

'I thought I would read while you get ready for bed.' He took a book from a stack he had set on a desk in the corner of the room.

She read the title: *The Victorian Pulpit*: Spoken and Written Sermons in Nineteenth-Century Britain.

'Isn't that a little old-fashioned for the modern church?'

'In places,' he conceded, 'but the Victorians had some sound theological ideas.' He sat down. 'How would you like to go to service in St Paul's in Sketty tomorrow? My mother and aunt always attend morning service and we can visit them afterwards. Perhaps even stay for lunch.'

Ideally Edyth would have liked to have spent the first day of married life lying in bed until the last possible moment before the hotel stopped serving breakfast, or even better, eating it in their room so they wouldn't have to dress. Then, a stroll on the beach or cliff path, depending on whether the tide was in or not, before lunch and an afternoon nap with the door locked, followed by an early dinner and a romantic stroll on the beach in the moonlight. But then Peter was a vicar. He could hardly miss church, and if they had to attend a service anyway . . . and she wanted to see his aunt's house.

'If you'd like to,' she acquiesced.

'I think morning service would be best. We could hire a taxi to get there, so we wouldn't have to get up too early. And, after we've visited Mother and Aunt Alice, we'll have the rest of the day free. If we lunch with them, we could either catch a bus or walk from Sketty to Mumbles, and have tea in one of the cafés on the front.'

'You seem to have it all planned out.'

'Mother appeared quite agitated this afternoon. And I do need to talk to her.' He looked away from her, unable to meet her steady gaze. 'Do you want to use the bathroom first?'

'No, you can.'

'I won't be long.'

She looked around the room after he left. He had unpacked his suitcase while she'd dressed earlier. It stood on its side in the corner next to the wardrobe. She lifted hers beside it and opened the drawer where she had placed her lingerie. She had chosen a white lace and silk negligée set but it was flimsy, and transparent in the light, so she had brought her satin robe for the hotel corridor.

She laid everything out on the bed then sat on it and tested the springs. It was firmer than her bed at home. Was that a good or a bad thing? She bounced up and down and the springs creaked.

'Edyth, what on earth are you doing?' Peter hissed after he had closed the door behind him.

'Testing the bed.' Without thinking, she added, 'It doesn't half make a racket.'

'So I heard. And I wouldn't be surprised if it was heard halfway to Swansea. You're not bouncing around with your sisters now. Didn't you think what it would sound like out in the corridor? The clerk and porter were sniggering down in reception.'

'Sorry.' She jumped up in embarrassment.

'The water's hot if you want a bath.' He set his toilet bag on the washstand.

'I think I will.' She couldn't stop looking at him. His dressing gown was dark-red lightweight wool, which suited his colouring, and his pyjamas were blue-and-white striped cotton. He smelled of the same shaving soap and cologne that her father and Harry used. But he wasn't her father or Harry, and there was a sudden rush of electrifying intimacy. She was finally alone in a bedroom with the man she loved, and he was dressed ready for bed.

He went to the window and pulled the curtains across it.

'Don't close out the moon and the sea,' she pleaded.

'But people on the road or the beach can see in.'

'Not if we switch off the light.'

'I'd like to read.' He picked up his book.

'How about a compromise?' she suggested. 'You can close them now, but I'll open them and switch off the lights when I come back. I'd like to go to sleep looking at the moon and the sea.'

'Is that what married life with you is going to be like?' he asked. 'A compromise?'

'Until we rub the rough edges off one another.' She moved close to him and planted a kiss on his lips. He stepped back. 'Is something the matter?' She smarted at his rejection.

'Just this place. When you go to the bathroom you'll see what I mean, Edyth. You can hear every sound in the building. People talking in the room next door, walking up and down the corridors.

I even heard someone coughing in the bar downstairs. The bed squeaking was the absolute limit.'

'I didn't think the walls were that thin.'

'Perhaps I'm being over-sensitive, but I think it's best we leave the start of our married life until we get home.'

Shocked, Edyth stared at him.

'You do understand what I'm saying?'

'A honeymoon without a honeymoon,' she said unthinkingly.

'You don't mind, do you? You are very young. Something like that can be painful – a shock to the system. Especially in strange surroundings.'

'Not according to my mother or Bella.'

'You discuss the intimate personal details of your life with them?' Now it was his turn to be shocked.

'Not personal to me, no,' she qualified, 'but the facts of life, sex and married life in general, yes.'

'I'll read until you get back.'

He'd closed the subject and she was unable to think of a single thing to say to re-open it, so she left for the bathroom and lingered there even after her bath.

She rubbed Nivea cream into her hands and feet to soften them; sprinkled essence of violets on her neck and behind her ears because Peter had told her it was his favourite perfume. She removed every trace of make-up with more than her usual care, put just the slightest dab of powder on her nose to stop the shine, brushed out her curls and studied herself in the mirror. She thought she looked reasonably attractive. Not stunning, but attractive. But what was the point when Peter didn't want to make love to her?

Was it her? Was she off-putting or ugly in some way that she hadn't noticed? Did she have halitosis? After she cleaned her teeth she put her hand in front of her face and breathed upwards, but all she could smell was mint-scented tooth powder.

Finally, having no more cause for delay, she gathered her towel, toilet bag and clothes together and returned to the bedroom.

'I've set the alarm for half past seven,' Peter said without looking up from his book. 'Will that give you enough time to dress and get ready to go down for breakfast?'

'Yes.' She went to the window. 'Can I switch out the light and open the curtains?'

'Switch out the light first but give me time to put my book away.' He folded his bookmarker into the page, closed the book and set it on the chest of drawers next to the bed.

She waited until he lay back on the pillows before pulling the switch and drawing the curtains. Moonlight streamed in through the window on to the bed, bathing the room in a cold grey light that painted the bed linen silver.

Heart pounding, Edyth slipped off her robe and went to the bed. Peter's eyes were shadowy enigmatic pools in the gloom.

'That is a very pretty negligée. It could be a fairy costume from *A Midsummer Night's Dream.*'

'I hoped you'd like it but I don't think I'm anyone's idea of a fairy. I'm far too clumsy.' She turned back the sheet. 'Peter,' she summoned her courage, 'are you quite sure that you wouldn't like me to undress completely?'

'No, Edyth. Aside from the feeling that the entire hotel is listening at the door, we've had a long day. Let's sleep. We have the rest of our lives to get to know one another.'

She slipped off her negligée and hung it and her robe on the back of the door. Sitting on the bed, she swung her legs up and pulled the sheet and blankets over herself. Peter rolled over and turned his back to her. She reached out to him but he moved away, evading her touch and effectively ending her hope that he would go to sleep holding her.

She lay rigid, fighting frustration and disillusionment, until she heard his breathing steady into a soft even flow. Only when she knew he slept did she close her eyes.

David climbed the steps of Pontypridd's most famous landmark, the old bridge, and stared down at the dark and swirling waters of the River Taff far below. The air was cold, and damp, the surface of the water gleamed, black like wet coal, and still he could see Edyth and Peter. They were drawing slowly, inexorably closer to one another in that Hollywood-style boudoir – their lips met, Peter closed his hand on Edyth's bare shoulder, she locked her arms around Peter's neck . . .

Closing his eyes against the image didn't help, he could still see them. He lifted first one foot then the other on to the parapet, straightened up, leaned forward and jumped. And then, finally, he saw them no more.

The alarm trilled into life at seven-thirty. Edyth looked around the room in bewilderment for the few seconds it took her to realize where she was. She sat up, ran her fingers through her hair to brush it back from her face and saw Peter sitting, dressed and shaved, in the chair in front of the window.

He turned to her and smiled. 'Good morning, Mrs Slater.'

'Good morning,' she answered shyly. 'You are up early.'

'I'm usually an early riser, especially when I sleep as well as I did last night. The combination of exhaustion, champagne and travelling proved an excellent sleeping pill. But I woke just as dawn broke over the sea. It's so long since I've seen it, I'd forgotten what a wonderful sight it is. How did you sleep?'

'Fine, when I managed to stop thinking. Peter, what you said last night, about us waiting. I—'

'It will be different when we are in the privacy of our own home, Edyth. Now, if we are going to be in good time for breakfast you'd better dress.' He set his book aside. 'I'll go downstairs and order us a taxi to take us to the church. It will be an extravagance, but then a honeymoon is a once-in-a-lifetime experience.'

'Can we afford it?'

'On special occasions, but we won't be able to make a habit of it.' He left his chair and kissed her cheek. 'If my aunt's chauffeur can't bring us back here, we'll walk to Mumbles from Sketty through the park. We certainly have a fine day for it. The only cloud is over the sea, and we can always order a taxi in Mumbles, or even, if you're up to it, walk across the headland to here.'

'I'd enjoy a walk if the weather stays fine.'

He went to the door. 'Meet me in the dining room?'

'I'll be half an hour.'

She looked out of the window after he left the room. The sun was shining but the wind was whipping sand across the beach. She opened the wardrobe and lifted out a dark-green woollen suit before going to the bathroom. She washed, dressed and applied her make-up mechanically. All she could think of was Bella's confession that she and Toby hadn't been able to keep their hands off one another – and Peter's wish to postpone their lovemaking.

As he refused even to discuss it, all she could do was wait until the end of the week when they would go to the vicarage in Tiger Bay. But that thought didn't prevent a tight knot of apprehension from forming in her stomach. Peter was charming and polite, solicitous even. But she could hear Harry's voice ringing in her ears: '*Some men don't make good husbands and I have a feeling Peter Slater may be one of them . . .*'

The front doorbell rang out as Harry was running, light-footed and whistling, down the stairs early the next morning. He turned and shouted up the passage, 'I'll get it, Mari.'

To his surprise, one of his parents' oldest friends, local constable Huw Davies, was on the doorstep.

'Good morning, Uncle Huw. You've come round early for a cup of tea on a Sunday morning and in full uniform, too. Have they run out at the station?'

Huw stepped inside and removed his helmet, revealing his thinning ginger hair. I'm sorry, Harry, I'm afraid I'm not here for Mari's tea. Is your father in?'

'There hasn't been an accident, has there?' Harry froze as he thought of Peter and Edyth. 'My sister—'

'It's not your sister,' Huw reassured quickly.

'Huw, I heard your voice. How nice of you to call.' Lloyd walked down the stairs in shirtsleeves and waistcoat, still fastening cufflinks into his cuffs. 'Come in.' He opened the door to the sitting room. 'Harry, ask Mari if she'll make us some tea, will you, please?'

'I'll leave the tea, if you don't mind, Lloyd.'

'This has to be a first, a policeman refusing tea.' Lloyd waited for Huw to enter the sitting room and followed him.

'As I was just saying to Harry, this isn't a social call, Lloyd. I only wish it were. It's about your brother-in-law, Harry.'

'My brother-in-law,' Harry repeated in surprise. 'All three are upstairs sleeping.'

'The younger two may be, but David isn't. I recognized him from your wedding. I'm sorry I couldn't make Edyth's but—'

'Edyth understood, Huw,' Lloyd interrupted. 'It's not always easy to get leave at short notice.'

'I'll check David's in bed.' Harry went to open the door.

'He's not, Harry,' Huw said firmly. 'We had an attempted suicide in the town last night. It was definitely David. He jumped off the old bridge.'

Harry stared at him in bewilderment. 'David . . . Are you sure?'

'I saw him jump and hauled him out of the river. He picked a bad spot. The water's not deep enough to break a fall at that point. Or drown in,' he added.

'Is he alive?' Lloyd dared ask the question Harry couldn't bring himself even to phrase.

'Just about. He's under guard in the Graig Hospital. He's broken bones in both his legs, ankles and pelvis.' Huw turned his helmet over uneasily in his hands. 'You know my views on charging unsuccessful suicides, Lloyd. If it had been up to me I would have turned a blind eye. But unfortunately I wasn't the only one to see him jump. The sergeant was with me and we both watched David climb up on to the parapet, so there's no question of an accidental fall. When the sergeant told the Superintendent, he insisted that David be formally charged with attempted suicide as soon as he comes round.'

'Has he said anything?'

'He hasn't regained consciousness yet, Harry.' Desperately unhappy at having to deliver the news, Huw continued to look down at the helmet in his hands. 'He's in a bad way. The doctors are not expecting him to come around for at least twenty-four hours.'

'But he will live?' Harry had grown to love his brother-in-law in spite of his obstinacy and occasionally wild ways, but he knew that Mary loved him more.

'That, as the doctor told me this morning, is in the lap of the Gods.'

'Can we at least see him?' Lloyd pleaded.

'Strictly speaking, no. But, as I reminded the Super this morning, procedure demands a formal identification by a close relative.'

Huw didn't have to say any more. Quicker than Harry, Lloyd opened the door and reached for his and Harry's hats and coats.

'If he does come round, and can give us a good reason as to why he should have been on that parapet and jumped from the bridge – anything at all that I can use to placate my superiors – I promise you I'll do everything in my power to get the charges dropped, Lloyd.'

'Thank you, Huw. You're a good friend.' Lloyd set his hand on Huw's shoulder.

'As I said to the sergeant, David's a farm boy. I thought I saw a shadow leave the water and crawl on to the bank when I went in to get him. If he saw a dog and tried to rescue it . . .'

'Being a farm boy, David has a harder attitude than most to animals. Especially ones he doesn't know,' Harry dismissed.

'Oh no, he doesn't,' Lloyd contradicted, instantly understanding what Huw was trying to do.

'But he does—'

'If he was rescuing a dog, Harry, it couldn't be attempted suicide, could it?' Huw always spoke slowly and Harry had often wondered if it was a deliberate attempt to make people think he wasn't very bright. For the first time he realized it was exactly that.

'I'll go and tell Sali where we're going. Harry, you'd better tell Mary what's happened.' When he saw Harry hesitate, Lloyd said, 'Better it comes from you than anyone else.'

'Yes, Dad.' Harry had never been so reluctant to comply with an order from his father. But he went into the hall and walked back up the stairs.

# Chapter 16

'I TOLD ALICE you would be at church this morning,' Florence Slater said triumphantly, gazing at Peter and Edyth before shaking her table napkin out of the 'slipper' the maid had folded it into.

'More fool them.' Alice straightened her fork. 'Theo and I found better things to do the morning after we were married than go to church.'

'We had to attend church anyway,' Peter said quietly, 'so I thought we may as well sit in your pew, Aunt Alice.'

'Vicar or no vicar, I'm sure God would have forgiven you for missing service this one Sunday.' Alice rang the bell for the maid to start serving the meal.

'Alice, that is blasphemous,' Florence reprimanded.

'No, it isn't,' Alice contradicted. 'I'm only applying the philosophy of the good book. God is all-seeing, all-knowing, all-forgiving – or so you keep telling me.'

'Not when it comes to deliberate sins,' Florence lectured.

'I think we've all had enough sermonizing for one day, Flo. Much as I like Reverend Hastings, he goes on and on *and* on. More than half the congregation were sitting with their eyes closed this morning. I'm sure I heard the choirmaster snoring. I was so bored, I caught myself counting the hairs on his head when it fell forward. He has fifty-seven left, and they were so thickly plastered with Macassar Oil it was easy to see every one. Now,' she turned to Edyth and Peter before Florence could protest any further, 'are they looking after you at the hotel?'

'Very well,' Edyth assured her.

'And the food?'

'Dinner last night was wonderful.' Edyth glanced at Peter but he seemed happy to leave the conversation to her.

'Excuse me, madam, ladies, sir.' The maid came in with a tray that held four steaming bowls of cauliflower soup.

'Tell me, what did you eat?' Alice demanded once the soup had been served.

'Oysters followed by roast duck with plum sauce, mashed and roast potatoes, vegetables, cheese soufflé, pears in red wine, cheese, coffee and brandy,' Peter answered.

'And to drink?' Alice's eyes sparkled mischievously.

'You know what we had to drink, Aunt Alice, because I had it on good authority from the wine waiter that you insisted on going down to the cellar to choose the champagne yourself.'

'Champagne?' Florence said. 'I know you gave Peter and Edyth the honeymoon at the Caswell Bay Hotel as a wedding present, Alice, but champagne really is an unwarranted extravagance. Just think what they could have done with the money.'

'Phooey,' Alice dismissed. 'In my experience, unless people are destitute they always find money for essentials.'

'It was very generous of you, Aunt Alice,' Edyth said gratefully, hoping she wouldn't antagonize Peter's mother further by expressing her gratitude.

'Just make sure they serve you the same vintage every night,' Alice warned. 'Don't you dare put up with anything inferior, no matter what they tell you about short supply. It's a jolly good drink. I always share a bottle there with a few members of my bridge club after our monthly inter-club tournaments. They have a decent cellar in the Caswell Bay – provided, of course, you know your wine and aren't prepared to be fobbed off with rubbish. And price is no indication of quality. Remember that, Edyth. Take the trouble to study wines and vintages. It could save you a great deal of money and, more importantly, your palette, in future.'

'I hardly think a vicar's wife is likely to need any knowledge of wines, Alice, expensive or cheap. Peter and Edyth are in no position to stock a cellar.' Florence fragmented her bread roll with a venom that suggested she wished it were her sister she was crumbling.

'You're such a wet blanket, Flo. Vicars might not be the richest of men but I'm sure Peter and Edyth will be able to keep a good table. So, let's hear it.' Alice looked expectantly at Peter. 'What do you two have planned for the week?'

'If the weather holds, walking,' Peter said resolutely.

'And if it doesn't?'

'A trip or two into Swansea,' Edyth said.

'*Disraeli* with George Arliss is showing in the Plaza and there's a musical, *The Whirl of the World*, playing in the Grand this week. I suggest you enjoy yourselves while you have the time to do it. Salt?' Alice handed Edyth the cruet.

'Thank you.' Edyth took it from her.

'Peter should be spending his time preparing for his return to his parish,' Florence said primly.

'I spent the last month preparing for this week's leave of absence, Mother,' Peter reminded her mildly.

'You know what your father used to say. You can never put too much preparation into a sermon. The more effort you expend, the more likely you are to introduce God into the lives of your flock.'

'I remember, Mother.'

'Oh goody, fillets of beef,' Alice cried out childishly, when a second maid brought in the next course, as the first maid cleared away their soup bowls.

'You will come and see us again, Peter?' Florence pressed.

'Of course we will, Mother.'

Edyth's heart sank. Much as she was enjoying the excellent meal and Alice's company, she found her mother-in-law irritating and Peter's meek responses to his mother's edicts even more so.

'When?' Florence demanded.

'We'll call in to say goodbye before we leave at the end of the week.'

Edyth's spirits soared.

'But we have things to talk about, Peter. I've contacted one carrier but I'm by no means certain that he is the cheapest, or the most secure.'

'He comes highly recommended, Flo.' Alice pushed a cut-glass bowl of horseradish in front of Edyth. 'Although I think you're making a terrible mistake. Young people need to be left to get on with their lives. Especially when they're first married.'

'You talk a lot of nonsense at times, Alice.' For the first time since they had sat down to the meal, Peter's mother's voice rose above her customary soft intonation, and acquired a sharper edge. 'I have a great deal of experience at managing a parish. I helped Arnold run Mumbles smoothly for over twenty years. Both Peter and Edyth will find my help invaluable.'

'Am I missing something?' Edyth set her knife and fork on her plate and gazed at her mother-in-law.

'I am going to move in with you and Peter, Edyth. Where else would a mother live other than with her son and daughter-in-law? Didn't he tell you?'

The ward sister showed Harry, Huw and Lloyd into a side ward where David lay, white-faced, in an iron-framed hospital bed. He was so still that Harry leaned over to check his brother-in-law was still breathing.

'Constable Davies.' A uniformed sergeant rose from an upright chair placed discreetly behind the door.

'Sir, this is the family of the patient, come to formally identify him.' Huw hung back behind Lloyd and Harry.

'Is this man David Ellis?' The sergeant removed a notebook from his tunic pocket and looked to Harry.

'He is,' Harry asserted.

'You will visit the station and sign a statement to that effect?'

'Of course.' Harry bent even closer to David and whispered, 'Davy, it's me, Harry.'

'He's heavily sedated, Mr Evans. He can't hear you.' The sister lifted David's arm from the bed and took his pulse.

'Can we talk to his doctor?' Lloyd asked.

'Doctor John won't be here again until tomorrow morning, unless we have an emergency. The patient's broken bones have been set.' She indicated the cages that had been placed over David's legs, ankles and hips to take the weight of the blankets that covered him to his chin. 'We'll take further X-rays in a few weeks to see if any of the damage is permanent. Until then, the only prescribed treatment is care and rest.'

Refusing to be deterred by the sister, who was already holding the door open to show them out, Harry again whispered, 'Davy.'

David's eyelids flickered.

Encouraged, Harry repeated, 'Davy.'

David opened his eyes, only to close them before focusing.

'Can I stay with him?' Harry pleaded.

'Visiting hours are strictly regulated, Mr Evans. One hour on Sunday afternoon and half an hour on Wednesday evening. For close family only. No more than two visitors allowed for each patient,' the sister recited mechanically.

'Please,' Harry looked pointedly at the sergeant, 'I won't disturb David or anyone else on the ward. I'd hate for him to wake surrounded by strangers.'

'Rules are made for a reason, Mr Evans, and you have been here quite long enough,' the sister declared finally.

'I'll take over from you if you like, sir,' Huw said to the sergeant.

'I thought you were off duty in an hour, Davies.'

Huw shrugged his shoulders. 'I'm a friend of the family.'

The sergeant didn't argue. Huw Davies was a bachelor who lived with his elderly father, a retired policeman. His brothers had all moved away from the town and his only sister, a young war widow, was fiercely independent and known to resent Huw's interference in her children's upbringing. Consequently, the constable had acquired the reputation of being a soft touch when it came to swapping shifts or taking over from another officer who had a personal emergency.

The sergeant left the chair. 'Be my guest, Davies, but there won't be anyone here to relieve you until two o'clock this afternoon.'

'That's all right, sir, I didn't have anything planned for today.' Huw took his place.

'Not even sleep?' the sergeant enquired drily. 'Goodbye, gentlemen. I hope the young man makes a recovery.'

'Thank you.' Harry watched the officer walk down the corridor.

Ignoring the nurse, he leaned over David and whispered his name again.

David could hear Harry calling him. He was also aware of people and movement in the background and, from the distant clatter of crockery, and footsteps echoing over hard floors, he knew he was in a strange place. But he preferred to remain in the grey, fuzzy cocoon of semi-consciousness that enveloped him, than blink his way upwards to the light – and pain. He was aware of hurting, although his body felt strangely numbed.

'Davy, come on, I know you can hear me, open your eyes.'

Harry's voice penetrated the cocoon and David remembered standing on the bridge – and jumping. Strangely dispassionate, he wondered if he were dead. But if that were the case, then why was Harry with him?

'I really must ask you to stop trying to rouse the patient, Mr Evans,' the sister protested.

'His eyes are flickering,' Harry demurred. 'Davy . . .'

'Edyth,' David mumbled.

'She's fine, Davy,' Harry murmured, with a backward glance at Huw and his father.

'Tell her . . . tell her I love her, Harry . . .'

'The dog's fine, son, I saw it leave the river,' Huw said loudly for the benefit of the sister, who was still holding the door open.

'The patient needs quiet.' The sister exercised the authority of her position. 'And no more questions, constable, not until the doctor gives you permission to talk to him.'

'Yes, sister.' Huw removed his helmet and stroked his bald head.

'David's in good hands.' Lloyd nodded to Harry, who left the room.

'Thank you, Huw,' Lloyd said gratefully. 'We really appreciate you taking over here.'

'If he comes round again while I'm here, I'll call in and see you on my way home.'

'I'll tell Mari to keep the kettle on the boil and bake a cake.'

'That will be worth calling in for.' Huw smiled at the sister, but she ignored him and swept Lloyd out of the room.

'So this is where you're hiding yourself, dear.' Alice Beynon pressed one of the brandies she had carried outside the house into Edyth's hand.

'No, thank you, Aunt Alice.' After Peter's mother had announced that she was moving in with them, Edyth had left the dining room. She knew that if she stayed, she would only say something that would upset Peter's mother – and probably Peter. She was beginning to wonder if she knew the first thing about him after hearing that he had invited his mother to live with them without consulting her.

One of Mari's often repeated maxims during her childhood had been, 'If you say nothing you can't be asked to take it back later.' So, she had simply risen from the table, walked out of the room and, feeling the need for fresh air, made her way into the garden.

'You've had a shock, Edyth, you need it,' Alice persisted.

'If I drink that, I'll be squiffy for the rest of the afternoon,' Edyth protested.

'That might be the best state to be in. You can't think too hard or get really angry when you're squiffy.' Alice walked over to a bench set in a sheltered spot overlooking her rose garden. 'Come and sit down, dear. I spend hours here in summer when the blooms are out.'

'It is lovely,' Edyth complimented absently.

The bushes had been gorgeous in July and one or two withered blooms still clung to the branches, relics that Alice's gardener referred to as the 'ghosts of summer past', but the skeletal trees and shrivelled, blackened leaves were hardly lovely now. However, Alice allowed Edyth's comment to pass.

'Peter didn't tell you that his mother was moving in with you?'

'Not a word.' Edyth sat on the bench and stared blindly down at the brandy.

'What would you have said if he had asked you?' Alice pulled a pack of small, thin black cigars from her pocket. She offered Edyth one. Edyth shook her head. 'Go on, it will annoy Flo – and Peter,' she coaxed.

Edyth took one. 'Before I met Mrs Slater' – after the way Peter's mother had made the announcement that she was moving into the vicarage in Tiger Bay with them, Edyth couldn't bring herself to call her Mother' – I probably would have agreed. After all, she's alone and she's lost everything: her home, her husband and, to some extent, even her son.'

'Rubbish, sons grow up and marry; it's what normal men do. Although I admit I never expected to see the day that Peter would take a wife. If they try to hang on to their mother's apron strings they're laughed at by every right-thinking person. Flo has me, and she's hardly roughing it in the workhouse,' Alice pointed out caustically.

'Your house is beautiful,' Edyth complimented.

'It's taken a lot of time and money to get it this way,' Alice dismissed the subject. 'But how do you feel about having Flo to live with you now that you have met her? The truth, mind.'

'I just wish Peter had consulted me.' Edyth sipped the brandy. She found it warming, given the chill in the air. 'I thought the vicarage was to be my home, mine and Peter's. It was selfish of me, but it never crossed my mind that Peter's mother would want to move in with us. Peter speaks so often about your generosity towards her, I assumed she was settled here.' She suddenly realized that, for all her apparent sympathy, Alice was Florence's sister. Had she said too much?

'Flo has never settled with me,' Alice divulged. She produced an elaborately embossed gold lighter, lit Edyth's cigar and then her own. She saw Edyth looking at it. 'This was my husband, Theo's. But he didn't buy it and it wasn't to his taste.' She fingered the bull embossed on the front. 'The managers of his butchers' shops, God bless them, clubbed together and gave it to him on his fortieth birthday. Little did they, or I, think that it would be his last.' She returned the lighter to her pocket. 'Theo didn't like Florence, either – or Peter's father, come to that.'

'How did you . . .' Edyth stammered into silence.

'It's as plain as the very pretty nose on your face, my dear. But don't worry; your secret is safe with me. Or at least, as safe as it can be, given that some looks speak a thousand words. And, to your credit, you gave Flo one of those before you left the dining room. Flo never has been what you might call lovable.' Alice set her brandy glass on the ground.

They sat in silence for a few seconds. Then they heard Peter talking to his mother. His voice was low, reproachful; hers was soft, languid.

'You knew that I wanted to tell Edyth in my own time, Mother.'

'When, Peter? I am moving in with you next week . . . '

'They're in the sitting room,' Alice whispered. 'Would you like to see my greenhouse, Edyth?' she asked in a louder voice. 'It's not at its best at this time of year, but the gardener has just planted the Christmas roses and they're coming well. Not in bloom yet, but the buds are plentiful.'

'I'd love to.' Wanting to get as far away from Peter and his mother as possible, Edyth followed Alice to the back of her house. Her 'greenhouse' was the largest conservatory Edyth had seen. Only one small area had been given over to seedlings. Half a dozen chairs, two chaises longues and a bamboo table in Raj-style cane stood in the centre, surrounded by pots of rubber plants, geraniums and trailing vines.

'I confess I'm to blame for Flo moving in with you, dear. I haven't put myself out or changed my ways to accommodate her since the day she arrived here. In fact, truth be known, I've gone out of my way to annoy her. Revenge for her sanctimonious attitude towards me and Theo over the years.' She drew on her cigar and blew a puff of blue smoke in the direction of one of the Christmas rose bushes. 'Good – or rather bad – for the greenfly; they hate cigar smoke, which gives me an excuse to light up in here,' she explained briefly. 'I know from the frequent and tedious sermons Flo has positively relished giving me over the years that she believes cards, alcohol, tobacco and novels, with the exception of a few – very few – classics, to be the work of the devil.'

'I remember you mentioning that you belong to a bridge club,' Edyth recalled.

'Not just belong, dear. I insisted they meet here twice a week after Flo moved in. Before that we used to meet in an upstairs room in the Bush Hotel. Although we still hold the larger tournaments in the Caswell Bay Hotel, which is why they know me so well there. I enjoy planning our buffets with the manager. He and I have very similar tastes. Then there's drink. Theo always insisted on having a good bottle of wine with dinner and a brandy afterwards, and I saw no reason to change the tradition after he was buried or when Flo moved in.'

'Peter drinks wine.' Edyth drew on her cigar. The tobacco was stronger than she'd expected and she coughed.

'Put it out it if you don't like it, dear. They are an acquired taste. And yes, I was successful in developing Peter's taste when it came to alcohol, but not in all things,' Alice mused. 'But to get back to Flo, God only knows where she got her sanctimonious, holier-than-thou attitude from. Listen to me blaspheme, that's something else I do to annoy her, but sometimes I think Flo was born pious. She hates me calling her Flo, by the way, because it reminds her of our working-class upbringing, which is why I never call her anything else. But she can hardly argue with an older sister, especially one whose charity she's been living on for the last fourteen years. Our parents were shopkeepers. They weren't religious, far from it. Our father owned a tobacconist and we all worked in it. My mother, Flo and me. That's where I met my husband.'

'And where Peter's mother met his father?' Edyth asked.

'Good Lord, no. Peter's father never allowed wine, tobacco, spirits or, I suspect, Flo's lips to touch his. As I was saying, Flo always did have a bit of a religious bent. When she was thirteen she developed a crush on a Sunday School teacher. She started to dress like her, talk like her and, I believe, even think like her.' Alice finished her brandy. 'She started going to church three times every Sunday. Morning and evening services and Sunday school. At fifteen she became a Sunday school teacher herself. Peter's father was appointed curate to the parish and she fell head over heels in love with him. It wasn't surprising. He was the handsomest man you ever saw and every unmarried girl in the church was after him.

The only mystery was why he picked Flo. She never had great looks, but she did know how to pray. And he did have an odd way about him. Nothing you could put your finger on – just odd, not normal. You know what I mean?'

Edyth didn't but she nodded anyway. 'Does Peter take after his father?' she asked curiously.

'In looks and unfortunately, in my opinion, his dedication to the Church in Wales. He was a bright boy. He could have done well in any field he chose – medicine, the law, even the army – but Flo wouldn't hear of him entering anything except the Church. And Peter's biggest fault is a tendency to take too much notice of his mother. But in all fairness, he doesn't appear to have inherited his father's arrogance. Reverend Slater senior would have been very shocked and annoyed if he reached Heaven and discovered that the Good Lord hadn't set aside a particularly saintly and holy cloud just for him. But for all his self-importance, Peter's father never had the gumption to stand up to Flo. Sadly, Peter's just as lacking in that department.'

'But Peter's parents did love one another?'

'I think they did, in their own peculiar fashion.' Alice ground out her cigar and immediately lit another. 'I was married by the time Flo started courting. Every time I saw Mam and Dad they complained that all Flo could talk about was Reverend Slater. My parents weren't too happy about it, but they couldn't stop them from getting engaged on Flo's eighteenth birthday. That was when Flo decided her future husband's vocation was hers. Eventually she wore Mam and Dad down. They married when Flo was nineteen. But Peter didn't put in an appearance for over twenty years. That's why he's so old-fashioned in his outlook. Old parents bring up old children, or so I've always thought.'

The description of Peter's parents' courtship was so similar to hers and Peter's, Edyth couldn't help thinking that history had repeated itself. 'I've often considered some of Peter's ways Victorian, but he told me that his parents were middle-aged when he was born.'

Alice laid a dry, arthritic hand over Edyth's. 'You can count on one ally in the family, my dear. You have any trouble with Flo, come to me and I'll do what I can to sort her out.'

'I couldn't possibly.'

'Yes, you could.' Alice rested her cigar on the amethyst ashtray on the table. 'I've tried every ruse I can think of and I couldn't sway Flo an inch from her determination to move in with you. But I'll do whatever it takes to stop her making your life a misery. And mark my words, she will if you let her. She's a deceptively soft-spoken, tyrannical hypochondriac who likes to have the whole world running round after her. Start as you mean to go on, dear. Be firm, don't put up with her nonsense. And if things get too much for you, come and stay here, or invite me down for a visit.'

'I couldn't impose.'

'Yes, you could.' The old lady's eyes sparkled with mischief. 'I can imagine just as many ailments as Flo when the mood takes me. And I'm just as capable of demanding my nephew's hospitality as a right. Now,' she leaned heavily on her cane and hauled herself upright, 'let's go in, finish lunch, drink coffee and eat petits fours as though all's right with the world. That will throw Flo. She likes nothing better than to create a scene, then sit back and enjoy it, while pretending she had absolutely nothing to do with instigating it.'

'I knew David was fond of Edyth but I had no idea he'd do anything like that,' Mary murmured when Harry sat on the edge of her bed and watched her feed their new son. 'Are you sure that he jumped deliberately? That he didn't fall?'

'We're sure, love,' Harry broke in softly. 'Huw Davies and another officer saw him climb on to the parapet. And it was Huw who fished him out of the river.'

'But David is going to be all right, isn't he?' She fought back tears as she looked to Harry for reassurance.

'I told you he came round when we were there. He has a lot of broken bones and he doesn't look too good now, but you know David. He's as strong as a Welsh pit pony and he's come through worse.' Harry recalled the beating David had survived when he'd been forced to work on another farm before he and Mary had married and he had managed to secure her family home.

'David kept telling me that he didn't want our farm. I thought it was a phase he'd grow out of, but now this . . .'

'You're not to blame for what David did, Mary,' Harry said firmly. 'It's not your fault any more than it's Edyth's for marrying Peter Slater. We all knew David was fond of her but he's only eighteen, and I doubt he's seen her more than a dozen times in the four years since we married, apart from that week she spent with us three years ago. And that's no basis for marriage. If you want my opinion I think he fell in love with the idea of being in love, not Edyth.'

'We didn't see that much of one another before we married, Harry,' she reminded him.

'Ah, but it was the quality of the sightings.'

She was too upset about David even to listen. 'I was stupid to try to keep David at the farm. Don't you see? He fell in love with Edyth because she's the first girl he's really known who's the same age as him. If I'd let him travel as he wanted to do, met more people . . .' She looked down at the baby at her breast. 'No matter what you say, Harry, it is my fault. I put the family farm before David . . .' Her voice broke as tears welled in her eyes again.

'I don't want to hear another word like that from you, darling.' Harry cradled both her and the baby in his arms. 'For the last time: it is not your fault. David is the one who climbed on that bridge and jumped. He probably drank too much at the wedding, got maudlin, went out for a walk and did something stupid on impulse because he wasn't capable of thinking straight.'

'If he recovers—'

'*When* he recovers,' Harry corrected emphatically, 'we'll talk to him.'

'And let him do whatever he wants?' she pleaded.

'Within reason. I draw the line at letting him join the Foreign Legion.'

'Harry—'

'Sorry, darling, bad joke.'

'Martha, Matthew and Luke need to be told.' Mary sniffed back her tears.

'My mother told them that David's in hospital after a fall. They don't need to know any more for the present.'

'And Edyth? She's going to feel dreadful.'

'My father and Uncle Joey have already left for Swansea. We talked about it, and decided it was too much of a risk to try to keep it from her. People are always travelling from here down to the coast and Dad didn't want to tell her on the telephone. So you see,' he forced a smile, 'you have nothing to worry about except yourself and little Will there. My mother and the girls are enjoying fussing over Ruth. Martha, Matthew and Luke are having the time of their lives tearing around the park with Bella and Toby, and Mr Jones is running the farm like clockwork. He told me so on the telephone not half an hour ago, when I rang him to warn him not to expect us back for a few weeks.' Mr Jones was the farm manager they had employed to 'help' David. 'The time to concern yourself with David is when we manage to get him home. He's going to need a lot of nursing and I have a feeling that he isn't going to be the easiest of patients to look after.'

Harry kept the police threat to prosecute David to himself. If Huw Davies's ruse worked, Mary need never know about it. If it didn't, David's future didn't bear thinking about. Used to living outdoors, prison would crush his spirit and finish what he had begun when he had taken that leap from the bridge.

'Why didn't you tell me that your mother was going to move in with us?' Edyth had waited to broach the subject until she and Peter were walking through Singleton Park on their way from his aunt's house to Mumbles. The clouds they had seen over the sea early that morning had blown inland, darkening the sky and threatening rain. Alice had offered them the services of her chauffeur to drive back them back to the hotel. But, wanting privacy to talk, Edyth had insisted they walk.

'I was going to mention it,' he mumbled shame-facedly.

'When?' she questioned evenly.

'Some time this week. It wasn't the sort of thing I wanted to put in a letter.'

'I can understand that it needed some discussion, which is why I'm unhappy about the way I found out about it.' She took a deep breath and braced herself. 'Was it your mother's idea or yours?'

'It was always . . . sort of assumed between us that when I had my own place she would leave Aunt Alice and live with me.'

'To keep house?'

'If you had told me when I received my posting to Pontypridd that I would be married by October I would never have believed it, so the answer to that is yes. Probably to keep house for me.'

'So, you knew that your mother intended to move in with us the day you came to Pontypridd and bought my wedding and engagement rings?'

'Yes, but we were having lunch with the Bishop and Reverend Price. Edyth, you're not unhappy, you're angry.'

'Yes, I am.' She stopped and looked at him. 'I am angry that you didn't consult me.'

'Mother's frail. You've met Aunt Alice, heard the way she talks. She likes company and an active social life. Mother is more refined; she prefers to spend her time contemplating, reading and meditating. You won't even know she's in the house, I promise you. And don't forget, we'll both be busy with parish business. Mother can keep an eye on Mrs Mack and see that the house is run properly.' He tossed off the last remark as an afterthought.

'Knowing that Mrs Mack is a poor cook and, from the state of the house when I saw it, a dismal housekeeper, you told her that we would keep her on?' she asked incredulously.

'Yes.'

'I was only there for a short time but the vicarage was dirty, Peter. There was dust everywhere and the tiles in the passage looked as though they hadn't been washed in months.'

'She was busy looking after Reverend Richards. I could hardly throw her out, Edyth. She's been at the vicarage for forty years. And—'

'And?' she pressed, furious that he had not only arranged for his

269

mother to move in with them but also engaged an incompetent housekeeper.

'. . . And she's a friend of the Bishop's wife's cousin,' he finished lamely. Large, fat raindrops fell heavily from the sky. He opened his umbrella and held it over her. 'We can stop in the Mermaid Hotel for tea, if you like.'

She thought of the last time she had been in the Mermaid Hotel with her parents. 'No, thank you,' she said abruptly.

Offering her an olive branch, he said, 'We can go anywhere you like, Edyth. I'm sorry. I should have been more open with you.'

'Yes, you should have.' She pulled her hat down as far as it would go to protect her hair. 'Did you think that I'd refuse to allow your mother to live with us?'

'I hoped you wouldn't.'

Forced to accept that Mrs Slater had outmanoeuvred her, she resolved to make the best of the situation. 'Peter, she's your mother. Of course we can offer her a home as she has none.' She took his arm. 'Let's go to the George Hotel. And, if this rain doesn't let up, we can get a taxi from there back to the Caswell Bay.'

'Thank you.' He kissed her cheek.

'Just one thing, Peter,' she clung to his arm as he headed for a belt of trees that offered a little shelter as the downpour escalated into a cloudburst, 'from this moment on, we discuss everything that affects our married life.'

'I promise, Edyth.' He clutched her gloved hand. 'I'm sorry. I know it's not much of an excuse, but I've been a bachelor for so long, I'm not used to considering the wishes of others. Have a little patience with me?'

She quickened her pace to match his. They had what was left of this week and one whole week to put the vicarage in order before his mother descended on them. And if she took the opposite tack to Aunt Alice and went out of her way *not* to annoy Florence Slater, perhaps she could make a friend of her, after all.

Even as she formulated the thought, she suspected that putting her idea into practice was going to be difficult, especially as she doubted that Peter's mother would make any concessions to her position as Peter's wife and mistress of the vicarage.

The clerk left his reception desk and met Edyth and Peter at the door of the hotel. 'Reverend Slater, Mrs Slater, two gentlemen have called to see you; they insisted on waiting. I showed them into the Residents' Lounge.'

'Did they say what they wanted?'

Edyth didn't wait for the clerk to answer Peter. She ran into the lounge, tripped in the doorway and, to her astonishment, saw her father and Uncle Joey sitting at a table with pints of beer in front of them.

'Falling over as usual, I see, Edyth.' Joey left his seat and kissed her cheek. 'Hello, Peter.' He shook Peter's hand when he joined them.

'Dad? Uncle Joey? What on earth are you doing here?' Edyth looked at her father.

'What's wrong?'

'Sit down, Edie. You too, Peter.' Lloyd closed the door and told them in as few words as possible what had happened to David.

Peter sat, outwardly at least, unperturbed, but Edyth clutched her handkerchief to her mouth as her eyes rounded in horror.

'You really think David tried to kill himself because I married Peter?' she asked her father.

'No,' Lloyd assured her. 'It's as Harry said. David's spent practically all his life on the farm. He doesn't know many people and, as a result, he put far more store by the friendship you offered him than you did, that is all.'

'How is Mary taking it?' Peter asked.

Lloyd turned to his son-in-law. 'As you'd expect, Peter, badly. She and David are very close. But we have to concentrate on the good news. David spoke and recognized Harry when we went to see him this morning. He's in excellent hands and everything that can be, is being done for him.'

'We came because we didn't want you reading about it in the newspapers or hearing it from someone else,' Joey explained.

'People from Pontypridd visit Swansea all the time, commercial travellers and the like. You know how people gossip.'

'I do, and I'm glad you came to tell me.' Edyth clasped her father's hand.

'Are you staying the night? Because if you are, I'll get you a room.' Peter left his chair.

'No, we both have to work in the morning.' Lloyd glanced at his wristwatch. 'The trains leave Swansea for Cardiff on the half-hour.'

Edyth glanced at the grandmother clock in the corner of the room. The hands pointed to five o'clock. 'Give me half an hour to pack and I'll come with you, Dad.'

'Don't be silly, Edyth, this is your honeymoon,' Lloyd emphasized. 'I would never have come here if I thought you'd interrupt it.'

'No, Mr Evans, Edyth is right,' Peter said to Lloyd and Joey's surprise. 'Edyth's place is with her family at a time like this. I know her. She won't rest a moment until she sees Harry and Mary. And David, if that's possible. And, as her husband, my place is at her side. I'll go and book out of the hotel and telephone my mother and my aunt to let them know we're leaving. I'll just say that a member of your family has been taken ill, Edyth.' He clasped her shoulder.

She laid her hand over his. 'Thank you,' she said gratefully.

'You certainly won't be able to see David for a while, Edie,' Lloyd warned, recalling the ward sister's attitude.

'But I will be able to see Mary and Harry, Dad, and I need to. If you won't wait for us, I'll only catch a later train.'

'I don't doubt you will, Edie,' Lloyd agreed wryly. He looked from Peter to Edyth, and recognized the tell-tale signs of obstinacy on his daughter's face. 'Very well. Both of you go and pack, and tell the hotel and Peter's mother that you're leaving. In the meantime I'll order some sandwiches.'

'We had a very good lunch, Dad.' Edyth went to the door.

'You might have, miss,' Joey said, 'but we certainly didn't.'

# Chapter 17

BELLA CARRIED A CLEAN NIGHTDRESS, vest and nappy into Harry and Mary's room. Believing herself to be alone, she lifted them to her nose and sniffed them before laying them on the end of the bed.

'Let me guess, they're warm from the airing cupboard and scented with lavender water.'

Bella turned and saw Edyth curled on the window seat. 'I didn't see you there. Five years ago you would have jumped out and shouted boo to scare the living daylights out of me.'

'Ah, but now I'm all grown up.'

'And married,' Bella reminded.

'Do they smell of lavender water?'

'Of course.' Bella straightened the sleeve of the long cotton and lace nightdress.

'The smell of our clean nighties when we were little is one of my happiest memories. Bedtime, cocoa, cheese sandwiches and stories read by Mam or Dad.'

'More often by Mam than Dad. I must ask Mari exactly how much lavender water she sprinkles over the laundry so I can get ours to smell the same way.' Bella sat in the nursing chair Harry had carried up from their mother's study. 'You all packed?'

'Just about.'

'Some honeymoon you and Peter have had,' Bella sympathized.

'I would have had a wretched time if I'd stayed in Swansea. I'd have worried about what was happening here the whole time,' Edyth answered. 'And, as Peter said, we can honeymoon any time. It was more important that I spend this week with Mary and Harry. I feel awful—'

'Don't, and stop it,' Bella broke in. 'We've talked David's stupidity over until I'm sick of it. I agree with Harry, he must have been drunk to do what he did. And you heard Dad and Harry when they came back from the Infirmary on Wednesday. David is going to recover.'

'Yes, but it's going to take months and he may never walk the same—'

'But thanks to Uncle Huw, he won't be going to gaol,' Bella said strongly.

'I suppose that's something,' Edyth allowed grudgingly, although she was amazed that anyone, let alone Huw's superiors in the police force, had believed that David had jumped off the old bridge to rescue a dog. If he really had seen one struggling in the water – which she doubted – it would have made more sense to run down the bank and wade in, not jump off a high bridge.

'And here's our gorgeous little man.' Bella gave Edyth a warning glance to drop the subject, before swooping down on Harry as he carried in Will, who was damp and wrapped in a towel.

Harry set the baby on the bed and tickled him under the chin. I'll leave you two to adore my son. Just make sure Mary doesn't do too much.' He looked sternly at his wife who walked in with Ruth. 'I still don't think that you should be out of bed, let alone bathing Will and playing with Ruth.'

Mary's response was to laugh and kiss him. 'Go on, off to work in the store.'

'You will be back for lunch?' Edyth asked Harry.

'I wouldn't miss your farewell lunch for the world, sis. Ruthie darling,' Harry lifted his daughter into his arms, kissed her and deposited her on the bed next to Will, 'look after your brother and Mam for me while I've gone, will you?'

She wrapped her arms around his neck and clung to him.

'You've soaked my waistcoat, little miss. I think you bathed yourself as well as Will,' he complained.

'I'll change her. Come to Auntie Bella, Ruthie.'

'And I'll take these soggy clothes down to Mari to wash.' Edyth took the frock and vest Bella peeled off Ruth.

'She's only had them on five minutes.' Mary rubbed a stain on the front of the bodice, smearing it. She sniffed it. 'Chocolate?' She looked from Harry to Ruth. 'And who gave you chocolate?'

Ruth huddled close to Bella, stuck her thumb in her mouth and muttered, Can't 'member.'

'Can't 'member indeed,' Mary smiled. 'It was Daddy, wasn't it?'

Ruth giggled.

'I'm innocent,' Harry protested. 'Try Glyn.'

'Off with you.' Mary pushed him to the door. 'You're cluttering up the place.'

'See you at lunchtime, darling.' Harry wrapped his arms around Mary, lifted her off her feet and kissed her long and lovingly.

'What a sight, and before lunch, too,' Bella teased.

'Retaliation for the displays you and Toby subject us to. Mary and I may have been married for four years but we're not past it — yet.'

Bella set Ruth on the bed. 'Two minutes and I'll be back with a clean frock, poppet.'

'Pink one?' Ruth asked hopefully.

'If there's one clean.'

Mary saw Harry to the door. Edyth waited with Ruth and Will until Mary returned, then she went out on the landing. Bella hadn't got as far as Maggie's room where Ruth's cot had been placed the day Will had been born. She was standing in the doorway on tip-toe, her arms wrapped around Toby's neck, her lips glued to his.

Edyth tried to creep past but Toby saw her. He lifted an eyebrow but made no attempt to release Bella, although he did stop kissing her.

'Sorry we're behaving as if Bella and I are the honeymooners, not you and Peter, Edyth. Just so you know, we're not trying to steal your thunder.'

'You're not,' Edyth muttered in embarrassment.

'You'll be back for Edyth and Peter's goodbye lunch?' Bella asked Toby.

'I will, Bopsy. But much as I'd like to stay and keep you

company this morning, I have to go and work on the portrait of Mr Moore's dog.'

Bella frowned. 'I thought you were painting his granddaughter.'

'I am,' he grinned.

'Just be careful someone other than Edyth doesn't hear you calling her that. If they do, it might be the last commission you get from the Moores.' The goodbye kiss she gave him escalated into another full embrace.

Edyth ran down the stairs and saw her father at the front door showing out Huw Davies.

'Hello, Uncle Huw. I didn't know you were here.'

'And hello and goodbye, Edyth.' He shook Lloyd's hand. 'You'll remember what I said, Lloyd. There's no truth in the rumour.'

'I'll remember, Huw.'

'What rumour?' Edyth asked her father as they watched Huw walk down the drive.

'That his superiors told him he'd never be promoted for sticking to his story that David jumped into the river after a dog.' He closed the door.

'It's not true?' she asked.

'I'm afraid it is, my sweet,' Lloyd said thoughtfully. 'Huw Davies has sacrificed a great deal for this family.'

'For his principles.' Sali came out of the sitting room and took Lloyd's arm. 'Ruth's clothes?' she asked Edyth, looking at the bundle in her hand.

'She helped Harry and Mary bath Will. I'm taking them to Mari.' Edyth glanced back down the passage when she reached the kitchen door. Her father's arms were locked around her mother's waist and they were kissing just the way Bella and Toby had been.

Wondering if every man in the world was a romantic except for her husband, she flung the kitchen door open only to hit Peter, who was coming out, on the nose.

He grimaced in pain and wiped his nose with his handkerchief to check it wasn't bleeding. 'Is there a fire, Edyth?'

Edyth! He never called her anything except Edyth — not 'sweetheart' as her father did her mother, or 'darling' as Harry usually addressed Mary, or 'Bopsy' as Toby had nicknamed Bella – not that she would have particularly wanted to be called 'Bopsy', which reminded her of the dolls she and Belle had christened.

'No, there isn't. Sorry, I didn't know you were behind the door.' Feeling her temper rising for no good reason, she handed Ruth's clothes to Mari. 'Ruth helped to bath Will.'

'So I see.' Mari shook out the frock. 'And she managed to spread that chocolate Harry gave her all over herself.'

'Harry blamed Glyn.'

'He gave it to both of them.' Mari ran a sink full of cold water and plunged the clothes in it. 'The parents make more work than the children in this house,' she grumbled good-naturedly.

Peter held up a tin. 'I'm taking one of the fruit cakes you made yesterday down to Reverend and Mrs Price.'

'Good idea. A goodbye present and a thank you for their dinner last night, all in one.' Edyth hadn't eaten much of the dinner but Peter had out of politeness, and suffered for it afterwards with a severe case of indigestion.

He pecked her cheek. 'See you at lunch, Edyth. I've finished my packing and locked my case.'

'Wonders will never cease, a man who can fold his own shirts,' Mari mused.

'I've been a bachelor for so long, Mari, it's nice to have a woman fussing over me.' Peter winked at the elderly housekeeper, and Edyth felt suddenly, unaccountably and ludicrously jealous. 'You'll remember to finish your packing, Edyth?'

'I will, and I'll be ready to catch the two-thirty train, Peter.'

'Good, see you at lunch.' He opened the door warily and walked down the passage.

'You and Belle up in Mary's room?' Mari asked.

'Yes.'

'I'll bring up tea and some of my spice biscuits.'

'That would be nice.'

'What would be nice, Edie?' Sali walked in.

'Elevenses in Mary's room,' Edyth explained.

Sali slipped her arm around Edyth's waist. 'I was just saying to your father that I'm going to miss you girls when you go to Cardiff and Mary and Harry go back to the farm.'

'Surely Harry and Mary won't be leaving for a while? Will is only just a week old and David's in hospital.'

'Harry said they'll stay for at least another week but it will soon pass. Lunch under control, Mari, as if I need to ask?'

'All under control, Miss Sali, you can go to the shop with Harry with a clear conscience. It will be on the table at one sharp so the newlyweds can leave shortly after two.'

'See you then, darling.' Sali kissed Edyth and received a hug from her daughter in return. Sali frowned. Was it her imagination or was Edyth's embrace more intense than usual?

Edyth saw her mother and Harry out then walked back upstairs. Ruth was giggling and pretending to run away from Bella, who was having no success in dressing her.

'Mari is bringing up elevenses and- spice biscuits,' she announced, 'but only for little girls who are dressed.'

Ruth ran to Bella and obediently held her arms up straight. As Mary was busy with the baby, Edyth returned to the window seat. As soon as Ruth was dressed she left Bella and climbed on Edyth's lap.

'There's no use looking in my pocket,' Edyth said to her niece, 'I haven't any hidden chocolate like your father.'

'I knew Harry had given it to her.' Mary tucked the nightdress around Will's legs.

'And Glyn apparently, but Mari said Harry waited until after breakfast.'

Bella sat in the nursing chair. 'As Will's fed and bathed, can I nurse him to sleep?' she asked Mary.

'Practising?' Mary handed him over.

'I hope, although there's no sign of any babies as yet.'

'You've only been married two months.' Edyth watched the raindrops beating down on the window pane. It was a grey, overcast, miserable day, and she couldn't help thinking that it matched her mood.

'Just as long as you don't beat me to it, Edyth.' Bella glanced across at her sister.

Edyth buried her face in Ruth's hair so Mary and Bella wouldn't see the expression on her face. Peter had behaved no differently in her parents' house than he had in the hotel, insisting that he wanted to leave the beginning of their married life until they were in their own home. She was beginning to find his behaviour not only frustrating but infuriating.

'You look very pensive for a bride, Edyth,' Mary commented.

'She's thinking that as of today she's going to be a vicar's wife and she's dreading it,' Bella suggested.

'Are you dreading it?' Mary asked in concern.

'Not at all,' Edyth refuted. 'From what Peter told me, the parishioners are all lovely people.'

'There's bound to be at least one old bat, like Mrs Hopkins, intent on making the new vicar's wife hell just because she's young.' Bella stroked the baby's cheek with her little finger. 'But if you have any trouble, just let us know and Toby and I will come down and sort them out for you.'

'And how would you do that?' Edyth laughed.

'You'd be surprised,' Bella said darkly.

'I think I would.'

'Want to see Mari.' Ruth climbed off Edyth's lap and peered at her brother, who was already sleeping soundly in Bella's arms, before going to the door.

'No more chocolate, Ruthie,' Mary warned.

Ruth shook her head

'Or more than one biscuit or you won't eat your lunch.'

Ruth nodded solemnly; Edyth opened the door and let her out of the room.

'Here, Edie, I'm being selfish.' Bella left the chair and handed her the sleeping baby.' You can have a last cuddle. I'll be able to nurse him tomorrow and the day after.'

'Thank you.' Edyth took the chair Bella had vacated.

'So how is married life, Edyth?' Bella took Edyth's place on the window seat.

'Don't embarrass the poor girl.' Mary was disconcerted at the way Harry's sisters discussed the most personal and intimate aspects of their lives. 'We all know what married life is like.'

'Yes, we do,' Bella smiled broadly. 'I knew it was going to be good, but not this good. Sex on tap any time of the day or night – I'm sorry, Edie, I didn't think. I can wander into Toby's studio and interrupt him any time, but you can hardly do that if Peter is talking to his parishioners. Not unless you want to give them an eyeful, that is.'

'I'm not sure what our life in the vicarage is going to be like – yet,' Edyth murmured. The tone of her voice prompted Bella to change the subject.

'Another month and we'll be in our own house. Harry can have his back – that's if you and he want to move in there. I'm sorry, Mary, that was tactless of me but I thought you might want to be near to David, that's if they keep him in the Infirmary that long.'

'I do want to be near him.' Mary's face fell. 'I can't wait to see him but the doctor won't allow me to visit while I'm nursing Will for fear of picking up an infection in the ward and, as there's little likelihood of David coming out for a month, I suppose I'll have to content myself with writing letters and sending messages via Harry.'

Realizing she'd upset Mary, Bella changed the topic of conversation again. 'So, Edyth, tell us: which side of the bed does Peter sleep on?'

'The right.'

'As you look at the bed or as you're lying in it.'

'Belle . . .' Edyth didn't bother to conceal her irritation.

'Haven't you thought that it's just about the most important thing that's happened to us and we're not supposed to talk about it?'

'Yes,' Edyth said abruptly.

Mary's cheeks flamed crimson.

Bella leaned back against the frame. 'Just the way you feel about your husband, how you can't wait to see him, to tear his clothes off . . .'

'You tear Toby's clothes off?' Edyth wondered if she should try that approach with Peter, then remembered his sterile pecks on the

280

cheek and decided she might not get the response she was looking for if she tried.

'No, not really,' Bella confessed, 'he always takes them off before I can tear them off. Do you tear Harry's clothes off, Mary?'

Mary turned a deeper shade of vermilion. 'The evidence of Harry's and my private life is downstairs cadging biscuits from Mari and lying in Edyth's arms.' She indicated Will.

Disturbed by Bella's conversation, Edyth gazed pointedly at her watch. 'Look at the time, I promised Peter I'd be packed so we can go to the station right after lunch.'

'Please, put him down in the cot, Edyth,' Mary asked when Mari bustled in with a tray. 'If you don't, he's going to be spoiled, and I won't be able to do any work at all when I get him home.'

'In my opinion, you can't spoil a baby with love, only with chocolate,' Mari chipped in.

'I heard what Harry did, Mari, I'm sorry about Ruth's dress,' Mary apologized.

'Don't give it another thought. That husband of yours has always kept a secret supply since he was a boy. Joey used to sneak it to him before he was old enough to buy his own.' She looked at Edyth and frowned. 'You all right, Miss Edyth?'

'Fine, Mari,' Edyth lied. 'I just have to go and finish my packing.'

'There's no going back now, Edyth,' Belle warned. 'The honeymoon's over, real life is about to begin.'

Edyth fled the room before Bella could see the apprehension in her eyes.


'Well, Reverend Slater, Mrs Slater, you've had terrible weather for your honeymoon, if Swansea's been anything like Cardiff.' Mrs Mack stood in the porch of the vicarage to welcome Peter and Edyth when they arrived in the taxi Peter had hired at Cardiff station.

'The weather wasn't very good, Mrs Mack.' Peter didn't explain that they had spent most of the week in Pontypridd. He dropped their cases in the hall and darted back out in the rain to pay the driver.

'I wasn't expecting you until this evening, but I suppose I could make you some afternoon tea if you want it,' the housekeeper conceded ungraciously.

Accustomed to Mari, who was used to catering for any number of friends and family at no notice, Edyth was stunned by their housekeeper's offhand attitude. Especially when she considered that Mrs Mack was employed by them.

'We would like tea, please, Mrs Mack, and biscuits,' she added, thinking of Peter's sweet tooth.

'I'm making a nice warming leek and potato soup and hotpot for dinner. I thought they wouldn't spoil no matter what time you arrived.'

'That's fine – for dinner.' Edyth looked around the hall and noted that the tiles were no cleaner than they'd been on her first visit. 'But we would like tea now.'

'You can have tea, but there are no biscuits in the house except plain. I suppose I could put some cheese on them.'

Edyth had never expected subservience from a housekeeper but she was shocked at Mrs Mack's response. 'If you would, Mrs Mack.'

'Where do you want it?'

'In the sitting room, please.'

'It'll be twenty minutes.'

Edyth wondered why it would take twenty minutes to make tea and a few cheese biscuits, but decided against demanding an explanation. She had a feeling that she and Mrs Mack were going to have words soon enough – and before Peter's mother arrived. But they could wait until she'd looked around the house.

The upper wall in the hall had been papered in small-patterned beige wallpaper, the dado varnished in brown to match the paintwork. It wasn't what she would have chosen, but she could live with it. Aside from the tiled floor, the carpet-runner on the stairs, and even the newly painted stairs either side, could do with a good scrub. Slivers of gummed wallpaper dropped by the decorators had caught in the stair rods. She laid her hand on the banisters and discovered that even they were sticky with gummy residue.

She walked into the living room. The walls had been papered in cream, patterned with pale-blue roses. Reverend Richards's furniture had been removed and replaced with Peter's mother's 'Regency' pieces: a walnut-framed uncomfortable-looking upright sofa and easy chairs, a walnut sofa table, a large bureau bookcase, and a set of matching shelves that had been filled to capacity with Peter's books – leaving no room for hers. A hideous, and barely recognizable, oil painting of Mumbles Head hung over the fireplace. The fire was laid, however. She lit a spill from a box of matches on the mantelpiece and touched the flame to the newspaper rolled beneath the sticks.

'Mrs Mack wouldn't have thought to light the fire because she wasn't expecting us until later.' Peter had left his hat, coat and gloves in the hall. He rubbed his hands together to restore the circulation, before holding them out to the thin flames that licked upwards through the coals.

'Hopefully the room will soon warm up.' From the chill in the air Edyth knew she was being optimistic.

'Do you like Mother's furniture and the changes that have been made, Edyth?'

'It's an improvement,' Edyth replied guardedly.

'Wait until you see the dining room.' He led her across the passage into an equally large and gloomy room, which also faced a high wall. The table and chairs were Regency – late Regency, judging by the ornate carved scrolls and curlicues. A silver bowl stood in the centre of the table and an array of heavily embossed antique silverware was set out on the sideboard.

She recalled the clean, elegant and simple lines of the beautiful, modern pieces Bella and Toby had bought for them in Tiffany's. Not only would they jar when set against these antiques, there wasn't enough room left to display them, even if she'd wanted to.

She went to the sideboard and opened the door. Both cupboards had been filled with fussy, gilt-rimmed, rose-patterned china. The drawers were packed to the brim with hand-embroidered tablecloths and napkins.

'Aren't you glad now that I told you to wait before buying anything?' Peter asked smugly.

'I'm just wondering where we're going to put our wedding presents.'

'I expect you'll find somewhere,' he said airily. 'Let's have tea. The sooner I get started on that sermon, the sooner I'll be free to enjoy our first evening in our new home.'

Mrs Mack must have heard them go into the sitting room because a few minutes later she wheeled in a trolley and set it next to where they sat huddled, as close to the fire as they could position the uncomfortable chairs.

'Would you like me to pour the tea, Mrs Slater?'

'No, thank you, Mrs Mack.' Edyth knew she was being irritable and unreasonable, but she couldn't wait for the woman to leave the room.

'Mrs Richards always liked me to pour, sugar and milk the tea, and serve it.'

'I'll pour, thank you, Mrs Mack,' Edyth reiterated firmly, recalling what Aunt Alice had said about starting as she meant to go on, and deciding it could apply just as easily to the housekeeper as Peter's mother..

'In that case, if that's everything for now, Mrs Slater, I'll get on in the kitchen.' The housekeeper made sure they knew that her feelings had been hurt.

'It is. Thank you, Mrs Mack.' Edyth poured the tea but her hand shook.

'I've made up the beds in the back and front bedrooms, Reverend Slater. Shall I make up the bed in the master bedroom for Mrs Slater senior?'

'No, thank you, Mrs Mack, my mother won't be arriving for a week.'

'Then I'll keep the sheets and blankets in the linen cupboard so they'll get a good airing.' She shuffled out of the room.

'You told Mrs Mack that your mother was moving in with us?'

She helped me to arrange the furniture and put things away in the cupboards. I hope you don't mind but I gave Mother the largest bedroom. Your parents have bought us that small modern suite and as Mother's is so much bulkier, it made sense to give her more space. And she wanted her desk in there as well as her washstand. I tried telling her that we had a bathroom, but she insisted she couldn't do without her washstand. Besides, the largest bedroom is at the back so it will be quieter for her. Mine is at the front but as I'll be the one to get up when people call in the night, it won't matter so much if I'm disturbed.'

'Yours?' She suddenly recalled Mrs Mack mentioning that she had made up two beds. One in the front bedroom and one in the back.

'I'm used to sleeping alone.'

'Peter . . .'

'And I'll more often than not work late at night and early in the morning. Apart from writing sermons, people will want to see me at all sorts of odd hours. Especially if they are working. Being a vicar is not a nine until five job, Edyth.' Seeing her hand poised over the sugar bowl, he said, 'I take two sugars and a splash of milk.'

'After the number of times you've drunk tea in my parents' house, I know. Peter, about the bedrooms—'

'We'll talk about them when we go upstairs to look at the arrangements I've made. If you don't like them, we'll change them.' He took the tea she handed him and helped himself to a cracker and cheese.

'Hardly a sumptuous repast for our first meal in our home,' she said, 'but at least Mrs Mack has promised us a hot meal for dinner.'

Peter took a bite and made a face. Edyth picked up a cracker and examined it.

'Don't eat it, Peter. The cracker's so old it's soggy.' She poked at it, then sniffed it. 'The butter's rancid, the cheese too strong and,' she sipped her tea, 'the tea's stewed.'

Peter shrugged his shoulders. 'Mrs Mack's catering, I'm afraid.'

'And you told her she could keep her job!' she exclaimed crossly.

'She's been here so long . . .'

Edyth was beginning to feel that it had been days not hours since they had entered the house. The place was dirty, cold and unwelcoming for all that it had been freshly decorated. The food their housekeeper had served was stale and obviously of inferior quality even when it had been fresh, and to top it all, Peter had announced that he wanted separate bedrooms. Her temper finally snapped. As the housekeeper was the easiest target she chose to fire her first broadside at her. 'Mrs Mack will either mend her ways or go.'

'Edyth, please, I told you, she's a friend of the Bishop's cousin—'

'Then the Bishop or his cousin can offer her a position in their house,' she said flatly.

'She's been here for over forty years.'

'No wonder. If she serves food like this she'll see out any number of incumbents in this vicarage.'

'If you don't mind, I'll go and work in my study.' He left his chair.

'You promised to show me the rest of the house.'

'So I did. But first I need to put away the books I took to Swansea.'

Edyth almost asked why, then thought better of it. She had far more serious things to discuss with Peter than when he should or shouldn't put his books away. 'The door to your study is the one immediately left of the front door?'

'It is.'

'And the kitchen is at the end of the passage opposite the front door?'

'That's right.'

'I'll come and find you after I've spoken to Mrs Mack.'

'Don't upset her, Edyth.'

'Why? We pay her wages to do a job, don't we?'

'Yes, of course, but—'

'She needs taking in hand, Peter. It's plain that she's been doing exactly as she likes. She can't serve food like this and expect to stay in our employment.' She left her chair, and after resolving to dig out a thick sweater from the trunks she'd had sent from home, she placed the dishes and teapot back on the trolley and wheeled it down the freezing corridor.

Mrs Mack was sitting in one of two deep-cushioned comfortable chairs next to the brand-new range, a recipe book and a brown medicine bottle on her lap, and a faraway look in her eye. There was a strong smell of paint, and Edyth could see that the room had recently been refurbished. There were green and white painted cupboards, a large sink with a gas geyser for hot water above it, a scrub down pine table and sturdy pine chairs, which she guessed had also belonged to Peter's mother, and, to add insult to injury, the room was deliciously warm, in sharp contrast to the rest of the house.

Mrs Mack jumped up when Edyth wheeled in the trolley. She held up the medicine bottle. 'I have a sore throat.'

'I'm sorry to hear that.' The news didn't make Edyth feel any more sympathetic towards the woman. Inedible food was unacceptable, whatever the condition of the person who'd prepared it.

Mrs Mack looked at the untouched trolley. 'Is something wrong, madam?'

'Mrs Slater will do, Mrs Mack. And yes, there is. The tea is stewed, the cheese and biscuits are stale, and the butter is rancid.' Edyth went to the pantry.

'Can I help you with something, Mrs Slater?'

'I'm checking the stocks.' Edyth opened the door. Lifting the cover from the milk churn on the marble slab next to the door, she sniffed the contents. Then she looked at the meat safe, and the rest of the shelves.

'There is very little food here. None of it is fresh and all of it is poor quality.'

'Mrs Richards never complained about my housekeeping or marketing, Mrs Slater,' Mrs Mack protested in an injured voice. 'I don't know what you're used to, but a vicar's household is not a rich one. I have had to practise certain economies over the years.'

'You need no longer concern yourself with marketing economies, Mrs Mack. I will buy all our groceries from now on.' Edyth took a toasting fork from the rack of utensils. 'Please fill the kettle and boil it, Mrs Mack, and make a fresh pot of tea. The one you served us is undrinkable. In the meantime, I'll see if this cheese tastes any better toasted.'

Edyth balanced the tray on her knee and entered Peter's study. 'I'm not sure this is any better, Peter, but I've done the best I can with what's in the larder. If there are shops open, I'll go out—'

'Edyth, what on earth do you think you're doing?'

'Bringing you tea and cheese on toast,' she answered in confusion.

'Never, *never* walk into my study without knocking.'

As her father's study door was always open to the entire family she stared at him in amazement. 'But, Peter, we're married—'

'And I could have visitors. A newly bereaved widow, a couple about to embark on marriage, parishioners entrusting me with confidential information. Imagine how they would feel if my wife waltzed in without as much as by your leave to bring me tea.'

Feeling justly rebuked, Edyth murmured, 'I'm sorry, I didn't think.'

'No harm was done this time, but please, always knock in future, even if you think that I am alone. It is as well that you don't develop bad habits.'

She set the tray on his desk. 'I'm going upstairs to look at the bedrooms and bathrooms. You'll join me?'

'As soon as I've eaten this.' He shuffled through the letters he had been opening. She had been dismissed, and she felt exactly as she had done when the headmistress of the grammar school had told her to leave after a particularly unpleasant interview.

'I heard you on the stairs, Mrs Slater.' Mrs Mack joined Edyth on the landing as she was looking at the doors and debating which one to open first. 'Reverend Slater had the bedroom suite your parents bought you put into this bedroom.' She opened the door to a back bedroom. It was situated above the sitting room and just as gloomy because the wall of the church extended beyond the height of the window. The pale beech wood suite would have looked better set against plainer wallpaper, but the bed linen was all wrong. The bed was covered in a crimson draped and gathered satin bedspread. Edyth turned it back. The linen was thick and coarse.

'I'd like this bed made up with the linen we were given as wedding presents, Mrs Mack,' she said shortly.

'I made the beds up according to Reverend Slater's instructions, Mrs Slater. He knew exactly where he wanted everything to go.'

Edyth saw her trunks and packing cases stacked in the corner of the room. She was tired after travelling but she was determined to unpack all their things in the morning and set them out. 'Show me the other bedrooms, please, Mrs Mack.'

'Mrs Slater senior will be next door to you, Mrs Slater.' The housekeeper opened the door on a room Edyth suspected had been arranged exactly like another in a vicarage in Mumbles many years earlier. The bed was a four-poster. The writing desk, chest on chest of drawers, washstand, bedside cabinet and wardrobe were all of dark-stained mahogany, the bedspread a carbon copy of the one in her bedroom, only in navy-blue.

'This is Mother's room.' She looked up. Peter was in the doorway.

'So I understand. That will be all, Mrs Mack. Reverend Slater and I would like to eat as soon as dinner is ready, please.'

'Soup and hotpot won't be hurried, Mrs Slater.'

'As soon as you can make it,' Mrs Mack,' Edyth repeated in a strained voice.

She waited until she heard the housekeeper walking over the tiled hall before turning to Peter. 'Did you give orders for the beds to be made up in your mother's linen?'

'Of course. I assumed that you'd want to unpack our wedding presents yourself. Surely it won't hurt to use mother's linen for a week or two until you have a chance to get the house as you want it?'

'No, of course it won't.'

'You're tired, Edyth, it's the strain of the last week,' he avoided mentioning David's name, 'and the travelling, coupled with the unfamiliarity of the house. You're determined to find fault with everything because it's so different from your parents' house and

Mrs Mack's ways are not the same as Mari's. But don't worry, you'll soon settle in.'

'I hope so.'

She wished she could be as convinced as Peter seemed to be. But she wasn't accustomed to Mrs Mack's ideas of 'economies' on food or cleaning, and she had a feeling she would never accept them as adequate.

Peter wrapped his arm around her shoulders and she rested her head against him for a moment. If only he would always hold her this way. She moved closer to him and he stepped back.

'Come and see the bathroom. It's so clean and bright.'

'Bright?'

'I'll grant you the two bedrooms on this side of the house are gloomy, but then all you and Mother will be doing is sleeping in them.' He opened the door to the bathroom, which was tiled in black and white chequerboard tiles. He was right, it was clean and bright, and smelled of soap.

She rubbed her finger around the bath. 'This at least looks clean,' she commented.

'It should do. The people who installed it cleaned it. I told Mrs Mack that she should continue to use the washstand in her attic room and the outside lavatory, to leave the bathroom solely for our use. Is that all right?'

'Yes.' She smiled at him. 'Thank you.'

The bedroom Peter had reserved for his own use was lighter and brighter than the two at the back of the house. It was so spartanly furnished it reminded Edyth of Micah Holsten's room, with a single bed, wardrobe, chest of drawers, bookcase and small desk all in oak, and a crucifix above the bed. Then she realized none of the furniture was new.

'This was your furniture when you were a boy?' she asked.

'It was.'

'But most of the time you'll sleep in my bedroom?'

'That's the doorbell. I told Mrs Mack to ask the carriers to put most of the things that were transported from your parents' house into the box room. But you'll have to wait to see them. We're about to have our first visitor.' He left the room and ran downstairs without answering her question.

# Chapter 18

'EDYTH, COME DOWNSTAIRS. Quickly, please,' Peter called above a hubbub of voices in the hall.

Edyth ran down the stairs to see him ushering in a delegation of a score or more small children, who were being shepherded by three older girls. If the knife-edge, ironed creases on the boys' shorts, their pressed shirt collars and the starched frills on the girls' frocks were anything to go by, they were in their Sunday best. The smallest girl was carrying a bunch of flowers almost as large as herself, and another was struggling beneath the weight of a basket of fruit. Behind the group stood a dozen men of varying ages in dark suits, white shirts and sober ties.

'The church council and Sunday school have come to welcome you to your new home, Edyth.' Peter beamed at everyone.

'Please, do come in,' she invited. 'I'll call Mrs Mack. Hopefully we can find some biscuits for the children.' She made the offer out of politeness. There had been tins in the pantry, but after she'd spoken she realized it was doubtful that anything edible lurked in their depths.

'No, please, Mrs Slater.' One of the girls stepped forward.

'This is Prudence Smart, she's only fifteen but she teaches the infants' class in our Sunday school, Edyth.' Peter moved to make room for the men to enter alongside the children. Rain was hammering down, and they closed their umbrellas outside, shaking the worst of the water from them before depositing them in a brass umbrella stand in dire need of polishing.

Edyth shook the girl's hand. 'I'm very pleased to meet you, Prudence.'

'Please, don't put yourself out for us, Mrs Slater. My mother said you must have a hundred and one things to do in the house. The last thing we want to do is hold you up, but if you can spare a few minutes, the children have been practising a hymn they'd like to sing for you.'

Edyth tried not to look relieved. 'In that case, all of you must come to tea another day.'

'Soon?' the little girl holding the flowers asked hopefully.

'Very soon, in the next week or two,' Edyth promised.

'Will there be jelly and blancmange?' a small boy asked.

'Nigel!' Prudence reprimanded.

'It's all right.' Edyth stroked the boy's curly hair. 'There most certainly will be jelly and blancmange, Nigel.' She made a mental note to add both to the shopping list she intended to write that evening. She took the flowers and basket of fruit. 'For Reverend Slater and me? How very nice and thoughtful. You're spoiling us.' She stood next to Peter while the children sang 'All Things Bright and Beautiful'.

Halfway through their rendition, which was amazingly accomplished considering they had no instrumental accompaniment, she felt the weight of Peter's arm around her waist. She leaned against him, wondering if this was what he intended their life to be; public shows of affection concealing private remoteness in separate bedrooms. Surely not. But every time she thought of Harry and Mary, Bella and Toby, and her parents, she knew something was wrong between them.

'That was charming. Don't you think so, Edyth?' Peter nudged her.

Edyth realized the children had stopped singing. She clapped enthusiastically, hoping they hadn't noticed that her mind was elsewhere. 'Absolutely charming,' she reiterated. 'I look forward to getting to know all of you during the coming weeks. Thank you again for these beautiful flowers and the fruit.'

'See you tomorrow in Sunday school, Mrs Slater.' The older girls rounded up the children and led them outside.

'My study is too small to accommodate the full council, so we'll use the dining room for our meeting. That's if you don't mind, Edyth?'

'Not at all, Peter. Don't forget to set a match to the fire.' She only wished the room was cleaner and more welcoming.

'This is Anthony Jones, the youngest member and secretary of the council.' He introduced her to a fair-haired, good-looking young man. Edyth knew she had seen him before, but it took her a few moments to recall that he was one of the policemen who had rounded up Anna Hughes and the other 'ladies' the night she had arrived at the vicarage.

'Very pleased to meet you, Mrs Slater.'

His smile wasn't as friendly as it might have been. Ever-sensitive, Edyth assumed he disapproved of her.

'Mr Williams, chairman of the council.'

'My wife, Eirlys, and I would be delighted if you would come to tea tomorrow between services, Mrs Slater.'

'How kind.' Edyth looked to Peter.

'Edyth and I would be delighted to accept your invitation,' Peter answered for her.

'Shall I ask Mrs Mack to serve you tea, Peter?'

'Please, Edyth.' He stepped back, watching the last of the council walk into the room ahead of him. 'We will have a quiet evening together, I promise you.'

Wondering if all the problems between Peter and her were in her imagination, Edyth waved off the Sunday school children. She was just about to shut the door when Micah Holsten walked around the corner. Ridiculously pleased to see a familiar face after so many strangers, she called out to him, 'Micah, how lovely of you to visit us on my first day in the vicarage.'

He produced a small bunch of flowers from behind his back. 'They pale into insignificance set against those.' He fingered the enormous bunch she was holding. 'Someone must have raided every garden in the Bay to supply you with them. Not to mention a couple of fruit and vegetable shops,' he added, eyeing the basket.

'These are from the church council and Sunday school. But I love heather; it reminds me of the mountains in Pontypridd. And it's white heather, too.'

'Lucky heather. I bought it off a gypsy in Loudon Square. She blessed the recipient but you'd better not tell Peter,' he added in a dramatic whisper. 'I don't think High Anglicans go in for gypsy blessings.'

'I'm sure they don't,' she laughed, feelingly suddenly preposterously happy. The combination of the flowers and Micah's smiling face had somehow put all her problems into perspective. There was nothing that she couldn't sort out — given time to talk to Peter. 'Please come in. Peter's holding a church council meeting in the dining room but you're welcome to wait in the sitting room until he's free.'

'I give you fair warning: if I step over that doorstep, I'll drip all over your floor.'

'It could do with some water on it.'

'It doesn't look too clean,' he conceded, looking down at it. 'But no doubt, like most housewives, you'll soon remedy that.' He stood on the cork doormat and slithered out of his dripping mackintosh. She hung it in the porch. His trilby was sodden and he shook it outside the door. 'Perhaps I should leave this out here?'

She took it from him and set it carefully on the newel post so it wouldn't dry out of shape. 'You haven't an umbrella?'

'I hate them. You can't see where you're going when you're walking under one, or what your neighbours are doing, and I was born nosy.'

'I have no idea how long church council meetings last.'

'Aeons and aeons, I should think,' he answered mischievously. 'But it's not Peter I've come to see, it's you.'

'Really? Please, you must know where the sitting room is, go on in. I'll ask Mrs Mack to bring us some tea.'

'Must you?' He made a wry face and she laughed again before remembering that the members of the church council could probably hear her.

'You'll be wanting tea, Mrs Slater?' Mrs Mack materialized in the kitchen doorway.

'For the church council in the dining room. And Pastor Holsten and myself in the sitting room, Mrs Mack. Make sure both pots are freshly made.' She went into the sitting room and closed the door behind her. Micah was sitting bolt upright on one of the wooden-

295

framed easy chairs. He looked as though he would have been more comfortable on a park bench.

'Sorry, the furniture is my mother-in-law's,' she apologized.

'I'm glad to hear it. I'd hate to think it was your taste. You seem far too nice and considerate to want to give your guests backache.'

'From what you said, I take it that you have drunk Mrs Mack's tea before?'

'I think she makes it in the morning and leaves it warming on the range all day. As I've discovered to my cost, some people in Wales believe that's perfectly normal, which is why I usually drink coffee.'

'I looked in the pantry earlier, I didn't see any coffee, but I will buy some just as soon as I've had a chance to go shopping. However, there's no need to worry about Mrs Mack's tea. I had a word with her about it. The pot will be fresh.' She sat on the sofa. If anything, it was even more uncomfortable than the chairs. It certainly didn't encourage relaxing and it was impossible to loll on it the way she and her sisters did on the ones at home. *Home*. She forced herself to remember that this was her home now, for all that it didn't feel much like it at the moment.

'You're attempting to knock Mrs Mack into shape?' Micah said admiringly. 'I've already taken my hat off to you, so I bow to your courage.' He left me chair and gave her a theatrical, three-circle hand movement, Shakespearean bow. 'No one on the Bay has ever managed to make that woman do an honest day's work. She has to be the idlest person of my acquaintance. But then, I've never known a drunk to be industrious.'

'Drunk?' Edyth repeated in astonishment.

'You didn't know? Well, you'll no doubt see her with a brown medicine bottle, for a cold she can feel coming on, or sciatica, or—'

'A sore throat.' Edyth recalled the bottle she'd seen Mrs Mack nursing in the kitchen.

'That's a new one. If you dared to take the bottle from her – and I'm not advising you to try, because she'd probably turn vicious – you'd discover the contents are odourless but not quite tasteless. She buys homemade vodka by the litre from the Russian

296

seamen when they come into port. Which is why no one ever smells drink on her breath. It doesn't have a distinctive scent like whisky.' He left his seat. 'This chair is not made for someone as long or thin as me. In fact, I'm not sure who it was made for. Possibly a deportment school that tortures young girls in the belief they're being turned into ladies?' He took a cushion from the chair, sprawled on the floor next to the hearth, stretched his long legs over the rug and, pushing the cushion behind his back, leaned against the wall. 'That's better. You should try the other side. Perched up there, you remind me of one of those American pole-sitters who stay on tiny platforms for days.'

'I feel like one.' She did as he suggested and sat on the floor on the opposite side of the hearth to the one he had taken.

'If the tea is drinkable we can put it next to the coal scuttle. That way any spillages can be easily mopped from the tiles.'

'You seem to know a great deal about Mrs Mack.' As Edyth arranged her skirts over her legs, a disturbing notion occurred to her. She was more relaxed and happier in Micah Holsten's company than she was in her own husband's. She pushed the disloyal thought from her mind.

'Everyone who's lived for any length of time in the Bay knows Lizzie Mack for what she is.'

'Scottish?'

'Probably, I've no reason to believe her accent isn't authentic. But she turned up here long before my time. She used to run a house.'

'A house?'

'One lived in by several ladies of the Anna Hughes ilk. You recall the lady you met the night you came to the Bay to look for Peter?'

'I do.' She blushed at her own naivety.

'Age forced Mrs Mack into retirement. But not before, or so rumour has it, she amassed "a tidy bit of money", which her drinking habits undoubtedly drain, although Russian vodka is generally cheap enough. About two years ago, Mrs James, who runs the seaman's lodging house in Bute Street, took Mrs Mack on as a housekeeper. She put up with her for six months before ordering her to leave. Then Mrs Mack took a caretaker's job in Moore's shipping offices, in exchange for living accommodation and a small salary. Mr Moore senior is a tough man; he had her out in three weeks.'

'But she told Peter and me that she'd been with Reverend Richards and his wife for over forty years, that she's a friend of the Bishop's cousin.'

'And you believed her?' He exploded with laughter.

'We had no reason not to.'

'More fool the pair of you. Sorry, I didn't mean that,' he apologized, but clearly finding it difficult to keep a straight face. 'You weren't to know. And she has pulled the wool over many people's eyes in her time, including, I'm ashamed to say, me. Among her many and varied qualities Mrs Mack is an inveterate liar. Fantasy at short notice is her speciality. And she can be convincing. She conned me on my second day in the Bay six years ago. I believed her story that she had lost her home and job when the family who employed her had moved out of Loudon Square. I even gave her ten shillings from the mission's poor box. But you have to hand it to the woman. She knows how to pick gullible victims. Isn't that so, Mrs Mack?' he asked when she carried in a tea tray.

'What, Pastor Holsten?' She eyed him warily.

'You know how to pick your victims,' he repeated.

'Why are you both sitting on the floor?' she asked, instantly changing the subject.

'Because it's more comfortable than the furniture.' Micah sat up, took the tray from her and laid it in the hearth. 'I was just telling Mrs Slater that you've had many jobs in and around the Bay, and been with Reverend Richards for . . . oh . . . I'd say about eight months, wouldn't you? Before he went into hospital, that is.' His eyes shone with suppressed humour when he turned to Edyth. 'Old Mrs Arnold, who *was* Reverend and Mrs Richards's housekeeper for over forty years, left him when Mrs Richards died. She thought there'd be gossip about a widow keeping house for a widower. Although, as she was well over seventy and he was over sixty and in failing health, I can't imagine what she thought people would say about them. Or more to the point, what they'd get up to.'

Mrs Mack pulled herself up to her full height. 'I might not have been Reverend and Mrs Richards's housekeeper for all that time, Mrs Slater, but I "did" for them.'

'You helped Mrs Arnold occasionally on Saturdays when she cleaned the range and gave the house a good going-over ready for Sunday because Reverend Richards didn't like anyone working in the house, not even to cook the dinner on Sundays,' Micah corrected.

'I . . . I . . .'

'That will be all, Mrs Mack.' Edyth felt sorry for the housekeeper. Although, from the defiant expression on Mrs Mack's face, the woman was preparing to argue with Micah.

'Reverend Slater asked for biscuits, Mrs Slater. I told him straight, Reverend Richards didn't have a sweet tooth.'

'Reverend Richards is no longer the incumbent here, Mrs Mack, and Reverend Slater does have a sweet tooth. I will make cake and biscuits just as soon as I have had an opportunity to go to the shops to buy the ingredients,' Edyth broke in, wondering what the woman was building up to.

'If you give me some money I could go to the baker's in Bute Street and see if they have any cakes left.'

'We'll manage until Monday, Mrs Mack. I'll do some baking then. You have our dinner to cook,' she reminded her.

'Yes, Mrs Slater.'

Edyth shivered in the draught Mrs Mack created when she opened and closed the door. The sitting room was a little warmer than when she had put a spill to the fire, but there was still a definite, damp chill in the air.

'I'm sorry,' she apologized to Micah. 'This room isn't at all comfortable.'

'It didn't occur to Mrs Mack to warm the house for your return? Thank you.' He took the tea she poured him.

'Evidently not.' Edyth handed him the sugar bowl and milk jug.

'I have wondered if she behaves the way she does simply to be perverse, or if she genuinely likes to upset people and make them suffer.' He sipped the tea. 'Still, that's enough of Mrs Mack, who you have taught to make a decent cup of tea. Edyth, the miracle-worker, I salute your superior skills.' He replaced his cup on its saucer.

'I didn't teach her anything, just told her to make fresh when people wanted it.'

'It sounds simple, but I used to visit Reverend Richards after his wife died and Mrs Mack never took any notice of the orders he gave her. To change the subject, did you enjoy your trip? The weather was dreadful, but perhaps that doesn't matter on a honeymoon.'

'It started raining on Sunday and hasn't let up since, but Swansea and the Gower are beautiful even in the rain. Not that we saw much of it. We had . . . an emergency at home. Harry's brother-in-law, David, had an accident, so we returned to Pontypridd on Sunday evening.'

'David – I met him at your and your sister's wedding. He is all right?' he asked solicitously.

'He will be. He fell and broke his legs, ankles and pelvis. Harry's wife Mary was dreadfully upset, but everything was more or less back to normal when Peter and I left my parents' house this morning.' She firmly closed the subject. 'Tell me, how are things on the Bay? I wasn't sure what kind of welcome I'd get, but so far it has been wonderful.' She looked at the fruit and flowers she'd laid on the sofa table.

'There's no one like Bay people for welcoming and accepting strangers into their community. And I'm sorry to call on you so soon, but when I heard that you'd returned to the vicarage . . .' He gave her a deprecating smile. 'You can't limp in the Bay without someone from two streets away rushing to offer you a bottle of Sloane's liniment,' he explained. 'I hoped you'd consider doing me a favour. It's not for me, it's for someone else. But please don't feel that you have to do anything about it if you don't want to.'

'After what you did for me, I'm hardly likely to refuse you any reasonable request, Micah.'

'It's Judy Hamilton.'

'The singer in your band? The one whose grandmother died the night you rescued me from the police station.'

'Rescued might be a bit strong; the police weren't about to birch or hang you. But yes, that's the girl. She's had a terrible time the last few weeks. Her grandmother left her the contents of her rented house, not that there was anything particularly valuable in it. But her long-lost father — who abandoned her when she was a baby and returned to swindle her — sold it all. The buyer came when most people from the Bay were at Pearl King's funeral, so there was no one around to stop the men from cleaning out the place. Judy was left with the clothes she stood up in. And the woman who employed her as a housekeeper sacked her shortly before her grandmother died.'

'That's dreadful.' Recalling the frock she had given Judy at Bella's wedding and remembering they were the same size, Edyth began to mentally sort through her wardrobe for clothes she could do without.

'She's living with her uncle — you know him, Jed King — at the moment. But his house is small and full to bursting with his family. Judy has looked for a live-in position in the Bay and Cardiff, but jobs are rarer than reindeer around the docks these days, especially for girls. Two days ago I met her in the street. She'd just registered with one of the agencies that send Welsh girls to London as domestics. She was upset because they warned her she couldn't expect as much money as a white girl, that's if they found her a position at all.'

'Talk about kicking someone when they are down,' Edyth cried indignantly.

'The coloured people who live in the Bay and rarely venture out of it have no idea of the prejudices they are likely to encounter outside. People are simply people here, not Afro-Welsh, Asian, Chinese, Arab, or Maltese — or any name other than their own. They're simply known as Dai who lives up the road or Mary who runs the corner shop or Judy who sings. Judy's seen a little of what it can be like for coloured people on the outside and not just in the agency. She's been turned down at auditions because of the colour of her skin.'

'That's appalling.'

'I've read newspaper articles about your father and I can see you're his daughter,' Micah said drily. 'I haven't said anything to Judy, but I thought that perhaps you and Peter might be thinking of taking on another maid.'

'We certainly need good help.'

They were disturbed by a knock at the door. Edyth scrambled to her feet and opened it.

'I came to see if you've finished your tea.'

'Not yet, Mrs Mack. I'll carry the tray into the kitchen when we have,' Edyth answered.

'I just happened to catch what Pastor Holsten was saying just now—'

'By listening at the keyhole, Mrs Mack?' Micah enquired bluntly.

She folded her arms across her flat chest. 'We don't need a maid in this house. Especially a coloured girl.'

'That is for me and Reverend Slater to decide, Mrs Mack, not you,' Edith said firmly. 'And let's get a few things clear from the start. First, you do not eavesdrop on my or the Reverend Slater's private conversations. And secondly, in this house the only thing that matters is a person's character. Not their colour, politics or religion.'

'I'd like to hear you say that to Reverend Slater's face.'

'I beg your pardon?' Edyth said icily, stunned by Mrs Mack's effrontery.

'If a coloured girl sets foot in this house, I'm packing my bags and that's final.'

'You've just given me one more reason to employ her, Mrs Mack.' Edyth met Mrs Mack's stare head on. The housekeeper was the first to turn aside. Muttering, she retreated to the kitchen.

'Do you mean it?' Micah asked. 'You'll take Judy on. I don't mind telling you, I was expecting a much harder fight.'

'I need to employ someone who knows what a duster and scrubbing brush are.'

'Judy's grandmother taught her to cook and clean. Pearl King came to the Bay as a kitchen maid and her cooking was superb.'

302

'You don't have to sell Judy to me, Micah,' Edyth laughed. 'But it will be as much Peter's decision as mine.'

'Why, you're the lady of the house, aren't you?'

'Yes . . . yes, I am,' she said decisively. 'And if Judy coming here means Mrs Mack will go, we can pay Judy Mrs Mack's wages and I can work alongside her to get the house as I want it.' She thought through the idea. 'If Judy can cook, that will have Peter convinced. He's had too many inedible meals put in front of him lately to want any more. And if she can't cook all the dishes he likes, I can teach her.'

'You can cook?' Micah asked in surprise.

'You thought my father brought up his daughters to be ornamental just because we have help in the house?'

'It happens.'

'Not in the Evans household. Mari is one of my mother's oldest friends, and we have two maids because there are so many of us and my mother works full-time as a buyer in Gwilym James.'

'The department store?'

'Yes.' As always with people outside of the family, Edyth didn't tell him the store was part of Harry's enormous trust fund.

'In that case, I apologize. I had you down as being one of the idle rich.'

She laughed again when she returned to the carpet next to the hearth. 'You knew I intended to go to college and train as a teacher.'

'So you did.'

'How soon can Judy start?'

'Ten minutes ago.'

'I thought you hadn't said anything to her?'

'I haven't, but I told her that I'd look around.'

'If she's going to live in I ought to go upstairs and check the attic rooms. I know Mrs Mack sleeps in one, so presumably that is all right, but I have no idea what condition the others are in.'

'In this weather they are going to be cold and damp,' he said, 'but with luck there'll be fireplaces in them. I can lay a fire in the room to air it, and if there's a mattress on the bed we can prop it in front of the fire.'

'And if there's no bed and no mattress?'

'She can have mine until you get a chance to buy both.'

She looked at him in surprise. 'You really do care for Judy, don't you, Micah? Is she Lutheran?' She wondered if finding jobs for people was all part of the service Micah offered as Pastor of the Norwegian church.

'She's Catholic, but I hate to see people getting a rough deal in life, whatever God they worship. And Judy's had a streak of bad luck through no fault of her own. Jed's wife means to be kind, but she has a houseful of children of her own to look after and another on the way. She's overworked and irritable, and Judy is an easy target. It's not her fault or Judy's, but they'd both be better off out of one another's company. You know what it's like, or if you don't, you can imagine. Two women trying to share the same kitchen inevitably leads to quarrelling.'

Edyth decided the news that Peter's mother was going to move in with them couldn't have reached the Bay yet. So Mrs Mack had to be close-mouthed about some things. 'Even if I manage to sort out a room for Judy, I still have the problem of what to do with Mrs Mack, that's if she doesn't walk out in a huff.'

'She won't,' Micah predicted. 'She has too cosy a berth here to jump ship, despite her threats to do just that.'

'I don't like the woman but I hate the thought of her having to go into the workhouse.'

'She won't,' Micah replied confidently. 'I told you, she has a nest egg. She'll find lodgings soon enough. There are always people willing to take in paying guests to make a few extra shillings. Even a Mrs Mack.'

Among the many important things Edyth had earmarked to discuss with Peter was money. He had continually told her that they wouldn't be rich but she had no idea what his stipend was. He had mentioned that his father had left him an annuity, so they couldn't be that badly off. She didn't even know what he was paying Mrs Mack. Her mother's maids earned twenty pounds a year plus their keep, Mari more than twice as much. She could start Judy on twenty pounds a year and raise it later if the girl was worth extra. And she had savings of two hundred pounds, so if

Peter objected to paying the girl's wages as well as Mrs Mack's – if the housekeeper stayed – she could always pay Judy herself.

'Do you think Judy would accept an offer of twenty pounds a year plus keep? On a month's trial during which she could leave or I could terminate her employment?' she asked Micah.

'That sounds more than fair to me. There are girls from the Bay living in as maids who get only six pounds a year plus keep.'

'Given my father's history of organizing strikes for better working conditions and a decent living wage for everyone, he would never forgive me for exploiting someone.'

'Edyth . . . Micah, what on earth are you doing?' Peter stood in the doorway and stared at the sight of the two of them sitting on the floor.

'We decided that your chairs are too grand for us to sit on, Peter.' Micah climbed to his feet and offered Peter his hand.

'The suite isn't very comfortable, Peter,' Edyth said quietly.

'It encourages people to sit up properly, so it may take a little getting used to.'

Edyth could hear Florence Slater's voice behind his explanation. 'We thought you were in the dining room with the committee.'

'The meeting finished ten minutes ago.'

'I didn't hear the men leaving.'

'Probably because you were too busy laughing and gossiping in here. We could hear you all through the meeting.'

'I hope we didn't disturb you.'

Clearly agitated, he chose not to answer her question. 'I've just left Mrs Mack crying in the dining room. She says you're replacing her with a coloured girl.'

'I never said replacing. Micah asked me if I could find a place for Judy Hamilton, the singer with the Bute Street Blues Band—'

'The last thing we need in this house is a singer,' Peter declared.

'She's not a professional, Peter,' Micah explained. 'She's lost her position as a daily housekeeper.'

'Why?' Peter asked abruptly.

During the time it took Micah to explain Judy Hamilton's background, Edyth had decided that no matter what Peter said, she would employ the girl. She had given in to all of Peter's demands –

that his mother live with them, that they employ Mrs Mack, that they defer the consummation of their marriage until they move into their own house, that they have separate bedrooms, she hadn't exactly agreed to the last one; it was still up for discussion as far as she was concerned – but if the vicarage was to be her home, then she would employ whom she liked.

'I have already told Micah to offer the girl the job, if she wants it, Peter.'

'No matter what Mrs Mack says.' His expression grew chilly.

'You did say I could run the house any way I wanted to.' He hadn't actually but she knew he wouldn't argue the fact in front of Micah. 'Give me ten minutes to check the attic, Micah. If one of the rooms up there can be made ready for Judy, she can move in right away.'

Edyth left the men in the sitting room and ran up the two flights of stairs to the attic. There were four doors on the poky, windowless landing. One was locked and she presumed that was Mrs Mack's, although she thought it odd that the housekeeper felt it necessary to lock her door.

One opened into a room full of boxes and tea chests, marked Dining Room, Sitting Room, Kitchen, Bedroom 1, Bedroom 2, Maid's Room and Peter's Room. They were comparatively dust-free, and she knew she had stumbled across the cases that had been used to ferry Peter's mother's goods from storage to the vicarage.

The other two rooms were furnished identically. Both held a single iron bedstead with thin, dustsheet-shrouded mattress, aluminium washstand and chest of drawers. There were no wardrobes, and no room for one in either, but there were hooks on the backs of the doors.

Micah had said that Judy had lost most of her possessions so she was hardly likely to need a great deal of storage space. There was also a fireplace in each room. Trusting that the chimneys had been swept recently she went downstairs and into the kitchen.

'Light a fire in both of the attic rooms that are furnished, please, Mrs Mack.'

'Both?' Mrs Mack questioned.

'It's cold and damp up there. The whole floor could do with an airing.'

'It's a lot of trouble to carry coals up two flights of stairs and I've never seen the need to light a fire in my room,' Mrs Mack protested.

'Please do so now,' Edyth requested firmly. 'Miss Hamilton will be moving in this evening. I have decided to give her a month's trial.'

She left before the housekeeper could make another comment. Taking a deep breath, she braced herself for Peter's disapproval and turned the knob on the door of the sitting room.


'It's very kind of you to give me a job and take me in, Mrs Slater.' Judy dropped a battered shopping bag in the hall. It was bulging, but not very large, and it was the only luggage she had brought.

'Not at all, Judy. In fact, I think you are going to be an absolute godsend,' Edyth blurted unthinkingly. Thankfully Peter was in his study, so he didn't hear her blaspheme and she resolved to watch her language more closely in future.

Judy looked around the hall. 'I could start right away, Mrs Slater. Those tiles could do with a good scrubbing with powdered brick and washing soda and, after they've been cleaned, coating with wax.'

'Let's get you settled first, Judy. I've only been in the house for a few hours myself. The first thing I want to do is go into every room and make a list of what needs doing and then put the jobs in order of priority. For the moment, I'll show you to your room so you can unpack.'

Judy picked up her shopping bag. 'That won't take long.'

'Mr Holsten told me what happened to your belongings. I'm sorry. But as well as unpacking, you'll have to make up your bed. It's on the top floor. You can take either of the empty rooms with fires burning in them, whichever you prefer. You can go on up if you like,' she said at a knock on the door.

Judy went up the stairs. Edyth opened the door. Micah Holsten was on the step.

'I'm not coming in, just came to drop off Judy and say thank you again. You will give her time off if she gets the chance of another audition?' he checked. 'If she is going to make anything of herself it will be through her singing and, although you've seen no evidence of it, her dancing.'

'Of course I will, Micah.'

Peter opened his study door. 'Problems, Micah?'

'I only came to drop Judy off.' Micah pointed to his van, which he'd parked in the yard. The engine was still running. 'And remind Edyth that there's a meeting of the Bay youth committee on Monday evening at six o'clock.'

'What's that?' Edyth asked.

'I forgot to tell you, Edyth?' Peter slipped his hand around her waist again. 'I've left all the Sunday school and youth work to you. Micah has set up an interfaith youth committee that works with all the churches, mosques, synagogues and temples in the Bay. I thought you could be our representative on it.'

'See you on Monday in the mission at six o'clock. Don't forget. We've all the Christmas holiday events to plan for. Every place of worship joins in. No matter what the denomination there's some festival or other around that time.' Micah ran back to his van.

'I'm sorry, I meant to mention the committee, but this last week you were so busy with David and your family—'

'I know, Peter. And I'm very grateful to you for allowing me to interrupt our honeymoon. But,' she smiled determinedly, 'we're home now and we can have a very long talk about the parish, the house and everything else. Does over dinner tonight suit you?'

'Of course, and afterwards we'll listen to the radio in the sitting room.'

To Edyth's surprise he kissed her, just as Mrs Mack walked into the hall. It was only one of his pecks on the cheek, but in front of the housekeeper it seemed bizarre.

Determined to do everything she could to please him, she ran lightly up the stairs.

# Chapter 19

PETER SAT at the head of the dining table, picked up his spoon and looked down at the bowl Mrs Mack had placed in front of his chair.

'Some things should not be discussed at meal times,' he glanced at Mrs Mack, 'money is one of them.'

Edyth took the hint. 'I'm sorry, I wasn't thinking.' She watched him carve a dent in Mrs Mack's leek and potato soup, which was as thick, floury and unappetizing as the one Mrs Price had served them in the vicarage in Pontypridd. It seemed like years ago, rather than a couple of months. 'It was kind of the church council and Sunday school to bring us those flowers and fruit.'

'It was.' He made a face as he struggled to swallow the soup.

'I think more people have walked through the doors of this vicarage than Cardiff station in the couple of hours since we returned.'

'I warned you what our life here would be like,' he said, taking her remark as a criticism.

'You did.' She left her chair and closed the door when Mrs Mack returned to the kitchen. 'And I don't mind holding open house for every member of the church. But as well as helping you in the parish, I want to run the vicarage efficiently, and in order to do that I have to keep a tight control on the kitchen. This is inedible.'

He dropped his spoon into the bowl. It fell with a dull plop and rested on top of the jelly-like soup. 'You seem absolutely determined to find fault with everything Mrs Mack does.'

'It doesn't bother you that you can't eat the food she serves, or that the house in dirty and neglected?' she asked flatly.

'It's not that bad—'

'Peter, I'm not making a fuss over nothing. I wouldn't be able to find fault if Mrs Mack did her job properly. I can't possibly allow her to continue to do the marketing and cooking. Not after seeing the quality of food in the pantry, the state of the kitchen and the meals she slops up.' She pushed her bowl away from her, to emphasize the point she'd made.

'She *is* the housekeeper.'

'For the moment,' Edyth muttered darkly.

'I won't give you leave to sack her, Edyth, no matter what Micah Holsten told you about her,' he warned. 'And while I've agreed to your request that we give Judy Hamilton a position here, I will not allow you to make her our housekeeper over Mrs Mack.'

Edyth was seething, but she kept her thoughts to herself. 'I'll need to know how much you pay Mrs Mack.'

'I'll look it up tomorrow.'

'Why not simply hand me the household account books and let me work out everything for myself?' When he didn't answer her, she risked antagonizing him further by venturing, 'Have you any idea how irritating your silences can be, Peter?'

'We are eating, Edyth. How can I digest my food if you persist in quarrelling with me over domestic arrangements I've already made.'

'You're determined to keep Mrs Mack on no matter what?'

'I was brought up to believe that a man is head of his own household. My father was in sole charge of the all the decision-making in our family and, to my knowledge, Mother *never* questioned his authority – not once.'

Edyth checked her temper when Mrs Mack returned to clear the soup bowls, but it remained simmering beneath the surface. And it didn't help that she knew she was being touchy, possibly even petulant, and certainly on the verge of her first serious quarrel with Peter. 'Bring in the hotpot, Mrs Mack, and leave it on the table. I will serve it. And please close the door behind you when you leave. Reverend Slater and I have things to discuss.'

'As do I.' The housekeeper stood, hands on hips, and confronted Edyth. 'That half-caste—'

'Mrs Mack.' Peter rose to his feet and looked down at her. 'Please refer to the maid as Miss Hamilton. I never want to hear that expression in this vicarage again.'

Despite the words they'd exchanged, Edyth could have kissed Peter for reprimanding the housekeeper.

'Whatever she is,' Mrs Mack continued unabashed, 'She's clearing the bookshelves and bureau bookcase in the sitting room.'

'I asked her to do it, Mrs Mack.' Edyth spoke to the housekeeper but looked at Peter.

'Why?' Peter frowned.

'Because I need space to store and display our wedding presents and my family photographs,' Edyth explained. 'I also intend to pack away the china and silverware in here on Monday morning to make room for the sets Harry, Mary, Bella and Toby gave us.'

'I suppose you expect me to stand back and watch that girl undo all my hard work of the last two weeks?' Mrs Mack glared at Peter.

'There's no need for you to do anything, Mrs Mack.' Edyth deliberately lowered her voice in contrast to the housekeeper, who was shouting belligerently. 'I'll get a man in to carry the packing cases down from the attic. After we've filled them, he can return them to the box room.' Edyth looked across the table at Peter. 'I take it there is a jobbing handyman around Tiger Bay that I can employ to do a few hours' work?'

'There is Alf Roberts, the verger. He's a retired seaman who takes care of the church,' Peter informed her. 'He saw to the heavy work that needed doing in both the church and the vicarage in Reverend Richards's time.'

'Then I'll ask him to find the help he needs to transfer the boxes of wedding presents and empty packing cases downstairs, and the full cases back up again after Judy and I have packed your mother's things away.'

'Mrs Mack, we're waiting for our hotpot,' Peter reminded the housekeeper, who was standing, open-mouthed, listening to their conversation.

The housekeeper left and Peter sat back down. Although Edyth was glad to see that he could be assertive with Mrs Mack when he chose, she refrained from passing comment in case he regarded her remarks as patronizing.

'Please don't pack away the silverware, china and ornaments in the sitting room, Edyth.' Peter picked up his napkin from the floor where it had fallen when he'd left his chair.

'Why not?'

'Because Mother is looking forward to seeing all her old things again. This vicarage is similar to the one I grew up in. With Mrs Mack's help, I managed to place her furniture and ornaments more or less just as they were in Mumbles.'

'But this isn't the vicarage in Mumbles, Peter.' Edyth felt as though she and Peter were speaking different languages. 'This is *our* home, Peter. Yours and mine. People have been kind enough to give us beautiful wedding presents—'

'They have,' he interposed sharply. 'Mother gave us every single possession she owns. The entire contents of her house.'

'Exactly, Peter – *her* house. This is ours.'

'Hotpot.' Mrs Mack barged in without knocking. There was a jubilant look on her face, and Edyth knew she had been listening at the keyhole again.

'Would it hurt you so much to leave the silver on display and the china and cutlery in the sideboard until Mother arrives? That way the two of you can discuss where you want everything to go. After all, this is now home to you both.' Peter's suggestion sounded so rational that Edyth felt as though she was being unreasonable.

Deciding to employ the same tactics on him that he used on her, Edyth didn't answer him. She took the tray that held the tureen from Mrs Mack, set it on the table and handed the housekeeper the barely touched soup bowls in return.

'Thank you, Mrs Mack, I'll serve.' She spooned out a portion and handed it to Peter. The hotpot looked even worse than the leek and potato soup, but she persevered, filling her own plate as well as Peter's, the whole time conscious of Mrs Mack standing, bowls in hand, behind her chair, watching every move she made. 'That will be all, Mrs Mack, you may return to the kitchen.'

Mrs Mack left and closed the door. Edyth replaced the serving spoon in the tureen, glanced at Peter, then, without warning, whirled around and opened the door. Mrs Mack was standing in the hall, staring intently at a cobweb on the ceiling.

'That ceiling could do with a brush-down,' she slurred.

'The entire hall could with a damned good scrub,' Edyth said angrily.

'Edyth!' Peter reprimanded.

'I am sorry I swore, Peter. Mrs Mack, please don't ever let me catch you listening outside a door in this house again. If you should—'

'You'll what?' Mrs Mack stared coolly back at her.

'I'll reconsider your position in this house.' Edyth looked pointedly at Mrs Mack's apron. The outline of the bottle could be clearly seen in the pocket.

Mrs Mack leaned forward and looked around the corner at Peter. 'I'd like to hear what the Reverend Slater has to say about that.'

'You're slurring, Mrs Mack,' Edyth said.

'Am I, Mrs Slater?' Mrs Mack waited a full insolent minute before walking off down the passage. Edyth didn't return to her seat until she had seen the housekeeper close the kitchen door.

'Did you hear what she said to me, Peter?'

'You knew she was listening at the door?' The colour had drained from Peter's face.

'Yes,' she returned to her chair. 'Micah Holsten and I caught her doing the exact same thing when he called this afternoon. She even had the gall to open the door and interrupt us. Now will you allow me to sack her?'

'Let's eat. I have an extremely busy day tomorrow – as do you.'

Edyth clenched her fists. She had to find a way to break through Peter's maddening silences and point-blank refusal to discuss anything important – or intimate. She suspected that if she didn't succeed, their marriage was doomed to failure.

She picked up her knife and fork and poked at the hotpot. 'This is even worse than the soup. I doubt there was any meat on these mutton bones when Mrs Mack bought them. They're not fit for dogs let alone humans.' She speared an oyster with her fork and lifted it to her nose. 'The oysters are off, the mushrooms shrivelled . . . don't touch it, Peter.' She left her chair and piled her plate and Peter's on the tray that held the tureen.

'What are you going to do?'

If she hadn't known better, she would have said that he looked afraid. 'There has to be a fish and chip shop around here somewhere and, as it's a Saturday night, it's bound to be open until late. I'll send Judy to get some.'

'For all of us?' Peter asked.

'No, not for all of us,' Edyth opened the door and picked up the tray ready to carry it out. 'Just for Judy, you and myself. Mrs Mack can eat her hotpot.'

Judy returned to the kitchen after taking Peter's fish and chips to him in his study and saw that Edyth had laid two place settings of cork mats, knives and forks on the table.

'Sit down, Judy. I have plates warming on the rack on the range. We can eat right away.'

'I can't eat with you, Mrs Slater. Not even in the kitchen, it's not right.'

'Rubbish, Judy, the old mistress and maid relationship went out with Noah's Ark.' Edyth unwrapped the two remaining news-paper-wrapped parcels of the three Judy had brought from the fish shop and set them on the plates.

Edyth had elected to eat with Judy in the kitchen because Peter had insisted on being served his fish and chips in his study. He had told her that he liked to go to bed early on Saturdays and still needed to revise his sermon for the morning, something he had intended to do after dinner – if she hadn't refused to allow him to eat it – which suggested that he blamed her for their spoiled meal, not Mrs Mack. But she suspected that his main reason for retreating to his study was to avoid listening to her criticism of their housekeeper.

Fortunately for her and Judy, Mrs Mack had also refused to listen to complaints about the hotpot and, after announcing that she had worked quite enough hours for one day, swept up the stairs.

'These fish and chips look really excellent, Judy.' Edyth set the cruet and vinegar bottle on the table and sat down to eat.

'Best on the Bay, from the Sophia Street shop,' Judy said with a rare smile. She moved her place setting to a chair lower down the table, further away from Edyth's.

'We may as well sit opposite one another so we can talk.' Edyth put the teapot on the table, filled two glasses with water from the jug and set them next to the cups and saucers she had laid while Judy was out.

'What would you like me to do tomorrow, Mrs Slater?' Judy asked shyly.

'Apart from the essentials that have to be done every day – cleaning out the fire grates and laying the fires, dusting the hearths and mantelpieces, filling the coal and stick scuttles, cleaning the bathroom and kitchen, and laying the table – nothing.'

'Nothing?' Judy repeated in astonishment.

'Well, not exactly nothing because I would like fires laid and lit in every single room, including all the attics. This house feels so cold and damp I think it must be months, if not years, since it had a good airing. But just to warn you for the future, Reverend Slater doesn't believe in anyone working on a Sunday. So, from now on, all the cooking and baking for Sunday will have to be done on a Saturday and our food heated up on the day. But we have to eat something tomorrow. I don't know what. I checked the pantry again while you were out and found virtually nothing edible in it.'

'Lunch won't be a problem, that is, if you're prepared to pay for it,' Judy said cheerfully, finally cutting into her fish after Edyth had started eating hers. 'I'll take one of your saucepans down to Mrs Josefina's in George Street. She makes the most delicious Spanish salt fish stew you've ever tasted and fills a pot for two shillings.'

'She cooks for her neighbours?' Edyth asked in surprise. To her knowledge no one did anything like that in Pontypridd.

'She's turned her house into a sort of café. The sailors know that whatever the time of day they can always get a meal in her back kitchen. And Mr Goldman the Jewish baker will be baking fresh bread and bagels in the morning. His Sunday is Saturday, if you know what I mean. If there's a tin of salmon in the larder I can make bagels for breakfast. And I'll buy a loaf for you to eat with the stew.'

'I didn't see any salmon.' Edyth wasn't quite sure what bagels were, and the idea of eating them with tinned salmon for breakfast sounded positively exotic after the usual breakfast fare Mari served.

'Then I'll call in the corner shop run by Mr Mohammed when I go to the baker's first thing and get one. That only leaves tea and supper.'

'Judy, you're a miracle-worker. Reverend Slater and I have been invited out to tea tomorrow but if the baker has something you fancy you can buy it for yourself, and for supper—'

'I'll find something in the Arab shop or the baker's. Will a simple meal, like cheese on toast or potted beef rolls do?'

'Very nicely, I should think,' Edyth said in relief. 'First thing on Monday morning I'll go shopping and you must come with me.' She cut into the remaining half of her fish. The crisp golden batter concealed perfectly cooked, flaking white flesh. She'd had no idea how hungry she was until she'd started eating, but then, she'd spent more time talking than eating at her and Peter's farewell lunch in her parents' house.

'What about the housework, Mrs Slater?' Judy asked. 'I won't be able to do any if I go shopping with you on Monday.'

'I haven't even had time to start making the list of things that need doing in the house, Judy. But before I do anything else, I need to sort out a good grocer, greengrocer, butcher and baker, and as you've lived on the Bay, you're the best person to advise me on that. It appears we already have a regular milkman, although I'd like the churn in the pantry to have a good scouring before it's filled with fresh on Monday.'

'I'll do it tomorrow evening,' Judy offered.

'Don't let Reverend Slater catch you.' Edyth was ashamed of herself when she realized she was already planning to keep secrets from Peter.

'I'll go to early mass in the morning. That will leave me free to do some housework tomorrow evening when Reverend Slater is at Evensong.'

'I remember your Uncle Jed saying at Bella's wedding that your family are Catholic.'

'That won't be a problem, will it, Mrs Slater?' Judy asked anxiously.

'Not at all,' Edyth reassured. 'If I manage to organize regular deliveries of food, we can order in our goods every week and that will save time on shopping. When we come back on Monday, we'll make a simple lunch and start on the hall. It's the first place people see when they call here and I'm ashamed of the state of it.'

'It is grubby,' Judy agreed.

'I'll put an ironmonger on the list of places to visit. I'd better check the cleaning materials so I'll know what to buy before we go.' Edyth felt as though she were being crushed beneath the weight of tasks waiting to be done. But as there was nothing she could do about the house or the shopping until Monday morning, she cleared her mind of all practical considerations and thought of Judy.

She was finding the vicarage strange and uncomfortable after life at home and her brief holiday in the hotel. Judy must be finding it doubly so, especially in the light of Mrs Mack's hostility towards her.

'Micah – Mr Holsten – tells me you have an audition lined up, Judy?'

'I do.' Judy sprinkled more vinegar on her chips. 'For a part in the chorus of a touring musical, *The Lady Does*, at the beginning of next month. But Mr Holsten, Uncle Jed and the rest of the band have more faith in my talent than I do. I don't for one minute expect to get it.'

'You sing beautifully, and I wouldn't tell you did if you didn't.'

'So do a hundred other girls.'

Edyth sensed that Judy meant 'white girls'. 'Mr Holsten told me you'd been turned down for a few jobs and why.'

Judy shrugged. 'The first dozen rejections were the worst. I'm used to it now.'

'You shouldn't have to get used to it,' Edyth protested.

Judy forked the last chip from her plate into her mouth. 'Even if

I wanted to, there's nothing I can do about it, Mrs Slater. If I make a fuss, I'll never be given another audition, much less a job.'

'You're probably right, Judy, but injustice always makes me angry.'

'So this is where you are hiding?' Peter carried in his tray and looked disapprovingly from Edyth to Judy. 'You didn't eat in the dining room, Edyth?'

She knew it was a reprimand not a question. 'I cleared the table when Judy went to fetch the fish and chips. It didn't seem worth laying it again just for myself.' She took his tray from him.

'I'm going to bed. You haven't forgotten that you're running the Sunday school tomorrow, Edyth?'

'No.'

'I will look in on you about halfway through to check everything is all right. I won't be able to stay, though. I promised to help the choirmaster audition new members in the vestry. He has a full programme scheduled for this winter. As well as the Christmas carol concerts, there's the twelfth anniversary of Armistice Day. And there's the interfaith concerts you'll be helping Micah organize.' He went to the door. 'You haven't forgotten we've been invited to tea by the chairman of the church council and his wife?'

'Mr Maldwyn and Mrs Eirlys Williams.' Edyth had made a point of memorizing the name of every member of the church council. 'Should we take anything?'

'A bunch of flowers, perhaps?'

'We have no garden. Is there somewhere where I can buy flowers on a Sunday?' she asked Judy.

'One of the greengrocers usually has a few bunches.'

Peter unbent enough to say, 'Goodnight, Judy. Goodnight, Edyth.' He didn't add, 'see you in the morning', but Edyth felt that he was about to.

Edyth stacked the dishes on the table. 'You can go on up, too, Judy. You're sleeping on your feet.'

'I haven't had a full night's sleep since I moved in with Uncle Jed. His youngest two wake every hour on the hour.'

'I had a baby brother who did that for six months. I used to threaten to put his cot on the roof. Go on,' she said, kindly to Judy, 'go on up. I hope you'll be warm enough in that attic.'

'I will be. I've never had a fire in my bedroom before. It will be a real luxury.'

'If Mrs Mack gives you any trouble, my bedroom door is directly opposite the bottom of the upper staircase.'

'She hasn't said a word to me since I arrived, just sniffed a lot whenever I'm around.' Judy left her chair. 'Are you sure about this, Mrs Slater? I could wash the dishes. It won't take me a minute.'

'Or me, Judy. Goodnight.'

Judy went to the door, but she hesitated and turned back. 'Thank you again for giving me this job, Mrs Slater. If you hadn't, I would have had to leave the Bay. That's if I'd found anything at all.'

'I've a feeling it's me who's got the best end of the bargain, Judy. If I only had Mrs Mack to help me, I suspect that Reverend Slater and I would live in freezing cold squalor all winter. Sleep tight, see you in the morning.'

After Judy went to bed, Edyth squeezed a last cup of tea out of the pot, sat and looked at the dishes. She had two pounds and some coins in her purse and nothing else besides, except her savings. Her father might be an MP, but unlike most Members of Parliament he had no private means. His expenses were met from the funds of the mining unions and, knowing how little most of the members had to live on, he never spent a penny more than he absolutely had to. Most of the cost of her family's day-to-day living was met by the salary her mother was paid for working in Gwilym James.

Lloyd Evans had been a miner himself before management had singled him out and sent him to study engineering in one of the 'mining schools' that had been set up in the South Wales Valleys; in his case, Treforest. His father had been a miner in the days when the work had still been well paid and Billy Evans had invested every spare penny of his own and his sons' money in houses that they had rented out. They had used the rents to buy even more houses and, when Billy died, the houses had been divided between Lloyd and his brothers. Victor's share had bought him his farm, Joey still had some of his properties, although he had sold a few when he had purchased the house he lived in with his family in Pontypridd, and Lloyd had sold all of his and used the proceeds to buy the family home.

Harry might have inherited wealth – or rather would in five years when he reached his thirtieth birthday and his trust was dissolved – but her parents had been careful not to touch it. And her own savings were an accumulation of all her birthday and Christmas money, the percentage her parents had insisted she set aside from her weekly pocket money, and the money she had earned in the school holidays by cleaning the stockrooms and working in the staff canteen of Gwilym James.

All her parents had promised her and her sisters was an education that would enable them to earn a living that would hopefully keep them in the style in which they had been brought up. If she and Peter really were desperately short of money, and she couldn't see how they could be because she was sure that Peter would be paid at least as much as the Reverend Price – and the Prices could afford to employ a tweenie – then she would have no choice other than to dip into her savings.

She had enough money to pay Judy's wages for a couple of years, but there was still Mrs Mack. The woman was not only unfit for her job, she was ill-mannered and rude. Why wouldn't Peter get rid of her?

With thoughts whirling senselessly and fruitlessly around her head, she finished her tea, left the table, ran a sink of hot water, washed their plates, knives and forks, and wiped down the work surfaces. Her temper flared again when she saw the dirt trapped in practically every dark corner. It was a disgrace, especially when she considered how short a time had elapsed since the renovations, and she wondered if Mrs Mack did anything besides sit next to the warm range, nursing her 'medicine bottle'.

She was exhausted when she finished. She left the kitchen and checked that all the fires had been banked down for the night, and the fireguards hooked in front of the grates in the downstairs rooms before going upstairs.

The door to Peter's single front bedroom was closed. She went to the bathroom, washed, dressed in her negligée set and walked along the landing. She tapped Peter's door softly. When there was no reply she turned the handle. Then she knew for certain that he'd locked himself in — and her out.

Edyth rose at seven the next morning. She'd expected to be the first one up in the house, but when she went downstairs, she discovered Judy had seen to all the fires, laid the breakfast, filled the kettle and set it on the range to boil. She had also left a note on the kitchen table to say she was going shopping after attending early mass but expected to be back around quarter past eight.

Edyth made tea, intending to carry a cup up to Peter in bed, but when she went into the hall she saw that his study door was open and he was at his desk.

He looked up at her. 'Good morning.'

'Good morning, Peter.' As his door was open she went in and laid his tea on his desk.

'Did you sleep well?'

'Yes. Would you like breakfast?' It was only after she asked that she realized there wasn't any.

'I never eat breakfast before morning service on a Sunday.'

'Afterwards?'

'Please.'

'In that case I'll leave Judy a note and tell her to have it ready for us.'

'Did I tell you that Mrs Mack has asked for every Sunday off? I told her that would be all right as there is no housework to be done on Sundays.'

'Except the fires, and Judy has already seen to those,' she reminded him.

'You don't mind?'

'About Mrs Mack, no. I only wish the woman would stay away permanently.' When Peter didn't comment, she said, 'What have you taken for your text today?'

' "Let he among you who is without sin cast the first stone." '

'I'm looking forward to hearing it.' She didn't have the courage to ask him if it was a reference to her attitude towards Mrs Mack.

Throughout the service Edyth was conscious of the attention she was attracting among the congregation. Afterwards, there were so many people to meet, hands to shake and pleasantries to exchange, it was closer to lunch than breakfast time when she and Peter finally managed to return to the vicarage.

After Peter had eaten the salmon bagels Judy had prepared, he went to his study. Edyth sneaked off to the kitchen with Judy, where they checked the pantry and started a list of everything that had to be done to bring it up to her standard of cleanliness, or rather Mari's, which Edyth regarded as normal.

Fortunately Peter liked both the salt fish stew and bread Judy had bought from the Jewish baker and, by the time Edyth left for Sunday school, she was marginally happier and less irritable than she had been the day before. After writing lists with Judy and finding it somewhat satisfying to place things in order of priority, she began to formulate a mental list of what she considered to be the most serious problems between Peter and herself.

She had to find a way to make him talk to her and tell her why he wouldn't sleep with her. And, on a more practical note, she had to sort out a budget for housekeeping – and persuade him to sack Mrs Mack.

She was mulling over the approaches she might use to prompt him into discussing their love life – or rather lack of it – when she walked back into the church for Sunday school. A sea of small faces turned to look at her. Most of the teachers had already collected their groups and sat them in their pews.

A few of the younger children were enthusiastically swapping wax crayons and drawing pictures of what looked like Joseph's coat of many colours, some of the older ones were studiously reading texts, but there was a group of about half a dozen women and ten or so children hanging back behind the door. Edyth looked around. No one was making an effort to approach them. As Peter had placed her in charge of the school, she assumed the responsibility.

She noticed that although all the women were soberly dressed, every one had dyed hair, some peroxide blonde, some blue-black, but the woman standing slightly to the front had red hair bordering on crimson. She was of middle height, thick-set and tough-looking. But it wasn't until Edyth was standing in front of her that she recognized her as Anna Hughes.

Two small girls clung to her skirts. They were clean and neatly dressed in matching long-sleeved white woollen frocks, and white socks. Their mousy brown hair had been braided into plaits, fastened with large white bows, and their shoes were patent leather.

'Can I help you?' Edyth said. Close up she could see that the women's faces had been scrubbed clean, but there were traces of eyeblack around the eyebrows and lashes, and their noses and lips were shiny with the residue of the cream they had used to remove their make-up.

'You don't remember us, do you?' the woman with red hair asked.

'Yes, I do, Mrs Hughes.'

'Don't suppose there's much point in saying sorry we beat you up now, although we are. If we'd known who you were we wouldn't have touched a hair on your head.'

'You should have said you were going to marry the vicar,' a blonde woman reproached in a pronounced Irish accent.

'I believe I tried, but you weren't listening,' Edyth commented drily.

'You don't hold a grudge, do you?' Anna asked.

'It's forgotten, by me at any rate,' Edyth answered, insincerely.

Anna pushed forward the two girls who were trying to cling to her. Both were shy and plain. The younger of the two gazed up at Edyth through enormous brown eyes.

'Me and the girls,' Anna began, 'well, we got to talking and we thought we'd like the kids to go to Sunday school. Reverend Richards didn't like us coming to church. None of us. He tried to make us feel like dirt, said he didn't even want our money polluting the collecting plate. I suppose you and Reverend Slater think the same.'

Edyth remembered the text of Peter's sermon that morning. '*Let he who is without sin among you . . .*'

'Reverend Slater made it plain from his sermon this morning, Mrs Hughes, that God's church is open to everyone.'

'See, told you.' The blonde Irishwoman elbowed Anna out of the way and held out her hand to Edyth. 'I'm Colleen.'

'Edyth Evans . . . Slater,' Edyth corrected. 'Sorry, I've only been married a week.'

'We'll forgive you. So will you take our kids in Sunday school or not?' Anna challenged.

'I'd be delighted to have so many new scholars.' Edyth looked around at the classes. 'Have they been to Sunday school before?'

'No, told you, Reverend Richards didn't want them.'

'Then suppose I take them as one class now to see how we get on before disturbing the other classes, and at the end of the lesson, I'll put them in with the others in their age groups, so they can start fresh next Sunday.'

'You going to teach us about Jesus, miss?'

Edyth kneeled down so she was on the same level as the children. 'Not today. What's your name?'

'Daisy Hughes.'

'No, not today, Daisy. Today I'll tell you about a man called Noah who built an ark.'

'What's an ark?' one of the older boys asked.

'Trust my James. He's always asking questions,' Colleen said proudly.

'It's a sort of ship,' Edyth answered.

'Like we see in the dock?'

'Yes, James, exactly like the very biggest we see in the dock.'

'What time do you want us to come back for the kids, then?' Anna asked.

Edyth checked her watch. 'An hour.'

'You know something, Mrs Slater, you're all right.'

'Thank you, Mrs Hughes'

'Just Anna will do. I'm nobody's missus.'

Edyth shepherded the children to a quiet corner at the front of the church.

'Call in and have tea with us tomorrow,' Anna shouted. 'We're only round the corner and it's always quiet about three o clock in the afternoon.'

'I'm not sure what I'll be doing then,' Edyth said tactfully.

'We'll buy you a cream cake,' Colleen promised.

'In that case I'll definitely come.'

Five minutes after Anna and the other women left the church, Eirlys Williams settled her class and joined Edyth just as she was beginning her story of the great flood.

'Mrs Slater?'

'Yes, Mrs Williams?' Edyth looked up at her.

'Can I have a word?'

'Of course.'

'These children——.'

'You heard Reverend Slater's sermon this morning, Mrs Williams?'

'Yes.'

'I'm putting it into practice, Mrs Williams.' Edyth turned back to the children. 'And God spoke to Noah——'

'Why Noah, miss?' James asked.

'Because he knew he'd listen, silly,' Daisy said. 'Now don't interrupt the teacher again. Carry on, miss.'

# Chapter 20

'THANK YOU FOR THE TEA, Mrs Williams,' Edyth said gratefully as she and Peter made their way down the stairs from Mr and Mrs Williams's 'rooms' above their boot and shoe store in Bute Street. 'It was thoughtful of you to invite us so soon after we returned. And you really must give me your recipe for fruit scones.'

'Reverend Slater did seem to enjoy them.' Eirlys Williams pressed a jar of raspberry preserves into Edyth's hand. 'He enjoyed these, too, and I made far more than we can use. We always go fruit-picking on my sister's farm in the Vale for a week in July. This year's crop was very good.'

'Thank you very much. I'll put it to good use.' Edyth slipped the jar into the shopping bag that she had used to carry the potted crocus bulbs Judy had bought that morning for her to give to Mrs Williams. 'I'm afraid our house is not ready to receive guests yet, but it will be in a week or two, and the moment it is, you will be among our first invited visitors.' She stood in front of Mr Williams so he could help her on with her mackintosh. The rain that had poured down relentlessly for days showed no sign of abating, and the Williams's house was a good fifteen-minute walk from the church and vicarage.

'We'll look forward to accepting your invitation. Thank you so much for coming. It was a pleasure to have you here, Mrs Slater, Reverend.' Mrs Williams shook hands with Edyth then Peter. Peter continued to grip her hand after he had shaken it.

'You do understand what I said to you about Anna Hughes's children, Mrs Williams.'

'The key to Christianity is forgiveness, and the return of the prodigal.' Mrs Williams was tight-lipped but she repeated the essence of the argument Peter had expounded when she and her husband had tackled him about Edyth's inclusion of the prostitutes' children in the Sunday school.

'Thank you for an enjoyable afternoon, Mrs Williams, Mr Williams. A most welcome respite on my busiest day; I look forward to seeing you both at Evensong.' Peter stepped out of the house ahead of Edyth and put up his umbrella.

Edyth thanked them again and, on impulse, kissed Mrs Williams's cheek before taking Peter's arm.

Peter peeled back his glove and peered at his watch after the Williams's had closed their front door. 'Only an hour before evening service begins.'

'It's been a busy day.'

'I'm afraid this is typical of what our Sundays are likely to be from now on. I've been thinking over what you said, Edyth—'

'About the bedrooms?' she broke in eagerly.

'About the housekeeping,' he amended. 'Supposing I put a fixed amount into your bank account every month? I will pay Mrs Mack and Judy Hamilton's wages directly to them and also the gas and electricity bills. Do you think ten pounds a month sufficient for food, coals, boot and shoe repair, clothes replacement and incidental household expenses?'

'I'm not sure. Coals will be expensive, especially this month, as I have asked Judy to keep a fire burning in every room. The house is very cold and damp. It feels as though it hasn't been lived in for years. I don't think Reverend Richards could have used many rooms.'

'Just his study, bedroom and dining room before I arrived, and I've never known the dining room to be anything other than freezing. I thought I'd pay in ten pounds tomorrow to cover the first month. If it isn't enough, we can go through the figures together and either find ways to cut costs, or up the amount, although I warn you it won't be easy to find any extra.'

'We're not going to have a joint bank account?'

'No, Edyth, I really think financial matters should be left to the man in the family.'

She knew from the tone of his voice that his decision was final.

'In that case, I'll detail where every penny is spent from tomorrow.'

'Good.'

'Thank you for backing me over allowing those children into Sunday school.'

'It's sound common and theological sense.' He looked down at her and smiled, and as always when they were discussing anything that wasn't personal to them, she felt close to him. 'No good can come of excluding them. It would build ideas of superiority in the minds of the other children and make the ones who weren't allowed in resentful. As it is, you, and the other teachers have an opportunity to counteract the malign influences those children are being subjected to. They won't live with their mothers for ever and who knows what you might inspire them to do when they make their own way in life? Or what heights they may reach as a result of your teaching?'

'There may be a budding vicar in young James. The Irish woman's son,' she explained. 'I've never heard a child ask so many questions.'

'You were able to answer them?'

'More by luck than by education. He really made me think about some of the things I've always taken for granted. I enjoyed teaching him.'

'Perhaps you should have gone to college after all,' he said quietly.

'Peter—'

'If we hurry we may have time for a cup of Judy's excellent tea. I take back my reservations about employing her, Edyth. We would never have eaten so well today if we'd relied on Mrs Mack. Perhaps we can keep Mrs Mack on to do the washing and the cleaning and promote Judy to cook.'

Edyth quickened her pace to keep step with him. After only a week of marriage she knew that was the closest she would get to an apology from Peter regarding his intransigent attitude towards Mrs Mack. But she still couldn't understand why he insisted on employing her when her housekeeping skills were even worse than her cooking.

Edyth woke cold and shivering before seven the next morning. She slipped on her robe and went into the bathroom. Peter's toilet bag and shaving kit were neatly laid out on a shelf next to the bath. She felt the brush in the shaving mug and opened the tin of shaving soap. Both were damp so she knew he was already up and, she suspected, working in his study. She bathed and dressed, then went downstairs to find the door between the kitchen and the washhouse open and Mrs Mack sorting through the laundry bags they had brought with them from Pontypridd.

'The girl's cooking the Reverend's breakfast,' Mrs Mack barked abruptly.

'Good morning, Mrs Mack,' Edyth said pointedly in the hope of inculcating some manners in the woman. 'I presume you're referring to Miss Hamilton?'

'The Reverend told her to carry on, even after I came down,' Mrs Mack continued as if Edyth hadn't spoken.

'Reverend Slater and I have decided that Miss Hamilton should take over the cooking,' Edyth informed her.

'Did you now? You could have told me. Anyway, I thought I'd make a start on the washing.' Mrs Mack straightened her back and adjusted the hosepipe she was using to fill the gas boiler from the cold tap.

'Can you wash?' It was only after Edyth blurted out the question that she realized how tactless it sounded.

'I've been washing for over fifty years. And as you've had your way and stopped me from cooking for the Reverend, what else should I be doing?' she demanded crossly.

'Cleaning, Mrs Mack,' Edyth suggested. She bent down and scooped up her fine silk underclothes and woollen frocks from the floor.

'I cleaned this house before you came. You've only been back a day. That's not enough time to dirty it.'

'All the paintwork needs washing down, Mrs Mack. You can start in the hall. And as soon as you've finished the paintwork there, you can give the floor a good scrub.'

'The tiles are damaged,' Mrs Mack declared. 'You won't get them no cleaner than they are, and as for the paintwork, the entire house has only just been decorated. Everyone knows you shouldn't wash new paint. If you do, you'll damage it.'

'Not if you use soft soap and water,' Edyth countered. 'And the paintwork needs washing because there's wallpaper paste and bits of paper left by the decorators all over the skirting boards.'

'The washing needs doing first.' Mrs Mack continued to heap Peter's white linen shirts, dog collars, cotton vests and pants into a pile.

Edyth held her breath and counted to ten in an effort to control her temper. As Peter was intent on keeping Mrs Mack on, it made sense to give the woman something to do. She consoled herself further with the thought that there wasn't anything the house-keeper could do to ruin white cotton and linens – unless she chose to boil them with coloureds that bled out their dyes. But if Peter hadn't bought his underclothes and shirts pre-shrunk, they shouldn't be boiled at all, not if they were to keep their shape and size. However, if Mrs Mack should ruin Peter's clothes it would annoy him. He might even see sense and get rid of the woman.

Edyth bundled her own clothes together and looked around to make sure she hadn't missed any. 'You may do the Reverend Slater's washing, Mrs Mack, but not mine.'

'Please yourself. Although I would have thought you had enough to do without rinsing out your own frillies and fancies.' Mrs Mack fingered an oyster silk camisole draped on top of the bundle Edyth had made.

Edyth examined the washhouse. It ran half the length of the back of the house. The roof was glazed like a conservatory as were the sides, but because of the high walls that surrounded most of the house it was as dark and gloomy as the sitting room and dining room. Two lines had been strung across the full width, both ornamented with the type of dolly peg sold by gypsies, but given the lack of light and warmth Edyth could imagine wet washing hanging there for days, all the while gradually growing colder, damper and, in time, mildewed.

'Is this the only place you have to dry the washing in winter, Mrs Mack?'

'You want the sun to shine in the Bay in late October just for you, Mrs Slater?' the housekeeper enquired caustically.

Edyth decided it was time to let Mrs Mack know that she didn't have a monopoly on sarcasm. 'All the year round, Mrs Mack, but as that's impossible in Cardiff, we'll have to improvise. I noticed there's an airing rack in the kitchen above the range.'

'You can only put clothes on that once they stop dripping.'

Edyth wondered if it was her imagination or if Mrs Mack had spoken with marginally more respect. She looked around the washhouse again. There was an enormous sink with a single cold tap – no gas water heater as in the kitchen and bathroom – the gas boiler, two tin baths, several buckets, a scrubbing board, wooden dolly, tongs and no other utensils that she could see. 'You have no mangle?'

'We did, but the Reverend Richards's brother took it.'

'You can't wash without one, especially in this weather.'

'Arms were made before rollers.'

'Wringing clothes wears them out, Mrs Mack. I'll buy one this morning and ask them to deliver it as soon as possible. Don't wring the clothes. Leave them in the rinsing water until it comes.'

The doorbell chimed down the hall.

'The problem with this vicarage is the parishioners never give you a moment's peace,' Mrs Mack grumbled.

'I'll get it.' Edyth walked through into the passage. Peter had left the breakfast table and was standing in the hall, napkin in hand.

'Who is it?' he asked, when he saw her leave the kitchen.

'I could only tell you that if I could see through walls, Peter.' She opened the front door. A taxi had parked outside and the driver was helping a woman out of the back. He was holding an umbrella low over her head, concealing her features, and he didn't lift it until they reached the step.

Peter's mother looked up at Edyth and gave her a cold, hard smile.

'I decided to come a week early and surprise you, Edyth. I expect that you can do with all the help you can get to put the house in order.'

'Of course you want to use my things, Edyth.' Florence Slater dismissed Edyth's protests the moment she began to make them. 'That way, you can keep your wedding presents wrapped for best. The time to use them will come soon enough, after you've worn out all my poor old china, linen and glassware. By the way, Edyth, I put rice corns in the salt cellar.' She lifted up the silver cruet that had been hers. 'It was *so* damp. I shook and shook and nothing came out. You obviously have many things to learn before you become a competent housewife. And this house is *so* cold and damp.'

'Which is why I ordered Judy to light fires in all the rooms,' Edyth said testily.

'I ordered her to rake them out in the attics, Edyth. That was sheer extravagance.'

'But Judy only moved in yesterday and the room had been empty for months, probably years—'

'Peter?' Ignoring Edyth, Florence looked across the dining table to her son. 'I have had the most marvellous idea about the Mothers' Union. You remember what a success I made of the one in Mumbles?'

'Of course, Mother.' Peter turned to Edyth who was sitting on his right because his mother had taken her place at the opposite end of the table to his own. 'The Bishop said it was the most dynamic Mothers' Union in the diocese.'

'I will do the same here. I'll put the ladies to work raising funds for good works in the parish. With so many unemployed men in the area, they can start a clothing club. We'll begin with baby clothes. They are so small you can turn out the most wonderful garments from the tiniest scraps of material. From there, we'll progress to school age children. And we'll lobby the shopkeepers for donations to make up hampers for the destitute. I saw so many shops in Bute Street. I had no idea the area was so large or the buildings so grand . . .'

'Mother is a wonderful organizer,' Peter whispered to Edyth.

'I can believe it,' Edyth said feelingly. She had returned from her shopping expedition with Judy to discover that not only had Florence well and truly settled into the vicarage, she had also assumed the position of lady of the house.

Florence had ordered Mrs Mack to lay the table for lunch and instructed her to set her place in future in the one traditionally occupied by the wife. She told Mrs Mack to make a Spanish omelette from the goods Edyth had bought, which had arrived back at the vicarage before Edyth and Judy, who had been held up in the ironmongers. And she had stood over Mrs Mack, watching every move the woman made to ensure that the lunch was cooked to her precise and strict specifications.

As if it wasn't bad enough that she'd been relegated to a side place at the table, Edyth had discovered that all the books Judy had taken from the shelves in the sitting room and the ornaments she had put to one side ready to be packed and carried up to the attic had been replaced in exactly the same positions as before.

'Edyth, Mother is speaking to you,' Peter reprimanded.

'Sorry, Mother.' Edyth didn't know why she was apologizing. She wasn't in the least bit sorry that she hadn't listened to Peter's mother. In fact, the less attention she paid her, the less likely she was to disagree with her.

'I was saying how thoughtful it was of you and Peter to arrange our bedrooms next to one another, so I can call on you in the night, if I should need you.'

'Why should you need me?'

'I suffer from rheumatism and my sore throats are agony. Especially at night. Sometimes a hot drink can help me to get back to sleep. It was so inconvenient in Alice's house. The maids slept on the top floor and Alice wouldn't allow any of them to move down close to our bedrooms although there was a perfectly serviceable box room that would have been adequate for a maid. Should I need a drink or anything else, you will now be on hand to get it for me.'

'If you'll excuse me, I have to sort out Mrs Mack's and Judy's duties.' Edyth left the table.

'So soon? I thought we could talk over coffee, Edyth,' Florence remonstrated. 'Peter told me that there is a meeting of the Mothers' Union tonight. I intended to outline some of my plans to you so you could implement them with the Young Wives. Two church groups working towards the same common aim would get twice as much work done.'

'I need to make sure that both Judy and Mrs Mack will be kept busy while I am out. And I wanted to let Mrs Mack know that Judy is taking an hour off this evening. She has an appointment with her uncle and the police to discuss the theft of furniture from her grandmother's house,' Edyth explained, in case her mother-in-law thought she was in the habit of giving her servants time off in the evening. Florence had already subjected her to one lecture on lax household management and waste after unpacking the boxes of groceries, taking great delight in scrutinizing every single item, complaining about its cost and suggesting cheaper alternatives that Edyth should switch to, and all of it within Mrs Mack's earshot.

Edyth had managed to listen in silence but she knew that if she stayed and talked over anything with Florence Slater now, she would end up quarrelling with her.

'You're not doing your digestion any good, Edyth, rushing about like this,' Florence warned.

'It can't be helped,' Edyth said through gritted teeth. 'I have a meeting arranged.'

'The interfaith meeting in the Mission doesn't start until six o'clock,' Peter reminded her.

'I promised to call in on some parishioners at three.' Edyth hoped Peter wouldn't ask their names. 'I also need to check the new mangle.' She left the room, closed the door behind her and leaned against it for a moment.

She took a deep breath, looked down and saw Judy on her hands and knees scrubbing the tiles with a wire brush and, from the smell wafting from the bucket next to her, a strong solution of caustic soda. Judy gave her a tentative smile, but the look in her eyes was unmistakable: a mix of sympathy and commiseration. But then she recalled Micah telling her that Judy too had suffered the indignity of being relegated to 'second position' in another woman's house.

She had been a fool to think that it could be possible for her and Peter's mother to live in harmony together in the same vicarage.

*

'I never thought I'd see the day when we'd entertain a vicar's wife to tea.' Colleen carried a brown earthenware teapot over to the hissing kettle and filled it.

Edyth looked around the room. She was aware of what went on in the house and knew exactly how the women made their money. Her mother had even talked to her and her sisters about what sex could be like for a woman when love wasn't involved. But she still hadn't quite known what to expect from a 'house of ill-repute'.

That the women would be sitting around in their underclothes or half-naked, waiting for men to come along and choose one of them? That there would be red lampshades everywhere and crimson wall hangings, as described in the lurid novels that she and Bella had managed to lay their hands on, despite the efforts of their parents and teachers to censor their reading.

In fact, everything was crushingly normal. The kitchen was large, scrubbed, and cleaner and more comfortable than hers in the vicarage. There were four easy chairs and a large pine table. The cushions on the chairs were covered in wool-worked needlepoint covers and the tablecloth was blue and red checked cotton. A jug of white dahlias stood in the centre of the table, next to it was a plate of assorted cream cakes. Edyth smiled when she recalled Colleen promising her one.

'Your tea, Mrs Slater.' Colleen poured it, but a young girl handed her the cup.

'Thank you.' Edyth took it from her.

'Gertie's just joined us,' Colleen explained. 'She's from Maerdy and she wants to be here, don't you, Gertie?'

'Yes,' Gertie answered enthusiastically. 'I want to make money and I can make more in a week here than I would in six months if I went into service.'

'Most of us choose this life,' Colleen said as though Edyth had asked what they were doing there.

'I see,' Edyth murmured, not knowing what else to say.

'It's nice to have a woman visitor for a change.' Anna offered Edyth a plate and the cakes.

'Thank you.' Edyth picked up a chocolate éclair.

'I know what you're doing, Mrs Slater,' Colleen said archly.

'You do?' Edyth looked at the Irishwoman in surprise.

'You're wondering if we have any naked men chained to the bedposts upstairs.'

'Leave it off, Colleen,' Anna snapped. 'Mrs Slater's married. She knows what goes on here. And the fact that she's here means she's broad-minded, so there's no need for you to make her out to be anything else.'

'I'm not trying to make her out to be anything,' Colleen bit back. She sat next to Edyth. 'Respectable young woman like you, Mrs Slater, is bound to be curious. Newly married — just found out what fun four bare legs in a bed can be, and what two people can get up to when there's no one to stop them. You must be curious about the extras we give that tempt a man to stray from his wife's bed. And come back to us time and again for more. Maybe we haven't the Reverend Slater calling on us yet—'.

'Nor are we likely to,' Anna interrupted, giving Colleen a warning glance.

'Oh, I don't know. People like a change. One man even had the gall to tell me he came calling on me because his wife was perfect and it palled after a while. He liked a bit of rough and tumble as contrast.'

'What are the Reverend's tastes?' Gertie asked naively.

'As if she'd tell us,' Colleen laughed. 'But I bet now you've found out what they are, Mrs Slater, you must wonder what it would be like with someone else. And there are plenty of good-looking young men around the Bay. Although I'll grant you not many can hold a candle to the Reverend. He is very pretty.' She raised her eyebrows and puckered her lips.

'I . . . I . . .' Edyth could feel her cheeks burning as colour rushed into them.

'Happy now you've succeeding in embarrassing her, Colleen?' Anna reprimanded. 'I don't know what you're trying to achieve. We can all remember what it was like to be a bride. Even me. When we were first married, my Patrick and I couldn't keep our hands off one another.' She smiled at the memory. 'Not even in church. I remember him sliding his hand up my skirt during a sermon. But then it was a very long one and most of the congregation were asleep – at least, I hope they were because he went home with my drawers in his pocket.'

Edyth barely heard the end of Anna's sentence. There was that phrase again. The same one Bella had used when she'd talked about Toby: *Couldn't keep our hands off one another.*

'You were married, Anna?' Edyth asked, sensing everyone expected her to say something when the room fell silent.

'We all were at some time or another. Why the surprise?' Anna finished her cream doughnut, lit a cigarette and leaned back in her chair.

'What happened to your husbands?'

'One of three things,' Colleen answered. 'They died, left us, or we left them.'

'My Patrick was killed in the Senghenydd pit disaster.' Anna's eyes darkened with a grief Edyth suspected she had never come to terms with. She knew just how few miners' bodies were brought to the surface for burial after an explosion or fall in a pit. The owners generally thought it uneconomic to dig them out. And at Senghenydd 440 had been killed.

'I'm sorry,' Edyth murmured, wishing the words didn't sound so inadequate.

'It was seventeen years ago this week,' Anna said briskly. 'You'd think I'd have forgotten it by now, wouldn't you? He was only eighteen. Sometimes I sit and wonder what he would have been like if he'd lived. He came to Wales from Donegal when he was fourteen because he heard there was work in the pits. I was skivvying in the house he lodged in. We lied about our ages and got married. Did all right too for a while. Rented a house, I did the housework, he brought home the money. We were looking forward to the baby I was carrying. He was born three months after Patrick went. I called him Patrick after his father. But he didn't last long, neither. Died in the workhouse of scarlet fever before he was a year old.' Anna shuddered. 'But a lot of water has flowed in and out of the docks since then.'

'I had a boy when I was fifteen,' Colleen said.

'James?' Edyth asked, struggling to keep her voice even after hearing Anna's story.

'Not James, Tom. I named him for his father, but that bastard up and left me. I heard he's living with a woman in Liverpool now. My Tom went to sea as a cabin boy when he was ten. He's an able seaman now,' she said proudly. 'He's somewhere in the Pacific. I had a letter from him two days ago. James is the son of one of my regulars. He's bright because he takes after his father, who's real crache and kind, not like some. Gives me money for James, as well as myself.' She saw the bemused expression on Edyth's face. 'We all have regulars, every one of us.'

'Change your tune, Colleen,' Anna rebuked. 'This is no conversation to be having with a vicar's wife. Perhaps it was a bad idea to invite you here, Mrs Slater. Someone seeing you walk through the door could put two and two together and make a hundred and four, if you get my drift.'

'Please, call me Edyth, and I'm sure that everyone who knows me would realize I am only visiting you and the other . . .' she hadn't meant to hesitate but she did, 'ladies.'

'Well,' Anna said doubtfully, 'I suppose it's all right in here. But I don't want you – none of you,' she looked at the women assembled in the kitchen, 'talking to Mrs Slater outside, lest anyone thinks she's become one of us.'

'Given what the Reverend Slater—'

'*Enough*, Colleen.'

Anna silenced Colleen so quickly Edyth wondered if Peter had come into the brothel before they married. Surely not. If he had, he wouldn't be so reluctant to come to her bed, unless he had picked up one of the 'diseases' people whispered about. Was that it? Had Peter visited the brothel and caught something he was afraid of passing on to her?

'You take any nonsense from anyone about letting our kids come to Sunday school?' Anna changed the subject.

'No,' Edyth answered. 'My husband thinks it's a good idea. One of the things he wanted to do when he came down here was to open the church to everyone on the Bay.'

'He's certainly done that,' Anna agreed.

'We all want our kids to be educated so they can have chances we never had.' Colleen tore a piece from a newspaper, twisted it into a makeshift spill, pushed it in the fire and, when it flared, lit a cigarette. 'This isn't a bad life but it's not easy to bring up kids when you're working. On the other hand, none of us can turn down the chance to make a few bob, because we all know how short a working girl's life can be.'

'Why short?' Edyth asked.

'When your looks go, you're out because there's always up-and-coming fresh competition.'

'But that doesn't mean the scrap heap,' Anna chipped in. 'I've almost enough money put by to buy a shop like Jenny Fish.'

'She worked in a house for twenty years, now she owns a fish and chip shop,' Colleen explained.

'Not in Cardiff, mind, Llandaff.' Anna spoke as if Llandaff was somewhere exotic, not a village four miles up the road.

'And then there's Llinos Bakewell, she's a real success story.' Colleen drew heavily on her cigarette. 'She went home to Carmarthen and passed herself off as a widow. She had a tidy bit of money and bought herself a nice house and shop that she rented out. Every widower and bachelor for miles started courting her but she ended up marrying the local doctor. Talk about landing on your feet.'

'Or on your back, and that's where we're all headed if we're lucky, girls.' Anna left her chair and glanced at the clock on the wall. 'I heard Llinos caught him with her winning ways between the sheets. He thought he was in God's pocket marrying a widow with readies and a bit of experience. Wonder if she'll ever tell him just where she gained the experience. It's time for us to go to work, Mrs Slater – Edyth – and time for you to leave. You don't want to bump into any of our clients. Like I said, if they see you here they might get the wrong idea.'

'I like the ones who leave work early.' Colleen flicked her ash into the range. She mimicked an English accent. ' "Just off to the bank before I go home, Miss Smith." ' *Sotto voce* she added, 'Via Anna Hughes's for a spot of jiggery pokery.'

'You can set your clock by our clients.' Anna smiled. 'The ones who come before seven.'

' "Sorry, dear, must go into the office early. I have letters to write before the meeting. No, don't disturb yourself; I'll get the girl to bring you a nice cup of tea in bed." ' Colleen dropped the accent. 'Then it's a quick whiz round here for a bit of mattress-bouncing for half an hour to set them up for the day.'

'The real bosses come round mid-morning because they can afford to extend their elevenses into lunch,' Anna observed.

'Unlike the clerks, who steal ten minutes from their lunch hours for a quickie.' Colleen stretched her arms above her head, throwing her breasts into prominence.

'Followed by the crache who come after lunch and like a snooze before going back to the office.'

'And the four o'clockers who will be here now.' Anna added pointedly.

Edyth gathered her coat and handbag from the chair where she had left them.

'The casuals arrive from six onwards, but the real moneyed crache come down here on a weekend, drunk as lords and looking for the good times they've heard they can get in the Bay, which was why we were so pissed off when we saw you standing on the street corner.'

'Language, Colleen,' Anna rebuked.

'Thank you for the coffee and cake, ladies.' Edyth was strangely reluctant to leave. She would have liked to have heard a few more of Colleen's stories about the mysteries of sex. Despite the women's coarse turn of phrase, which she suspected was down to the way they made a living, there was a genuine warmth about them that she found endearing, and she could have stayed in the kitchen for hours listening to them talk about their gentlemen friends – and four bare legs in a bed.

'You must come to the vicarage for tea,' she said as Anna walked her to the door.

'Oh no, Edyth, that won't do. It's one thing to allow our kids into Sunday school, quite another to have us in your home, especially as I heard that the Reverend's mother moved in today.'

'How did you know?' Edyth wound her muffler around her neck and unclipped her umbrella.

'The taxi driver's a regular. We give him a couple of free ones a week to show our gratitude for the trade he brings in. Thank you for seeing our kids all right in Sunday school. You're welcome to call round whenever you want a chinwag, but make sure it's our quiet time.'

'Thank you for the tea and cake.' Edyth felt as though she were being thrown out.

'See you around, Mrs Slater, thanks for the Bible talk, sorry you couldn't convert any of us,' Anna said in a loud voice for the benefit of a passer-by.

Edyth heard the door close behind her but there was no 'click' of the latch and she suspected that most of the 'regulars', as Colleen had called them, simply walked in.

She turned back and looked at the house when she reached the corner. A man was walking through the door. It was Charlie Moore.

Edyth shuddered. Four bare legs in the bed were all well and good – provided you could choose the owner of the other two legs.

She looked around the street. Although it was only just four o'clock, a thick grey twilight had fallen. There had been no let-up in the rain, and it was two hours before she had to be at the meeting in the Norwegian church. She turned towards the vicarage then stopped.

She had a sudden vision of her mother-in-law presiding over the ornate Victorian silver tea service she loathed. Florence was pouring tea, monopolizing Peter's conversation and feeding him the cakes and biscuits that she had bought in the baker's that morning because she knew she wouldn't have time to bake that day.

Feeling restless, angry and needing to think, Edyth set her face to the sea and headed down the Bay towards the docks.

# Chapter 21

EDYTH TURNED HER BACK on the canal, where lines of coal barges, waiting their turn to be unloaded at the quays, basked like fat slugs in a cabbage patch. She walked up the street, absorbing the sights and sounds of the place that, she reminded herself, was now 'home'. A horse snorted and pawed the tarmac when the boy driving it reined it in every few yards for the housewives to come to their door at his cry: 'Bak–er.'

The fishmonger was standing, leaning on his cart on the corner, his gleaming wares open to the teeming rain while he dropped a handful of coins into a woman's hand. Eirlys Williams had told her that the tradesman was the unofficial money-lender on the Bay, and frequently 'subbed' seamen's families until the ships came in.

Two women dressed in blackened, flowered overalls were filling buckets from a mound of coal that had been delivered to their front door. Edyth watched them carry it through the house and wondered why it hadn't been delivered down the lane to the back gate. But then she hadn't walked at the back of this particular terrace of 'two-ups, two-downs' and perhaps, like Pontypridd, only some of the houses had a back yard.

Car engines roared ahead of her in Bute Street as bankers, merchants, businessmen and their clients drove to and from the imposing offices. And in the distance, the faint banging and grinding of wagons crashing into one another resounded from the railway shunting yards.

Inside open doors, toddlers were crawling and watching their mothers negotiate with the delivery men. And down a lane, she spotted a crowd of men, crouched on their haunches, staring intently at the ground. Rain obviously didn't affect the open-air casinos that abounded in the Bay.

She felt surrounded by noise and people, and she wanted to be alone. That meant circumventing the busiest part of the docks where the large ocean-going vessels were berthed, and the Pier Head where day-trippers embarked on the pleasure boats that sailed across to the Devon port of Ilfracombe and around the Welsh coast, although she knew there was little likelihood of seeing anyone she knew on a wet Monday afternoon in October.

She reached Bute Street and passed cafés filled with Filipino and Somali seamen, talking in their native tongue and playing dominoes and cards to while away the time before they managed to secure a berth on a vessel out of Tiger Bay. She spotted lookouts posted near the doors to warn of approaching policemen, who couldn't always be counted on to turn a blind eye to illegal gambling. And the whole time she returned the greetings of men, women and children she had seen in church.

Already she felt that she was accepted as a resident of the Bay with a job to do. It was what she had told her father she wanted. But when she had spoken to him, she had assumed that she would have a normal marriage – and be mistress of her own house.

She reached the sea and a comparatively deserted area where small boats bobbed alongside their moorings. Further along to her left she could see the dry dock yards. Two massive ships had been winched out of the water and they looked larger beached than she had ever seen a vessel on water.

She stood for a few minutes and admired the graceful, elegant lines of a tall masted sailing ship moored out in the bay. A lovely relic from a slower, more romantic age that towered, in every sense of the word, over the squat, ugly steam ships spawned by the industrial era. She recalled the stories she had read about ships and sailors, from her childhood favourite, *Treasure Island*, to Richard Henry Dana's *Two Years Before the Mast*, and imagined herself back in a time where schooners and ships powered solely by the wind were the only ones that sailed the seas.

A resounding catcall shattered her daydream and reminded her that she was within sight of the workmen painting a hull in one of the dry docks. She put her head down, pulled her umbrella even further over her face and continued on her aimless way. A rickety, wooden-planked walkway stretched down from the quay, jutting into the rows of small boats, and she stopped again, mesmerized by the sound of a lone saxophone.

The melody was new to her. Sad and yearning, it captured the essence of the grey day. In it, she could hear the spasmodic rhythm of the rain falling on to the sea; the roll of the small boats as they bobbed in the swell of the tide, abandoned and forlorn, waiting for their captains to bring them to life; the relentless, determined ploughing out to sea of the larger vessels, which had places to go and goods to deliver; and, permeating every tuneful phrase, her own dark, restless mood.

She leaned on a post and continued to listen until the final note was drowned in the rasping blast of a steamer. Three more blasts followed in quick succession, sending the gulls screaming high into the air. Her blood ran cold. The eerie, raucous noise was similar to the colliery sirens in Pontypridd that not only marked the beginning of the colliers' shifts, but also sounded the alarm whenever there was an accident or fall underground.

She was still standing, staring at the wash of the steamer, when Micah Holsten emerged from below deck of the smallest, shabbiest boat moored off the walkway. He was dressed in a seaman's dark coat and peaked cap, an instrument case tucked under his arm. He waved to her and she waved back.

'Edyth, what are you doing in this deserted corner of the docks?'

'Listening to music. Was that you playing the saxophone?' she asked when he drew closer.

'It was,' he admitted warily. 'Are you going to report me for cruelty to your ears? Or to a bird society for frightening the gulls?'

'Neither. It was a lovely piece.'

'Thank you from the bottom of my heart,' he rejoined flippantly. 'I come down here to practise because people complain long, loud and bitterly if I play in the mission. They say it interferes with their concentration and they can neither read nor play chess. Helga says it curdles the waffle batter and Moody agrees with her. However, I had no idea I had an audience out here.'

'An appreciative one. What was the piece?' she asked. 'I haven't heard it before.'

'That's because you caught the world première. I've only just written it, and christened it "Rainy Bute Blues".'

'I had no idea you composed music.'

'It's a hobby. Cheaper than gambling and drinking, and emotionally safer than women.'

'It's beautiful and exactly how I feel.'

'I hope not. It's a sad piece.' He ducked beneath her umbrella. His blue eyes shone warmly into hers; his face, damp and smiling, was so close she could smell the toothpowder on his breath. 'It's wet out here.'

'That's stating the obvious.' She returned his smile.

'Can I tempt you with a cup of coffee?'

She looked around. 'You could if there was a café. But there's none in sight.'

'Oh, but there is, and a very exclusive one.' He offered her his hand, she took it, and he led her down the walkway. He jumped ahead of her on to the deck of his boat, then reached out and lifted her across. 'Welcome to my cave.'

'Your cave looks suspiciously like a boat to me, Pastor.'

'No, it's my cave. Like bears, every man needs a retreat, and this is mine.'

Edyth didn't know anything about boats, but Micah's was even more dilapidated close up than it had appeared from the quayside. Half a dozen people couldn't have stood on top without elbowing one another dangerously close to the edge. It was also in poor condition. The deck floor was splintered, there was hardly any paint on the surfaces and what little there was had curled back from the sodden wood like the skin of a dried orange.

'You go to sea in this?' she asked in concern.

'I value my life too much. The *Escape* – aptly named, don't you think? – floats here, just. But I have a feeling that even if it had an engine, and I managed to set course for the open sea, both I and the boat would end up beneath, not on, the waves.'

'It doesn't have an engine?' she asked in amusement, looking around for sails.

'I exchanged it and what was left of the ragged sails for a month's sugar ration for the mission. We don't get through that much sugar but then it wasn't a very good engine. But it did have some scrap value.'

'Was this boat ever seaworthy?'

'Not that I know of. I inherited it from a friend. He bought it at auction and intended to renovate it, but died a week later. Some say his end was hastened when he realized how much work he had taken on. However, if not luxurious, the cabin is watertight and it gives me what I need: privacy to play my saxophone and think for an hour or two away from the bedlam the mission frequently degenerates into, especially when the Scandinavian ships are in port.'

'A floating cave,' she suggested.

'Exactly. Climb down into the cabin; there are only a few steps.' He stood back and she recalled what he'd said about always allowing a lady to go downstairs ahead of a man.

She reached a door no more than five feet high. She opened it and ducked down. She had expected mildew and the sour stench of damp, but the place was clean, if faded, and warm, and smelled of fragrant, freshly ground coffee. Two small sofas set in alcoves on either side of the area took up most of the space. Their cushions were upholstered in oriental tapestry, bleached with age but intact. A table stood between them covered with a green linen cloth. A brown clay bowl filled with wrinkled winter apples and a music stand were set on it.

'Let me take your coat and umbrella, you're soaking wet. And your shoes are squelching.' Before she had time to protest, he had relieved her of her umbrella and placed it in an enamel bucket, removed her coat and hung it on a hook on the back of the door. She took off her hat and brushed it with the back of her sleeve.

'The lady has diamonds in her hair.'

'That's a poetic way of saying my hair is wet, but it will soon dry. It's warm in here.'

He pointed to a metal brazier in the corner that radiated

warmth. 'I've only just smothered the coals. I can't play with cold fingers. Take off your shoes and stockings.'

'I couldn't—'

'Sit around in wet feet and you will get pneumonia,' he warned.

She sat on the edge of one of the couches and removed her shoes. He took them from her, tore up a newspaper, scrunched the pieces into balls and stuffed them into the toes before placing them close to the brazier. 'Now your stockings.'

'They'll be fine.'

'Women and their modesty. They will not be fine, but if you won't take them off, dry your legs as best you can with this.' He handed her a towel. It was threadbare but clean.

The cushions at her back were the same size as the cushions on the seat of the couch and she guessed that if the table was removed they could be rearranged into a bed.

'Please, make yourself comfortable.' The ceiling was too low for Micah to stand upright. He leaned over a scrap of a kitchen area that held a bowl, a spirit heating ring with a kettle balanced on top, and a spirit lamp. He struck a match, lit the ring and the lamp. The cabin was instantly bathed in a soft, golden glow at the expense of a nose-stinging odour of paraffin. He lifted the lid from an enamel jug and filled the kettle with water.

'What are you doing out on an afternoon like this so far from the vicarage?'

'Walking.'

'If you were going to the interfaith meeting it doesn't start for over an hour and a half.'

'I know.' She watched him unscrew a glass jar. His hands were fine, his fingers long and tapered, his movements slow and deliberate. He spooned ground coffee into an enamel jug, opened a cupboard and removed a tin of evaporated milk, a jar of sugar and two mugs.

'So, why were you really out in the rain?' he pressed.

'I needed fresh air so I thought I'd explore Tiger Bay, seeing as how it's my new home.'

'In this downpour?' he said sceptically.

'I've lived all my life in Wales. If I let rain bother me I'd never go outdoors.'

'I suppose that's true enough.' He didn't sound convinced.

By dint of breathing in and sliding sideways, she managed to move behind the table. She leaned against the side of the alcove, lifted her legs on to the seat and dried them as best she could.

He set the mugs on the table. 'I heard your mother-in-law turned up at the vicarage before the fishing boats brought in their catch this morning.'

'Does everyone know everyone else's business on the Bay?' she demanded, allowing her irritation to surface.

'Pretty much,' he said easily. 'Why? Who else has mentioned her arrival?'

'Anna Hughes.'

He let out a long low whistle. 'You've talked to our Anna Hughes after what she did to you?'

'*Your* Anna Hughes?'

He laughed. 'If that disapproving glare is intended to make me blush, it's failed. Anna is not mine specifically,' his smile broadened at the implication, 'but the Bay's in general. She's quite a character, is our Anna.'

'I noticed. I had coffee and cream cakes with her and her . . . ladies before I came down here.'

'Does Peter know you've been hobnobbing with her?'

'No, but he wouldn't mind,' she replied, hoping she sounded more confident than she felt.

'Someone told me that you had allowed Anna's and the other women's children into your Sunday school.'

'More gossip?'

'The Bay's riddled with it. It's the principal hobby of the residents. You can pick it up and drop it at will. Expend as much or as little time on it as you like. And, if someone takes the trouble to embellish it, rumours can be more entertaining and sensational than a novel. Plus, there's always the chance that you'll be able to feel superior at the expense of your neighbours' failings. If you want to keep up with what's happening around here, you'll have to learn to gossip.'

'So it would seem.'

'What did Peter say to the new pupils you took on?'

'Welcome,' she said shortly. 'He wants to build up the congregation. He thinks their attendance at Sunday school will benefit the school's existing pupils as well as them.'

The water began to boil and Micah tipped it on the coffee. 'Good for Peter, but allowing Anna and the other girls' children into Sunday school isn't quite the same as allowing his wife to drink afternoon tea in a brothel.'

'We sat in the kitchen and there weren't any customers around.'

'I should hope not, otherwise they may have taken you for the newest recruit to Anna's academy.'

'I'm married to a vicar,' she reminded him.

'That doesn't give someone as young and pretty as you the right to be above suspicion like Caesar's wife.'

'People would have to be petty-minded to make something out of nothing. Working for the good of the parish means visiting all kinds of people.'

'And gives you an excuse to get out of the vicarage. Is your desire for fresh air and a walk an indication of trouble in paradise?' he asked bluntly.

'Define paradise.'

'You sound like a schoolteacher delivering a lesson on analysis.' He dropped a spoon into the jug and mixed the coffee and water.

'I was a pupil until July.'

'So you were. But to get back to the subject, doesn't every honeymooner believe they've reached paradise?' When she didn't comment, he continued, 'Let me guess: you and your mother-in-law don't get on.'

'I could complain about her, Micah, but I'd rather not even think about her. I'll be seeing her soon enough.'

'It's that bad between you?'

'Worse.'

He finished stirring the coffee and strained it into the mugs. 'Then why invite her to live with you?'

'I didn't.'

'Peter did?'

Needing to change the subject, she looked at his music case. 'Would you do me the most enormous favour?'

'I would say anything for a lady with the blues, but remember that Peter is my friend.'

'I know you two are friends, what of it?' she asked surprised at his sudden sombre tone.

'Nothing in particular, just reminding you.'

'I was going to ask if you'd play that piece of music again. What did you think I was going to ask you to do?'

'I wasn't sure. And playing music is not a favour. Don't you know that every musician is constantly in search of an audience?' He pushed one of the mugs across the table towards her, together with the jar of sugar and pierced tin of milk.

She put one sugar and a splash of milk into the coffee and gripped the mug tightly, siphoning the warmth from it into her hands.

He sipped his coffee before lifting his case on to the table. He unclipped it and gently brushed a smudge from the polished surface of the saxophone before taking it from its bed. While he prepared the mouthpiece, she curled up in the corner of the bench seat and closed her eyes.

He started playing softly, gradually increasing the depth and breadth of the notes until he created a symphony that filled the small space, leaving no room for anything other than the music. For Edyth, the world outside ceased to exist. All her problems, all her worries, were obliterated by the seductive melody.

The bitterness and resentment she felt towards Peter's mother dissolved into indifference. The concern she'd never voiced, and barely acknowledged – that Peter had never loved her, and had only used her to obtain the promotion he'd so passionately wanted – died as she was swept up in a swell of emotion engendered by Micah's music.

The mood of the piece changed without warning, becoming even more evocative and beguiling. Visions rose unbidden to her mind, so tangible, so real, she could taste and feel them. She revelled in the sensation of warm, sensuous lips pressed against hers. Entwined her naked body with that of a man. Felt the flat of his hard, muscular stomach pressed against hers. Thrilled to his touch as he lightly caressed her breasts.

She was finally making love, just as she'd imagined she would on honeymoon and it was exactly how her mother had told her it would be. Surrender and submission to a passion greater than she could have ever imagined. She felt herself drowning in the depths of his blue eyes, exchanging long, loving glances that needed no words. Evidence of perfect love and harmony . . .

*Blue eyes. Peter's were brown.*

'Edyth!'

She looked up and saw that Micah had finished playing and was looking anxiously down at her.

'Are you all right?'

'I . . . I . . .' Hot, burning pain rose in her throat, choking her. A pain that went beyond tears. How could she have been so blind as to have married Peter without realizing that he didn't love her? He had never loved her the way she loved him.

Micah set the saxophone on the table, took the mug from her trembling fingers and bent over her. Afterwards she realized he'd probably intended to raise her from the seat. But by then it was too late. She had already kissed him.

'No!' Micah closed his hands over hers, prised them from his neck and pushed her away. She fell back on to the seat.

'I'm sorry.' It was little more than a whisper and by then he had turned his back to her and was facing the door so she couldn't be sure that he'd heard her.

He kept his face averted from hers as though he couldn't bear to look at her. 'Why did you do that?' His voice was harsh, condemnatory. 'Things can't be that bad between you and Peter, surely? Not when you've only been married for nine days.'

She didn't want to answer him because she couldn't, not without being disloyal to Peter, her *husband*. Just over a week ago she had promised to love honour and obey and now – now she had kissed Micah.

He finally turned and looked at her. 'They aren't that bad, are they?' he reiterated.

'I'm sorry,' she stammered, so ashamed she wanted to crawl into a corner and hide from Micah and everyone else who might suspect what she had done. How could she possibly go home and face Peter? Behave as if everything was normal? But then it wasn't normal between them. Had never been normal . . .

'Do you want to talk about it?'

'Only to say I'm sorry. I don't know what came over me. It must have been the effect of your music,' she apologized.

'You must have a reason for doing what you did.'

She felt that he was trying to pressurize her into admitting something. But she didn't know what. 'No reason beyond the music and the fact that you were there.'

There was anger and something else in his eyes, something she couldn't decipher. 'Married women shouldn't continue to behave as though they're single, *Mrs* Slater.'

'I didn't go around kissing every man in sight when I was,' she countered angrily, upset that he thought so little of her. 'Please, pass me my coat.'

He handed it over. She left the seat and slipped it on. It was cold, wet and clammy.

'You're leaving?' he asked as she bent down and picked up her shoes.

'Yes.'

'You're overwrought.'

'I behaved like a fool.'

'Forget it, and forget the interfaith meeting. Let me walk you home and you can spend a quiet evening with Peter.'

'No.'

'No to what?' he pressed.

'All of it,' she answered illogically.

'You don't want to forget you kissed me?' he enquired sardonically. He fingered his lips and she wondered if he was trying to scour them clean. As if her touch had somehow defiled him.

'Yes, I want to forget it.' Even as she said it, she knew she wouldn't. It wasn't her first kiss, but it had felt like her first grown-up kiss. And that, coupled with the music, had created a moment, a memory, she wanted to cling to, treasure and savour.

'About the meeting,' he switched abruptly to practical considerations, 'Christmas is months away. At this stage of the committee people simply argue about who's going to do what. If you don't go, I can volunteer you for every boring task no one else wants to do and then the meeting will be over in record time.'

She pulled the newspaper put of her shoes and slipped them on. 'That doesn't sound ideal from my point of view.'

'But it's brilliant from everyone else's. Interfaith committee meetings can be as tedious as—'

'As tedious as?' She forced herself to look at him but he could no longer meet her gaze. They had enjoyed an easy, friendly relationship but she had destroyed it. Furious with herself for succumbing to the stupid impulse to kiss him she picked up her hat.

'. . . I was going to say a vicar's sermon before I realized that I can't say that to you. Look, if you do go to the meeting you won't achieve anything and everyone will see that you are upset. That will give rise to gossip. Can't you just hear the old wives?' He mimicked a shrill woman's voice. ' "Have you heard? The vicar's wife isn't happy? Is it the mother-in-law? Is it the work she's expected to do? Is it Mrs Mack's tea? I heard the vicar beats her . . ." '

'Peter would have to acknowledge my presence to beat me.' The moment the words were out of her mouth she regretted them. But just as Mari had warned her so often, once out, there was no taking them back.

He breathed in sharply. 'I see.'

'No, you don't, Micah. I may be a very new wife but I have learned one thing in a week. The only people who can possibly know what a marriage is like are the people inside it.'

'It might help to talk about it,' he said, after a moment's strained silence.

'There's no point.'

'Try me. I'm a good listener and a pastor, which means anything you tell me is as good as speaking in a confessional.'

'You're Lutheran not Catholic, and I don't need a religious mentor. I have one at home – remember.'

'Who, it appears, you can't talk to.' He sank down on one of the couches. 'The same rules of confidentiality apply to the ministers of all the Christian religions, and I could speak to Peter for you, if you want me to.'

'There's no point in talking to Peter. He doesn't listen.' She set her hat on her head.

'If ever you need to get away, or want to be alone, you can come here any time you like.'

'After what I just did?' She looked at him again and that time she caught him looking back at her.

'I never come here in the morning. You're welcome to use it then.'

'No, thank you. I think it's best that I make this my first and last visit to the *Escape*.' Hurt at her offhand rejection of his offer was mirrored in the depths of his deep, blue eyes. And she realized then just whose blue eyes she had seen in her vision when he had been playing the music.

She took her umbrella from the bucket and pretended to study it intently.

'Please, Edyth, let me take you home?'

She opened the door.

'You're upset. I can't bear the thought of you walking back through the Bay alone in this mood. I won't rest until I know that you have reached home safely.'

'I'll be fine,' she asserted. 'You don't need to worry about me.'

'I'll make your apologies at the meeting then. Tell everyone that you had to make your mother-in-law a proper welcoming tea — with arsenic.'

She tried to laugh at his stupid quip but a lump in her throat prevented her. She walked up the steps and on to the deck. Grey dusk had turned to dark, overcast night. The black sea glittered with the silver, gold and crimson reflections of shore lights and those on the boats.

Someone was singing on the quayside in an old man's wavering voice. Edyth couldn't make out the words but she recognized the rhythm of a sea shanty.

Micah's hand closed around her arm. 'Please, let me walk you home.'

'No.'

'It's forgotten.'

She found the courage to say what she suspected he was thinking as well as her. 'It will never be forgotten, not by either of us.'

'I need to know . . .'

'What?' she asked when he didn't finish his sentence.

'You and Peter – is your marriage a sham?'

It was then she realized he was as attracted to her as she was to him, but with all the other complications in her life she couldn't bear to think what that might mean. Not now.

'It doesn't matter whether it is or it isn't, Micah. You were there at the ceremony. We're joined together by God, for better for worse. "Let no man break asunder . . ." '

'Edyth—'

'Goodbye, Micah.'

Edyth ran off the boat, away from the dock and into the maze of back streets. She thought that if she kept the sea at her back and headed in more or less a straight line she would soon reach the vicarage, but whether it was the darkness, the street lights or the thoughts that kept intruding and demanding her attention, she managed to lose her way.

She saw the pyramid-capped towers of the church half an hour before she reached them. Twice she found herself facing high brick walls that blocked what she was certain was the most direct path to the vicarage. She would have asked someone, but the heavy rain had kept most people indoors and she was wary of approaching the few men she saw.

She tried to take her mind off what had happened by concentrating on the house, the tasks that needed doing, the cleaning, polishing and rearrangement of china and glass. She decided to confront Peter's mother and insist that she be allowed to use her own things. Then she recalled how Florence always managed to freeze her out of the conversation and that Peter invariably bowed to his mother's demands, and realized she had absolutely no chance of succeeding.

She finally walked past the church hall, saw the lights on, heard a hubbub of women's voices and remembered the Mother's Union meeting. At least she wouldn't have to cope with Peter's mother right away. She walked down the lane, slipped her key into the lock and opened the front door quietly. Mrs Mack was crouched on her knees outside Peter's study door, her ear to the keyhole.

'Mrs Mack! What on earth are you doing?'

There was a resounding crash from inside the study.

Alarmed, forgetting Peter's directive that she never walk in on him without knocking, she ran to the door, pushed Mrs Mack aside and turned the knob. It was stuck fast. She pushed it.

'Edyth, is that you?' Peter called.

'Yes, I just caught Mrs Mack eavesdropping outside your door.'

'I'll be out in a moment.'

Edyth turned and confronted the housekeeper who had climbed to her feet. 'Go upstairs and pack your things.'

The housekeeper swayed slightly and crossed her arms across her thin chest. 'No.'

'What did you say?' Edyth couldn't believe the woman's refusal.

'I said no. I'm not going.'

Edyth took a deep breath and braced herself. 'There is no "not going", about it, your behaviour is unacceptable.'

Peter opened the door. His face was red, his hair dishevelled, his dog collar crooked. 'Edyth, what's all this noise?'

'I caught Mrs Mack on her hands and knees crouched outside your door listening through the keyhole.'

'I was just about to ask if you and the young man would like some tea.' Mrs Mack gazed coolly at Peter.

Edyth looked past Peter. The young constable Peter had introduced to her as secretary of the church council was sitting on a chair that had been pulled in front of Peter's desk. He turned and glanced at her. 'Mrs Slater.'

'Constable Jones, isn't it?' She smiled, but his eyes remained cold.

'She,' Mrs Mack jabbed her finger in Edyth's direction, 'told me to pack my bags, Reverend.'

'We'll discuss this later, Mrs Mack, after Constable Jones and I have finished our council business,' Peter said shortly.

'Didn't you hear me, Peter? I said she was eavesdropping outside your door—'

'I said later, Edyth.'

He shut the door in her face. The front door opened and Florence Slater walked in.

'Edyth, you're dripping over the floor.'

It was only then Edyth realized that she had yet to take off her coat or put her umbrella in the stand.

'Mrs Mack,' Florence Slater held out her arms and the housekeeper helped her out of her coat, 'we'll have tea in the sitting room. I trust you've made up the fire.'

'Yes, Mrs Slater.' Mrs Mack smiled triumphantly at Edyth. 'Would you like toast or tea-cake with your tea, Mrs Slater?'

'Buttered toast, Mrs Mack. Edyth, your umbrella has dripped all over the floor. Mrs Mack has enough to do without clearing up unnecessary messes.'

Edyth dropped her umbrella into the stand and shrugged off her coat.

'The meeting was very successful. I have a great deal to tell you. Edyth, where are you going?' Florence demanded when Edyth set her foot on the stairs.

'To bed,' Edyth said shortly. 'It's been a very long day and I'm tired.'

'I'm not sure that you are strong enough to be a vicar's wife, Edyth. You need to be in good health and, as I said earlier, if the groceries you bought are indicative of the way you've been brought up to eat – shop-bought cakes and the like – it's hardly surprising you're not up to doing a full day's work. It's just as well I came here a week early.'

Edyth carried on walking up the stairs.

'Edyth, I'm speaking to you.'

'I heard, Mrs Slater,' Edyth finally snapped, 'but I chose not to answer.'

# Chapter 22

KNOWING JUDY AND MRS MACK were busy in the kitchen, Peter left the breakfast table and opened the front door at the second ring of the bell.

'Surprise!' Bella kissed Peter on the cheek and walked into the hall. 'Sorry to interrupt your breakfast, but we've asked and asked you and Edyth to visit us, and you're always busy. So, we thought we'd come down and surprise you.'

'And whisk you and Edyth off to lunch in the Carleton in Queen Street, to dine in "sophisticated surroundings with beguiling background music",' Toby quoted the Carleton's advertisement from the *Glamorgan Gazette*.

'Sorry,' Peter muttered, 'I have a funeral in half an hour.'

'I suppose that's the problem with being a vicar,' Toby sympathized. 'Unlike me you can't say, "I don't feel like working today, so push off and bury yourself." '

'I have no idea who you are, young man, but that comment borders on blasphemy.'

Anxious always to be the first to know what was going on in the vicarage, Florence had left the dining room ahead of Edyth to join Peter in the hall.

'You remember Edyth's elder sister and her husband from our wedding, Mother,' Peter reminded her.

'Mrs Ross, isn't it?' Florence looked down her long nose at Bella, as Edyth embraced her sister.

'Yes.' Bella held Edyth at arm's length. 'Are you all right, Edie? You look very pale.'

'I'm fine,' Edyth answered unconvincingly.

'Well, if we can't take the two of you out to lunch, we'll just take Edyth,' Toby announced cheerfully.

'That is out of the question. Edyth and I have to attend a meeting of the altar flower circle in an hour,' Florence announced flatly.

'Please, don't stand there, Belle, Toby,' Edyth opened the sitting-room door. 'Go on in. I'll ask Judy to bring you coffee.'

'The maid, Edyth,' Florence reprimanded. 'How many times have I told you not to refer to the girl by her Christian name? You're far too familiar with the servant.'

Drawing strength from Toby and Bella's presence, Edyth said, 'I prefer to call her Judy.'

'I'm sure the ladies of the altar flower circle can do without Edyth for once, Mother. After all, the group looks to you for inspiration and advice.' Peter softened his suggestion by adding a compliment. 'And this is the first time Edyth has seen any of her family in over a month.'

'I suppose we could manage without her,' Florence said ungraciously.

Edyth took Bella and Toby's hats and coats and hung them on the stand before going into the kitchen. She turned to see her mother-in-law at her elbow.

'If you do go to lunch with your sister you'll have to be back here by half past two,' Florence warned.

'Why?' Edyth lifted a tray down from the top of a cupboard and handed it to Judy, who had already put the kettle on to boil.

'The Mothers' Union tea is being held in the church hall this afternoon . . .'

'Not until three o'clock and you are chairman. I don't even qualify as a member,' Edyth added pointedly with a backward glance into the passage, but Peter had disappeared.

'I need you to help serve the tea.'

'Judy or Mrs Mack could assist you.'

'They're servants, dear. Besides, you know full well that the maid goes to the grocer's on Monday afternoon and Mrs Mack always takes a few hours off between lunch and dinner.'

Edyth was convinced that Mrs Mack used the 'few hours' to

sleep off the effect of the drink she downed in between her morning chores. And she couldn't understand why Peter still categorically refused to sack the woman, when she grew more insolent by the day towards her and Peter, and ever more subservient towards his mother.

'Think how it would look, Edyth dear, if you weren't at the tea,' Mrs Slater drawled.

'It would look as though I have taken a day off to visit my family, which I have tried to do every week for the past three weeks without success,' Edyth replied.

'You really are unbelievably selfish, Edyth.'

'Selfish! I—'

'Edyth, could you come here for a moment, please?' Peter called from his study.

'Take tea into the sitting room for three, please, Judy,' Edyth went to the door.

'I take it I am not invited to join you and your sister and her husband?' Florence murmured in a hurt tone.

'I assumed that you would want to go upstairs to write letters as you usually do after breakfast. Mother, please excuse me, I have to see what Peter wants.' Reining in her temper, Edyth left Judy laying the tray and went into Peter's study. Peter was sitting behind his desk. She closed the door behind her.

'Edyth, please, can't you have a little patience with Mother?' he asked.

'I and my patience are exhausted, Peter.' She sat on one of his visitors' chairs and leaned her elbow on his desk. 'This is our house, but you wouldn't think it from the way your mother behaves or from the way she insisted on furnishing it. I . . . I . . .' Mindful of Mari's dictate about not having to take back what had been left unsaid, she bit her lip.

'You're what, Edyth?'

She looked up at him, saw concern in his eyes and decided that for once she was going to tell him exactly how she felt. 'Angry, frustrated and furious. When I married you I assumed that we'd have a normal marriage, which included you sleeping in my bed

360

and didn't include your mother living with us and taking over my role as mistress of the house.'

'Keep your voice down,' he pleaded.

'Why should I, when Judy, Mrs Mack and your mother know we sleep in separate rooms, and you and Mrs Mack take more notice of what your mother says than me? I want children—'

'Edyth, please. I have a funeral in half an hour—'

'There's always something in half an hour,' she dismissed, her anger getting the better of her. 'A funeral, christening, wedding, churching, confirmation, communion or special service. How can I make our marriage work when you won't even discuss our private life?' When he didn't say anything in his own defence she finally voiced the suspicion uppermost in her mind. 'Are you ill? Is that it? Do you have a contagious disease that you're afraid of passing on to me?'

He looked at her. There was no anger in his eyes only a pleading for understanding that she chose to ignore.

'I am going into the sitting room, I am going to drink tea with Bella and Toby, and then I am going out with them for the day. And frankly, the mood I'm in, I might not come back.'

'And if I promise you that we'll talk – really talk – tonight if you do?'

'Not just over the dinner table with your mother sitting in pride of place?'

'Of course not at the dinner table. But I have scouts this evening—'

'After scouts,' she interrupted. 'I will come in here, sit down and face you across this desk like one of your parishioners and discuss my problems with you. And you'll listen, even though the only problems I have are with you, your mother and Mrs Mack,' she added vehemently.

Florence knocked the door once and walked in. 'Peter, I think it might be an idea for you to host the Mothers' Union tea if you can spare the time—'

'Peter doesn't like people walking into his study, Mother,' Edyth reminded her.

'I could hear you, Edyth, so I knew that you two were alone.'

'We would like to continue our discussion in private.'

'You weren't discussing anything with Peter, dear, you were shouting at him, and your sister and her husband could hear you in the sitting room. Really, Edyth, I thought you'd have more consideration, if not for yourself, then for Peter.'

'Mother, Edyth and I have decided that she should have a day to herself once a week,' Peter said before Edyth had time to think of an apt retort to his mother's comments.

'Are you sure that's wise, considering all the things that have to be done in the parish?' Florence said even more softly than usual.

'Yes, I do, Mother. And now I have to go to the church to prepare for the funeral. Will you be back for dinner, Edyth?'

'No,' she said decisively, determined to stay away from Florence for as long as possible, although she doubted that she'd find her any less irritating on her return. 'But I will be back by nine o'clock. Scouts will have finished by then and we'll have that talk.'

'I'll see you then. I'll just pop in and make my apologies to Bella and Toby. Mother,' he smiled at Florence, 'I'll see you at lunch.'

Edyth knew her mother-in-law was furious that she'd been thwarted in the plans she'd made for both of them for that day. But much as she wanted to, she didn't allow herself a smile of triumph. Not even a small one.

Toby jumped out of the taxi he'd hired to drive him, Bella and Edyth from the vicarage to the centre of Cardiff. He held the door open and kissed Bella's cheek as she passed. 'Do some serious shopping, Bopsy. I'll meet you both in the Carleton at one.'

'You're not coming with us?' Edyth asked.

'Have to meet a new client who wants to be painted for posterity, but I'll be through by lunchtime. See you then.' He kissed Edyth's cheek, then Bella's again, and stepped back in the taxi.

'Coffee in Gwilym James's tea shop first?' Bella asked.

'So you can interrogate me?'

'You don't have to talk if you don't want to, Edie. But everyone in the family is worried about you. Your letters aren't a bit like you. All about church meetings and functions and no mention of anything personal. And you're always promising us a visit and never turning up.'

'So Mam and Dad sent you down here?' Edyth guessed.

'Toby had to come anyway and I have some news.'

Edyth looked into her sister's face. She wasn't just happy and smiling, she was positively blooming.

'You're having a baby?' she guessed.

'I am. Toby's over the moon, and Mam and Dad . . .' Her face fell slightly. 'The last thing I want to do is crow, Edyth.'

'And you're not.' Edyth flung her arms around her sister's neck. It would be churlish of her to begrudge Bella and Toby their happiness just because her own marriage hadn't worked out the way she'd expected it to. 'I'm so happy for you and Toby. I'm going to be an aunt again.' She wiped a tear from her eye.

'Come on, Edyth.' Bella wrapped her arm around her sister's shoulders. 'Let's find a quiet table where we can talk.'

It was still early, and the tea shop was deserted. Bella took possession of a table in the furthest corner from the door and the kitchens, divested Edyth of her hat and coat, and ordered scones and tea for two.

Edyth pulled her handkerchief from her pocket. 'I suppose you heard me shouting at Peter this morning.'

'Toby and I couldn't help it, Edie,' Bella said apologetically. 'I thought your mother-in-law was difficult at your wedding, but she's a living nightmare. How long is she staying with you?'

'She's moved in.'

'Permanently? And you let her?' Bella cried indignantly.

'It was understood between her and Peter that she would move in with him as soon as he had a place of his own.'

'And you went along with it?'

Edyth shrugged. 'What else could I do? Tell Peter his mother wasn't welcome in his house?'

'It's your house, too, and frankly, if I had a mother-in-law who behaved the way Mrs Slater does, I'd do just that. Did you know that she was going to move in when you spent most of your honeymoon at home?'

'Yes.'

'And you never said.'

'There didn't seem to be any point. How is David really?' Edyth asked, wanting to change the subject.

'As I've said in my letters, and told you this morning, on the mend. Harry's hoping he'll be allowed out of hospital in a couple of weeks. Mam and Dad are pressing Harry and Mary to stay with them until after Christmas, and then go home with the children afterwards. It would be wonderful if you and Peter could come, too. There's bags of room, between our house and Mam and Dad's.'

'It's Peter's busiest time.'

'You won't even be home for Christmas?' Bella cried in disbelief.

Not trusting herself to speak, because she couldn't bear the thought of spending Christmas anywhere but at home, Edyth shook her head.

'Edyth,' Bella lowered her voice to a whisper, 'Toby and I overheard what you said to Peter this morning about separate bedrooms . . .'

'He hasn't made love to me if that's what you're wondering,' Edyth revealed. She hadn't realized how desperate she had been to talk to someone about her problems with Peter until that moment.

'You have to ask him why,' Bella advised strongly.

'If you heard that much you must have heard us making arrangements to talk this evening.' Edyth was amazed that Bella wasn't more surprised by the revelation, but then, she had overheard the argument.

'Have you any idea why he won't sleep with you?' Bella asked quietly.

'Only what I said, that he's ill. I have no idea if it's true but it's the only explanation I can think of that makes sense. Other than I'm so disgusting he can't bear to come near me.'

'You know that's not true, Edie.'

Edyth reached across the table and grabbed her sister's hand. She held it until the waitress brought their order. Glancing around the room, which was still more than half-empty, she saw Harry striding towards their table.

'Why do I get the feeling that I've been set up?' Edyth looked from her brother to her sister.

'I own this store – remember?' Harry pulled a chair out from under the table and joined them. 'Tea and scones for me too, please, Eira.'

'Yes, Mr Evans.' The waitress scurried away.

'You knew where to find us?' Edyth asked.

'Bella happened to mention that you might come shopping here this morning to take advantage of the family discount,' he said lightly.

'Happened to mention?'

'All right,' Harry conceded, 'we're concerned about you.'

'I get the message. But I married Peter. The problem is mine and I'll sort it out,' she said firmly.

'The sooner the better from the look of you, Edie,' Harry said soberly.

'What do you mean?' she asked indignantly.

'You've lost an alarming amount of weight in a month, your hair's scraggy and in need of a good cut, and you look tired.'

'The hair we'll remedy this morning,' Bella said cheerfully. 'I've already booked appointments for us at the salon upstairs. You'll meet us at the Carleton, Harry?'

'If the board meeting I called finishes in time. If not I should make coffee.'

'And then Edyth and I—'

'And then Edyth will go home,' Edyth interrupted Bella.

'You told Peter that you wouldn't be back until after dinner. I heard you.'

'My mother-in law has a Mothers' Union tea.' Edyth dropped two sugar cubes into her cup and stirred it. 'She asked Peter to call in, but he won't, because he can't stand the vice-chairwoman. So he'll be alone in his study. Judy will be out shopping and Mrs Mack will be taking a couple of hours off, so we'll have the house to ourselves. It will be a good time to sort out our problems.'

'And when you have, you'll come and visit home soon?' Harry pressed.

Edyth smiled at her brother and sister. 'I promise.'

'And if you want me to talk to Peter, I'll be here all day—'

'That won't be necessary, Harry.'

'But you have the telephone number of the store, just in case.'

'You two know something, don't you?' She looked from Bella to Harry.

'We don't *know* anything you don't, Edie,' Harry assured her.

'But you suspect something,' she persevered.

'Talk to Peter. Whatever is wrong between you should be discussed by you two and no one else,' Harry declared. 'I hope I'm wrong about Peter. But if I'm not, I'll never forgive myself for not stopping you from marrying him. But you have to hear it from him, Edie. Not me.'

Edyth walked from the city centre to the docks after lunch. It was a cold, dry day and she was enjoying the fresh air and the prospect of a few hours to herself. Her newly cut and permanently waved hair was safely tucked beneath her hat and after spending the morning with Bella and eating lunch with her sister, Toby and Harry, she felt confident enough to tackle Peter and the world. She was also angry with herself for not confronting Peter sooner and for allowing him to move into a separate bedroom.

She tip-toed past the church hall, lest anyone hear her passing and drag her inside. Judging by the noise, the Mothers' Union tea was in full swing.

She opened the front door of the vicarage and stepped inside. The house was so deathly quiet she could hear Peter's mother's clock ticking in the sitting room. She hung her coat and hat on the stand and carried the bag of underclothes and cosmetics she had bought upstairs. She opened her bedroom door and froze. Peter was lying in bed with Constable Jones. They were clinging to one another, kissing the way a man did a woman.

Hating herself for watching, yet unable to move, she continued to stare into the room, at Peter and the young man. The clothes — shirts, trousers and underclothes — scattered around the bed . . .

Peter looked over the young man's shoulder. He saw her and his eyes widened in horror. 'Edyth . . .'

She hung her head and turned her back to him.

Mrs Mack was behind her, blocking her path. An evil smile of pure delight lifted her crabbed features.

'Now perhaps you can understand why your husband doesn't want you in his bed, Mrs Slater.'

She dropped her bag and fled down the stairs. She heard Peter cry out her name behind her. She lifted her hat and coat from the rack and wrestled with the lock that refused to open.

She heard Peter shout, 'That's the end of your blackmailing, Mrs Mack. Pack your bags and leave.'

Finally she managed to wrench the door open and ran out of the house and across the courtyard. She could hear the slap of Peter's bare feet chasing after her. His voice, high-pitched and anguished, calling her name.

She didn't know where she was running to. Harry? Bella? A pain gripped her side. She paused to catch her breath and saw that she was in the street Anna Hughes lived in. A man was walking towards her from the direction of Anna's house. She recognized him and knew what she would do.

She would hurt Peter every bit as much as he had hurt her. She rushed up to the man and took his arm. He peered at her and she realized he was drunk.

'Edyth?'

'It is, Charlie.'

'Thought you didn't like me,' he slurred.

'I do now, Charlie.'

He gazed at her through half-closed eyes. 'What you doing here?'

'Didn't you know, Charlie? I live here now, and you and me are going to take a walk.'

'Where?' he asked suspiciously.

'Anna Hughes's house. Haven't you heard, Charlie? I'm working for her now. You want me, you can have me.'

He gave her a stupid drunken smile. 'How much?'

'How much you willing to pay?'

'That depends on what you are prepared to give.'

'Whatever you want, Charlie. All you have to do is ask.'

'And pay?' he checked.

'Whatever you think I'm worth, Charlie.' She heard a man shout behind her and pulled Charlie forward. 'Come on, it's cold out here and we're wasting time.'

'Mrs Slater, Edyth, I don't want any trouble . . .'

'You won't have any, Anna.' After weeks of turmoil, during which her problems had seemed insurmountable, Edyth felt amazingly calm. It was as though a veil had lifted and revealed her life for the sham it had been. There was no solution that she could see to the mess that was her marriage, but it was a relief finally to realize just why she had failed as a wife.

Peter's refusal to make love to her – his reluctance even to sleep in the same room. Mrs Mack's rude, overbearing attitude, and the hold she'd had over Peter. The Bishop's insistence that Peter could only become vicar of the parish if he were married. Harry's warning to her the night before her wedding: '*Some men aren't the marrying kind.*' Alice Beynon's remark when they had been talking in the garden after Florence had announced that she was moving into Tiger Bay with them: '*Sons grow up and marry; it's what normal men do. Although I admit I never expected to see the day that Peter would take a wife . . .*'

If only Harry had been more explicit. But if he had, would she have listened to him? Deciding the answer was probably not, she addressed Anna.

'Tell me which room is free, so Charlie and I can use it.'

'All our rooms are fully booked,' Anna said forcefully.

'Surely you have one free. Charlie will pay in advance.' Edyth dug Charlie in the ribs with her elbow. 'Won't you, Charlie?'

'What?' He stared blankly at her.

'Anna wants money.' Edyth held out her hand.

'Want money, do you . . .' He swayed precariously, and Edyth realized he was not only drunk but bordering on comatose. He slipped his hand inside his coat, missed his pocket twice and eventually, after a great deal of fumbling, found his wallet. Holding it out with exaggerated care, he flourished it in front of her eyes before opening it and removing a ten-shilling note.

'Foursh timesh your usualsh pricesh.' He bowed to Anna.

'Becaussh I like the ladyssh.' He stood so far back on his heels he would have toppled over if Edyth hadn't grabbed his waistcoat and steadied him. He wrapped his arm around her and grinned stupidly.

'We haven't any rooms,' Anna snapped. Unfortunately for her, Colleen chose that moment to burst in.

'Bloody man! Gave me two bob, nothing for the extras and kept me for over an hour . . .' She picked up on the silence in the room, turned around, and saw Edyth and Charlie standing together. 'What you doing here, Mrs Vicar?'

'We want a room, I take it yours is empty.' Edyth filched the money from Charlie's hand and handed it to Colleen.

'Ten bob!' Colleen stared at the note before holding it up to the electric light as if she couldn't believe her luck.

'Which one is it?' Edyth demanded.

'Don't take the money, Colleen. I told her all our rooms are fully booked,' Anna snapped.

'Ten bob's ten bob. Notes like that don't grow on trees.' Colleen rolled the money into a tube and pushed it into a button-down pocket on the side of the silk cami-knickers she was wearing beneath a sheer muslin robe.

'Colleen, give it back,' Anna ordered.

'Come on, Anna,' Colleen wheedled. 'I'll give you two bob out of it.'

'I don't want two bob. I want her and him,' Anna pointed to Edyth and Charlie, 'out of here. She's trouble and he's sozzled.'

'Charlie's always three parts to the wind and what's it to us if the silly bitch wants a thrill? One thing's for sure, she's not going to get one from her pretty boy husband. Mind you,' Colleen looked Charlie up and down. 'Doubt Charlie's up for much, state he's in. Looks like Gertie had the best out of him this afternoon.'

Shocked, Edyth stared at Colleen.

'Surprised we know your baby-faced vicar's taste in the bedroom?' Colleen took a cigarette from an open pack on the mantelpiece, lifted her leg on to a chair, struck a match and lit it. 'Everyone in the Bay knows, love. Before he carried you over the threshold, there were sailors queuing at his door every night. And they weren't there for Bible studies.'

Edyth had heard enough. 'Which is your room?'

'First door on your right at the top of the stairs. Don't walk straight ahead or you'll get an eyeful. Gertie's got two in with her.'

Edyth tugged Charlie's arm. Leering at the expanse of leg Colleen was showing, he ambled out behind her. When they were in the passage Edyth heard Anna speaking low, urgently to someone in the kitchen: 'Run as fast as you can, straight down to the Norwegian mission. Get Mr Holsten. No one else will do. Micah Holsten, got that? Tell him to get here as quickly as he can.'

Edyth didn't wait to hear the reply. It was a good half-hour walk to the mission and back, and by then it would be too late.

Edyth lay on the bed next to Charlie and stared at the ceiling. Darkness had fallen but she had left the electric light on. The plaster was cracked with a filigree network of grey lines, and there were cobwebs in the corners of the coving. But the neglect didn't extend to the rest of the room. It was clean and dusted, if cluttered. The thing that had struck her most about Colleen's bedroom when she'd walked in was how ordinary it was. Just like the kitchen.

The bedroom suite was cheap, veneered deal, and not particularly well cared for. There were white heat rings and stains on the surfaces of the cabinet and dressing table where cups of tea and perfume and cosmetic bottles had stood. A chair in the corner was heaped to overflowing with frocks, petticoats, silk stockings and robes. Another corner was filled with a pile of slippers, boots and shoes.

Charlie snorted loudly and began to snore, making more noise than the cows when they calved on her Uncle Victor's farm. Like her, he was lying on top of the beige satin bedcover. He'd point-blank refused to get into the bed, and had fallen flat on his face on the mattress after shouting, 'Donsh wnash to get in thoshs sheets donsh know whosh bensh in them.'

He'd struggled to his feet a few minutes later and tried to

unbutton his trousers, only to get so hopelessly tangled in the legs that she'd had to help him pull them off.

Unable to stand the noise Charlie was making another moment, she sat up, swung her legs to the floor and picked up her stockings from the foot of the bed where she'd left them. She rolled one on then the other, clipped them on to her suspenders, left the bed and went to the tallboy where she'd draped her woollen frock. She pulled it over her head and, by lifting her arms as high as they would go behind her back, managed to fasten the buttons. Her shoes were on the floor beneath the bed, her coat on a hook on the door. Her hat and handbag were stacked next to a litter of lipsticks, face powder, cigarettes, ashtrays and empty scent bottles on the dressing table.

She glanced around the room to make sure she hadn't forgotten anything. Then she looked down at Charlie, sprawled on his back, dressed only in his vest – and still snoring. She felt in her pockets and opened her handbag to look for something she could leave him as a memento. All she could find was a lace handkerchief. She upended her perfume bottle on it and dropped it on his chest. She opened the door quietly, closed it behind her and went downstairs.

The hall was tiny and, like most two-up two-down terrace houses, the front door was directly opposite the stairs with barely enough room for the door to open inward. She had just closed her hand on the doorknob when she heard, 'Hello, Edyth.'

She turned. Micah Holsten was standing in the kitchen doorway. 'I heard Anna asking someone to get you. I hoped you wouldn't come.'

'Someone has to talk sense into you.' He closed the door behind him and walked towards her.

'Why does it have to be you?'

'I'm an expert at making the wrong sort of friends and being in the wrong place at the wrong time.' He caught hold of her arm.

'Let me go.'

'No.'

'I'm not going anywhere with you,' she protested.

'Yes, you are.'

'And if I scream?'

'The police would be amazed if a woman in this house didn't scream. And I didn't give you an invitation. It's an order. For once in your life, you're going to think of someone besides yourself.'

'You think *I'm* selfish . . .' After everything Peter had done to her, the last thing she wanted to do was listen to someone else's hard luck stories.

'Peter's still your husband,' he reminded her.

'Why should I consider him after what he's done to me?'

'Because right now, he's sitting in the vicarage knowing that he has lost everything he has ever worked for: people's respect, a settled life, marriage – you. And possibly, if the Bishop ever hears what happened tonight, his career.'

'Peter doesn't give a damn about me.'

'That's where you're wrong, Edyth. He does care for you. Very much.'

Micah had parked his van outside Anna's house. He opened the door, pushed Edyth into the passenger seat, walked around to the driver's side, started the engine and drove down towards the sea. He parked on the quayside overlooking the marina of small boats where the *Escape* was berthed, switched off the ignition and turned to face her.

The weather had broken while she had been in Anna's. Rain was beating down, making rivulets on the windscreen, moving and darting in random patterns, sometimes sideways, sometimes upwards. Edyth found it easier to concentrate on the way the street lights reflected on the drops of water in the darkness, than to look at Micah.

'Peter never loved me.' She finally broke the silence that hung between them. 'He only married me to get his damned parish.'

'You're sure about that?'

'Of course I am.' She only thought about Micah's question after she had answered it. Sustained by her anger towards Peter, his mother, the barren, loveless life she had found herself enmeshed in, she blamed Peter entirely for the whole sorry mess of their marriage.

Logic dictated that she was as much to blame as Peter for

rushing up the aisle on such a short acquaintance. But she didn't want to be logical. Or think how things might have turned out if she'd stayed in Swansea when her parents had taken her to college instead of running to Peter in Tiger Bay.

'As I see it, you were the one who chased after Peter, not the other way around.' He offered her a cigarette, she took it.

'I didn't know you smoked.'

'Sometimes.' He struck a match and lit first her cigarette and then his own. 'Peter loves you as much as it is possible for a man like him to love a woman.'

'You expect me to believe that?'

'It's the truth. It's not Peter's fault that he is the way he is. He didn't choose to be a homosexual any more than you chose to be clumsy. He was born that way. Some men love women, some love men. And provided no one is forced to do anything against their will, there is absolutely nothing wrong with that.'

'The healthy liberal Scandinavian attitude to free love,' she sneered. 'I've read about your country's obsession with nudity.'

'Is getting everything out in the open any worse than criminalizing a man for something he can't help, and gaoling him for his passions, as you do in this country?'

'So you think it was all right for Peter to marry me to get his parish?'

'Of course not, Edyth,' he interrupted. 'But I believe that Peter felt he had no choice. You were the one who came down the Bay in the middle of the night and stayed until your parents gave you permission to marry him.'

'He'd already asked me to become his wife, because he wanted the parish.'

'I'm only his friend, and a comparatively new one at that, but when Peter first came down the Bay there was a certain amount of, not scandal exactly—'

'Gossip?' she finished acidly.

'Peter's reputation preceded him. We have a fair number of men like him living in the Bay. I don't know what I'm saying; living everywhere, and not just Wales or Britain – the world. And whatever you've heard, it's not a sickness, Edyth.'

'I didn't say it was,' she said sullenly.

'But the Bishop thinks it is. And he and the Dean forced Peter, under threat of losing his job, to go and see a doctor. What he did to Peter was barbaric.'

'What did he do?' she asked, needing to know.

'They call it electric shock aversion therapy. The use of pain, or in some people's opinion, including mine, torture. It's designed to make men conform to the pattern laid down by the Church and modern society. Just when Peter decided that he couldn't take any more of the Church's prescribed "treatment" the doctor declared him "cured" and told him to go off and get married to make sure he'd never stray again. Believe what you want to, Edyth, but I know that Peter married you loving you more than any other woman he'd ever met.'

She considered what Micah said. Recalled Peter's nervousness whenever she kissed him, his insistence they wait to consummate their marriage. The more she thought about their courtship and honeymoon, the more she saw anxiety in every move Peter had made.

'Edyth, you're kind and compassionate, you want to help the world and already you've made a difference to some people's lives in the Bay. You, not Peter, welcomed Anna and the other girls' children into Sunday school. You opened your home and your heart to Judy when she needed a home and a job.'

'It was those qualities that led me to marry Peter.' She was unable to keep the bitterness from her voice.

'Think about what he must be feeling now. Knowing what you have seen and that he has lost your respect—'

'How do you know what I saw?'

'Because I went to see Peter.'

'When?' she demanded.

'When Anna sent for me, I went straight to her house. You were upstairs. I didn't want to interrupt you, so I walked to the vicarage.' For the first time she detected emotion in his voice – anger and condemnation – and much as she would have liked to pretend it didn't affect her, it did. If Micah had any respect left for her after she had kissed him, it had certainly evaporated now.

'You told Peter where I was? What I'd done?'

'I told him you were safe with friends. He was in his study, worried sick about where you'd gone. I have never seen a man looking so lost or broken. Think what it must have been like for him to have lived a lie all this time, Edyth. Knowing that if he went out and sought a lover he could be sent to gaol. You do know that men can be imprisoned, even if they both consent and they make love in private.'

'I read the papers.'

'Do you still love Peter?'

'How can I? At the moment I feel that I have never really known him.' She recalled Bella's wedding, how envious she had been of Toby's love for Bella. How she had wished for a man who would love her as Toby loved her sister. And then she had seen Peter: young, good-looking, charming . . .

Had she fitted Peter into a Prince Charming mould to suit herself? Fallen in love with the idea of being in love, not with Peter himself? It had all happened so quickly between them. Even the night before they had married, she was conscious of how little time they had spent together. How little she knew him.

She had assumed it was pre-wedding nerves. How much heartache could she have avoided if she had listened to Harry and called off the wedding?

'Peter was terrified of hurting you. That's why he kept Mrs Mack on. She saw him with Constable Jones the day after the Reverend Richards went to hospital. She threatened to go to the police and tell you if he didn't raise her wages and allow her to carry on working as housekeeper in the vicarage.'

'He told her to pack her bags and go just before I left for Anna's,' she murmured.

'Then let's hope her next stop is in Scotland. Do you feel anything for Peter now?'

'Sorry for him.' She pulled the ashtray out of the dashboard and rested her cigarette on it.

'Then tell him just that. It would mean a great deal to him if you could forgive him for marrying you, Edyth.'

'If he thought he was "cured" it was hardly his fault.' She

laughed suddenly, surprising even herself. 'When you think of it, Micah, Peter and I made quite a pair. The naive schoolgirl and the almost equally naive vicar thinking that all he needed was a wedding certificate to change his life.'

'Can I drive you back to the vicarage?'

'Yes.' She stubbed out her cigarette and closed the ashtray.

'Just one more thing, Edyth. He doesn't need to know about you and Charlie.'

'No one needs to know about me and Charlie.'

'You needn't worry, Anna and the girls won't tell anyone about it. I checked.'

'Unless someone comes looking for the vicar's wife,' she said drily.

'I can't speak for Charlie,' he said quietly.

She pictured Charlie as she had last seen him, dead to the world, half-naked and snoring on Colleen's bed. She doubted he'd even remember what had happened. 'About Charlie—'

'You don't have to tell me the details, Edyth,' he interrupted harshly.

'No, I don't.'

'I'd rather you didn't mention it again.'

'I won't unless someone else brings it up. Please, Micah, drive me to the vicarage.'

# Chapter 23

MICAH STOPPED HIS VAN outside the front door of the vicarage. Edyth looked at him when he put on the handbrake, but he was staring resolutely straight ahead, at the lamp on the wall.

'Are you coming in?'

'No, you told me that the only people who know what is going on inside a marriage are the two concerned. This is between you and Peter.'

'I wouldn't be here if it wasn't for you, Micah.'

'You would have come to your senses sooner or later, Edyth. If Peter wants to talk to me, or thinks that I can do anything to help him, he knows where to find me.'

Edyth opened the door and stepped out. Micah released the handbrake and drove off. She stood and watched until the van turned out of sight, then faced the vicarage. The moment she opened the door, Judy ran into the hall and Edyth sensed she had been waiting for her.

'I'm so glad you're home, Mrs Slater. I think Reverend Slater is ill. I wanted to send for the doctor but he refused to let me telephone him.'

'Is he in his study?' Edyth took off her coat and hat.

'Yes.'

'Where's Mrs Mack?'

'I haven't seen her. But she could be up in her room. I haven't checked there.'

'Mrs Slater?' Edyth asked, wishing she had time to talk to Judy and explain what had happened. Better she hear it from her than someone else. And when she did, maybe she or her uncles wouldn't want her to stay on in the house. Not if Mrs Mack told everyone on the Bay just what she'd seen Peter doing that evening, and how much of a sham their marriage was.

'Mrs Slater senior came in from the Mothers' Union meeting about an hour ago. She wanted to see Reverend Slater but he wouldn't talk to her. I made her tea and a sandwich and she went up to her room. She asked me to remind you to call in and see her when you went upstairs. She said she could feel one of her sore throats coming on. I offered to make her a hot drink and poultice but she said she didn't want one.'

Edyth suspected that her mother-in-law had refused Judy's offer because she wanted to send her running up and down stairs in the early hours as punishment for going out to lunch with Bella and Toby. Anything to cause maxim upset and chaos when she'd been crossed in some way. But the last thing she wanted to think about was Peter's mother's hypochondria. As for the events of the afternoon, time and Mrs Mack would tell whether or not they could be kept from her.

'Thank you for looking after everyone, Judy, but I'm back now. You can go to bed.' Edyth went to Peter's study door. 'I'm sorry, I didn't even ask how your shopping went.'

'Fine, Mrs Slater. I hope you don't mind, but I called in at Uncle Jed's.'

'Of course I don't mind, Judy I told you that you can see him any time you like, as long as you do your work here.'

'The police called. They told him we're unlikely to get anything back from my grandmother's house. Neither my uncles nor the police have managed to trace any of my grandmother's things. It's horrible to think that I'm the daughter of a man who can steal from his dead wife's family. I can't understand why my mother ever married him. Not if she was like my gran.'

'Your father might have been different when he was young, Judy. People change and remember, your father is not you. You're kind, honest, pretty and talented. Forget your father and concentrate on the good people in your family. Your uncles and grandmother.'

'Uncle Jed keeps telling me that I'm just like my mother.'

'Then she must have been a really special person. Goodnight, Judy, we'll have a long talk in the morning.'

'You and Reverend Slater are in some kind of trouble, aren't you, Mrs Slater?'

Edyth braced herself. 'Yes, but I'm hoping it can be sorted, Judy.'

'If it would help, I'd work for my keep and nothing else. I'm happy here, you're kind—'

'It's not money, Judy,' Edyth said quickly, touched by the young girl's offer. 'And no matter what, I'll try to keep you with me. We'll talk tomorrow,' she repeated.

'Yes, Mrs Slater. Goodnight.'

'Goodnight, Judy.' Edyth knocked once, then, as his mother had done earlier, walked into Peter's study.

It was little wonder Judy had thought Peter was ill. He was sitting slumped over his desk, his head buried in his hands. Edyth called his name but she had to touch him before he realized she was there. He looked up at her with blank, uncomprehending eyes.

She took a chair and sat beside him, taking his hand in hers.

'You must hate me,' he whispered after a while.

'No, I don't hate you.'

'Where did you go? I looked for you. When you ran out of the house – the expression on your face – I thought I'd never see you again.' He held her hand tight but didn't dare look at her, and she sensed he was too ashamed.

'Micah Holsten found me. He explained some things to me that I didn't understand. I wish you'd told me that you couldn't love me the way I wanted to be loved from the beginning.'

A single tear ran unchecked down his cheek. She would have found it easier to bear hysterical sobbing. 'I believed I'd changed. The doctor told me I had. I so desperately wanted a normal life, with you and children, but above all I wanted you and Mother to be proud of me. The way she was proud of my father.'

Again Edyth pictured that small boy playing on the sands of Swansea Bay, his middle-aged parents watching him build sand castles, his father in a dog collar, his mother planning out every

379

detail of her son's life without sparing a thought for what he wanted.

'I am so sorry, Edyth. Can you forgive me?'

'There is nothing to forgive, Peter. We both made mistakes. I've been thinking that perhaps I didn't want to go college all along but just didn't realize it. Maybe I was afraid I'd fail, maybe I only said I'd go because it was my father's ambition not mine. Marriage to you gave me a very convenient escape route.'

'Do you really believe that?'

She knew he was clutching at the straw of comfort she'd offered him. 'Yes, I do.'

'Has Mrs Mack gone?'

'I don't know. Judy said she could be in her room. I wish you'd told me about her threats. If you had, I would have given her her marching orders the day I moved in.'

'She not only threatened to tell you, she threatened to go to the police. If she does I could be charged, tried and sent to gaol. As it is, the rumours might be enough for the Bishop to take the parish away from me and give it to someone else.'

She smiled at her blindness. Even now, with their sham of a marriage in tatters, and the threat of prison hanging over his head, all Peter could think about was the Bishop and the parish. But she looked for and found some of the compassion Micah had assured her she had.

'You're doing too good a job in the parish for the Bishop to get rid of you, Peter.'

'I wish I had your faith.'

'You are a brilliant, caring vicar. The Bishop will never find another one like you.'

A loud banging on the door startled both of them.

Peter leapt to his feet. The voice of the sergeant from the Maria Street police station boomed from outside.

'Reverend Slater, we know you're in there. Open up . . . please.'

'I'll go.' Edyth saw a shadow on the stairs when she went into the hall and she knew, without turning around, that Peter's mother was behind her.

Peter walked past her, opened the door and faced the officers. Edyth had never felt more afraid for him, or prouder.

'Reverend Slater, sir, we have to ask you to accompany us down to the station.' The sergeant glanced at Edyth. 'We can discuss the reason in the interview room.'

'Thank you for your tact, Sergeant, I'll just get my coat and hat.' Peter lifted both from the hall stand.

'Peter, what's this all about?' his mother demanded. She was standing barefoot, halfway up the stairs, her grey hair plaited into two braids that hung over her brown flannel dressing gown.

'I need to go down the police station with the sergeant and constables, Mother.'

'No, you don't.'

He turned and looked at her. 'Yes, I do, Mother.'

'Whatever it is can wait until morning,' she argued.

'I am afraid it can't wait, madam,' the sergeant interposed.

'Peter, go to bed. You must refuse to go.'

'They are not making enquiries, Mother,' Peter informed her bluntly. 'They are arresting me.'

'I don't understand . . .'

He continued to look at her. 'I think you do, Mother.'

Florence Slater turned from Peter to Edyth and screamed, 'This is all your fault, you . . . you trollop! If you had been a proper wife to my son, nothing would have happened'

'Mother—'

'Go, Peter' Edyth pitched her voice below Florence's screams. She kissed Peter's cheek, murmured, 'Take care of yourself,' then went to her mother-in-law. Florence had stopped screaming and fallen, sobbing, to her knees. Edyth put her arm around her. 'Come on, Mother, let's get you up to bed.'

Florence pushed her away. 'You ruined my son's life. I'm not going anywhere with you.'

'I'll take her, Mrs Slater.' Judy ran down the stairs, in a blue dressing gown and white flannel nightgown.

'Thank you, Judy.'

'I don't want you, neither, you . . . you . . . half-caste.'

'I won't have those words said in this house, Mother.' Peter went to the two constables. 'Goodbye, Mother.'

Florence Slater finally allowed Judy to lead her away.

The sergeant lingered to speak to Edyth after the officers had escorted Peter out of the yard. 'Your housekeeper Mrs Mack made a complaint. We also have a young man in custody. When Mrs Mack came to see us she pointed out your husband's – partner-in-crime, as it were,' he finished diplomatically. 'He's one of our constables. Mrs Mack mentioned that you were also there, Mrs Slater?'

'Pardon?'

'Mrs Mack said you saw your husband in bed with this young man.'

'I saw nothing, sergeant.' Edyth lifted her chin defiantly

'I'm not sure I believe you, Mrs Slater.'

'Are you calling me a liar?'

'Mrs Mack said you were in the doorway and you would have seen your husband and the other man. According to her, they were both stark naked and performing lewd acts.'

'Not that I saw, sergeant.'

'You did open the bedroom door?'

'I did,' Edyth acknowledged, 'but Mrs Mack started screaming behind me. I thought she was having hysterics. The next thing I saw was my husband trying to calm her.'

'Really?' He clearly hadn't believed a word she'd said.

'Really, sergeant,' Edyth reiterated, looking him in the eye.

'Well, it appears that Mrs Mack saw enough for both of you. Not that we need her testimony either. The young man has confessed.'

'I see.'

'I should warn you, the papers are bound to get hold of this. You'll have reporters camped on your doorstep and telephoning you. Your father is an MP, isn't he?'

'He is,' Edyth confirmed.

'Better warn him what's happened and what's coming his way, Mrs Slater. Not that there's much he can do about it, but it's as well to be prepared.'

*

Edyth was too busy for the next few hours to think of anything other than what had to be done immediately. She called the doctor for Peter's mother, who remained hysterical. She watched him give her mother-in-law a sleeping draught then, after leaving Florence in Judy's care, she returned downstairs, spoke to the telephonist at the local exchange and placed calls to Peter's Aunt Alice and her father.

Micah arrived at the front door as she was speaking to Lloyd. She opened the door to let him in and he sat on the stairs and waited for her to finish.

'. . . Please don't come right away, Dad, and tell Harry, Bella and Toby that I'm fine. There's nothing any of you can do. I have Judy here to help me look after Peter's mother, and Mr Holsten has arrived. I just wanted to warn you in case a reporter tried to question you . . . Yes . . . I'll see you in the morning . . . Love to everyone there . . . Take care.'

Micah waited until she replaced the receiver before speaking. 'I heard about Peter's arrest. I thought I'd go down the station and see if I can help him.'

'I'll come with you.'

'That's not a good idea, Edyth.'

'You heard me talking to my father. Judy is looking after my mother-in-law. Peter will need a solicitor.' She tried to remember all the things her father had said, which she hadn't thought of when the police had taken Peter away.

'I know a good one.'

'Will he come out at this time of night to help Peter?'

'On past experience, I'd say yes. I can telephone him if you like. If he is in, I'll meet him at the police station.'

'Please.' She handed him the telephone. 'I'll just check on my mother-in-law then I'll come down the station with you.'

She left him speaking to the operator. When she returned downstairs ten minutes later there was a scribbled note on the hall table: '*Stay here. Will be in touch with news as soon as I have any, Micah.*'

The Bishop took three cheese and cress sandwiches from the pile

Judy had made for everyone's lunch, heaped them on a plate and carried them over to one of the easy chairs. He arranged his bulk as comfortably as he could, given the limitations of Peter's mother's chair, sat back and sipped his tea.

'You do understand, Mrs Slater, the Church cannot afford to be tainted by this unfortunate affair. I appreciate this isn't a great deal of notice, but if you could clear the house of your and Reverend Slater's belongings in the next forty-eight hours, so the next incumbent can take up residence, we would be very grateful.'

'And what form would this gratitude of the Church's take, Bishop?' Lloyd enquired coldly. He and Sali had arrived at the vicarage in Tiger Bay an hour before Peter's Aunt Alice, who had been driven there by her chauffeur, but ten minutes after the Bishop and Dean, who had heard about Peter's arrest precisely as the sergeant had warned Edyth some people would – from a newspaper reporter.

'We will allow Reverend Slater to resign and we will pay his salary up until yesterday. Really, Mr Evans, given the circumstances, there's nothing else that I can do for Reverend – Mr Slater.' The Bishop demolished a sandwich in two bites. 'I telephoned Maria Street police station this morning. Peter Slater has pleaded guilty, as has his . . . accomplice. The Church has to distance itself from any criminal act. However, what Peter Slater has done is not only criminal; it is unspeakable and morally reprehensible.'

'I will try to clear this house tomorrow, Bishop.' Now that Peter's career was over, Edyth no longer felt any compunction to address the bishop as 'Your Grace', although she was tempted to call him something more derogatory after hearing Micah's account of the 'treatment' the Church had insisted Peter undergo.

'Thank you, Mrs Slater.'

Edyth watched the tea Judy had poured her grow cold on the table next to her. The visitors had started arriving at the vicarage before dawn. First reporters, then the police looking for Mrs Mack, who had disappeared after going to the police station, although she had managed to clear her room. But not of everything. Edyth had found the boxes of silverware that Bella and Toby had given her and Peter secreted beneath the housekeeper's bed, and she dreaded to think what else the woman had stolen – and taken – but she was too dispirited to look, much less make a formal complaint to the police.

Alice picked up the sandwiches and offered them around. The Bishop took another two, the Dean three, but Lloyd, Sali and Edyth all shook their heads.

'I'll telephone the firm Florence employed to look after her effects. I'm sure they'll collect them all and put them back into storage until you, or Peter, decide what you want to do with them, dear.'

'Thank you, Aunt Alice.' Edyth was grateful for Alice Beynon's tact. But once she left the vicarage she hoped that she'd never see another piece of Florence Slater's furniture or silverware again.

'I'll get one of the Pontypridd firms to pick up your things, Edyth.' Lloyd pulled his pipe from his pocket. 'Fred Davies is usually very helpful. With luck we should have the house cleared by tomorrow evening.' If looks could kill, the Bishop would have been lying stiff on the floor.

'I think you should come home with us now, Edyth,' Sali said. 'Bring Judy with you. We can always use another maid . . . '

'No, Mam. I know you and Dad mean well, but no.' Edyth shook her head. 'Micah said he'd try to arrange for me to visit Peter before they move him to Cardiff gaol tonight. I want to stay here in case he succeeds.'

'But you and Judy will come home with us tomorrow?' Sali looked anxiously at her daughter.

'We'll talk about it.' Edyth glanced at the Bishop, who was contentedly munching his way through the sandwiches alongside the Dean. 'At the moment I can't think further than the next few hours.'

'I understand, darling. If you'll excuse me, I'll go in the kitchen and help Judy to make a start on packing things away.'

'And I'll pack Florence's suitcase.' Glad to leave the clerics, Alice followed Sali.

'When you gentlemen have finished, I'll show you out,' Lloyd said pointedly when the Dean finished his tea and looked around as though he expected more.

'Yes, well, we should be going. We'll send an agent for the keys, Mrs Slater, or you can leave them with one of the church council members if you prefer.'

'I'll leave them with Mr Maldwyn Williams,' Edyth answered.

'That is satisfactory.' The Bishop eased himself out of the chair. 'Our commiserations, Mrs Slater.'

Lloyd walked to the door and held it open. The Bishop hovered in front of Edyth's chair. When she made no attempt to shake his hand, he left with the Dean. Lloyd walked out with them and returned within minutes.

'Bloody hypocrites,' he swore. He looked down on Edyth, who had left her chair and was kneeling in front of the bookcase. 'You'll have plenty of willing hands to help you, my sweet. Mari and the maids can come down with us tomorrow.'

'There's no need, Dad.' Edyth lifted a pile of books from a shelf. 'There are so many people out of work on the Bay I can get all the help I need. Besides,' she gave him a wry smile, 'all of our wedding presents and most of my things are still packed. Peter wanted us to use his mother's furniture, china and silverware. He was trying to recreate the rooms in the vicarage he'd grown up in.'

'And you were happy to go along with that?' Lloyd asked.

'No, but it's all academic now, isn't it?'

'I suppose it is. I'll see if I can get Fred to bring down a van tomorrow, I doubt we'll need a lorry. And then, my sweet, you can come home and forget about Tiger Bay.'

'And do what, Dad?' The one thing Edyth had found time to think about that morning, besides Peter, was her future. The rest of her life yawned in front of her and she didn't have a clue what she was going to do with it.

'Your mother and Uncle Joey can find you a job in Gwilym James,' Lloyd suggested. 'It will probably mean starting at the bottom of the staff tree, the way your Uncle Joey did—'

'No, Dad,' she interrupted. 'No family favours.'

'There might be some way you could still go to college.'

'No, there isn't, Dad, and I won't have any of your friends pulling strings for me either. No college will take a married woman. Besides, after the way I left Swansea, I doubt any of them will look at me. The principals do talk to one another, you know.'

'No decision has to be made in a hurry, Edie. You'll need time to get over this and put it behind you. And when you've succeeded, we'll think of something. We always do.'

Lloyd helped Alice's chauffeur carry Florence, who was still heavily sedated, downstairs. Alice piled rugs and pillows in the back seat of the car and made her sister as comfortable as she could, then closed the door on her. She hugged Edyth so hard she took her breath away.

'Don't become a stranger, Edyth, come and see me and stay as often as you can. We'll have lots of fun together.'

'I don't think so, Aunt Alice. Not while Peter's mother lives with you,' Edyth replied with more honesty than tact.

'Then we'll meet in Swansea behind Flo's back. Go and eat our way through the most expensive items on the lunch menu in the Mackworth.'

'I'd like that.' Edyth kissed the old woman's cheek.

'I have no one except you and Peter. Flo doesn't count. And whatever Peter's done and wherever they put him, he'll always be my nephew . . .' Alice blew her nose in the handkerchief Edyth handed her. 'You'll write?'

'I promise, Aunt Alice.'

'I know we haven't known one another long, Edyth, but you're like my own. I love you.'

'I love you, too, Aunt Alice.'

Edyth waved until Alice's car was no longer in sight then she returned to the house, where Judy and her father and mother were already hauling empty packing cases down from the attic.

Sali and Lloyd left at dusk. Edyth and Judy continued to fill tea chests with Peter's and his mother's things until well past their usual dinner-time. Realizing they hadn't eaten anything other than sandwiches all day, Edyth found her purse and asked Judy to fetch fish stew from Josefina's. The girl hesitated for a moment.

'If you don't mind waiting, Mrs Slater, I'll call in on my Uncle

Jed on the way, to ask him if I can move back in with him tomorrow.'

'There's no need to do that, Judy.' Edyth dropped a pile of old parish magazines that she had scavenged from Peter's study next to the case she intended to pack Florence's silverware into.

'But you'll be leaving here tomorrow.'

'My parents said they'd take you. They can always do with extra help in the house.'

'If that's the case, why haven't they already employed someone?' Judy asked astutely.

'Judy, please, let me think for a few days. It's not just your future, it's mine, too. To be honest, the last place I want to go is back to my parents' house in Pontypridd. I can see it now; everyone in the town will shake their head, and mutter, "poor Edyth", and behind my back point me out to their friends and whisper, "The second Evans girl. Did you know she married a vicar who fell in love with the local policeman?" Edyth began to laugh, and once she started she couldn't stop.

'Are you all right, Mrs Slater?' Judy asked, concerned that Edyth was becoming hysterical.

'Yes, Judy. I'm sorry. I didn't mean to frighten you. But put that way, it sounds so peculiar and – I can't help it – funny.'

Judy was still out when the doorbell rang half an hour later. Concerned in case it might be the reporters her father had already sent away twice that day, Edyth crept quietly into Peter's study and looked through the window. She had left the outside light burning. Beneath it stood a small boy dressed in ragged trousers and jersey. She walked briskly down the passage and opened the door.

'Pastor gave me this, missus.' He pulled a creased envelope from his pocket but he clung on to it. 'He said I was only to give it to the lady who lived here, and I'd know her because she's pretty with brown hair and big eyes like Claudette Colbert. Is that you?'

'From the description, I hope so.' Edyth took the note and opened it.

'*Be in my cave at 2 a.m.*'

'He said you'd give me a penny, missus.'

She reached into her overall pocket and fingered the change she'd thrust into it after counting out the correct money to give Judy to buy the fish stew. Staring at the note, she absently handed the boy a silver threepenny bit.

'A silver joey! Thanks a million times over, missus.' The boy ran off, leaving Edyth wondering what she'd done.

# Chapter 24

IT HAD finally stopped raining but the clouds obliterated the moon and stars. The only light came from the street lamps, but they failed to penetrate the thick mist that had fallen, heavy as smoke, over Tiger Bay.

Constables marched their beat, drunks lurched along the side streets, stray dogs fought in the gutters, and cats yowled, startling Edyth with their eerie cries, but she continued to walk quickly in the shadows of the high buildings of Bute Street. By moving swiftly and purposefully, and keeping her hat pulled low, she managed to reach the area where the small boats were berthed unchallenged.

Not knowing if the walkway was lit, she had dropped a small torch into her pocket and when she saw that the shore lights didn't reach the water, she blessed her foresight. The boats all looked the same in the unrelieved darkness; black, shapeless shadows. She shone the torch down at her feet and walked carefully, lifting the slim light to the hulls where the names were painted. Eventually she read *Escape* in faded, peeling letters.

The boat was in complete darkness. Her heart started pounding erratically again. The note she had received hadn't been signed, but the boy said the Pastor had given it to him. She'd assumed Micah had sent it. What if he hadn't? What if it had been sent by a murderer — Charlie even? No, not Charlie, he wouldn't have known about the *Escape*, but then neither would anyone else, besides Micah.

Trying not to make a noise that would carry to the shore, she stole on to the deck. She shone the narrow light of the torch on the steps, and walked down to the cabin, closed her hand over the door handle and pushed.

The lamp had been lit, but she had seen no light because the portholes were covered with sheets of snug-fitting brown cardboard. And there, sitting on the couches, were Micah, a man she had never seen before, Peter and the young constable.

Her hand flew to her mouth. 'Peter, what happened?'

'Some men don't like people who are different. And the police needed punchbag practice.' He fingered the cuts and bruises on his face before leaving his seat. She opened her arms and hugged him, holding him close.

'Can we go now?' the stranger asked Micah.

'Yes.' He looked at the young constable. 'Not a sound when we go up on deck.'

The young man nodded agreement. He looked at Edyth and, for the first time since she'd met him, there was no hostility in his eyes. She offered him her hand and he shook it.

Micah led the way outside.

'I thought you were being moved to Cardiff prison,' Edyth said when she and Peter were alone.

'I have no idea how Micah managed to arrange it, but he had the Black Maria that was taking us to the prison diverted down here. His friend has secured us berths on a ship bound for South America.'

'You won't be back.' It was a statement not a question.

'Not to go to gaol, Edyth.'

'It's a pity, you were a good vicar.'

'Micah has given me some rather impressive ship's chaplain's papers. I didn't dare ask where he got them from. But he warned me not to use them on the voyage out. You're looking at Ordinary Seaman Griffiths.'

'You'll write?'

'If and when he can, your friend Seaman Griffiths will. I've made arrangement for Micah to send annulment papers to the port. I'll get them back to you as soon as I can.'

'You'll need money.'

'Micah's given us each five pounds and we're working our passage.'

'But your bank account—'

'I've given Micah a paper signing it over to Mother. I'm sorry I can't give you anything to show for our marriage, Edyth.'

'You've given me a great deal, Peter, starting with wisdom.' She forced a smile. 'Doesn't it say somewhere in the Bible that's worth more than gold, diamonds and pearls?'

'Peter?' Micah hissed down from the deck.

Edyth kissed her husband lightly on the lips. 'God speed.'

'I loved you, Edyth Slater – Evans – in my fashion.'

'I know.'

Peter climbed up on deck. Edyth was standing looking around the tiny cabin when Micah returned.

She looked at him. 'Thank you.'

'Don't thank me until it's over. We're not out of stormy water yet. We have to row to the ship because we daren't risk starting an engine in case it brings the customs' officers and the coastguard down on us. The ship's leaving at three. And the port police might come on-board if the officers in Maria Street get a message to them in time to inform them that they've lost their prisoners. If that happens we're sunk, in every sense of the word. In fact, we may be better off at the bottom of the dock.'

'Peter will go to gaol.'

'Not just him. All four of us. Aiding and abetting escaping prisoners is a serious crime.'

'You've taken a terrible risk.'

'I told you, Peter's my friend, but I didn't just do it for him. There is something you can do, if you want to help.'

'Name it.'

'My friend in the rowing boat and I will need an alibi. Take down the cardboard after we've gone and stay here. Move about in front of the portholes, make up the bed, fold the table away and rearrange the cushions. There are rugs and pillows under the seats. Put pillows in the bed to make it look as though two people are sleeping in it. If the porthole is uncovered, I doubt the police will try to get in to check if they see your head on the pillow. But just in case, throw the bolt across the door after I'm gone. If you hear someone outside, start talking and use that.' He pointed to a wind-up gramophone. There was a record on the turntable. 'Saxophone music,' he explained.

'And in the morning?'

'I hope to be back by four. I'll go ashore and watch the boat from there. I won't return until it's out of the bay and I'm sure that Peter and the boy are safe. Our story is that my friend with the boat and I spent the night here drinking and playing chess.' He took a wooden chess set from a cupboard and put it on the shelf that held the lamp. 'My friend left before dawn; you stayed with me until morning. But I warn you, Edyth, giving me an alibi will cost you your reputation.'

'I've lost that anyway.'

He pulled up the collar on his thick navy seaman's coat and pulled his peaked cap low over his forehead. 'See you later – if everything turns out to be plain sailing.'

After Micah left, Edyth followed every suggestion he'd made. She threw the bolt across the door, removed the cardboard from the portholes, turned up the lamp, folded down the table and rearranged the cushions into a surprisingly large double bed. It covered every inch of floor space in the cabin. The only way she could get to the shelf that held the spirit lamp, chess set and gramophone was by standing on the cushions.

She found sheets and pillowcases, as well as two blankets, folded beneath the couches. She rolled the rug to look like a body and placed it in the bed, pulling the sheet over and fluffing it out so the 'head' couldn't be seen from any of the portholes. When she finished she glanced at her watch. It wasn't even two o'clock and Micah had warned he wouldn't return until four.

It was going to be a long two hours with nothing to do except wait – and worry. Determined to stay awake, she sat on the edge of the makeshift bed, but it was low and her calf muscles started aching. She lifted them up and rubbed them and, as she did so, she heard a noise. A creak that could have been a footstep on the planking.

The boat rocked.

Was it simply due to the natural movement of the sea or someone stepping on board?

Too nervous to start talking as Micah had advised, she kneeled on the bed and reached out to the gramophone. Her hand shook as she slid the switch on the turntable. It started rotating. Seeing that it was fully wound, she lifted the arm across the record and dropped the needle. The scratchy tones of a saxophone filled the cabin, blotting out all other sounds. In her present jittery mood it sounded like a discordant selection of notes. Anyone listening would know it was a record, but that didn't matter if Micah intended whoever he suspected of spying on him, to think that he was otherwise engaged — with her.

She played the record twice more, winding the player each time in between. After the third time she lifted the arm, turned the head upside down and stopped the turntable. She listened intently but all she could hear was the usual sounds of the sea: water lapping at the side of the boat; ships' sirens; sailors singing drunken dirges as they made their way back to their ships after a night in the dockland pubs.

Senses straining to their utmost, she kicked off her shoes and lay on the bed next to the rolled-up rug.

She woke with a start when she heard a quiet tap. When it sounded again she looked around in alarm. A white face peered through the porthole in front of her. She cried out before realizing it was Micah. Her limbs unnaturally heavy with sleep, she stumbled from the bed and crashed into the door, hitting her arm painfully before pulling back the bolt.

'I'm sorry—'

'It's all right, there's no one about that I can see.' Micah stepped inside and thrust the bolt back home.

She rubbed her eyes in an effort to focus. Whether it was lack of sleep or the paraffin fumes from the lamp, the cabin remained blurred. 'What time is it?'

'A quarter past four,' Micah said shortly.

'Then—'

'The ship's out of the Bay. Peter's as safe as he can be on-board a vessel heading for the Americas.'

He brushed against her and she jumped back. 'You're freezing cold and . . .' She reached out and felt his woollen coat, 'Soaking wet.'

'I tried to keep the boat steady at the foot of the rope ladder they lowered from the seaward side of the deck. Peter slipped and accidentally kicked me into the water.'

'You'd better get those clothes off or you'll get pneumonia. That was what you told me, and I only walked down here in the rain. I didn't swim here.'

'You're right. I'd like to leave them on deck but that would only give notice that I wasn't here all night, to anyone checking my movements.' He opened a small door; behind it yawned the space where the engine had been. He pulled out a pair of patched trousers and a crumpled shirt. 'My ship repairing clothes, the only others I have on board,' he informed her apologetically.

'You'd better put the wet ones in there. You don't want to soak the bed.'

'You sound as though you are used to giving orders.'

'With three younger sisters and a younger brother, I try, but I'm not always obeyed.' She sat on the bed and turned her back to him.

He lowered the wick on the spirit lamp, casting the cabin in shadow. 'It's freezing in here,' he complained. 'Why didn't you light the brazier?'

'Because I was too worried to be cold.'

'You can turn around now.' He was standing, shivering in the ragged trousers and shirt. He picked up the clothes he had dropped to the floor and tossed them into the old engine housing. They landed with a squelch. 'Expensive night. They were an almost new pair of shoes,' he grumbled.

'Expensive in more ways than one. Peter told me that you had given him and the boy five pounds each. But you must have paid out a lot more to buy their passage and false papers.'

'He told you about that?' He sat on the bed behind her. She could feel the cold emanating from his back.

'How much does he owe you?'

'The kind of favours money can't buy. It's the way life works on the docks.' He climbed under the blankets but he was still shivering. 'It's times like this that I wish I'd stayed in the Caribbean.'

'You've travelled?'

'Not as much as I'd like. You look ridiculous perched on the edge there. You're like a gull on a rock without the aptitude for balance. You may as well lie down. We can keep the fake me between us, if you're afraid I'll pounce on you. But I warn you, I'm too exhausted to do much in that line.' He patted the rolled-up rug.

She moved back into the space where she'd been sleeping when he'd arrived.

'I'm sorry I woke you.'

'I'm sorry I slept. I didn't mean to.'

'You've had a hard couple of days, Edyth, and tomorrow – or rather later today – won't be any different. I've a feeling that the police will be asking us a lot of questions about Peter's disappearance.' He stretched out, pulled the rolled-up rug closer to himself to give her more room, and turned to face her. 'So, we may as well sleep while we can.' He took off his glasses and laid them beneath his pillow.

'Have you any other spare clothes here?'

'No.'

'You'll set the whole of the Bay talking if you go to the mission dressed like that in the morning. People will think you've gone on the tramp.'

'Can't be helped,' he said carelessly.

'Yes it can. I'll go to the mission for you and ask your sister to give me some of your clothes.'

'You really are keen to lose what little is left of your reputation, aren't you?'

'You know something, Micah, I've gone past caring and it's a wonderful feeling to be totally free and not have to worry about what people are thinking or saying about me.'

He leaned back on the pillow and stretched out his arm. 'Sorry, did I hit you?'

'You did. You're so cold you can crawl into my space and steal my body heat if you like.'

'I'm too uncomfortable to turn down that offer.' He sat up, shook out the rug and spread it over both of them. 'Goodnight, or rather good morning, Mrs Slater.'

'I think I'll revert to Edyth Evans.'

'In that case, goodnight, Edyth.'

She closed her eyes. What could have been a minute or an hour later, he rolled closer to her and slipped his arm around her waist. Three-quarters asleep, the only thing that registered was the cold, and she snuggled up to him as she would have to Bella or one of her other sisters if they had been as icy.

Only he wasn't Bella or one of the others, and the next thing she knew, his mouth was pressed over hers and he was kissing her with a passion and urgency that sent the blood coursing headily around her veins.

His hands sought her skin beneath her clothes. He caressed her thighs above her stocking tops, her breasts through layers of clothes . . .

She moved away from him.

'Edyth, I'm sorry . . .'

Before he finished speaking she had stripped off her clothes.

He kissed her again, harder, roughly, thrusting his tongue into her mouth. When he finally lifted his head to draw breath, he said, 'I fell in love with you the first time I saw you laughing at the top of the stairs in your parents' house, holding a golden slipper in each hand. Looking inordinately pleased with yourself because you had frightened Harry.'

'You didn't know me then.'

'I don't know as much about you as I would like to now.'

'Please, Micah, no more words.' She caressed his entire body with the length of hers.

'Are you sure you want this to happen?'

'This is not the time for talking.'

'Say my name,' he commanded.

'Micah.'

Without any finesses, or attempt to caress her into submission, he kicked off his own clothes and thrust himself into her.

She gasped.

'Edyth . . . I thought I'm so sorry . . .'

'Please, Micah, don't stop.' She dug her nails into his back, treating his body as brutally as he was treating hers. 'Don't ever stop.'

Seconds later, just as her mother had promised, nothing mattered outside of the passion they had engendered in one another. Not her pain, not the unsettled traumatic past or the uncertain future. Only the fact that they were together, and it was everything she had ever dreamed of finding in love – and more.

When Edyth next woke it was to see Micah watching her. He looked strange and then she realized he wasn't wearing his glasses, although he must have turned up the lamp sometime while she slept, because the light was stronger, casting a gold tinge over the cabin.

'Good morning,' she smiled lazily.

'It is.' He returned her smile. 'Why did you want me to think that you had made love with Charlie Moore?'

'I didn't. You assumed I had, and refused to talk about it. But when I picked him up, Charlie was barely capable of standing upright. Anything more strenuous was out of the question. Possibly that's why I dragged him to Anna's. I never liked the man. Certainly not enough to do what I just did with you.'

'I couldn't bear the thought of you and him – together.' He stroked her body lightly, tantalizingly, with his fingertips. 'But this seems so right, doesn't it?' he asked as if he needed reassurance that she felt the same way.

'It does.' She lifted her arms and locked them around his neck, and for the next half-hour there was no need for any more words.

When Edyth next opened her eyes the hands on her wristwatch

pointed to six o'clock. She grabbed her petticoat, slipped it on and tried to leave the bed, but Micah grabbed her waist.

'Let's play at bears hibernating today and not leave the cave.'

'I can't, I have to clear the vicarage.'

'Move into the mission with me. We'll marry as soon as your annulment comes through.'

She wriggled free from his grasp and stepped out of his reach. 'No, Micah.'

He sat up, hitting his head on a cupboard door.

She leaned over him in concern. 'Did you hurt yourself?'

'No.' He caught her wrists and gripped them hard. 'Don't you love me?'

She smiled at him. 'Of course I do. And I want another night – morning – like this one as soon as you can spare the time.'

'Then move into the mission.'

'No, Micah. Try to understand. I went from school to marrying Peter. It's as though as I was frightened of being alone and making my own way in the world.'

'Were you?' he asked seriously.

'I don't know. What I do know is that I need to find my own life before I look for another marriage, so I can bring something to the relationship instead of leaning on my husband. It's too easy to live someone else's life instead of building your own, and that's exactly what I'd be doing if I moved in with you. I'd become an appendage to you and your job. Your friends would become mine. Your work would become my work and I don't want that. Not any more.'

He looked confused and she asked.

'Am I making sense?'

'Not the kind I want to hear.'

She finished dressing and walked over the cushions to the cupboard where he kept the sugar, tinned milk and coffee. There was no food, not even biscuits.

'Close your eyes, get another hour's sleep and I'll walk up to the mission and ask Helga to send down some clothes for you. Then I'll go up to the vicarage, have a bath and change, and on my way back I'll buy breakfast in Mr Goldman's bakery. We'll eat it here and talk about ways in which I can achieve my independence. I haven't a clue how to go about it.'

'I confess I'm not thrilled at your choice of topic. I can think of far better things to discuss.'

She blew him a kiss. 'Or not, as the case might be.'

'You won't be long?' he pressed.

She shook her head. 'An hour at most.'

'A real kiss before you go?' he pleaded.

She kissed him, he held her tight and she said, 'I had no idea a lover could be so possessive.'

'Get used to it, Edyth, because it's the way I intend to behave with you for the rest of my life.'


Forty minutes later, bathed, changed, her hair and make-up in place, Edyth left Judy packing Florence's china in the vicarage and walked down to Goldman's. The Jewish baker was putting the fourth lot of bread rolls in his window that morning. He saw her, waved enthusiastically and smiled. Half-expecting him to ostracize her because of the scandal involving Peter she wondered if he had heard about it.

'Sit down, Mrs Slater.' He pushed a chair towards her when she walked into the shop. 'My wife and me, we heard about your trouble, and we're sorry for you and your husband. Everyone is made different and thank God for it, I say. It would be a dull world if we were all the same. Have a cup of coffee – on the house. It's the best coffee you'll get on the Bay.' He set a cup and saucer on the counter in front of her.

She thought of Micah waiting for her in the *Escape* and almost refused, but decided ten minutes either way wouldn't make much difference. Her mother had warned her that she and her father wouldn't arrive early because he had an appointment with one of the local councillors that he couldn't postpone.

'Thank you, Mr Goldman, I'd love a cup of coffee.' She couldn't help but contrast his attitude with that of the Bishop.

'If you've come for rolls, they're good today. We have some good cakes, too, and bagels.'

'Fresh fish bagels?' she asked.

'Lox.'

Before Edyth knew what she was doing she had bought enough bagels, rolls and doughnuts to feed half the Bay.

'Hello, Edyth, how are you bearing up?' Eirlys Williams walked in carrying a shopping bag. 'Maldwyn and I were sorry to hear about Reverend Slater. We don't care what anyone says about him, he was good for the parish.'

'Thank you.' Tears started in Edyth's eyes. She knew she was being silly but she couldn't help herself. She found it hard to take people's kindness after the Bishop's attitude. It didn't make sense, but she had found it easier to cope with criticism of Peter's behaviour than understanding.

Mr Goldman saw that she was overcome with emotion. 'You were expecting people to be unkind about you and your husband? Well, it won't happen, not on the Bay. You and Peter were kind to your neighbours and that's what matters most.' The baker served Eirlys and two other customers with bread and biscuits, and topped up Edyth's coffee and his own. 'People here – well, we're not so quick as people outside to condemn because we all have something wrong with us. If we didn't we wouldn't be here.'

'Speak for yourself, Mordecai Goldman.' His wife bustled in with a tray of pasties and dropped it on a shelf in the window.

'What do you think is wrong with you, Mr Goldman?' Edyth asked in amusement after his wife had returned to the kitchen.

'You got an hour, I'll tell you.' He picked up his cup, leaned over the counter and began relating his family history. 'My whole family are Jewish; that wasn't so good in Russia when the Cossacks started murdering us for sport, so my father went to Poland and set up a bakery there. But the Poles,' he shrugged, 'they're not so fond of Jews either. So, when I married my beautiful Leila, I decided it was better for our children to come here. Only problem was my wife and I had no children, so I should have stayed in Łódź to look after my parents.

'Now my father has just had a heart attack, and my mother can't manage to run the shop. My brothers and their wives have all up and gone to America. I'm the nearest to Poland, so I have to go back and take care of the family business. But I'm going to miss the

Bay. You take half the families here. They're not Jew, Hindu, Muslim, Catholic, black, white, yellow, Arab, Somali, Pakistani or whatever, but a mix of everything human under Jehovah's sun, and the only place they all fit in is the Bay. That's why I love it here.'

'But you have to go back to Poland?'

'Just as soon as I can find someone to buy my business.'

Edyth looked around the baker's shop. 'How much do you want for it, Mr Goldman?' she asked suddenly.

'Why?' he replied suspiciously. 'You interested in buying?'

She suppressed a rising tide of panic. 'I might be,' she ventured, desperately trying to quell the thought that she knew absolutely nothing about running a business.

'Well, it's not just the business, there's the rooms upstairs. The wife and me, we have it comfortable here. We'd want to sell our furniture to the buyer to save trouble. It's all quality goods. And there's the goodwill. Our customers come here every day because they know they're going to get the best bread on the Bay. And I don't disappoint them. I have a good apprentice. He needs managing but he bakes all right. Although I don't tell him that. I'd want him kept on. It's only fair; he's been with me since he's twelve.'

Micah's brother-in-law, Moody, stuck his head around the door that led to the kitchen. 'Hello, Mrs Slater, nice morning.'

'It is, Moody.' His smile was infectious and Edyth couldn't help but return it.

'You want me to bake more fairy cakes today, Mr Goldman?' he asked.

'Yes, Moody.' The baker turned back to Edyth after Moody disappeared. 'He's young, he's black, but I tell you, after what I've taught him, that boy is an honorary Jewish baker.'

'How much do you want for the house and the business, Mr Goldman?' Edyth was conscious that she knew even less about baking on a commercial scale than she did about business. But how hard could it be to learn? It could be months if not years before she found another ready made, successful business to buy.

'I couldn't let it go for less than two hundred and fifty pounds. I'd be robbing myself blind if I did.'

Edyth's face fell.

'How much you got?' Mr Goldman asked.

'Two hundred but not a penny more, and I'd need fifty contingency funds to run the place.' Edyth knew that if she asked, Harry or her father would lend her the money. But she wanted to do something entirely on her own for once, and not have to rely on the family to help her.

'Tell you what I'll do, for a nice lady like you who will look after Moody and my customers for me. You pay me one hundred and fifty pounds cash upfront and you give my sister-in-law a pound a week. That will square things up. We'll get the papers drawn up all legal. You won't miss a pound a week from the till but it will keep my sister-in-law going. She married an Arab seaman but she hasn't seen him in four years. I keep telling her he has a wife in every port, move on, find yourself another man. All she says is, "He'll come back." '

'How long do you want me to keep paying her?' Edyth asked cautiously.

'Three years.'

'But that's fifty-six pounds interest on a hundred pounds over three years. That's an astronomical rate,' she protested.

He shrugged his shoulders. 'My wife's sister could die six months from now.'

'She's ill?' Edyth asked.

'No.'

'How old is she?'

'Thirty-five.' A ghost of a smile played around his mouth. 'Take it or leave it.'

Edyth didn't hesitate. 'I'll take it, Mr Goldman.'

'First you look at the room upstairs and the building, so I can show you how sound it is. Then tomorrow we go to the solicitor, and afterwards the bank, and you pay me the one hundred and fifty pounds.'

She looked at the bag of rolls and bagels. 'I was going to have breakfast with a friend.'

'Pleasure can wait,' he said firmly. 'If you don't put business first, you'll be bankrupt in a week.'

'Can I borrow your errand boy?'

'Be my guest. And a pencil and a piece of paper?'

'At no extra charge,' she cautioned.

'You're learning, Mrs Slater. One day you may even be ready to do business with a Jew.'

Edyth took the brown paper bag and pencil Mr Goldman gave her. She thought for a moment then scribbled, '*Bought breakfast, but was delayed. Sorry, can't make it back – enjoy the food.*' She paused for a moment debating whether or not to put '*love Edyth*'. Instead she added, '*Thank you for last night.*'

Micah, or the police if they managed to intercept the note, could interpret the message any way they wanted to.

# Chapter 25

'READY, MOODY?' Edyth called into the bakehouse.

'Yes, Miss Evans.' Moody carried the first tray of steaming rolls out into the shop. Edyth took them from him and began to stack them in the window. She had never known there could be so many different kinds of breads and rolls; white, brown, rye, corn, poppy seed, oatmeal, milk, wholemeal, bagels, soda, sultana, French . . .

'Butter and sandwich fillings.' Judy carried them out of the kitchen and set them on the counter. 'I'm going to enjoy making them to the customers' orders, especially the man Mr Goldman told us about who likes corn beef and strawberry jam. But then, he hasn't put in an appearance yet. Do you think Mr Goldman was joking about him?'

'I never knew when Mr Goldman was joking and when he wasn't. Let's just hope we keep all his customers and his books didn't look better than they were.' Edyth stood back and looked around the shop. She hadn't stopped working for the last three weeks and in all that time she and Judy had only managed to spend two days in Pontypridd.

They had moved into the Goldmans' spare bedroom as soon as Edyth's banker's draft had cleared. And shortly afterwards, the mistress and the maid situation between her and Judy had died from an overdose of friendship. It was difficult to be standoffish with someone or address them formally as Judy had done in the vicarage, when they divided the work that had to be done equally between them during the day and shared a bed at night.

After the Goldmans left on a ship bound for Gdansk, Edyth and Judy had cleaned the upstairs rooms, and Edyth conceded that Mr

Goldman had been right. They hadn't needed to do anything to make them habitable. There was even – the most unimaginable luxury – a small bathroom in the rooms behind the shop, put in next to the kitchen at great expense, or so Mr Goldman had assured her.

She took the milk rolls Moody had brought in and began to arrange them in the window. Half past five in the morning and she had already been working for an hour. She was loving every minute of it.

'Good morning.'

She looked up and saw Micah watching her. She gave him a cautious smile. She hadn't seen him since the night they had spent together on the boat and, although she had written to him – twice – to explain why she was so busy, he hadn't replied. 'Good morning, Micah,' she replied. 'Can I help you?'

'I confess I only called in to find out if it was true that the baker's is under new management.'

'As you see.'.

'Bakers work cruel hours,' he observed.

'Judy and I have just finished our elevenses,' she teased. She winked at Judy, who laughed before tactfully disappearing into the back.

Micah took a sample of fruit cake from the counter and ate it. 'You made this?'

'You know full well Moody did. I've been forced to increase his wages. I'm terrified he'll get a cook's job aboard a ship before I'm ready to let him go.'

'Can't you follow a recipe?' Micah asked.

'Not Mr Goldman's, I can't. Some of it runs along the lines of "you know how much to put in of that" or "one pinch on cold days and two on warm days" and my absolute favourite – "Go outside, look at the sky and you'll see how much time to give the dough to rise from the colour of the clouds." '

Micah laughed. 'I loved that man.'

'I hope to see him again one day.'

'Well, if it's any consolation, my shopping list is straightforward. Two milk rolls, two poppy seed and two French, please.'

Edyth picked up a pair of tongs, chose the rolls, slipped them into a bag and handed it to him. 'On the house.'

'Keep doing that and you'll go bankrupt,' he warned.

'It's only for the first customer.'

'Of the day?'

'Ever. In fact, he gets free shopping for the rest of his life. Just returning a favour,' she added.

'Next thing you'll be telling me is that you have no intention of moving from the Bay.'

'I don't. I've put every penny I have into this business.'

'And what does the lady do for entertainment?'

'She goes to bed early – very early.'

'In that case, would you like to come round to the mission for a late tea or an early dinner, whichever suits, when you shut up shop tonight?'

'No.'

'I see.' He failed to conceal his annoyance at her rejection.

'The mission is always – how did you put it? – bedlam. On the other hand, you could come round here for an early dinner. Judy has an audition – in London this time. I'll be taking her to Cardiff station later this afternoon. She's staying overnight as it looks promising.'

'Jed told me, it's for the chorus of 'Blackbirds', an all-black show that's going on tour.'

'It is, although I dread to think what I'll do for help if she gets it,' she said seriously.

'I know a few promising young girls looking for jobs.'

'I bet you do.'

'So dinner tonight, I accept your invitation. What time do you want me here?'

'Is six o'clock too early?'

'That depends on what time you want me to leave.'

'That is entirely up to you.'

He looked around to check no one was about. 'Edyth, that night on the boat . . . this could lead to—'

'Babies? I hope it does. I'd like dozens.'

'But we won't be able to marry until your marriage is annulled. And me visiting you on a regular basis—'

'Is bound to lead to gossip. In fact, it already has. The police didn't believe a word of the alibi I gave you. But they couldn't disprove it either. So, if you intend to keep visiting me, you'll have to learn to be discreet, Pastor.'

'Edyth, be sensible. The man is rarely ostracized. But a child born outside marriage would ruin you.'

'Not on the Bay, which is why I've decided to stay. The respectable, kind-hearted people like Eirlys Williams would pretend any child of mine was Peter's no matter how long the gap between him disappearing and the birth. The kind-hearted, but not quite so respectable people like Anna Hughes wouldn't give a damn whether the child had a father or not, so long as it was clean and cared for.'

'And you?' His blue eyes were serious.

'I've already picked out the father of my children, but he'll have to allow me to keep my independence.'

'And what will he get in return?'

'My love and affection for the rest of his life. A key to my door, space to put some clothes in my wardrobe and chest of drawers. Will six o'clock tonight suit you, Micah? You can bring your pyjamas, although I really would prefer it if you didn't wear any.'